For Lord and Liege

tinctaculum

Also by Birgit Constant

The Northumbria Trilogy

Prequel: *Squire and Sword*

Book 1: *Warrior of two Kings*

Book 2: *For Lord and Liege*

Find out how the story continues:

The Minstrel's Quest. Book 3 of the Northumbria Trilogy

Coming in 2026

About the Author

Birgit Constant writes historical fiction for language enthusiasts and is particularly interested in hidden histories of less well-known people and places.

She has a PhD in medieval studies, has learned eleven languages and worked her way through translation, IT and Public Relations internationally before ending up in the world of books.

Subscribe to her monthly newsletter *Medieval Motes* for exclusive reading material and a bonus e-book at www.birgitconstant.com/newsletter.

BIRGIT CONSTANT

For Lord and Liege

THE NORTHUMBRIA TRILOGY

BOOK TWO

Birgit Constant, c/o Literatur- und Kulturlounge, Mainzer Str. 6,
55276 Oppenheim, Germany

www.birgitconstant.com

ISBN: 9783911199063 (e-book) / 9783911199070 (paperback)

Book Cover by Damonza
Editor: Miranda Summers-Pritchard
Maps by John Wyatt Greenlee of Surprised Eel Maps

N
W
E
S
ESCOCE
Bebbanburh
Noef Chastel
Dunholm
NORTHUMBERLAND
Riche Munt
Use
Euerwic
De
NORTHGALES
Snotingeham
Lincolia
MERCE
Trente
Burg
Elig
Sauerna
Waruuic
Use
EST ANGLE
Grentebrige
Tamise
Melduna
Londres
WEST SESSOINE
Wincestre
Cantwarebyri
Sandwice
Wiht
Pevenesel
Hæstinga
ENGLAND
AD 1070
NORMANDIE

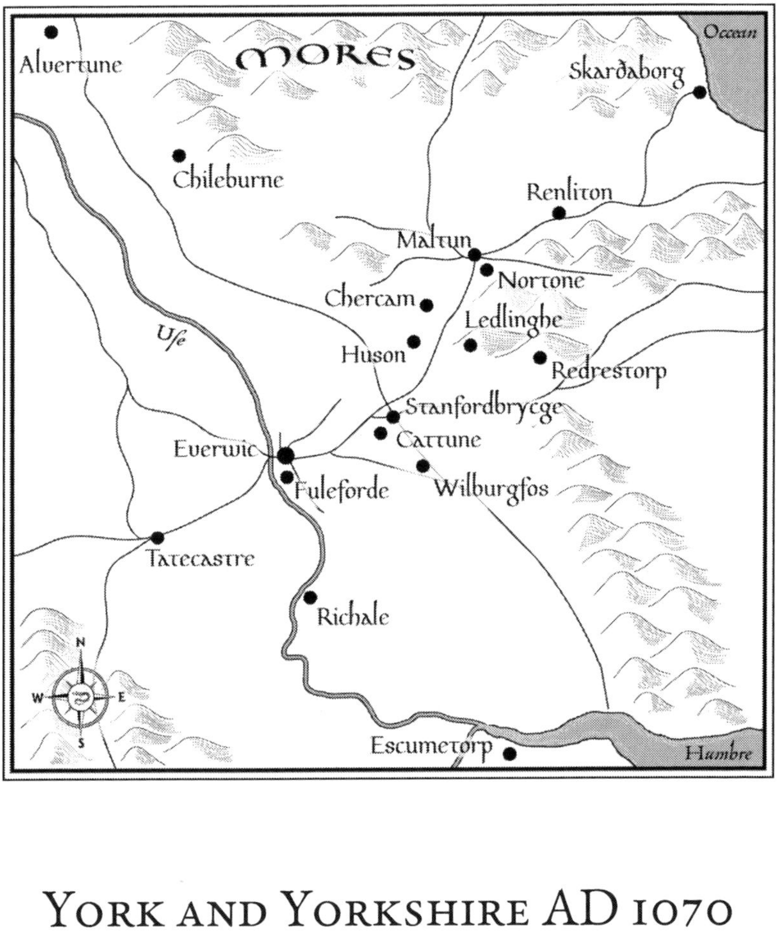

York and Yorkshire AD 1070

Cast of Characters

Historical persons are marked with an *

Wilburgfos

Roger/Hroðgar: son of the liege lord
Geoffrey de Bernaium, Norman liege lord of Wilburgfos, and
Edeva, English noblewoman and healer: his parents
William and Adelais: his half-siblings
Isabel and Tankred: his sister and brother

Roger's friends
Richard de Perci*: youngest son of William de Perci*
Joscelin and Drogo: Norman squires
Brandolf and Bjarni: Danish brothers

Other residents
Oswulf: master of arms
Hugues de Borre: bailiff
Frederic de Lisieues: seneschal
Walter Fossard*: son of Nigel Fossard*
Father Leofric: priest from Cattune

English servants
Emma: kitchen maid
Hild: healer woman
Cenhelm: cupbearer

Residents at the Benedictine priory
The prioress
Gwennaol: Breton girl
Morwenna: nun and Gwennaol's grandmother
Sister Agatha: vice prioress

People outside Wilburgfos
Osbern*: liege lord of Scornesbi
Gilbert FitzOsbern: his illegitimate son
Picot de Perci*: younger brother of William de Perci* and liege lord of Sudtone (together with Nigel Fossard*)
Simon de Kyme*: seneschal of Picot de Perci* in Sudtone
Robert de Monbrai*: Comte de Northumberland and nephew of Geoffroi de Monbrai, Bishop de Constantia (Coutances)
The deputy of Ralph de Paynel*, shire reeve of Everwicscire
Nicholas Beaumont: vassal of Robert de Monbrai*
William "Als Gernuns" de Perci*, vassal of the Comte de Cestre, tenant-in-chief Hugues d'Avranches*, and liege lord of Geoffrey de Bernaium, Osbern de Scornesbi* and Picot de Perci*

Kings and high nobility
William I*: King of England and Duke of Normandy
William le Rous*: second surviving son of William I*, later King of England
Robert Courteheuse*: eldest son of William I*, Duke of Normandy
Bishop Odo de Baieus*: Comte de Kent and half-brother of William I*
Robert de Mortain*: Norman duke, brother of Odo* and half-brother of William I*

King Philippe I*: King of the Franks
Alain le Rous*: Breton tenant-in-chief of William I* and II*
Comte de Cestre*: Hugues d'Avranches*, tenant-in-chief of William I* and II*

For old/foreign-language expressions and locations, please refer to Places and Glossary.

Part 1

WILBURGFOS, OCTOBER IN THE YEAR OF OUR LORD 1085

Chapter 1

Roger's hands and toes sank into the soft ground as another squire placed a bucket full of water on his back. The autumnal cold crept from the muddy earth into his fingers that only recently had caressed Emma's smooth, warm skin. Sighing, he bent his arms and lowered his straightened body until the tip of his nose touched the dirty tufts of grass.

"An Engleis crawling in the dirt beneath my feet – what a delightful sight!"

Although Roger would have loved to hurl a load of mud at his elder half-brother for this comment, he didn't even bother lifting his eyes. Instead, he continued to count each push-up while taking care that the bucket did not shake.

"Much as I would relish watching you crumble from exhaustion, I'm afraid I have to proceed with my fight."

Out of the corner of his eye, Roger watched William resume his place on the battleground where weapons practice was taking place.

Ðunres hamer on þe heafod! Would that the god of thunder teach his brother a lesson, if his opponent couldn't.

"Give me that!" thundered a man nearby.

Roger looked up.

The bailiff, Hugues de Borre, snatched something from a young boy's hand and threateningly waved it in front of a woman's face. "So, you wanted to steal from your liege lord, did you?"

"Look at the apple," said the woman, clasping the crying child in her arms. "It's a tiny, shrivelled thing, and worm-eaten too. We wouldn't use it in the kitchen anyway."

"That is not for you to decide!" Hugues de Borre threw the apple into the basket and pointed at the great hall. "Go take these apples to the kitchen! If I catch you stealing again, you will not escape your just punishment."

Roger glanced back at the blades of grass approaching his face. On the battleground, the two panting fighters were prancing and moving about until one of them let out a muffled scream.

"Well, who's the better one of us – again?" asked William, loud enough for everyone to hear.

"You were lucky today," answered his opponent with a deep breath. "But next time, you lose."

"You know as well as I do, mon cher Walter, that this is very unlikely to happen. After all, who could possibly take me on?"

"Someone with a mouth as big as yours," Roger hissed through his teeth, while pushing himself up again with shaking arms.

Two leather boots appeared by his side. "This exercise seems to be too easy for you. Why don't you try it with one arm only?"

A kick jerked Roger's arm away. With a thud, his face slammed into the mud, the bucket tilted, and the ice-cold water splashed over his head and shoulders. Spitting and coughing, Roger sat and wiped the muck from his face.

As he made to rise and pounce on his brother, Oswulf, the master of arms, stepped between the two. "You fight very well, William. Perhaps you would like to find out if you are ready to be dubbed?"

"I certainly would. Who will be my opponent?"

Oswulf beckoned to a squire to bring a wooden practice sword and a shield. "I myself shall put your fighting skills to the test."

William raised an eyebrow. "Don't you think someone younger should do this?"

"Didn't you just say that none of the others can take you on?"

"Well, yes, but—"

"Then let's try and see how long *I* can hold out against you, shall we?" said Oswulf as he took the sword and shield.

Roger stood and wiped the mud off his tunic. His long hair was dripping, but luckily, most of the water had simply trickled off his woollen garment. How he would have regretted missing this fight had he left to put on some dry clothes!

For a long time, William repeatedly attacked Oswulf, but the master of arms always managed to defend himself.

"Given your age, you're still going strong," said William as the two fighters paused briefly.

"I do what I can."

Was there a mischievous glint in the eyes of the master of arms? Roger didn't have much time to think about this question, for suddenly, it was Oswulf pushing forward and attacking William. All he could do was to back off and helplessly try to evade or thwart the attacks. A blow against his leg made William wince. The thrust to his belly caused him to jump back. As Oswulf threw all his weight into his shield and smashed it against his opponent's breast, William at last uttered a sound somewhere between surprise, rage and a rather impolite name for the English master of arms. With the other onlookers appalled and Roger delighted, William toppled backwards into the muddy ground with a splash.

Oswulf placed the wooden sword at his side and stroked his large moustache. “Looks like you’ll be staying with us as a squire for a bit longer, don’t you think?”

With his lips pressed together, William threw away the practice weapons and got up. “I’ll see you in the next lesson,” he said through gritted teeth.

With a grin, Roger watched him stomp off.

On his way, William pushed a maid aside who was walking towards the great hall with a bowl in her hands.

She stumbled, dropped the bowl and just about caught herself from falling. She shouted after William, but he just continued as if nothing had happened. With a look of despair, the woman turned over the bowl. Whatever had been in there could probably not be used anymore, for she shook her head, put the bowl down and reluctantly picked up what lay on the ground.

Hugues de Borre rushed in from the side.

Roger turned away. William’s kick had saved him from having to serve out his full punishment, but Oswulf would not hesitate to make it double if he didn’t get on with the weapons practice.

As they were storing away the equipment in the armoury, a servant told Roger that his father wanted to see him right now.

The autumn sun shone through the narrow openings under the roof of the great hall and threw a faint glimmer on the dark wooden beams. William, their father, Sire Geoffrey, and the bailiff, Hugues de Borre, were standing by the fire in the middle of the hall, disdainfully watching him approach.

"You were late for weapons practice," said Sire Geoffrey, "and you knocked the baskets out of a servant's hand because you were angry about your punishment."

"A full bowl of eggs and two handfuls of pears," added the bailiff.

"I did not! Who said so?"

"William can testify to it," answered the liege lord.

"What? It was *he* who pushed the woman aside."

"That's not what William says."

"Then he does not speak the truth. I didn't touch the woman. Why don't you ask her yourself?"

"Are you saying I'm a liar?" asked William.

"I do, for I was on the battleground at that time. Oswulf and the others can confirm this."

Hugues de Borre snorted. "It wouldn't surprise me if it was you."

"And it doesn't surprise me that you think so." Roger clenched his fists. "But is it not your duty to gather evidence instead of jumping to conclusions? Did you even question the woman at all?"

"I know my duty very well." Hugues' wild hair seemed to rise like the puffed-out fur on the arched back of a cat getting ready to defend itself. "Of course I questioned her."

"So? What answer did you get?" Roger relaxed. Now, William would no longer be able to deny what he had done.

"What do we care about the idle chatter of a servant?" asked William. "It wouldn't be the first time you've taken out your anger over a punishment somewhere else, mon cher Roger."

"Lygewyrhta! It wasn't me! Why don't you admit that you did it?"

"Asez!" said Sire Geoffrey. "Everybody knows your tantrums and their consequences. How you think you're going to run a manor one day, I do not know, but at least it will not be mine." He looked at William, whose sneer widened. "In order for you to learn how to handle food supplies, in particular before winter, you will work as a page during mealtimes for a week."

"You must be joking! I'm not a child anymore."

"You behave like one," said the liege lord, turning to go. "Cenhelm will instruct you."

Chapter 2

As Roger stood, stunned, watching the three men leave, he felt someone touch his shoulder. He turned round and looked into his mother's kindly face.

"Cum, min sunu," said Dame Edeva, beckoning him to follow her into the private chamber on the first floor. She closed the door behind them, took a small leather pouch from a wooden chest, pulled out a golden ring and presented it to Roger. "See if it fits."

"A ring? For me?"

Roger took the shiny object and looked at it from all sides. Like strings in fine fabric, a multitude of delicate lines ran along the entire shank all the way to the round head of the ring. On the top, oval chain links framed a patterned background that was dominated in the middle by a cross formed by a tree, an axe and a longsword – a seal that Roger had never seen before.

"This is Kjetil's ring. It belongs to the rightful heir of Wilburgfos, who cares about its people, not about what his favourite son claims. I wanted to give you the ring two years ago with Kjetil's scramasax, but it would have slipped off your finger." She struggled to smile. "It is the last thing I have left of him."

"Don't you want to keep—"

"No, Hroðgar, I don't. A ring should be worn, not forgotten in a dark corner. Put it on!"

"Are you sure?"

"I want you to wear it. Kjetil would have wanted it too." She pressed her lips together.

Roger pushed the gold ring onto the little finger of his left hand. *It belongs to the rightful heir of Wilburgfos.* The ring fitted as if it had been made especially for him. "What do the symbols mean?" he asked, regarding the head of the ring.

"The tree is the trunk of Yggdrasil, the world ash, which stands for the eternal connection of all things. The sword represents protection, justice and wealth; the axe strength, courage and power."

Roger nodded. He knew Kjetil only from what his mother had told him. They weren't related, nor had they ever met. And yet, Roger felt an unusual closeness to this man. He had already inherited Kjetil's short sword, and now, he also received his signet ring. His mother had loved Kjetil, and if she entrusted Roger with such precious keepsakes, she probably loved Roger at least as much, even though he was the product of her marriage to Kjetil's murderer.

"I thank you, Mother. You do me great honour with this gift." Roger rose and, after one last glance at the ring, lowered his hand. "I will wear Kjetil's ring with pride and prove that I am worthy of it."

Dame Edeva smiled. "You will, when you're a little older." She put the leather pouch back into the chest and gathered her floor-length blue tunic as she stood up.

Roger followed his mother down the stairs into the great hall and let his gaze wander. The servants were dressing the tables for the upcoming first meal of the day and brought earthenware mugs and jugs with wine that they put on the tables. A little away from the hustle and bustle, his father and half-brother were absorbed in a board game.

Out of nowhere, Hugues de Borre appeared by the stairs. "Was there something important to discuss?"

"I don't think you need to know what a mother discusses with her son, munsire," answered Dame Edeva.

"It depends on what it is, Dame."

"Well, if it puts your mind to rest, let me tell you that I have given my son initial instructions on how he will serve his punishment as a page."

"Then I wonder why you had to retire to your private chamber. Those instructions must have been confidential indeed."

"If you are insinuating something, Hugues, then say it out loud. If not, begone. I would like to eat."

"As you wish, Dame." The bailiff bowed ever so slightly while squinting suspiciously at Roger.

A bawdy laughter suddenly filled the hall as a white-blonde youth rumbled through the door. Roger rolled his eyes but couldn't help grinning. His friend, Brandolf, had a habit of making himself heard.

Approaching the kitchen, the young Dane fondled the bottom of a maid along the way. She let out a shriek and turned round, grumbling.

Shaking his head, Roger watched the scene.

"Oh, there you are!" said a young voice at his side, and two big, blue, inquisitive eyes looked at him.

"Richard, mon ami. Did you miss me?"

Roger patted him on the shoulder. He was fond of the little red-head, who was, like him, the son of a Norman and an Englishwoman. Richard was like a little brother, eagerly awaiting the next year when he would become a squire and would at last be allowed to compete in weapons practice against Roger.

"Yes, no, I mean, we were actually only looking for you because you had suddenly disappeared, and we didn't know where you were."

Roger tousled the little one's hair. "Your concern for me does you honour, but there is no need to worry. Look what my mother has given to me." Not without pride, he showed him the ring on his left hand. "It's from my mother's first husband. She wanted me to wear it."

"It looks different from the ones I know. There's no lions or initials anywhere." Richard grinned mischievously. "A special ring for my special friend."

Roger smiled. Was he really special? It almost sounded presumptuous, but he knew he was different in certain ways. If only his elder brother didn't always exploit this in his own favour, as he had today!

Part 2

WILBURGFOS, APRIL IN THE YEAR OF OUR LORD 1086

Chapter 3

"If you had a beard, I'd shave it off you now!" With a yell, Brandolf threw himself forward. His sword crashed onto the round shield that Roger had lifted above his shoulder, just in time.

"At least you'd be able to find my beard." With his full force, Roger swung the shield to the side, yanking his opponent's arm and sword. "Yours is not even visible, milksop."

He lashed out at the Dane's open flank. The blonde one cried out. Roger jumped behind him and drilled the blunt tip of the sword into his back. "Can you see the doors of Valhǫll, Viking? In you go!" He lifted his knee and gave the Dane a good kick in the butt.

With the others laughing out loud, Brandolf thumped onto the ground, followed by very audible Norse cursing. Roger raised his shield and sword up in the air and let the audience applaud him.

The Dane picked himself off the ground, threw the wooden sword and shield away and rubbed his side. "Stinkin' leftie!"

Grinning, Roger wiped the sweat off his brow with the sleeve of his linen shirt. "Father Leofric might see it as a curse, but it does have its advantages, my dear Brandolf. Besides, you ought to know by now that Vikings always lose against the English and the Normans."

"No, they don't!" protested Brandolf's little brother, Bjarni, with all the sense of justice of an eight-year-old. "You're lying!" Defiantly, he pushed his lower lip forward and stabbed the bark of a nearby tree with one of the little knives he always carried on his belt.

Wiping the dirt from his crooked nose, Brandolf sauntered up to Roger. "You're as proud as your father."

"I'm not like my father at all!" Roger slumped into the grass and put his arms around his knees. "That's William's prerogative."

Brandolf grabbed the water bottle from Drogo and looked down at Roger. He took a long gulp, wiped his mouth with his sleeve and grinned as he held out the flask to Roger. "At least your hair's better than his."

Stifling a smile, Roger took the water pouch. With his long hair, he did in fact resemble the two Danes, Brandolf and Bjarni. This was one of the few respects in which his mother had prevailed over his father. He would have preferred the hair of his second-eldest son to be the bowl cut of a proper Norman.

"Roger has reason enough to be proud," said Richard. "He is courteous, well educated and always willing to do his best." He picked up the shield and sword. "I'd be glad to be able to fight like you, Roger."

A voice with a pronounced Norman accent made the boys look up.

"I don't think your father would like to hear this, mon cher Richard."

Two riders were approaching on the path that led from the manor house through the small wood to the clearing. Had his half-brother been by himself, Roger would have remained seated, but since his friend, Walter Fossard, the son of a mighty vassal, accompanied him, Roger was forced to stand up.

William halted with a side-glance at Roger.

"My half-brother is still a little... short-tempered with weapons. Too much feral blood."

"What do you want, William?" asked Joscelin, the oldest squire, who was in charge of the whole group.

William pursed his lips. "Walter and I watched you for a while. We thought we might learn something new. I see you're playing with little wooden sticks."

"We're not playing, William," corrected Richard, "we're practising."

William nodded. "Oh, right. You're *practising* with little wooden sticks."

Roger growled. "You know very well that we mustn't use sharp weapons out here while practising."

"And that's how it should be," said William, "if there's one like you around."

"What are you insinuating?"

"Mon cher Roger, we all know that you're still unable to control your rage."

"Not everyone can be as perfect as you."

"Of course not. Father and I would still appreciate it if you stopped letting off steam at our property all the time. After all, I don't want to rebuild and buy everything again when I take over Wilburgfos someday."

"Wilburgfos is not Sire Geoffrey's property," Richard lowered the weapons as if trying not to support his opposition with an offensive gesture. "He has received it as a fief from my father, but it's not his own."

"Whatever," said William. "In any case, I will take over the manor house one day. So you'd better learn quickly how not to behave like a savage, like your Danish friends there."

"*We* are savages?" asked Brandolf. "Who killed all the people in the north because he wanted the land?"

William let out a brief laugh. "You, of all people, are asking me? Your fellow countrymen can do nothing but pillage and plunder."

Brandolf's white-blonde hair seemed to light up as a flush of anger shot up his face. "At least we don't wipe out whole swathes of land like you Normans did! You slaughtered all of my family."

Roger grabbed his friend's arm and pulled him out of William's reach. "Why don't you get lost instead of disturbing us any longer?"

"My dutiful little half-brother! If only he spoke and acted so valiantly at other times! Unfortunately, someone needs to teach his friends better manners, too. What a shame you can't do this, mon cher."

"Oh, and you could, could you?" asked Roger.

"Why don't you get off your horse?" asked Brandolf, trying to push past Roger. Even as the latter stood in front of him with his arm stretched out, the young Dane simply pushed forward. He was smaller than Roger, but the force in his upper body left no doubt that the two-handed battle axe was his weapon of choice. "Then we'll see who teaches who some manners!" Brandolf threw himself about to shake off Roger's grip.

After a brief hesitation, William handed Walter the reins and dismounted. He adjusted the sword on his weapon belt and took his kite-shaped shield with him.

Walter looked at his friend in confusion. "We don't have time for this, William. The others are waiting for us."

William waved his words off. "I won't be long, Walter. Why don't you ride ahead?" Without waiting for his friend's reply, William walked to the other side of the battleground, turned round and pulled his sword.

"What are you doing, William?" asked Joscelin. "You do know that your father has forbidden fighting with sharp weapons out here. Do you want to defy your father's order?"

"He who wants to prove that he's a man should also fight like a man." William regarded the reflection of the sun's rays on the shiny blade of the sword. "But you might be afraid of the Normans, like your ridiculous King Svend Estridsen?"

Bjarni, who until now had been standing behind a tree, stuck his head out timidly. "Go on, Brandolf! Show him!"

All eyes were on the snorting Dane, who freed himself from Roger's grip and stomped towards the weapons.

"You can't do that, Brandolf!" Unable to move and feeling a little queasy, Roger watched his friend. "What if Oswulf finds out? It's also far too dangerous."

Joscelin put his hand on Brandolf's shoulder as the latter reached for the weapon. "Come to your senses, Brandolf."

Brandolf threw the white-blonde curls back and shook off Joscelin's hand. "Let go!" He grabbed his large axe and stood opposite William at the other end of the battleground.

The two opponents eyed each other while prowling to the side and forward. William stabbed first. Brandolf jumped back and swung the axe above his head. William easily dodged the mighty blow that followed.

So it went on for a while without either of them gaining a decisive advantage. Over time, however, Brandolf's movements slowed noticeably, and it seemed to take a lot more effort to lift his axe for an attack than at the beginning of the fight. William, by contrast, smoothly and nimbly circled his opponent and his mighty weapon.

Roger's gaze kept swaying between the battleground and Bjarni, who was biting his nails while pacing in front of the tree and whose cheers diminished until they stopped completely. It must have been terrible for him to watch helplessly as William, armed with his sharp sword, almost toyed with Brandolf.

"Aaaargh!" Brandolf's scream startled onlookers and horses. On Brandolf's left thigh, a red line made its way through the light-coloured breeches down to his knee.

William stood with his back towards Bjarni, a mere six steps away.

Out of the corner of his eye, Roger saw how the boy pulled out a knife and charged. "Bjarni, no!"

He raced after the little one and caught his arm, but the boy swung his second knife through the air. A sudden pain cut off Roger's scream in his throat. He winced with a hiss. His hand reached for the burning cheek, and Bjarni was free.

When Roger looked again, Brandolf was hauling his battle axe through the air. William was only watching Brandolf. He didn't see the boy behind him, who now rammed the knife into his unprotected back. William writhed in pain and lowered his guard for just one moment.

"William!" Covered in blood, Roger made one last step forward towards the battleground, where Brandolf's axe went down on William, severing his left arm and half of his chest.

Chapter 4

The sounds of the fight echoed in Roger's ears: Brandolf's groan as he whirled his axe through the air; William's scream and the grisly crunch as the deadly weapon sliced through his bones; the long, dull thud shaking his brother's body one last time before death sucked all movement out of it. And then, silence. Nothing, and no one budged. Not a sound could be heard. Even the birds had stopped chirping.

Roger fell to his knees beside William. His cheek was burning. *Eala, Willelm!*

A red lump bulged over the blade of the axe stuck in the body and made William's skin appear almost translucent. Roger reached out for his brother, but before touching him, he pulled back his hand.

"Par Deu!" Walter croaked at last.

Roger gulped as he pressed the folded cloth of his sleeve, already a deep crimson colour, against his right cheek. Only vaguely did he make out Brandolf's features when he looked up at the Dane. "You killed my brother," he whispered.

Clinging to Brandolf's lower arm and in a voice that betrayed disbelief rather than pride, Bjarni said, "You won."

"You killed a Norman!" cried Walter.

"He insulted us!" hissed Bjarni, pressing himself even closer to his brother.

"Teis toi!" said Walter. "Had it not been for your cowardly attack from behind, your own brother would be lying there now."

"We must take him home," murmured Roger, dazed by the double pain he felt about William's death and Brandolf's deed. Shaking, he turned to Walter and held out his blood-smeared hand to him. "Give me the horse. I'll take William back."

Walter regarded Roger closely then nodded. "A tun acort."

While Richard helped Roger to his feet, Joscelin took the reins of the dapple-grey stallion.

"You will get the punishment you deserve," Walter said. "I'll see to that."

With a disparaging look at Brandolf, he turned his horse and trotted off towards Wilburgfos.

When Roger was sure that Walter was out of earshot, he turned to Brandolf. "Đu eart unwita! What were you thinking?"

"Your brother started it! What was I supposed to do?"

"You were so eager to get your axe. Practice weapons are not enough for you."

"Should I have battled your brother with a stupid wooden stick?"

"Perhaps," Roger said bitterly. The prospect of coming face to face with his father this time sent a tremor through his intestines. "Then he wouldn't be lying in the grass, sliced in half, and I wouldn't have to tell my father that his favourite son is dead."

Joscelin had picked some ribwort leaves and went on to secure them on Roger's cheek with a strip of cloth. He nodded towards a row of tall trees near the clearing. "Let's go get some strong branches and a few hazel rods over there. We need to build a stretcher to get William home. Drogo and Brandolf, you come along and help me. You others, get William ready." He took his sword and made a movement with his head towards the dead body. "Don't forget your axe, Brandolf! We'll need it."

Brandolf stood feet apart beside William, grasped the handle of his battle axe and pulled strenuously. Some flies which had settled on the gaping wound flew up, buzzing. After some jerking, the axe came smacking away from the huge gap, which was immediately filled by blood and entrails. Bjarni clamped his hands over his mouth and just about reached the large rock before retching sounds were followed by an audible gush of liquid.

While the others disappeared between the rows of trees, Roger and Richard turned to the dead body, on whose open wound the flies had greedily retaken their places. Richard wrinkled his nose and looked as if he was about to make a second puddle behind the large rock. He tied the horse to a tree and regarded Roger.

"You look terrible."

Roger inspected himself. The linen shirt stuck to his upper body as if it were tied to it by a wide, deep-red bandage whose colour matched that of Richard's hair. Roger let his fingers cautiously follow the crimson trail upwards. His throat was both greasy and encrusted with sweat and blood, leaving little trace of his light skin and his fine features that his mother so loved. He palpated the makeshift dressing on his right cheek, under which the tips of the leaves stuck out over cheek and chin bones.

"At least you're still alive," Richard added in a low voice.

"My father would have preferred it the other way round."

"You mustn't say that!" Richard handed Roger the light woollen cloak that he had put on this morning when they rode out to the clearing. "Take that to tie him up." He put William's sword on the side and slid the shield off William's left arm.

"Give me a hand, Richard." Roger spread the cloak beside William and showed his friend where to pull. When they had moved the body onto the cloak, Roger knotted the cloth around his brother's upper body and arm so that it looked as if William had thrown a short mantle over his left shoulder. Then he helped the other squires as far as his strength would let him to finish the stretcher while Richard collected the practice weapons in two woollen sacks.

Finally, four of them carefully lifted William onto the stretcher. Joscelin fastened it to William's horse and added his sword and shield. Brandolf took his blackened battle axe and lifted it onto his shoulder.

"What will you do now, Brandolf?" asked Joscelin.

Brandolf blew a strand of hair from his face. "Why? What am I meant to do?"

Drogo wildly flourished his hands. "William's dead, man! How are you going to explain this to Sire Geoffrey?"

Joscelin nodded. "You know what the laws stipulate for the killing of a Norman, don't you?"

"It was an accident." Brandolf apologetically lifted his hand. "I was only defending myself."

Roger slumped onto the rock, exhausted and taking a deep breath. His right cheek stung with pain, and he could still feel how Bjarni's knife cut through the flesh. "My father won't believe you."

The young Dane rolled his eyes. “You were all there. You can testify to it.”

Roger, Joscelin and Richard exchanged a glance. Joscelin folded his arms in front of his chest. “True, but the question remains, how it could happen out here – after all, we’re only allowed to use practice weapons for fighting outside the manor house.”

“There… there are riders.” Drogo froze.

“Again?” Joscelin frowned.

“Five Normans,” said Richard.

“Ic hine wergðo on mine sette!” Roger growled. “This will be Walter’s doing.”

“Fiz a putein!” Drogo alternately looked at the riders and Roger. “What are we going to do?”

Roger’s heart was pounding in his throat. He had to do something, but he was still paralysed with numbness and pain. He could already hear the hoofbeats of the horses.

His otherwise brash and daring brother-in-arms stood as if petrified. Soon, the group of riders would be reaching the woods around the clearing. Frightened, Bjarni clung to his big brother and buried his face in Brandolf’s arm and upper body.

“You need to go, Brandolf!” said Roger, but the Dane did not move.

He didn’t even seem to notice how his little brother was tugging at his sleeve and talking to him.

The leaves on the bushes rustled as the five horses galloped over the narrow path onto the clearing and came to a snorting halt around the youths. The leader of the pack, Hugues de Borre, spurred his stallion towards those surrounded and, without a word of greeting, pointed at Brandolf and Bjarni. “Seisisets tut deus!”

Four spears and all eyes were on the two brothers from all sides.

"Drop your axe, Daneis!" ordered Hugues.

Brandolf hesitated briefly then slowly put the axe on the ground.

"Wait!" said Roger. "I can explain."

"You can do that when they are brought before court." Hugues didn't even bother looking at him to answer. "Aluns!" He gave a hand signal and steered his horse back on the path.

Roger and the others had to watch helplessly as the men drove the two prisoners towards their fate with the tips of their spears.

Chapter 5

They left the woods and followed the narrow path along the Fors Bekkr, which accompanied the funeral cortege of the youths with an eerie hissing and gargling.

Although the snow had melted some weeks ago, foam crests were dancing atop the thunderous water. Many years ago, Roger's friends had only just been able to pull him from the torrential river and avert a disaster. Back then, no one died. Today, it was different.

The stream meandered through the flat green landscape like a dirty ribbon until it turned to the southwest and vanished behind the heavy palisade of Wilburgfos manor.

With his heart racing, Roger eyed the roof of the great hall, which was lying in wait behind the fence for their arrival. Just a short ride downstream of the manor house rose the formidable wooden structure of the Benedictine priory of Wilburgfos, whose steeple towered over the modest peasant huts. Roger gulped. What would his half-sister, Adelais, say when he brought her the news of her brother's death?

A few children craned their necks as the boys passed the small, decrepit huts of the settlement and through the palisade gate to get to the square in front of the great hall. The sun was high up in the sky. On an ordinary day, the morning work would have been finished by this time and the bustling preparations for dinner would start. Then, all sorts of sounds would fill the manor: the murmur and eating noises at the long tables in the hall, the hissing and rattling in the kitchen nearby, the nattering of the maids on their way between the kitchen and the storerooms, the soft tones of his mother and the commanding thunder of his father.

But today was no ordinary day. Roger felt as if he had buried his head under a down pillow. The chapel stood lonely and lost near the great hall. No neighing was heard from the stables, nor any banter about horses, equipment or war strategies. The door of the armoury, usually a noisy and bustling crossroads for young men, was closed and sulking gloomily. The other huts anxiously huddled up to the wooden fence.

People with uneasy expressions on their faces hurried off as soon as Roger gazed upon them. Others put their heads together, turned away with their hands covering their eyes or crossed themselves, looking down. The odd, hasty whisper reached Roger's ear, but he could not make out what people were saying. Fingers pointed reproachfully, sometimes at William, sometimes at himself. Only Drogo vociferously complained in the background about the obtrusive flies that buzzed relentlessly around the dapple-grey and William's body.

Roger had just brought the stallion to a halt in front of the great hall when his younger brother, Tankred, darted out from it. He was barely a year younger than Richard and looked like a small version of his elder half-brother with his light-blue eyes and bowl-cut reddish blonde hair.

"William? William!" Tankred threw himself half onto, half in front of the stretcher, digging his fingers into the cloak and tearing at it as if he wanted to shake William back to life.

"What have those felons done to you? Why did they do it? William! Get up! You mustn't die. You can't leave me!" His outburst of rage dissolved into violent sobbing.

"It seems Walter has been busy since he left us," Joscelin murmured in Roger's ear.

Drogo put his hand on the boy's shoulder. "Calm down, Tankred."

The youth startled and knocked Drogo's hand off. "Don't touch me!" His face contorted with rage, and he looked at the others. "Why didn't you help him? Did you just stand and stare like you are now? You are to blame for his death. Without you, he would still be alive. It's your fault. I hate you!"

"I tried—" said Roger.

"Oh, you!" Tankred panted. "You could never stand him. Because he could do everything better than you. Because I adored him for it. You never were and never will be the one I look up to."

"I wanted to save him, b—"

"Don't make me laugh." Tankred wiped his nose with his sleeve. "You were just waiting for William to die so that you would become the oldest son. I hate you!"

Roger clenched his teeth. Tankred was accusing him, of all people, that he hadn't helped William? Of course he had wanted to save him, and if it hadn't been for Bjarni's knife, he certainly would have succeeded. But William was dead, and he himself was badly injured – the inevitable scar would remind him, and everyone else, of this day forever.

All of a sudden, people's attention moved from the three brothers to the entrance of the manor house, from which now emerged Roger's younger sister, Isabel, with quick steps. Her straight, reddish blonde hair flew like a veil behind her, revealing her fitted, moss-green tunic, which hugged her feminine curves.

When she spotted William's stretcher, she stopped, clasping her mouth and nose with her hands. "Par Deu," she breathed, briefly closing her eyes and crossing herself as a tear ran down her cheek. Lifting the cloth of her tunic off the ground, she swayed towards William's body and knelt down awkwardly beside Tankred.

"Aluns!" Roger beckoned the others, who were watching Isabel's every move with open mouths. "Let's take him into the great hall."

Crying, Isabel stroked her dead brother's hair. Joscelin and Richard detached the stretcher from the horse and laid it on the ground. Without saying a word, Tankred stood by, sulking, while Drogo helped Isabel to her feet.

It was only now, with the stretcher flat on the ground and Richard leading the dapple-grey to the stable, that Isabel caught sight of her second-eldest brother. She gasped in horror. "Roger! You're covered in blood everywhere. You didn't actually—"

"Bjarni caught me with his knife. He wanted to help his brother. Like me."

They followed the others into the great hall and entered the spacious room made from massive dark wooden beams. As they were approaching the fireplace in the middle, the smell of burning wood infused the stale air around them. Delicate trails of smoke twirled into lofty heights where a big hole in the roof and a few narrow slits just below let the fumes sneak out and the light creep in. Here was where, at other times, the inhabitants ate and celebrated, the landlord saw to his courtly and other administrative tasks and kinsmen and servants slept – it was the central place of life at the manor. But today, there was no trace of life. Instead, the hall was heavy with the sense of death and transience.

On a dedicated table along the side of the hall lay the stretcher with William. Sire Geoffrey was gazing at his dead son with an expression on his face as if he had gulped down a whole jug of bitterwort potion in one go.

With his thick fingers, he lifted the shield, loosened the cloak and lifted it to look underneath. Not a single word nor tear, not even a reproachful look at those who had witnessed the accident. For a fleeting onlooker, it was impossible to tell what the father was feeling at this moment, but Roger very well noticed the barely visible, repeated tensing of the jaw muscles. Without doubt, a thunderstorm was brewing inside his father and would sooner or later erupt over someone.

Roger swallowed hard.

Right beside the liege lord, Hugues de Borre was looking not at the dead, but at the living who kept a reverential distance from him. In a dark corner stood Oswulf.

Clad in a floor-length, green dress, Dame Edeva fluttered over to her husband and Hugues de Borre and regarded her step-son at the table. She crossed herself, knelt down and folded her hands. After some time in silent mourning, she rose and looked among those standing by. When she spotted Roger, she gathered the folds of her dress and hurried to him.

"Eala, Hroðgar! What happened to your cheek? Why didn't anyone tell me? Cum, min sunu! I need to have a look at your wound." She gestured towards the staircase that led to the bedchamber. "Can you manage the stairs?"

Roger nodded and took a deep breath. Richard helped him climb upstairs and supported him in front of the bed while Dame Edeva pulled the soiled clothes from Roger's body. She told a maid-servant to bring boiling hot water and fresh linen then fetched her medicine kit from the heavy chest beside the bed. Richard covered Roger and left the room with a sorrowful look on his face.

After removing the blood-stained bandage and leaves, Dame Edeva cleaned the wound with a cloth as the maid-servant poked the fire under the pot of water she had brought.

"How are you, Mother?" asked Roger.

"I should ask you that. Besides, you shouldn't speak while I clean the wound."

Roger winced in pain and hissed.

Dame Edeva shook her head so that her veil swung sideways. "Your father has always been convinced that William would one day take over the manor. Every man wants his eldest son to follow in his footsteps. Yet fathers often overlook that their sons make the same mistakes as them."

After wrapping a bandage over the top of Roger's head and around his chin, she squeezed the water from the cooked yarrow, placed the herbs on the bandage and fastened them with another piece of cloth. "There you go, my boy. This will prevent the wound from festering. You should now sleep a little."

Roger looked into her light-green eyes, in which he had so often found solace when he had lost courage. "I tried to help him, Mother, but I failed."

Dame Edeva tenderly stroked his blonde hair. "You're a good boy, Hroðgar. I'm sure you tried everything to save your brother. Your wound is proof enough." She leaned over to him and kissed him on his forehead. "I know I can count on you. You did not fail."

As Roger entered the great hall the following morning, his father was sitting at the far end on a heavy wooden chair, drumming his fingers on the table. Beside him were his closest confidants, including Hugues de Borre, whose gooseberry eyes closely monitored the arrival of the hated son.

A few steps in front of his father, Roger stopped, lifted his chin and waited.

Both men eyed each other without saying a word. In Sire Geoffrey's light-skinned, clean-shaven face lurked two ice-blue eyes whose glance alone could pierce an opponent. As always, Roger looked in vain for a sign of human emotion in his father's face, but today, there was more than just coldness in his gaze. Was it worth a try to explain the situation? Would he be able, and willing, to muster at least a shred of understanding or even pity for Brandolf?

"William's dead," Sire Geoffrey said at last.

"I know, Father." *That's all you care about.* "I'm sorry."

"That doesn't bring him back to life."

"No."

Sire Geoffrey steepled his fingers and opened and closed his hands like a bellows. "I've been told that you disregarded my order and fought with sharp weapons."

"We had practice weapons until—"

"A Norman doesn't die from a blow with a practice weapon."

"William pulled his sword."

"One of you attacked him from behind."

"But he was the first to—"

"While another one slaughtered him from the front."

"William challenged him." Roger startled at the brashness of his reply.

"You defend your own brother's butcher?"

Roger bit his lower lip. How he hated conversations with his father! They resembled swimming in a torrential maelstrom into which someone throws a lifeline tied to a rotten branch. The maelstrom would continue to suck you further down into the deep, no matter how well you were able to swim. And if you started pulling yourself out using the lifeline, it was only a matter of time before the branch would break.

"No. What they did was wrong, but—"

"Good. That's why they will be convicted."

"What will happen to them?"

Sire Geoffrey propped himself up on the table with both hands, rose and let his gaze wander around the great hall. In a loud voice, he announced, "The laws of King William only know one single, just punishment for killing a Norman. We will pass sentence in two weeks' time at the next court session." Turning away, he stepped to the side.

Roger hung his head. If only he hadn't let go of Bjarni! "I'm sorry that I couldn't help him."

"You failed."

"I did my best to save him."

"It wasn't good enough."

"Not good enough? Bjarni slashed my whole cheek. I kept running, covered in blood, but it was too late. What else should I have done?"

"William wouldn't have hesitated to save you."

"Neither did I! Look at me! Would I look like this if I had hesitated?"

His father regarded him for a while. "I see a son who disobeys my instructions and whom I cannot rely on."

"I tried to save William!" Roger yelled. "My face will be disfigured forever because of this. The scar will remind me of this day for all my life. And you pretend as if I had merely stood there? As if nothing had happened?"

Sire Geoffrey's face remained free of emotion. "You live. William's dead."

The conversation was over. Sire Geoffrey turned away and marched towards the exit.

"You are a disgrace to your father." Hugues de Borre brushed past Roger to follow the landlord. "If only he had married a Norman woman again!"

The other kinsmen silently left with them.

Breathing heavily and with his mouth half open, Roger stood and watched them go. "Wordwringa!" He banged his fists on the table with all his might, as if it would help to suppress the tears of anger that welled in his eyes.

A dark voice made him spin around. "It's not your fault." The master of arms made a head movement towards the exit. "Come!"

Chapter 6

Roger slumped to the ground and picked up one of the two rolls of cloth. The light-coloured breeches tightened on his muscular thighs as he skilfully wrapped the brown cloth strips around his calves and fastened the ends. In his head, thoughts were buzzing around like midges at a pond in the setting sun. Over and over again, he lived through the events out there on the clearing, heard the screams, saw the blood, beheld the motionless body of his brother.

He stood and reached for his dark-blue tunic. The wound on his face was itching like mad – a good sign, so his mother said, that the flesh was still alive and healing well. For at least another week, she would be changing the bandage and putting on fresh herbs daily until everything had healed. Then, a scar as long as a man's finger would become visible and for all eternity, mark Roger as a living memorial to his brother. He shook his head in an effort to dispel the memories and focused his thoughts on the weapons practice ahead. For the time being, his mother had forbidden him from taking part in weapons practice, but Oswulf had insisted that he be present nonetheless, albeit only to watch, not to fight.

After extensive fighting with lances in the last few sessions, the master of arms had announced that he would be focusing on swords again today. Of course, Roger knew very well that the endless hours of practice were necessary to internalise techniques of attack and defence to be able to use them in combat. But the constant repetitions of the same movements bored him and did not make it easier to fight the images in his head.

The slitted collar of the tunic slid smoothly over his head, but it was a lot harder to squeeze in the rest of his body. When he'd put on this tunic for the first time at the age of fourteen, he'd had to fold it twice at the hip to avoid looking as if he were wearing one of the long tunic dresses of his sisters. Now, almost three years and hundreds of practice lessons later, the garment ended over a hand's width above his knee and tightly hugged his broad chest with every breath.

Roger smoothed out his tunic's rough fabric around his slender hips and strolled off while putting on his weapon belt, which was made of soft pig skin. On the left side, in an artfully decorated leather sheath, dangled Kjetil's short sword, the scramasax of an Engleis who cut many a Norman's throats with it before being himself slaughtered by the swords of the conquerors.

An icy hand crept over Roger's back. He pulled up his shoulders. What would happen to Brandolf and his brother? Bjarni was still a child, much younger than Tankred, who, despite his age, sometimes behaved as if he had only just left his mother's custody.

Roger looked at his left hand. He already wore the ring of the previous Lord of Wilburgfos. Would he one day, and against all odds, really replace it with the ring of the current owner of Wilburgfos?

A tug on his sleeve tore him from his thoughts. "I've called you twice," said Richard, "but you're not listening."

Roger took a deep breath. "A lot has changed in the last few days. And a lot hasn't."

"What do you mean?"

"Even if Father doesn't like it, I'm now the eldest son and, according to Norman law, the one to take over the manor house. He should be instructing me on how to manage it, but he cannot get William out of his head. As if he thinks it will bring him back to life!"

"You're impatient, Roger. It's only been a few days since your father lost his eldest son. He may not show it, but his mind is probably heavy with mourning and the loss of all his hopes. He'll eventually come to terms with the fact that you are taking William's place, but he needs time. So do you."

"You know, with the way you talk sometimes, you ought to have a long, white beard."

Richard grinned. "That won't help us if we don't show up on the battleground soon."

The two boys rushed to the rear of the manor, where the other squires and pages had already gathered. The English master of arms was pacing as usual with his head low and his hands on his back at the far end of the battleground as his pupils arrived. At last, Oswulf sauntered a few steps towards Roger and stopped in the middle of the square. Silent and without haste, he mustered his young counterpart. Although the sun was still low and the morning air crisp and cool, Roger started to sweat.

An eternal moment later, Oswulf finally broke the silence and addressed those present with his usual calm and sonorous voice.

"We're all devastated about what happened to William. But there's no place for mourning on the battlefield. Here, you must only think of fighting if you don't want to be next." He approached a few more steps and looked Roger straight in the eye. "It was an accident, Roger. I know I can trust all of you when you go out to practise on the clearing. Your father doesn't share my trust. He only sees that his heir is dead, and it blinds him to everything else. You must now go your own way and show him what you're made of." He fetched two wooden swords and threw one of them at Roger. "Let's start right away!"

Roger just about caught the sword and stumbled onto the battleground, where Oswulf circled him slowly with his sword lifted. However hard Roger tried, his ability to fight left him in the lurch today. A wrong step here, a slight lack of balance there, a parry just a moment too late – the master of arms punished each and every little negligence swiftly and ruthlessly. It didn't take long before a sizeable quantity of sand coated Roger's sweaty clothes, and the pains in his shoulder, arm and leg made it clear that his body would soon be covered in bruises. Roger resigned to the last blow into his open flank with a grunt. Then, Oswulf let him off the fight. Breathing heavily, Roger leaned onto the practice weapon.

Oswulf's moustache twitched sullenly. "You're not paying attention, Roger. Has William taken your fighting spirit and your ambition with him to his grave? You will take over cleaning the weapons for three days to reflect. Go!"

Cleaning weapons! For Roger, this punishment was part of the practice lessons, just like sword and shield were, as he regularly incurred it after letting off his anger at the wooden weapons or objects within his reach. The mere announcement of the punishment usually led to another outbreak of rage, but today, Roger gladly accepted this premature end of his practice time. He dragged the wooden sword through the sand, handed it to Oswulf and headed for the armoury.

THE CLASH OF metal behind him startled Roger as he was greasing a sword, lost in thought.

With a contemptuous look and a grim snort, Walter turned and stomped out of the room. He probably would have loved to throw a lot more to clean at him in order to vent his anger over William's death. Why Walter had a grudge against him, of all people, Roger didn't know. After all, Walter had watched the deadly fight himself.

Sighing, he turned his attention back to the sword.

Joscelin brought his equipment and laid it on the pile beside Roger. "Oswulf's right. You must forget what happened and look ahead, in particular, concerning who can help you now. You know that certain men are not well disposed towards you and would have preferred William as the successor."

Roger paused rubbing the sword. "You mean men like Hugues de Borre? What could he possibly do? Anyway, my father already considers me incapable of running a manor."

"But it's Hugues who provides him with the evidence," said Joscelin.

Roger nodded. "Yes, and he hates the Engleis."

Someone noisily cleared his throat at the entrance, startling the boys. In the doorway stood the master of arms. "Be careful what you say. This manor house has ears."

One after the other, the youths filed out of the armoury until only Roger remained.

Oswulf closed the door and sat on the bench beside him. "Would you like to tell me something?"

Roger leaned the sword on the bench and put the cloth aside as he tried to organise his thoughts. "I was distracted, Oswulf. I fought badly, but—"

"I saw that." Oswulf patted his hand on his chest where his heart beat. "What does it look like in here?"

Roger shrugged. "William and I never got on well, but the recollection of how he died still haunts me. The screams, the blood..." He looked down, wringing his hands. "I'm the eldest son now, and it is my duty to master everything that William was destined for."

"Are you afraid?"

"I had accepted that William would take over Wilburgfos and that I would have to fight for a fief somewhere else. Like so many others."

"You're taking on a difficult legacy. Your father is not going to make it easy for you."

"Neither is Tankred, but my mother and Isabel have my back. Tomorrow, I will let Adelais know that her brother is dead."

"Adelais lives in the priory, doesn't she?"

"She does, although it's not really the right place for her."

Oswulf rose to open the door. "Sometimes, we're at the wrong place and only notice it when it's too late. Beo gesund, Hroðgar."

Chapter 7

Every time the mossy, brown steeple of the priory emerged from the green landscape, it reminded Roger of the morning, six years ago, when he and his father took Adelais there.

Of all his siblings, she was closest to him, for both of them suffered from the "curse of their birth" as Adelais called it. Both had the bad luck of having been born under circumstances that had brought them their father's resentment through no fault of their own. Adelais seemed almost relieved to make her way to the priory and escape her domineering father. Roger, however, lost his soul sister on that day, and from then on, only spoke to her a few times a year on his visits. He was all the more happy to see her today, even if he had to bring sad tidings.

In front of the monastery, he tied his chestnut stallion, Modig Wiht, to a tree and knocked on the portal.

A nun opened. Her gaze wandered from his eyes to his cheek, most of which was still covered with a bandage.

"An accident," he explained. "I have an important message for Adelais."

The nun took his weapons belt and disappeared into the portico. As he waited, Roger strolled along the storerooms, the kitchen and other rooms in the courtyard. When he spotted the last door to the left, he heard the ghostly voice of his father.

William would have shown her how to conduct oneself towards a Norman.

A sudden pain shot through his toes as he kicked the door then shuffled to his father. *Of course William would have done so. He always does everything right, and I do everything wrong. And as long as he lives, nothing will change that. As long as he lives.*

A bright voice tore him from his memories. “Roger! What have you done?” From the side approached a young woman in a nun’s habit – a long black gown with a white coif under a black veil, covering the blonde hair and leaving only the face free.

Roger smiled. “Adelais! It’s good to see you.”

Adelais frowned at the bandage on his face. “Have you been in a fight with William again?”

It was the same look that Roger remembered from his mother’s face when he used to come home as a child, dirty and smeared with blood, even though there had been no weapons practice that day.

“No, I haven’t.” And with a serious undertone, he added, “William is dead.”

“Par Deu!” Adelais hastily crossed herself. “What happened?”

“Brandolf killed him in a fight.”

“But did you not once say that William was an excellent fighter?”

“He certainly is... was, I mean. It was an accident. William was distracted, and at that very moment...” He fell silent and tried to gulp down the recollection.

Adelais shook her head, folded her hands and lowered her gaze. “I knew it would come to this sooner or later with

William. May God have mercy on his soul... even though he deserves to rot somewhere else."

Roger struggled to stifle a grin.

Adelais looked at him. "How are you, Roger?"

"You're the first to ask me, big sister. Don't worry. I'm in good hands with my mother. She is a true herb witch. Oh, I'm sorry."

Adelais giggled. "That's all right. Your mother loves you. She will do anything to make you get better soon."

A bitter expression sneaked into her smile. Roger knew well what she was thinking of. He pressed his lips together and nodded.

She beckoned him to walk for a bit. "Tell me how the accident happened."

After listening in silence to Roger's explanations and nodding occasionally, she tucked her hands crosswise into the long black sleeves and stared into the open space.

"You know, Roger, Charlemagne's nephew, Roland, also thought he was invincible, and for a long time, he was. But when he was ambushed at Roncesvaux, his pride could not help him, and many valiant men had to die in the battle because of him. In the end, he realised he had made a mistake, but it was too late. And yet, three hundred years later, minstrels, like the reckless Taillefer, are still singing songs praising Roland. What for? To inspire the arrogance and the wish to kill in those who listen to them. What makes us better than our fellow human beings? Why do we look down on others? Where do we take the right to judge them?" She shook her head. "William is dead, but there will be others who act just like him. Everyone will ultimately reap what they sow. I will pray for William's soul, but above all, for his murderer, for Father's revenge will be terrible. May God help Brandolf and his little brother."

"I will be at the trial. Perhaps I can convince Father that it was an unlucky accident."

Adelais gave a hollow laugh. "So was my mother's death, and look what Father did to me because of it. As soon as I was old enough, he stuck me in a convent to get rid of the one who killed his beloved wife. The two Daneis will not get out of it so lightly. They are no women whom you can easily dispose of, and both of them are old enough to be punished according to King William's laws." She lowered her voice. "You know what awaits them?"

"Of course!" Roger answered, although he wasn't really sure what the laws demanded in such cases. Since he was twelve years old, he had been forced to attend trials at court, but his father had yet to deal with a murder. "And do *you* know?"

Adelais raised her eyebrows. "Do you think that I only read the Bible and sing songs in praise of God all day long?" She approached and whispered behind her hand, "This would be far too boring, which is why the prioress regularly borrows texts by worldly scribes from other libraries for me."

"Including King William's laws?"

"Absolutely. And in those, it is stated that the two Daneis face the punishment of mutilation, but you knew this anyway." An angelic smile lit up her face.

Roger nodded. "Yes, I've known this for a long time." Was he blushing?

"You must leave now, Roger. I am grateful to you for the news from home, even though not all of it was pleasant. My heart accompanies you on your way, for it will not be easy for you. Set a good example for little Tankred. Better than William did. A Deu, qe te gard cors e alme."

Roger watched Adelais until she disappeared through the inner portal into the part of the building that was only accessible to members of the priory. He then made his way back across the courtyard to the main entrance, where the nun who had let him in was already waiting.

From one of the front rooms, two women emerged and crossed Roger's path in the middle of the square. The older of the two was wearing the Benedictine black habit. When she spotted Roger, she briefly stopped and spoke to the other in an unintelligible language. The younger one was perhaps a year older than Isabel. Her dark, wavy hair fell loosely over her delicate shoulders and covered almost her entire back. She was wearing a floor-length dark red tunic underneath a pine-green woollen cloak, fastened at the shoulder by a brooch with three weirdly curled arms. From her small, round face, two sea-blue eyes looked up to Roger. If it hadn't been for the wrinkled nose, she would almost have looked curious.

Roger slowed his steps and watched the two women passing him by. What they spoke sounded familiar to Roger, even though he didn't understand a word of it. He had also seen the girl's face – that look – somewhere before.

However much he tried, he just couldn't remember when and where he might have met the girl before. But when he composed himself and opened his mouth to speak, the girl turned away and hastened after the older woman, who appeared rather impatient for a nun.

Chapter 8

A man with dark hair entered the chamber and bowed. "Greetings, Sire."

"I've been expecting you." Robert de Monbrai beckoned his servant to leave and waited until he had closed the door behind him.

"It looks like the king will be absent from England a little longer in order to take care of matters in Normandy. He has no peace and quiet with his vassals in the west and the south. What's more, his eldest son continues to assert his claim to Normandy with King Philippe as his ally. We don't know where he currently resides, but it seems that he is still outside of the country."

"Do you have news from the bishop?"

"Even in captivity, he's eager as ever to maintain his good connections."

A knowing smile spread across the faces of the two men.

Part 3

WILBURGFOS, FROM MAY TO NOVEMBER IN THE YEAR OF OUR LORD 1086

Chapter 9

"A dead person is a good omen – and a fine beginning."

"You think our time has come at last?"

"We've waited long enough. But the Wheel of Fortune turns, and there always comes a day when it goes down for those who feel a little too safe up there, above all others. They believe they can stay there forever, thinking themselves strong and superior to the rest of us. They claim a God-given right to abuse and oppress others. Yet, one day, they too will be dragged down and will have to atone for what they have done. How long I have waited and prayed for this day to come!"

"Should we give Fortune's wheel a little push to speed it up?"

"I like your thinking, but we must not rush it. Would you not also rather watch how they suffer, one by one, the slow and excruciating death they deserve? A quick, painless end would be… a pity. I want our waiting to be worth our while – and I will relish every single moment of their fear and suffering."

"Can I see her?"

"Have you no faith in me?"

"I prefer to make sure myself."

"She looks just like her."

"So, you have no doubt that our plan will succeed?"

“For years, I, we, have been waiting for this day. Now, it has come, and we will do everything we can to seize the opportunity. It could be the only one we have. This time, Fortune will be on our side.”

“I count on you.”

“And I expect you to follow my instructions. You owe me, for you did not keep the promise you gave me many years ago.”

“I was young and didn’t realise the danger.”

“What is done is done. You cannot change it. But you will pay for your failure by helping me achieve what I have been thirsting for all these years.”

“Rest assured that I will do all I can to satisfy you. I too have been loath to wait. So, it is with even greater pleasure that I finally begin what we have long wanted to finish.”

Chapter 10

The tall candles in front of the altar infused the air with a delicate scent of honey, which mingled with the spicy fumes from the censer into a sweet, warm fragrance. The priest had hardly any space fully to swing the precious vessel in the little chapel, for which Roger was secretly grateful. The smoke and the air, heavy with the breath and odours of the congregation, lay like lead on his chest with each and every inhalation.

With his head hanging low, Sire Geoffrey was standing near the stretcher and gazing at the pale face of his eldest son for the last time. A simple shroud enveloped the lifeless body that was laid out in the chapel of the manor, where today, family and the inhabitants of Wilburgfos bid it farewell in a solemn service. Hugues de Borre and the other barons stood away from the candlelight that engulfed father and son like a protective shell, watching the scene with sombre faces. Dame Edeva wiped a tear from her face with her hand. She had her other arm around Isabel, who sobbed uncontrollably. With a sullen glare, Tankred stood between his family and the Norman retinue. Roger, Richard and the other squires, right beside Dame Edeva and Isabel, exchanged furtive glances.

Father Leofric, a short and lean English priest with a dark habit and a silver-grey ring of hair, stepped up to Sire Geoffrey. After a brief glance from the liege lord, he nodded in Hugues' direction. Hugues made a gesture with his head, whereupon four of his men came forward and lifted the stretcher by its bars.

Leofric folded his hands around the Bible. Accompanied by an altar boy carrying the cup of holy water and the censer, he strode out with his head lifted high from the chapel towards the cemetery. He was followed by the men carrying William's body, Sire Geoffrey and Tankred and then Dame Edeva with Isabel and Roger. Last came the other vassals, the squires and the few servants who had been able to lay down their work at this time.

As the funeral procession left the chapel and crossed the courtyard, it was joined by Oswulf. The onlookers, crying, wailing or silently watching in awe, slowly returned to their day work or proceeded to prepare the funerary banquet.

Near the wall of the church of Wilburgfos, a freshly dug, flat grave was gaping in the cemetery. Hugues' men put down their load beside it. Leofric and the altar boy went to the western end while the mourners gathered round the grave. After praising William for his exemplary life and regretting how tragically early he passed away, Leofric sprinkled him with holy water one last time and swayed the censer again.

Exemplary life, Roger thought, breathing deeply. *Miserable hypocrite. Telling everyone what they want to hear – which is probably what saved your life when the Normans descended on your village.*

Two of the bearers grabbed the shroud which enveloped William and lowered the dead body into the earth.

Leofric took a small scoop and threw earth into the grave thrice. "For dust thou art, and into dust thou shalt return." He made the sign of the cross then said, "In the cross of our

Lord Jesus Christ be resurrection and salvation to you and to us all. Peace be with you."

The mourners crossed themselves. Sire Geoffrey and his family, one by one, scooped some earth onto the shroud.

Once the rest of the procession had taken their turns, Dame Edeva asked everyone to return to the great hall for the funeral reception.

There were tables, chairs and benches around the big fire in the middle of the hall. It smelled of wine, freshly baked bread and burning wood. Three honey-glazed ducks, which Sire Geoffrey had caught on the previous day's hunt, were roasting on a spit. Roger and Richard queued at the entrance to wash their hands before the seneschal assigned them and the other guests a place at the tables.

In the middle, the liege lord sat between Hugues de Borre and Dame Edeva, who offered Leofric the place beside her.

In joyful anticipation of the feast to come, the cleric gladly complied with her request. Yet his smile vanished when Roger appeared at his side. How often had Leofric tried in vain to convert him from his diabolic left-handedness! But the boy was stubborn, and so, when Leofric spotted him, he only ever closed his bony hand around his pectoral cross and prayed for the Almighty to protect him from evil.

"What a pleasant eulogy, Father," said Roger on sitting down. "You excel at talking about the dead."

The priest tensely watched Roger drink and put the cup back on the table. "It is my duty."

He seemed to expect another comment, but Roger only nodded, and it was not until a maid-servant approached with a bowl of juicy pieces of meat that the colour and also the smile reappeared in the cleric's pale face. After blessing the food for everyone, he eagerly dedicated himself to consuming all the culinary delights that he was served.

Meanwhile, Roger was keeping an eye on his father and Hugues de Borre. As their repeated side-glances in his direction suggested, they were talking about him, presumably not in a positive way. Since he was sitting too far away to overhear the conversation, he asked his mother what the two of them were discussing.

Dame Edeva shook her head. “They’re speaking too low. I don’t get much of what they say.”

Roger leaned forward and addressed his father, loudly enough to drown out what little noise there was in the hall. “Tell me, Father, what secrets are you discussing that even your wife must not hear a word?”

“It is no matter for a woman,” answered Sire Geoffrey.

“Maybe you want to tell me. After all, I’m now your eldest living son and will, one day, take over the manor. Should I not take part in your daily business?”

Sire Geoffrey exchanged glances with Hugues, whose eyes became even smaller. “Who decided for you to take over the manor?”

“William is dead. The next in line of succession is me.”

“You’re not suitable as a successor.”

Roger’s fledgling scar pulsated. “What do you mean, I’m not suitable? Who else should succeed you? Tankred?”

Sire Geoffrey pursed his lips. “Possibly.”

Roger jumped up. “You can’t be serious! Tankred is still a child.”

The voices stopped, and everyone stared at Roger.

He cleared his throat, smoothed down his tunic and sat down again.

Sire Geoffrey eyed him warily. "Tankred is young, but he has the heart of a Norman and knows how to control himself."

Ha! Like when we arrived in front of the great hall with William on the stretcher? Yapping like a rabid dog, he was. "I will prove to you that I'm a worthy successor."

"Don't make promises you can't keep."

With clenched teeth, Roger sprang to his feet and stormed from the great hall into the courtyard. As he was looking around to find something to vent his wrath on, he heard the voice of the master of arms behind him.

"That's not really how to convince your father."

Roger kicked the sand. A small cloud rose. "I know. Tankred will not speak a word to me for a while. He blames me for William's death, and now, I even call him a child in front of everyone."

"Can you count on the rest of your family?"

"I think so." Roger regarded the signet ring on his finger. *It belongs to the rightful heir of Wilburgfos.* "If it were up to them to decide, I'd naturally take William's place without having to prove myself first."

"The death of his eldest son will have hit your father hard. Everyone has their own way of dealing with the loss of a loved one."

Chapter 11

Roger stepped out from the cool stables into the yard where, from a cloudless sky, the sun was shining down on Wilburgfos and warming the sand beneath his leather shoes. He stretched his arms, closed his eyes and turned his face to the sun. A soft, vernal wind whispered through his hair, whose strands brushed his skin like tender fingers.

In front of the great hall, an unusually great throng of people had gathered. Everyone at the manor knew that today's agenda included more than the usual matters and petty crimes. Today's session would be different.

Roger shuddered as he remembered what Adelais had said. Was there really nothing he could do to help Brandolf and Bjarni?

Roger had not seen the brothers since Hugues and his men had taken them away from the clearing. No one was allowed to visit them or speak with them. The shed at the edge of the village, where his father had imprisoned them, was guarded day and night. Were they still alive, or had his father let them starve to death? Not likely. He'd be loath to miss an opportunity to demonstrate his power. The two captives probably had just enough to stay alive for their public conviction.

"Are they all here to attend the court session?" asked Richard and held his hand up to protect his eyes from the sun. "Even when my father judges major offences, there's never such a crowd."

Roger scratched his head. "I doubt that Wilburgfos has more men over twelve years old than Cattune. Your father might not have such a dutiful bailiff who does, in fact, punish anyone who dares not to attend court."

The two friends entered the great hall, which, for the first time since Roger took part in the sessions, was packed. It was like standing amidst a swarm of bees buzzing around him.

At the end of the hall sat Frederic, the seneschal of the manor, who gazed slowly, almost incredulously, across the room. He must have been around fifty years old, but his dark blue eyes had lost nothing of the friendliness and benevolence with which he had been presiding over the court sessions every three weeks or running the manor in Sire Geoffrey's absence for almost two decades now. Had he also been in charge of dispensing justice, Roger would have had more hope for Brandolf and Bjarni. But the final sentence would be pronounced by the twelve members of the jury, based on the investigations made by the bailiff, Hugues de Borre.

Roger, Richard and the other squires stood at one end in the first row, Walter and the older squires who, like him, would soon be dubbed or had recently been knighted, at the other end. Oswulf was watching from the wall behind the jury.

Frederic's gaze swept over those present while the noise in the hall slowly ebbed off. After exchanging a few words with the seneschal and Sire Geoffrey, Hugues de Borre sent off two men. Frederic rose and lifted his hands as a sign that the hearing was about to begin. When he considered it quiet enough, he sat down and called upon the reeve, who had both the voice and the shape of a large drum.

"Sire Geoffrey de Bernaium, messires, men of Wilburgfos. Before us lies today the difficult task of judging a most atrocious breach of the laws of our beloved King William and an attack on a member of the family of our highly esteemed liege lord himself. A breach that has shaken the order of this manor down to its foundations and thus, also the foundation upon which King William turned England into a kingdom of God. A breach whose outcome has caused unbelievable pain and suffering to our generous and honourable liege lord, whom we owe labour and life for his protection. Yet, I have no doubt that, after thorough consideration of the circumstances and the course of the incident, the honourable jurors," the reeve bowed to the slowly-nodding select twelve who would deliberate and decide the case, "will render a judgement that takes into account the outrageousness of the crime and brings the perpetrators to justice."

The few interjections from the audience got lost in the shouting from outside the great hall. Hugues' men were presumably conducting Brandolf and Bjarni through the cheering and jeering masses waiting at the entrance. Shortly afterwards, the two defendants appeared and were led forward amidst scattered whispers from the spectators.

Roger had heard the servants mutter something about the brothers being taken from the shed in the mornings in order to work in the woods or the fields all day long before returning to their prison with only a morsel to eat and drink. He only realised how little it must have been when he saw his friend and hardly recognised him. The chunky, lively Brandolf had turned into a haggard, shaggy fellow with hollow cheeks and a scruffy beard. His clothes, formerly hugging his taut body, were tattered and torn. God be praised, the wound on his thigh appeared not to have become infected, but a dark brown stripe of blood remained on his dirty legwear. Brandolf's clear eyes looked tired and dull as he wearily gazed at Roger. Similarly, Bjarni was only a shadow of his former self. Already a slim boy, he had lost a substantial amount of weight and teetered along with his head hanging low. Roger wondered anxiously if he could prevent the worst from happening – but what exactly was the worst?

Hugues' men pushed the accused all the way to the front. One of the warriors pulled Bjarni's head back by the hair, so that the boy looked at the judges. Bjarni let it happen. He was too exhausted and emaciated to protest.

The reeve circled round the brothers while proceeding with his charge. "These are the brothers Brandolf and Bjarni, sons of Ragnar the seafarer, who, at the behest of Dame Edeva, were allowed to stay at the manor after their parents died. But they betrayed the benevolence of our cherished liege lord, and in a practice fight outside the manor, they murdered Sire Geoffrey's eldest son, William, cold-bloodedly and perfidiously."

A murmur went through the crowd.

Roger leaned towards Richard. "What's he talking about?" he whispered. "They didn't want to *kill* William."

"They have also been charged with the forbidden use of sharp weapons during a practice fight without supervision by the master of arms." He stood with his legs apart near Brandolf and regarded him disdainfully. "What have you to say to this?"

With his eyes half closed, Brandolf glanced at him.

His guard rammed the sword pommel into his back. "Speak, Daneis!"

Brandolf groaned. "He pulled the weapon first."

Another murmur rippled through the audience.

Frederic placed a hand behind his ear. "You need to speak up, boy," he said. "We can hardly hear you."

With an effort, Brandolf straightened up and repeated just as slowly, but slightly louder, "He pulled the weapon first."

"Who?" asked the seneschal.

"William."

"Why should he have done so?"

"He insulted me and challenged me to a fight."

"As we have heard, this was a practice fight. Why did you have sharp weapons with you?"

"We always do when we leave the manor, but we always use wooden weapons for practising. Oswulf can attest to this."

Frederic looked for Oswulf, who nodded affirmatively.

"What does your brother have to do with all this?" the seneschal went on asking.

Brandolf turned his head to Bjarni, who was struggling to keep upright. "He wanted to help me." In his look lay all the pity of the world.

Roger's heart broke as he saw his friend and the younger brother standing there. Since the death of their parents, Brandolf had always taken good care of his little brother, but how could he now, with his own life hanging by a thread?

Hugues de Borre leaned forward on the table. "He interfered with a fight and stabbed a knife into William's back from behind, while you struck William dead from the front with your battle axe."

The unrest in the hall grew. A few shouted, "Shame!" and, "They'll need to pay for this!" before everything quietened down again so that the seneschal could continue the interrogation.

"Is this right, Brandolf?" Frederic asked calmly.

Brandolf shook his head. "I was angry with William, but I didn't want to kill him, seneschal. It was an accident."

"Liar!" someone cried from the back.

"He murdered him!"

Walter also jumped in: "It was no accident. You aimed your axe at William even though he was injured. You wanted to take revenge on him and deliberately and ruthlessly killed him."

Brandolf turned to Walter. "That's not true, and you know it as well as I do."

Roger stepped forward and held up his hand to draw the seneschal's attention. "Allow me to tell the jury how it all happened."

"That's not possible," said Hugues de Borre. "You're a friend of the accused."

"He is also William's brother and Sire Geoffrey's son," said Frederic with a side-glance to the bailiff. "Please speak, Roger."

"Thank you, seneschal."

Roger gulped. All eyes were on him.

He looked into the frozen face of his father, who had followed the whole trial in silence. To Hugues, who leaned back sulking after the seneschal's rebuff. To his friends, who watched him, full of hope. To Brandolf, who sighed softly and maybe thankfully for the support. And finally, to the jurors, whom he now had to dissuade from agreeing with the prevalent opinion in the great hall. What he said now could make the difference between life and death. What a terrible thought.

"We always carry our weapons with us when we leave the manor. You know yourselves that it is dangerous to wander outside settlements, and especially in the woods, without a weapon. As it is forbidden for us squires to practise fighting with sharp weapons if the master of arms is not around, we only fight with wooden practice weapons in the clearing. Oswulf himself has checked on us secretly several times to make sure that we obey this rule."

Oswulf shrugged and nodded again.

Roger pointed at Brandolf. "I've known Brandolf for many years. He's never been guilty of anything since he arrived at this manor, and he would never have picked up his battle axe of his own accord in a practice fight against one of us. But William repeatedly insulted and poked fun at him and also the rest of us. He was asking for a fight."

Sire Geoffrey slammed his fist on the table. "William would never have done that without a reason."

"What nonsense are you talking?" cried Hugues de Borre.

At the far end of the front row, Walter stepped forward, stuck his thumbs behind his weapons belt and planted himself in plain sight of everyone. "That's a lie," he said in a loud voice. "Brandolf told William to dismount because he wanted to teach him some manners."

Hugues gestured towards Walter. "Ço vus di!"

Joscelin appeared beside Roger. "His demand came only after William had called Roger and Brandolf savages."

"Actually, William taunted us all," said Richard, "because we fought with wooden weapons, as Sire Geoffrey had ordered."

"And when William got off his horse," added Drogo, "he pulled his sword because he and Brandolf should fight like men – with sharp weapons."

The judges looked baffled and surprised. Murmuring filled the hall. Walter's gaze swayed to and fro between the two groups as if he were looking for support for his words. A faint smile flitted across Brandolf's face when he glanced at Roger and his friends. Bjarni looked around in confusion while judges, jurors and those attending the trial eagerly conferred with each other.

Rising from his chair, the seneschal asked for silence. "The jury will retire to deliberate."

Roger and his friends took advantage of the interruption to get some fresh air. When the jurors returned and the trial resumed, the great hall was filled to capacity. News of what had happened during the hearing must have spread like wildfire throughout the village, for Roger was baffled to see many men who had not attended the first part of the trial.

While Frederic took his seat beside Sire Geoffrey, Roger felt a dull throbbing in his scar. His palms were sweaty.

Under the stern eyes of Sire Geoffrey and Hugues de Borre, the seneschal finally rose to ask for silence. "Sire Geoffrey, messires, men of Wilburgfos, we will now hear the judgement."

Taking a deep breath, he looked at the two brothers who stood still before him. "Brandolf, Bjarni: You are charged with the murder of the Norman William de Wilburgfos, son of your liege lord Sire Geoffrey de Bernaium. Hugues de Borre, bailiff of Wilburgfos, has investigated the circumstances of the incident and presented them to the jury. The jurors have also heard the accounts of the witnesses in court. Do you wish to say anything before I ask the jury for the result of their deliberation?"

Brandolf looked up. "It wasn't our fault, seneschal. It was an accident."

Frederic nodded then turned to the jury. “Have you reached a decision upon which you all agree, messires?”

The spokesman of the twelve rose and nodded. “Yes, munsire, we have.”

Roger held his breath like everyone else appeared to do in the great hall, which had suddenly become very quiet. He would have loved to cover his ears, too, but that would not prevent the judgement.

“We find the defendants, Brandolf and Bjarni, guilty.”

The silent tension burst into loud talking and shouting.

Roger closed his eyes. *All for nothing! God help them.*

“Silence!” shouted Frederic repeatedly, raising his hands to lower the noise before proceeding. “The jury finds the two accused guilty of killing a Norman. According to the laws of King William, you can prove your innocence through trial by fire or by combat. Which do you choose?”

Brandolf alternately looked at the jury and Frederic. “But everyone who was there can testify that we are innocent. Why don’t you ask the other squires? They all s—”

“Asez!” Sire Geoffrey jumped to his feet. “You will fight for yourself and your brother against one of my men.”

“With your permission, Sire, I’ll take care of it,” said Walter and stood in a wide stance.

Sire Geoffrey eyed him briefly and nodded. “So be it. Aluns!” He stomped ahead, followed by Hugues de Borre, Walter and the defendants, who were herded out of the hall by their guards.

Roger and the others set off after them before most of the spectators, still stunned, budged.

Looking up to Roger, Richard tried to keep up with his pace. “They can’t do that! Brandolf is too weak. He will lose.”

Roger shrugged helplessly. "They'll do it."

"But they mustn't. The laws of King William state clearly that an Engleis who is too weak or ill to defend himself may select someone to stand in for him. Would you fight for him, Roger?"

Roger sighed.

"Even if I wanted to, my father wouldn't let me. He has ordered Brandolf to fight himself, and there's nothing I can do to change that."

"And as you were saying, Richard," Joscelin interjected, "this law applies to the Engleis. If Brandolf, with his Danish ancestry, invoked this law, Hugues de Borre would immediately dispute it."

"That's splitting hairs!" Richard complained.

"That, mon cher Richard, is Hugues de Borre," said Joscelin with an unusual resignation in his voice.

When they arrived at the battleground, Brandolf and Walter were already facing each other with their swords drawn.

Many had gathered to watch the spectacle with their own eyes, and the rubber-necking crowds were soon satisfied.

Weakened as he was, Brandolf could not hold out against Walter for very long. The latter soon brought him to his knees and set the tip of his sword on Brandolf's throat.

The seneschal spoke one last time. "God has decided that you, Brandolf and Bjarni, are guilty of murder. You will pay a wergeld of one thousand two hundred shillings to the king and the family of the dead to compensate for the loss of a Norman vassal and a son."

"But their parents are dead, and the two of them have hardly any money," said Roger in a last effort to minimise the damage. "How are they meant to raise such a sum?"

"The inhabitants of the Hundred will pay for it if they can't," Sire Geoffrey answered.

A displeased murmur swept through the onlookers.

It's not enough that they get convicted. Everyone in Wilburgfos will hate them for this fine.

Frederic cleared his throat and tried to suppress the trembling of his voice as he continued. "Furthermore, Brandolf, you will be blinded and castrated for what you have done. You, Bjarni, will have your hand cut off as punishment. Both of you will then leave the manor, never to return."

Roger bit his knuckles. He couldn't even pray for want of words.

Walter pulled back his sword and looked down on Brandolf, who sat there slumped and staring into the void. "You're lucky to be sentenced already, Daneis. Otherwise, I would now give you the punishment that you deserve." Sheathing his sword, he turned away with a snort.

Hugues de Borre beckoned his men to come hither.

Only now did Bjarni seem to realise that everything was over. When a second guard grabbed his arm, the little one screamed and wriggled. "You can't do this! Leave me alone! Brandolf, help me! Help!"

But Brandolf knelt on the floor, petrified and not budging an inch. Even the screams of his little brother, his voice cracking from fear, could not move him from his stupor.

Devastated and deserted by all, he surrendered to his fate and did not offer the least resistance as Hugues' men pulled him up and along.

Roger watched Brandolf disappear for a long time. From afar, Bjarni's shrieks tore through the air. Sire Geoffrey and his vassals continued the court hearing as if nothing had happened. Most of the onlookers went back to their daily business at the manor. Silence fell on the battleground where Roger and his friends were left dumbfounded. Had they not done everything to save Brandolf and Bjarni? Why had the sentence still been pronounced against them?

Just as Roger was about to say something, the screeching of a child, followed by the blood-curdling roar of a sixteen-year-old, silenced him.

Chapter 12

The weeks passed after William's death. Sire Geoffrey went about his daily tasks as a liege lord, but the way he paused at times, when he would previously have called William in to confer, showed Roger that his father had not yet overcome what had happened.

The servants and peasants continued with their work as usual. They had more urgent problems to think about than past strokes of fate.

"The next winter will be hard, Roger," complained old Cenhelm, who looked after the supplies on the manor. "Cold and wet weather for so many months is not good for the harvest. The wheat rots, the vegetables grow poorly, and on many fruit trees, the blossoms fall off by the dozens." He groaned. "What little hay can be had from the meadows will hardly be enough to feed all the animals through the winter."

Roger knew from his friends that it was the same elsewhere. Joscelin had mentioned that his father's vassals doubted that they would get the same yield from their fields this year.

"It's a bad time to send commissioners for enquiries," Joscelin had added. "Many vassals will struggle to pay the levies that are already due. The barns and storerooms are empty, and the peasants worry that there will be a famine next winter.

They will scarcely welcome strangers who question them about every pig and each bushel of wheat, even if those strangers are envoys of the king."

The situation was bad indeed, but Roger had to handle such circumstances too, if he wanted to take over the manor.

Pondering Cenhelm's words and how he would proceed if he were the liege lord, Roger joined his family in the great hall for dinner. As he sat down, Sire Geoffrey looked over at him.

"I have something for you to do," he announced.

Roger took a sip. His father wanted to commission him to do something, for everyone in the great hall to see and hear? Well, whatever the task was, he had no choice but to accept.

He put down his cup and regarded his father, who was calmly chewing on a piece of meat. "So, what do you want me to do, Father?" he asked, torn between apprehension and expectation.

Sire Geoffrey finished chewing without haste, swallowed and wiped his mouth with the linen cloth over his shoulder. He grabbed his cup and drank a few sips.

Roger refrained from asking again and instead turned his signet ring back and forth. If he ever wanted to swap it for his father's one, then from now on, his behaviour had to be without blame, even though, at this moment, it was hard for him to hold back.

Sire Geoffrey put the cup down and turned to his son. "You know Sire Osbern de Scornesbi."

The grumpy guy from the neighbouring village? "I do, Father."

"William was to marry his daughter, Mathilda. You will ride to Scornesbi and tell Sire Osbern that the marriage will not take place. His pasture is worthless, all bogged down after the rain. You leave after dinner."

"Certainly, Father. I will do everything to your satisfaction."

With his dagger, Sire Geoffrey cut off a piece of meat and skewered it. "Don't disappoint me." He stuck the chunk of meat into his mouth. "After all, you want to inherit Wilburgfos."

A pleasant warmth flooded through Roger's body. Sure, he wanted this! He could, at last, prove himself and win his father's recognition! All his life, he had been waiting for this. He emptied his cup and jumped to his feet, full of verve and determined to fulfil his duty particularly well.

THE OLD VIKING settlement, Scornesbi, lay about half an hour's ride northwest of Wilburgfos on the other side of the Deorwente river. Where grain fields and many woods made up the landscape around Wilburgfos, here, it was the fertile pasture along the banks of the river.

With a wistful look, Roger passed the herds of cows and sheep that lined the path. *Wilburgfos could do with some of this land*, he pondered but did not dwell long on this thought, for after the heavy and frequent rain this year, the Deorwente had more than once burst its banks – and the first to be affected by such flooding were the inhabitants of Scornesbi. Roger had already been here a few times with his father and William, and he had no pleasant memories of these visits.

Even before he entered the village, he heard the barking of the hounds, mingled with men's voices shouting orders and the scattered neighing of horses. As he approached the manor, the pot-bellied liege lord and his men were preparing to go hunting.

Gilbert FitzOsbern, the only surviving bastard son of the liege lord, was leaning against the wall of a house, calmly watching the servants bustling around the yard. When he spotted Roger, he detached himself from the wall and took a few steps towards the new arrival.

"Well, look who's coming! A distinguished visitor from Wilburgfos."

Roger ignored him and headed for the middle of the courtyard where the horses stood – and, not far from them, Sire Osbern.

The latter scowled at the intruder. "What d'you want?" he asked in a voice like a dissonant fiddle.

Keeping his distance, Roger brought his chestnut stallion to a halt. Two of the hounds frolicked around his horse and curiously sniffed at the visitors. The stallion threw his head in the air and stamped his front leg, causing the hounds to jump sideways and trot off in search of other smells.

"Greetings, Sire Osbern. My father, Sire Geoffrey, is sending me on an important matter."

Sire Osbern turned a spear in his hand and inspected the tip. "If the matter is urgent, why doesn't he come himself?"

"My father has assigned the task to me."

The liege lord put the spear to the side and picked up a bow to fidget with the string. "He sends his milksop son? Where's William?"

"This is why I have come, Sire. Could I talk to you in the manor house?"

With a curled upper lip, the liege lord regarded Roger. "What's with your cheek?"

Roger's heart pounded. As if to brush off a fly, his hand flitted over the fresh scar which, as of late, was no longer hidden under a bandage. "Nothing, Sire. Just... a small wound from a fight."

Growling, Sire Osbern lowered the bow and walked towards the manor house. "So, are you coming or are you staying on your nag?" Without waiting for an answer, he shuffled on.

Roger dismounted and handed the reins to a servant.

Gilbert followed the two.

Although it was a warm day, a musty smell pervaded the great hall, which was darker and smaller than the one in Wilburgfos.

Two servants were clearing away the plates and leftovers from the last dinner.

Sire Osbern headed for a large wooden chair at the clean end of the oak table and slumped down in it with a groan.

Before Roger and Gilbert even sat, he leaned forward and looked at Roger with a crookedly raised upper lip that revealed a gap and two black teeth.

"I hope you have a good reason to keep me from hunting. It's the only pleasure I still have. The devil is an Engleis, and he has cursed this year. The malefic rain is swelling the Deorwente such that my pastures are permanently under water. I had a calf croak during the last flooding. Must have slipped on the mud and got caught in the creepers along the banks, stupid animal." He made wild gestures in the air. "It's dripping through the roofs of these cursed old huts at every turn, and those lazy peasants fall ill all the time."

Sighing, he sat up slowly. "Life in Scornesbi is awful. If it wasn't for the hunt... But you still haven't told me why you actually came here."

Taken by surprise that he could finally get a word in, Roger straightened up.

Gilbert, on the other hand, kept the same dumb expression on his face.

Roger cleared his throat. "It has been a while since you talked with my father about a union between Scornesbi and Wilburgfos."

With his mouth half open and one of his eyes half closed, Sire Osbern regarded him. "So?"

"You wanted my eldest brother to marry your daughter, Mathilda. However, William recently had an accident."

"He had an accident! And that's why you're bothering me and wasting my time?"

"It was a serious accident and..."

"And?"

"He can't marry Mathilda anymore."

"Quei? Why not? Mathilda's fifteen! It's about time she got a man to feed her! With this dreadful weather, this year's harvest will be poor, just about enough for the men. What am I to do with all the womenfolk at my manor? They're good for nothing except for filling it with more children." Moaning, he sank against the backrest of the chair. "How long until William's well again?"

"He's not going to get better. He's dead."

"Dead?"

Roger nodded.

Sire Osbern sat forward again, rubbing his rough hands so that they rustled. "Then she will marry you."

"What, me? Why?"

"That's why your father sent you, isn't it? You're the next male heir."

"I'm only the messenger. My father never mentioned that I should marry Mathilda."

"The wedding was arranged between me and your father. Your father needs the pasture. I need the money for my manor. So, the wedding will take place."

Droplets of sweat formed on Roger's palms. Had his father actually sent him to Scornesbi to introduce himself as Mathilda's future husband? Was it not at all about fulfilling an important mission in his father's name? Why had he not noticed for himself what consequences the news could have for him? He was trapped, courtesy of his own father!

His scar burned with hot blood. While inwardly wishing his father every ailment that his mother had ever mentioned, he feverishly wondered how he could dissuade Sire Osbern from considering him as the substitute husband for Mathilda. He didn't want to marry her. The mere thought of having to face Sire Osbern and his stupid son Gilbert each and every day made him sick.

"I guess that's settled then." Sire Osbern got up from his chair. "You may go and tell your father."

"I cannot marry Mathilda."

"What d'you mean?"

"Don't forget that my mother is an Englesse. Surely, you would not want your Norman daughter to marry a man who has English blood in his veins."

After a brief reflection, Sire Osbern waved it off and headed outside.

"Too late to worry about that now. As long as the money's right and I have one mouth less to feed. Let your father deal with it."

Roger jumped to his feet. "But, Sire! Think of Mathilda!"

"I do. I marry her to the son of a Norman whom this William Als Gernuns rewarded better for his service than me."

"But it's not yet certain that I will take over Wilburgfos."

"What are you talking about? According to Norman law, you are the next heir. Why should your father wish to change this?"

Roger would have loved to vent his anger about his father's idea of succession, but this was neither the right time nor place for it, and certainly not the right listener. "My father is considering Tankred as his successor. He's very much like William."

Sire Osbern stepped into the courtyard and turned to Roger. "Tankred? How old is the brat? Eleven, twelve? What would my daughter want with a man younger than her?"

Gilbert sneaked round to his father's side. "Perhaps Sire Geoffrey should compensate us for the cancelled wedding and the lost money. He could provide one of his daughters with a handsome dowry, and then I could marry her."

Roger scowled at Gilbert. "Father already has other plans for Isabel."

Gilbert grinned and made a gesture with his hand that Roger didn't like at all. "I have some plans for her too..."

"Keep your filthy hands off my sister!"

Sire Osbern scratched the stubble on his chin. "You have another sister, Edéis or something, don't you?"

"Adelais? She lives in the priory."

Sire Osbern nodded at his son. "I like your idea, Gilbert." He folded his arms and said to Roger, "Listen well to what you will say to your father from me: We deeply regret the premature passing of his eldest son, and it pains us that the union of our manors is no longer possible through the marriage of his son William with my daughter Mathilda."

Lygewyrhta. You only regret that your money pouch remains empty!

"Since we have refused other suitors for Mathilda after receiving Sire Geoffrey's firm promise, your father will understand that he is in debt to us. While I would normally insist that you, as the next in line of succession, marry my daughter, Gilbert has given me a much better idea..." he winked at his son, "for us. Your father will therefore give Gilbert one of his daughters in marriage."

Not as long as I live. "He will never do that."

Sire Osbern lifted his chin. "I'm not finished! Tell your father that I leave it up to him to decide which of his daughters he will marry off. If he chooses Adelais, let the convent return the sum he paid for her to enter. A fifth of it he shall keep, and I will have the rest."

"What? You cannot b—"

"Or he chooses Isabel. In that case, he is to give to me, for hunting, the largest patch of woods around Wilburgfos that is not part of the royal forest and has the most animals in it. After all, I will need to supplement my meagre supplies to feed another mouth."

Gilbert laughed. "And many more little mouths very soon, ha-ha!" He repeated the gesture he had made earlier.

"Galwræne yfelsacend! You lust even after a servant of God." Roger pushed Gilbert backwards, so that he crashed against the wall of the manor house. "Neither of my sisters deserves a man like you."

Gilbert's grin froze and turned into a snarl. "Fiz a putein! I'll show you."

He lunged at Roger, who took a step to the side and sent Gilbert tumbling to the ground.

The horses in the middle of the yard pranced.

The hounds came running when they heard the noise and encircled Roger with loud barking. One of them sniffed at Gilbert, who rose to his feet from the sand, and licked his cheek comfortingly.

"You'd better ride now," Sire Osbern slowly stroked one of the hounds over the head, "because I don't know how long I can hold my dogs back."

Pressing his lips together, Roger turned round and walked to his stallion.

"Don't forget to tell your father about my offer!" Sire Osbern called after him. "I expect his answer before the summer harvest begins."

Roger climbed into the saddle, throwing an angry glance at Sire Osbern and his son. "I will repeat your words to my father as you requested, but don't expect him to agree to any of your insolent proposals."

He spurred on his stallion and trotted back to Wilburgfos, trembling with rage.

"What's that face?" shouted Drogo as Roger arrived in the yard.

Raising an eyebrow, Joscelin said, "I smell trouble," then turned his attention back to his die.

Sat on the grass, his friends and some other squires were playing Tric Trac, Jonchet, and Merelle. He would have loved to have joined them, but his father was waiting for his return and Sire Osbern's response.

Richard, who had been anxiously watching Joscelin and Drogo's game, looked up. "What did Sire Osbern say?"

With a snort, Roger kicked the ground. "He's completely out of his mind. He wanted me to marry Mathilda in William's place."

"Lucky you." Joscelin struggled to stifle a laugh.

"That's the pettiest suggestion of all." Roger rubbed his stubble, lost in thought.

Joscelin threw the die in the air and caught it again. "Then you'd better get it over with. Your father returned from hunting in a good mood. Maybe it won't be as bad as you expect."

Richard jumped to his feet and grabbed the reins. "I'll take care of Modig Wiht."

"Do you know where I find Father?"

Joscelin pointed backwards with his thumb. "He's in the great hall with Hugues de Borre. Good luck."

Rolling his eyes, Roger set off. *Hugues de Borre, of course! It would have been a surprise to see my father without his shadow.*

The two men sat at a large table, absorbed in a board game.

What mischief comes next? First, I am to concede my right to succession to Tankred, then Father has Brandolf and Bjarni condemned, then he sends me to Scornesbi under false pretences to marry me off without warning, and now, I must propose to him to sell off one of his daughters with a rich dowry to a guy with the manners of an ox.

He stood next to the table and cleared his throat. "Father? I have news from Scornesbi."

With a nod to Hugues de Borre, Sire Geoffrey looked up and leaned back with his arms folded. "Speak."

In an effort to get the discussion over as quickly as possible, Roger only mentioned the two choices with regard to his sisters.

"Quei?" Sire Geoffrey jumped up and slammed his fist on the table. The chair crashed to the floor. "Is this your idea of getting a task done to my satisfaction?"

"I only repeat what Sire Osbern has told me."

Hugues shook his head. "Shame."

Sire Geoffrey was breathing heavily. The swollen veins protruded from under the skin on his throat. "I sent you to cancel a wedding, not to tell me what to do with my daughters."

"You wanted me to replace William and marry Mathilda."

"You were meant to fulfil a task, and you failed miserably."

"I have delivered your message as you requested."

"Then why do you come back with such undue proposals?"

"Because Sire Osbern says you owe him a compensation."

"Ha!" Sire Geoffrey threw his head back. "A compensation! Why did you not tell him that I owe him absolutely nothing?"

Roger's whole body stiffened. He was looking for an explanation but couldn't think of anything at all. "I... I don't know. His son suggested it."

Sire Geoffrey clasped his hands in front of his chest and looked upward. "His son! At least Sire Osbern has a son who has good ideas and is useful to his father." He bent down and picked up the chair.

Roger leaned forward to maintain eye contact. "You're not going to marry Adelais or Isabel to Gilbert, are you?"

"Of course not. I owe Sire Osbern nothing." Sire Geoffrey sat on the chair and pulled it towards the table. "I didn't expect anything else from you," he said without looking at Roger. "You're just not a true Norman like William."

So, that's what it was all about! It was a test, a game. Father knew from the start how everything would turn out.

Roger clenched his fists, turned around, huffing, and stomped through the hall to the door.

God sceal forlætan þe to ðam ecan forwyrde.

Chapter 13

"Will you still love me once you are Lord of Wilburgfos?" With her hand, Emma, the kitchen maid, shielded her eyes against the sun and squinted at Roger from her coarse woollen cape, which she sat upon on the grass.

Smirking, Roger pulled tight the leather strip of his breeches and regarded Emma. How pretty she was, with her wild red hair sweeping down to her shoulders in lush waves, her perfectly white skin – and all those freckles! And what fire was hidden behind the seemingly fragile exterior! The mere thought made Roger shiver with excitement.

"So, will you still love me then?" Emma sat.

"You shouldn't ask me such things." He smoothed out his linen shirt and tunic.

"Why not? You'll have to find a wife someday. If not now then later. When you are Lord of Wilburgfos."

She smiled, and all the freckles in her cherry-blossom-white face smiled with her.

Roger gave a brief laugh. "You have more faith in my father than I do. I don't seem to be getting anywhere since William's death. During hearings and trials, I am a tolerated guest; we no longer have to worry about incursions from Vikings, and everything's quiet in Wilburgfos. Nothing has changed except that William no longer lives at the manor. As if I only need to be patient and let everything run its natural course. Then everything will come as expected, and one day I will be Lord of Wilburgfos. I simply have to wait."

Emma tilted her head, her dark red curls swinging to the side. Her foot crept up Roger's leg, so that her garment slipped down to expose not only her thighs. "We could ease the waiting a little, don't you think?"

Roger's gaze wandered over Emma's body. The blood shot into his loins as her foot reached the middle of his thigh. His body quivering, he knelt down and stroked Emma's velvety skin with his fingers, starting at her foot and moving upwards. From afar, came the noise of children shouting, clapping, drumming and ringing bells, probably to scare away hungry crows from the freshly sown fields. But at that moment, it seemed to Roger more like they were cheering him on by loudly accompanying his hand on its way. He had almost reached his destination when a noise made him hark.

A voice rose above the nervous trampling of horses' hooves. "I bring news from Sire William de Perci on behalf of King William. Tell your master that I must speak to him."

Roger jumped to his feet and peered around the wall. "On behalf of the king! This must be important."

While putting on his weapons belt and throwing his cloak over his shoulders, he watched the three men who stood with the seneschal in the middle of the yard. The man without armour was probably the messenger. On top of the chain mail and the shields of the two others, the coats of arms of the respective commanders shone in bold colours. One warrior carried King William's white flag with a gold border framed in blue and a central, blue-edged gold cross. The emissary of William de Perci had five golden lozenges on a blue background.

"I must go," said Roger without looking back, leaving Emma alone behind the chapel.

The air was filled with white-grey swathes infused with the tang of meat and sausages that hung like garlands from the ceiling over the fire of the smoke hut. Roger and Drogo liked the smell, but Richard was always glad when the blood month was over because his eyes were constantly watering. Joscelin bore everything as calmly as ever. If there was no salt, the meat had to be preserved using smoke. Simple as that.

A few children, who had gathered firewood in the woods, squeezed past Roger, giggling. In front of them walked another group, whose baskets were filled with nuts, mushrooms and earth-encrusted roots. A blacksmith carried a load of tongs and knives back to his forge. Two servants conferred over a worn wicker basket that they examined meticulously from all sides, and two women dragged a huge basket full of sheep's wool that needed to be spun and woven.

Frederic stretched out his arm when he caught sight of Roger.

"You're coming just in time." He put his hand on Roger's back. "There is bad news from Normandy."

Together with Sire Geoffrey, his vassals and the master of arms, the riders sat down at the tables in the great hall. The messenger stepped forward.

"William de Perci sends me, messires. I bring news from King William, who is battling several traitors at once in Normandy. His eldest son, Robert Courteheuse, together with his ally, King Philippe, ruler of the Franks, continue to support the attacks on the possessions of Norman noblemen in Normandy. We have also had scattered evidence that four years in prison have done nothing to keep Bishop Odo de Baieus from encouraging such perfidious endeavours, again ignoring the limits of his power and his obligations to his own brother. It is our duty, as trusted vassals, to assist the king in his battle against his rebellious son and his allies. With the marriage of Princess Constance to Alain Fergant, Duke of Brittany, we have another powerful ruler at our side to fight the forces that are striving to destroy the Norman empire and to claim our and the king's lands beyond the water."

"How many riders does the king require?" asked Sire Geoffrey.

"Three warriors, plus equipment and horses. We will ride to Pevenesel in two days. You have until then to prepare."

Sire Geoffrey nodded. "I will personally be at your disposal, along with my bailiff, and will decide about the third rider."

Roger jumped up. "Take me with you, Father!"

Everyone stared at him.

"You're a squire," said Sire Geoffrey, "not an accomplished fighter."

Roger looked at Oswulf for help. "I could look after the armour and horses as I do in Wilburgfos."

"We need warriors, not grooms," his father said. "Besides, you are short-tempered and unreliable."

"He also has the wrong friends," Walter interjected. "He would be a danger to you and your entire army."

"Choose your men wisely, Sire," said the messenger. "You are responsible for them. Should one of them cause damage to us, I will hold you personally accountable for it in the name of King William."

"I am aware of that, munsire." With a fleeting glance at Roger, he took a large sip of wine. "It would have been a good opportunity for my eldest son, William, to prove himself in combat. Alas, to everyone's dismay, he was deviously slain in the woods in the spring."

"I am sorry to hear that, Sire." The messenger bowed his head.

"Why don't you let your eldest *living* son try?" Roger asked almost pleadingly.

"Silence!" The ice-blue eyes stared at him. "Your failure has already cost your brother his life. Who can say how many men will die on the battlefield because of you?"

Roger clenched his fists, turned away and marched out of the hall.

He left the manor through the palisade gate, headed towards the market and walked on for a while, silently fuming. Every now and again, he muttered some foul words that disappeared into the air amongst the sounds from the surrounding fields. He was so absorbed with what had just happened that he did not even turn round when he heard quick footsteps from behind. Only when someone, breathing heavily, caught up with him did he look up.

"Are you running away, Roger?" asked Oswulf.

Roger growled, fixed his gaze back to the ground and stomped on angrily.

"Do you think this will change your father's mind?"

"No."

"Do you think he would treat you differently in Normandy?"

"No."

"So, why are you running away?"

Roger paused. *Yes, why, actually?*

"Don't you think you could achieve much more if you stayed in Wilburgfos?"

Roger regarded the master of arms, whose expression demanded not an answer but an insight from Roger.

Oswulf gazed back at the manor. "No one can predict what awaits them in the Kingdom of the Franks and how long they will stay there." He turned to Roger with raised eyebrows. "Or if they will ever come back."

Roger frowned. "That never really crossed my mind."

"I thought so. You are eager to seize every opportunity to prove yourself to your father, but if you were to follow him to Normandy and die with him in battle, what would become of Wilburgfos? Tankred is too young to take over the manor. Wilburgfos would fall back to William de Perci, who would give it to one of his other vassals or hold it back for one of his sons. You have no choice. You must stay to secure your father's inheritance."

"Then why did my father just humiliate me in front of everybody? Could he not have simply said that I had to stay here in case something happened to him? He made me look like a stubborn, incompetent child."

"All the more believable after the exit you pulled."

"Ic eom unwita! How could I be so stupid? I should be glad that Father is taking along those who have always sided with William. Hugues de Borre, in particular, will not make my life difficult as long as he fights in Normandy."

The words danced in Roger's head like glowworms at dusk. Suddenly, it all made sense. By staying here, he not only secured the manor, *his* inheritance, but was also able, at least for a while, to avoid his father's yoke and the surveillance of the bailiff.

A heavy burden fell off his shoulders, and with a deep breath, he relished the new prospects that suddenly opened up before him.

"Life in Wilburgfos will be much easier for you," said Oswulf. "Frederic is well disposed towards you. He will gladly assign you important tasks and make sure that all who work at the manor will appreciate you and your work. Now, you can prove yourself an indispensable member of the manor – or do you want to pass up this opportunity and leave your rightful inheritance to others?"

"Absolutely not. It's much better for me and my future here at the manor if I don't go." He stretched out his hand to Oswulf. "You not only have a sharp sword but also a sharp mind."

Oswulf shook his hand. "Both will help you reach your goals – if you know how to use them."

Chapter 14

"Some kings die too early, and others seem to live forever." Filled with indignation, Robert de Monbrai stomped around in the great hall of his castle.

"The Danish king is dead. Long live the English king." Bored, the court fool twirled a glass cup in his hand and observed how the light broke into a thousand colours in the brightly-coloured glass. "A joy to the vassal aboard the king's vessel."

"Oh, shut up! The king knows how insecure his rule is these days. What other reason would he have to call all his vassals to Sarisberie to repeat their oath of allegiance to him?"

"The power of a king depends on the number of faithful, highly influential vassals and churchmen," purred the fool. "The strength of his enemies grows with each and every one that falls away from him."

He put the glass on the table. "He may be able to hold out by marrying his daughters to powerful princes, but as long as Robert Courteheuse and Bishop Odo are alive, they will stir up trouble in Normandy."

"It's a rebellion not only against the Duke of Normandy but also the King of England," shouted one of the men.

Another one slammed his fist on the table and rose. "We must protect our lands in Normandy and support King William."

"But if Robert defeats him, he will become Duke of Normandy," said a third. "We must not oppose him if we want to keep our lands."

"What if King William wins? We would look like traitors and lose our possessions in both Normandy and England."

Sire Robert beckoned to a servant. "Send for my messenger! I need some information."

Part 4

WILBURGFOS, FROM APRIL TO SEPTEMBER IN THE YEAR OF OUR LORD 1087

Chapter 15

"His hatred for the liege lord is growing. All his attempts to win him over have so far failed. In his desperation, he would do anything to secure his respect and hence, the manor."

"Good, very good. Then we'll make sure that he doesn't give up hope and keeps trying."

"I hope he likes what we have in store for him."

"Rest assured, there are few men who can resist such an offer for long. You, of all people, should know that."

"What if your... offer also attracts other men?"

"Then you have to make sure that they stay away. She knows what to do."

"Can we rely on her?"

"What are you trying to say? Do you doubt my sanity?"

"I would never dare, but can you be really sure that she will do as told? She's young."

"Leave that to me. Just see to it that everything runs as planned at the manor."

"As you wish. I'll do my bit in our plan, and you do yours."

"If I had a glass of wine, I would drink to that with you now."

"If everything goes as planned, we're bound to be able to do that soon."

Chapter 16

Shortly before the Feast of the Resurrection of the Lord, Sire Geoffrey, Hugues de Borre and their companion returned to Wilburgfos from Normandy at the end of March, and the expression on their faces did not bode well. Roger would have loved to know what had happened, but his father waved him off, saying he would find out everything tomorrow in the assembly.

On the following morning, after the practice session, Roger and the other squires entered the great hall, where all men fit for military service waited eagerly for what the liege lord had to tell them.

"King William has been in Roem for several weeks, negotiating with King Philippe," announced Sire Geoffrey. "He believes that he can bring back the Veuguessin, of which the King of the Franks has unlawfully taken possession, into his Norman duchy without a fight. However, not even he knows how long the negotiations will last. The king will celebrate the Resurrection of our Lord in Roem with his most important vassals and their men. He has sent everyone else back to England. He doesn't want to feed any mouths that are no use to him."

Sire Geoffrey's nostrils flared as he cast an irritated glance around the room. "The king is getting old," he murmured.

"He listens more to his doctors who tell him what to eat than to his vassals who administer and defend his land. We'll see what news we have from Normandy after the Feast of the Resurrection. Then we will decide what to do next."

"Do you think you will have to travel to Normandy again?" Roger asked.

"Did you not listen to what I've just said?" his father snapped back.

"Yes, I did, but I want to hear from you what you think of the situation."

"It is up to the king to do what he thinks is right. If he needs to reinforce his army again, we'll find out soon enough."

Hugues de Borre eyed Roger suspiciously. "Would you like to tell us why you are keen on seeing your father leave again?"

"I'm not keen. I only wanted to know if he thinks it possible."

"You can't wait, can you?" asked the bailiff. "And you would love to see me accompany him, wouldn't you? So you can play the liege lord here and pretend to be important."

"How dare you? It is the seneschal's duty, not mine, to manage the manor in my father's absence. But I do know someone who would leap at the chance to take the place of Lord of Wilburgfos – do you, Hugues de Borre?"

"I only know someone who doesn't know where he belongs at this manor – and that's you!"

"Oh, and where do you think I belong as the eldest son, if not in second place after my father, your liege lord?"

Raising his hands, the seneschal stepped between the two. "Messires, si vus plest! Let's talk about this calmly, without arguing. Roger has, in your absence, Sire, performed all his duties conscientiously and has willingly submitted to my orders and instructions." Turning to Hugues, he added, "So, he knows perfectly well where his place is at present, and he makes no effort to change it any time soon. I give you my word on that, munsire."

Pouting, the bailiff glared at Roger angrily.

Frederic beckoned. "Then let us go hunting now. It will be a welcome distraction for all of us."

In the yard, smoke from the houses twirled upwards as if it wanted to fill the blue patches in the sky with more light-grey clouds. The smell of damp firewood, freshly cleaned leather and excited horses, all tacked up, rose into Roger's nose. Dark male voices and high-pitched ones mingled with the clucking of fluttering chickens and the rhythmic clanging of metal. Roger was the last to mount his chestnut stallion before the hunting party set off from the manor to the market square in the centre of Wilburgfos.

On the wooden stalls, the peasants were offering the first spring spinach, herbs and wild plants, hand-woven baskets, knives and eggs.

Roger let his eyes wander over the market and the surroundings. Some girls they met on the way eyed him up or waved coyly. He smiled wistfully. His mother kept telling him what a handsome young man he had become and that his bright face and fine features proved his noble lineage to the outside world – and she cried whenever she thought of her first husband, who would have been so proud to have a son like him.

As they were approaching the market, Roger's gaze caught on a slender figure with long, dark hair. He squinted to try and make out her face, but she was still too far away. "Do you know that girl over there, Richard?"

Craning his neck, Richard looked around the market. "Which one? There are many."

Roger lifted his left hand, in which he carried his spear, and pointed straight ahead. "There. With the long dark hair."

Richard shook his head. "No, I don't know her. Why?"

"I have a feeling I've seen her before, but where?"

His other friends did not recognise the girl either. No one had ever seen her before.

While Sire Geoffrey and most of the other riders passed by the marketplace, Roger slowed down to get a better view of the girl who was regarding the goods at one of the stands.

Richard also reined in his horse, but Roger beckoned him to keep going.

"Ride ahead, Richard," he said, steering Modig Wiht to the side. "I would like to take a closer look at what's on offer."

As he approached the stand, he caught a glimpse of a long, deep-red tunic under the girl's dark green cloak as she walked. Hadn't the younger of the two nuns that he met in the convent worn a tunic of the same colour? This girl had the same clothes and also the endless dark curls.

He brought his horse to a halt behind the girl. "Don't I know you?"

The girl spun round and found herself nose to nostrils with Roger's chestnut stallion, who, softly neighing, stretched his head towards her. She answered his greeting with a gentle smile and stroked the horse's forehead. Judging by her lip movements, she was murmuring something to Modig Wiht, but it was impossible to understand what she was saying.

Roger cleared his throat excessively loudly.

The girl looked up, and all at once, her smile disappeared. The sea-blue eyes coldly examined him from top to bottom.

As Roger gazed back at her, he noticed the brooch with the three weirdly curled arms that fastened her cloak. "Didn't we meet in the convent last year?"

The girl was staring at his spear hand.

He raised the spear briefly, smiling. "You've probably never seen anyone carry their weapons with the left. I can also carry the spear with my right hand. A warrior needs to be able to wield his weapons equally well with both hands. It's important when you fight in a formation, such as a shield wall, or if your hand gets… well, in any case, I find it easier to wield weapons with my left. But I can also fight with my right. If I have to. But today, I'm not fighting. We're riding out to hunt, and it doesn't really matter in which hand I, well, I mean…"

Without saying a word or a wince, the girl regarded him.

"You're not a nun, are you?… Then why do you live in the priory?… Or do you not live there anymore? You don't want to become a nun, do you?"

The girl's silence tried Roger's patience. She was either mute as a maggot or stubborn as a mule. Or very simple-minded.

"Why don't you answer? Can't you speak? Or do you not want to?"

No sooner had he uttered the question than he regretted his tone. In the convent, the older nun had spoken to her in a strange language that he wasn't familiar with.

"Sorry." He pulled up one corner of his mouth in embarrassment. "I don't speak your language, but do you at least understand me?"

She nodded ever so slightly, still eyeing him up cautiously.

He breathed a sigh of relief. "Oh, good. So, you understand me, but you don't talk very much. Will you tell me your name?"

Her gaze wandered past Roger for a moment. "Gwennaol."

She grabbed the fabric of her tunic, turned away so that her long hair flew like a cape being thrown over her shoulders and hurried around the stands to the back end of the market.

"Wait!" Roger called after her, but she did not look back.

His father's stern voice made him whirl around. "Have you nothing better to do than chat to women at the market?"

Roger saw that the hunting party was waiting beyond the stands, probably because Richard had insisted on not leaving his friend behind alone. His concern for Roger's well-being was heart-warming.

"Who was that?" his father growled.

Shrugging, Roger turned his horse. "Gwennaol."

Sire Geoffrey frowned at his son as he also steered his horse back to the others. "What did you talk about?"

His father wished to know more about a conversation between his son and the girl he talked to? Roger smiled. What a shame he could not comply with this wish, even if he had wanted to! "Nothing. Apart from her name, she didn't say a word."

Silent, Sire Geoffrey spurred his horse to the front of the group and bade it follow him.

As Roger caught up with the others, Joscelin asked, with a deadly serious expression, "So, were the goods to your liking?"

Richard put his hands on his hips and snorted. "You lied to me. Everyone laughed at me when I asked them to hold on because you wanted to look at another market stall."

Roger smiled sheepishly. "I'm sorry, Richard. I didn't mean to embarrass you. But I wasn't sure whether I was confusing someone."

"Did you know the girl?" asked Joscelin.

"Not exactly, but I did recognise her. I saw her in the priory when I visited Adelais almost a year ago."

Joscelin raised his eyebrows. "The dameisele has certainly left a lasting impression on you if you still remember her after all this time."

Drogo rolled his eyes. "Lord help us! Can't you at least keep your hands off nuns?"

"She's not a nun."

"Then what's she doing in a cloister?"

"I dunno."

"Do you want to know?" asked Joscelin.

Roger fell silent, but he liked the thought.

Joscelin groaned. "Just as I suspected."

Confused, Richard threw a fleeting glance at Joscelin and Roger. "How are you going to do that? You can't ride to the priory all the time. Or do you want to become a monk? Even then, you wouldn't be allowed to stay there because it's a nunnery."

"Besides, you'll have to think about how you're going to edge out your stallion," Joscelin winked at Roger, "for she seems to like him more than his rider."

Roger picked up the reins of his chestnut stallion and looked around. "She might also prefer men who catch a full-grown wild boar on the hunt – like me, when I get to the forest before you, as usual."

With that, he galloped off, followed by a noisy bunch of exuberant youths on their horses, leaving Sire Geoffrey and his vassals behind in a swirl of clods of earth, wind and hooting.

Chapter 17

Ðunres hamer on þe heafod! He was supposed to clean weapons for a whole week? Roger gasped. He felt the urge to scream, but he gritted his teeth and slammed the battle axe into the soft ground with such force that it stuck without budging. With the others staring, he stomped off, jostling a lanky squire and almost tipping him over. A little apart, he sat down and leaned against the wall of a house.

While Oswulf pulled the students' attention back to the weapons practice, Roger looked around, plucked out a tuft of grass and tore the stalks into small pieces.

"Have you been dismissed from exercises again?" Cenhelm's amused voice sounded from above.

"Oh, Cenhelm, if you only knew how tedious those lessons sometimes are!" Roger groaned, making a sweeping gesture towards Oswulf and his pupils. "Just look at them there, going through the same steps all the time. What's the point of dancing around like that? I know how to wield a sword. I don't need any of those moves. The others can't win against me anyway, and Oswulf knows it. That's why he punishes me. Because I'm better than the others. That's why I have to clean weapons and do additional exercises for my strength and endurance. He does it to give the others the chance to fight without me, so that they can win for once."

Cenhelm growled, pondering. "In any case, the other squires obey the master of arms like sons do with their father. Oswulf's a good fighter. I am sure he has sound reasons for what he's doing, even if you don't seem convinced at the moment."

Roger flung the shredded grass to the side, put his arms on his knees and watched as the others went through the prescribed movements as one. "Yeah, yeah, just like Father. 'But you have to do it like this.', 'Can't you do it better?' Father patronises me like a little child, and Oswulf does exactly the same at times."

"It's not for me to judge your father, but I am sure he's doing what he thinks is right."

"Yeah, right, and that includes telling me over and over again how brilliant William was and how bad I am at everything. At least Oswulf doesn't constantly use my elder brother as a shining example for me, as Father still does. No wonder William was always his favourite son, as similar as the two were. Oswulf never liked him. But what could an Englishman like about a Norman? Especially one such as William, who had always considered himself the greatest and the best and also told everyone so every day."

A lump formed in his throat, and the scar on his right cheek was burning.

Cenhelm put his hand on Roger's shoulder. "You shouldn't say such things, neither about the living nor the dead."

"Such a fool! If only he had kept his big mouth shut. Just for once, for God's sake. Slaughtered like a pig." He buried his face in his hands and swallowed the tears that welled up in his eyes. He shouldn't cry like a woman in front of a servant, even if the servant was old Cenhelm.

"The Lord gives, and he takes away." Cenhelm squeezed Roger's shoulder. "You shouldn't take William's death so much to heart."

"That's easy for you to say, but even now, Father still finds opportunities to show me how inadequate I am as his heir. Why doesn't he just accept that William's not coming back and that an English-born son will succeed him? He can't help it anyway. I try hard to please him, and yet, he only ever sees my faults, everything I do wrong in his eyes. Again and again, I hear how exemplary William was in everything and that I am not a real Norman anyway."

"Well, you certainly aren't, but I guess that's true of a lot of sons by now. It doesn't make you a worse son nor a worse fighter."

Roger took his hands off his hot face.

Surrounded by his pupils, Oswulf was demonstrating a new sequence of evasive and defensive movements.

"Maybe that's why I get along better with Oswulf – we have more in common. Since William's death, he's been the one who listens to me and gives me courage when I've incurred Father's anger again. He's English, he's a fighter, and that's all that matters to him, not where someone comes from or who they are. He understands how I think, how I feel." A smile flitted across Roger's face as he ran his index finger through the sand. "He even wanted to know if I was in love the other day."

Cenhelm laughed out loud. "Hear, hear! Our Roger, in love? Who's the lucky girl then?"

"Me, in love? With whom? And I suppose you want me to marry her too, eh?" Roger paused. "Hold on. Why didn't *I* think of that before? Cenhelm, you should be part of the

Witan. I've got to get married! That's it! William never did because he..." He swallowed the thought and gazed across the sand as if the answer to his questions lay there somewhere. "Marriage. Good idea. Only, where will I find a suitable wife, if not here at the manor? One that Father would approve of, perhaps even a Norman woman. I must discuss this with Oswulf. Thank you, Cenhelm!"

Roger stood up and brushed the sand off his breeches. The grains fell on the lines he had drawn in the ground, which looked uncannily like a G.

After Oswulf had promised Roger to talk to him after the hunt, Roger prepared for the afternoon hunting trip with mixed feelings. On the one hand, he regretted that he had only been able to speak briefly with Oswulf. On the other, however, his pulse quickened, not only because a fast ride and a rewarding roast or two were waiting for him, but mostly because at first, they would ride past the marketplace, which made his belly tingle with delight. To drown in those sea-blue eyes again that were so mysterious and alluring – that was why Roger hungered for the rides into the woods even more than usual.

Oddly enough, his father seemed to have noticed this change in him, for Richard told Roger several times how Sire Geoffrey watched him while he stood with Gwennaol. Was this a good sign, as his father usually cared little who Roger spoke to or what he did when he was not on the battleground or sitting in court hearings? In any case, Roger wouldn't have much to tell him, for although he almost always spoke to Gwennaol when they passed the market, he mostly did the talking alone while she confined herself to listening. But Sire Geoffrey never asked what they talked about. He only watched silently from afar.

"I can't see her anywhere." Roger stretched his neck, searching the marketplace in all directions as the hunting party rode slowly past the stalls.

"Neither can I," said Richard. "Maybe she won't come today. Or she might come later."

Roger frowned. "But she's always here when we leave the manor."

"She might be sick," Joscelin said.

Roger continued to look everywhere, but there was no sign of Gwennaol.

"Maybe you're right. Otherwise, she would have come. She always has until now. She doesn't speak much, but she's there."

On the way back, Roger again kept an eye out for her, in case she had arrived late at the market, but she was nowhere to be seen.

When none of the nuns at their stall could – or would? – give him any information about Gwennaol, Roger spurred his horse and trotted forward to his father.

"Have you noticed that the girl wasn't there, Father?"

"What girl?" asked Sire Geoffrey without looking at him.

"Gwennaol. The girl we usually meet in the marketplace when we ride to hunt."

"Possibly."

"She wasn't there."

Sire Geoffrey shook the cloak off his arm like a pesky insect. "What's it to me whether some girl was at the market or not, why are you asking me about it?"

“What could be the reason for her not being there? Since I first saw her in the market, we’ve met her again on every ride, but not today. Don’t you find this strange?”

“No.”

“Perhaps she’s ill. Do you think I could find out at the priory?”

“No.”

“She lives there.”

“You’re not going there to ask about her.”

“Why not?”

“It’s no concern of yours.”

“But I—”

“You cannot take care of everyone you meet at the market.”

“I could ask Adelais if she—”

“You’re not going there, and you forget that girl!”

“But why?”

“Because I say so!” thundered Sire Geoffrey, so that drops of spit flew into Roger’s face. “And now, enough of this! I don’t want to hear any more of it. Aluns!” He beckoned his followers and spurred his horse.

Staying behind, Roger watched the riders gallop after his father towards Wilburgfos, as Richard and the other youths caught up with him.

“What did you say to your father that he was suddenly in such a hurry?” Richard wanted to know.

Roger shrugged. “If I only knew!”

“What did you talk about?”

“I asked him if he had seen Gwennaol, and he ordered me not to ask any more questions and to forget about her.” Roger’s gaze still lingered on the group of riders who were just reaching the gates of the manor. “I must find out.”

He steered his horse to the side and put it into a trot.

"Where are you going?" asked Richard.

"To the priory," Roger shouted and sped away.

A little later, he galloped through the palisade gate, threw his spear on the ground and jumped out of the saddle before Modig Wiht had even come to a halt. Without looking at anyone, he hastened into the great hall.

"Father? Father!" he called, weaving through the benches and chairs that the servants were setting up for the next meal.

Sire Geoffrey stood in a corner with Hugues de Borre and some other men who looked rather annoyed as they turned to face him.

Roger planted himself in front of his father and clenched his fists beside his thighs. "Father, I need to talk to you!"

The astonished murmur of the advisers was followed by a disparaging look from Sire Geoffrey. "I hope the matter is important enough to warrant your barging in."

"Can I speak to you alone?"

"I don't see why that would be necessary."

Roger gulped, warily eying the men, who stood there with narrowed eyes and furrowed brows.

"So?" Sire Geoffrey stared at him expectantly.

"I don't think they need to—"

"Just tell me why you burst in here like a vilein Engleis!"

"Very well, then. You've ordered that Gwennaol not leave the priory again. That's why she wasn't at the market earlier today."

"How do you know?"

"The prioress told me."

"So, you went to the priory."

"I did."

"Even though I forbade you." Sire Geoffrey's jaw muscles moved as if he were chewing a particularly sinewy piece of meat.

"You disregard the word of your liege lord," said Hugues de Borre. "Do you think that such behaviour shows that you yourself are suitable for this role?"

Roger bit his lip. Pondering, he turned the signet ring on his little finger back and forth. Why did he say how he knew? He should have kept his mouth shut. "Why did you forbid me, Father?" he asked softly.

"So, you don't want to take over Wilburgfos as a fiefdom."

"I do! But what has that to do with Gwennaol? Why did you have her locked up in the priory?"

"A liege lord must look after his lands and revenues. The head of a cloister cares for its members."

"I promise you that I will not neglect my duties at the manor because of Gwennaol. You will have no cause for complaint on my account. I only wish to speak to her, nothing more. Why does this anger you so?"

"William always knew how a future liege lord would have chosen."

It would have been the same, whatever William would have chosen. Whatever he did was good and right. Embittered, Roger nodded. "Then I guess I should follow his example."

"You've finally come to your senses."

"There's something else I wanted to tell you. I'm getting married."

Several astonished "Quei?" and "Excuse me?" burst out of the men.

Even the piggy eyes of Hugues de Borre were suddenly big and round.

Tuché!

Roger struggled to keep a straight face while inside, he was rejoicing.

"To whom?" his father asked.

Roger bowed deeply. "I will reflect on that decision like a true liege lord." He suppressed a grin and turned around, leaving a heated exchange of words.

Oswulf beckoned Roger to follow him into the botelerie next to the kitchen. It was a well-chosen moment for a private conversation in a place where nothing could usually be hidden from others. Sire Geoffrey and his advisers had ridden to the fields where a third sheep had been killed within just a few days, presumably by wolves from the neighbouring woods. The tables had been cleaned and put away, the kitchen tidied up and the remains disposed of. It was one of the few moments when silence filled the great hall. In a couple of hours, the servants would start preparing dinner. Until then, Roger and Oswulf had time to talk.

Roger sat at the narrow table that stood in the middle of the room.

The master of arms placed two mugs full of ale on the table and took a seat opposite Roger. "Wæs hal!" He raised his cup in the air.

"Drinc hal." With relish, Roger let the cool liquid run down his throat.

Oswulf put down the cup, wiped the foam from his moustache and leaned back. "So, you want to get married."

Roger nodded vaguely. The way the master of arms said it, his idea suddenly didn't sound quite as good as he had initially thought.

"How are you going to go about it?"

Roger clung to his cup, searching for an answer. His mind had gone blank – or rather, he hadn't actually thought about how he was going to deliver on his promise, nor whom he even wanted to marry.

"What did your father say?"

Roger ran his finger along the handle of his cup, following the movement with his gaze and smiling. "I think he was surprised."

"Did he approve of it?"

"Approve? That's not something he ever does where I'm concerned." He grimly regarded the surface of the table.

"Tell me, Roger, what's bothering you?"

Roger took a sip from his cup. His thoughts ran as wild as the furrows on the old oak table. "There's this girl I saw at the priory last year and a couple of times at the market. Some time ago, I approached her at the market and asked her name."

"Well?"

"She's called Gwennaol. I've never heard such a name before."

"Guen-na-ell." Oswulf let the name roll off his tongue. "That's a Breton name. Twenty years ago, many Bretons came across the sea to England with the Duke of Normandy and fought for him."

"An unusual name – just like herself. She's so... different from the women at the manor. She doesn't speak much. She's not even particularly friendly. Every other woman around here makes eyes at me, giggles like a fool when I pass by or blushes when I speak to her. With Gwennaol, all I get is contempt and one-word replies – if she does so much as look at me." He sighed.

Oswulf crossed his forearms. "You like her."

"Her eyes are like the sea, Oswulf." Roger stifled a smile. "Father has forbidden me from seeing her again."

"Is there a reason?"

Roger shook his head and stared at the table. "He never gives reasons for his decisions. But if I see Gwennaol again or ask about her, I will lose my inheritance."

"That's harsh." Oswulf calmly drank a large gulp. "Surely, there's more to it than your father wants to admit."

"What do you mean?"

"Perhaps your father wants to protect you from the girl."

"Protect me from a girl?" Roger laughed. "Oh, Oswulf. Sometimes you have funny ideas. Do you think I couldn't defend myself against a girl?"

The master of arms leaned forward. "What if she's a scinlæce?"

"Gwennaol a sorceress? An evil spirit? Impossible! The nuns would hardly shelter her in their convent."

"Then maybe she knows something about your father, and he doesn't want you to find out."

Oswulf put down his cup without taking his eyes off Roger.

"What would my father be hiding, and why would she of all people know anything about it? How? None of my friends know her or where she came from." Indignant at this crazy thought, Roger gulped down his ale. "Nonetheless, she might still be harbouring a secret that must not be revealed. After all, Father is very keen that I don't ask about her any more... I need to find out why it's so important to him."

"How are you going to do this? Your father has ordered that you not see her again."

"I know." Roger turned the signet ring round and round. "I'll have to think of something."

Oswulf raised his bushy eyebrows. "He has forbidden you not only as a father, but also as a liege lord." His voice softened. "You would violate your feudal lord's order just to speak to her."

He hadn't taken this into account. It was daring to disobey the order of a feudal lord.

"Father wouldn't hesitate to condemn me – his own son," Roger muttered more to himself than to Oswulf. "Even more so if he does actually have something to hide that is so terrible that I must not talk to Gwennaol. But what would I have done wrong in that case? I would have chatted with a girl. Could he have me convicted of that? Is it not something that all young men do?"

"Well." Oswulf leaned back. "The things we do for love."

"Love? What man could love such a sullen girl?" Roger washed the notion away with the rest of the ale in his cup. "I'm just curious to know why Father wants to keep me away from her."

Oswulf nodded. "You are brave, son of a Norman. Your father won't like it if you don't do as he says. But you're no longer a little boy who simply takes orders. You're becoming an æþeling, as befits your rank."

Roger's chest swelled with pride, making his tunic stretch even more than usual. That's right, he was too old to be pushed around by his father. He was almost eighteen and would be dubbed in three years at the latest. He had to make his own decisions. And this one was clear: he had to see Gwennaol again, even against his father's order.

Chapter 18

"Are you sure this is a good idea?" Richard put down the bucket with the ashes in front of the others.

Roger dipped the oil-soaked woollen rag into the ashes and rubbed it over the small rust stains in the rings of the chain mail. "I think it's brilliant. No one will suspect a thing."

Drogo set one spear aside and grabbed the next. "What if someone passes by and notices that you're not here?"

"Well, what then?" Roger rubbed on, unimpressed.

"What if he asks for you?"

"Tell them I needed to piss."

Joscelin threw the next coat of mail into the sand-filled barrel. "If your horse isn't there either, did it also go for a piss?"

"Why would anyone ask about me?" Roger rolled his eyes. "You worry too much when there's nothing to worry about. Everybody knows where we are and what we do there."

Joscelin rolled the barrel to and fro so the sand would trickle through the individual rings of the chain mail and grind off rust and encrusted dirt and blood. The metal banged on the wood with a loud clanging. "That's true," Joscelin said in a loud voice. "Nobody would become suspicious if we went off as usual."

"Will you be long?" asked Drogo as he twirled the spear in his hand to examine it.

Roger blew a strand of hair out of his face. “It depends on the prioress and how fast I can persuade her.”

Drogo put the spear to one side and snorted. “A left-hander looking for a bride in a convent? I don’t see why she would consent to that.”

“Why not?” asked Roger. “She knows me well.”

Drogo grinned. “Exactly.”

Roger gave him a friendly but firm kick in the shin.

Joscelin pulled the coat of mail from the barrel and then inspected it thoroughly. “Should she choose to do so, she would be defying your father’s order and thus undermining the authority of the liege lord under whose jurisdiction her priory falls.” He threw the armour back into the barrel and continued rolling it. “Your father would insist that she submit to his judgement rather than put his trust into a decision by the Archbishop of Everwic.”

Drogo picked up a sword and slumped on the bench beside Roger. “Emma may well appreciate what you have to offer, but for the prioress, you’ll have to think of something else to win her favour.”

Roger threw a side-glance at Drogo. “How do you know? Did you ask her?”

“It’s not me who wants to seduce a nun, it’s you.”

“She’s not a nun, and she’ll probably never be one.”

“Are you sure?” asked Richard. “She already lives in a convent. All she’s missing is the habit.”

“What Roger is trying to say is that even if Gwennaol ever had that intention, she would change her mind once she got to know him better.” Joscelin retrieved the chain mail from the barrel and shook it. “But you’ll have to get past the prioress first.”

In the morning, Roger and his friends rode as usual into the woods, north-east of the manor, where they would set out their nets for birds and fish in trees and on the riverbank, and then pass the waiting time with fighting exercises. While the others dismounted in the clearing, Roger rode on along a winding path to the priory.

"The prioress, you say?" The nun at the gate looked at him in surprise. "Wait here a moment. I will speak to her."

Roger lingered on in the courtyard and looked around. This was where he had met Gwennaol with the older nun for the first time. Would he see her again today? The sweet tingling in his stomach turned sour as he let his gaze wander to the storeroom at the far end of the courtyard. His vision blurred.

"Đis is laðlic!" Disgusted, he wiped his face with the sleeve of his tunic. That little toad had spat at him! "Ooh, just you wait!" he growled and stomped towards the storeroom. He pressed against the door to open it, but it seemed to be locked. "Open up, you little rat!" he ordered, hammering against the wood.

"Greetings, Roger," he heard the prioress say. "What can I do for you?"

The prioress? But she wasn't there when...? Roger squinted his eyes briefly then stared into the empty courtyard. Next to him stood the prioress of the convent – a small, chubby woman who was no more than ten years older than him and whose friendly, heart-shaped face looked rosy against her black Benedictine habit. "Forgive me, Reverend Mother Prioress." Roger bowed hastily. "I did not hear you come. Thank you for finding time for me. I have an important matter to discuss with you."

The prioress's eyes lit up. "An important matter? That sounds auspicious. Speak, my son! What is on your mind?"

"There's this girl called Gwennaol here in the convent. She's not a nun, and probably Breton." His little finger ached from the constant twisting of the signet ring. "I... I would like to..." He cleared his throat, but before he could say anything, the prioress relieved him of his agony.

"You wish to speak to her?"

"Yes!... I mean, if it's not too much trouble."

"I would very much like to give you leave to do so, Roger, but I must not. You know that your father has forbidden me."

Roger's hope sank like a shot duck in a dive. "Did he tell you why?"

The prioress regarded him benignly. "No. He only sent a messenger and ordered me not to let Gwennaol leave the convent again and to prevent any further contact between you both. I am sorry, Roger, but I must follow his order."

He knelt down in front of the prioress, took one of her small, cold hands between his and looked up at her. "Please, Reverend Mother Prioress! It is important that I speak to Gwennaol. She knows a secret about my father that he doesn't want me to find out. That's why he has told you not to let her leave the priory. I must see her. Isn't there some way I can talk to her?"

A mischievous glint flickered in the eyes of the prioress. "A secret about the liege lord of Wilburgfos behind the walls of this convent? Now, there's something that certain other people would like to know too."

He clasped her hand even tighter.

"I do not yet possess much that I can offer you in return, but I swear by Saint Michael that I will reward you richly when I take over Wilburgfos from my father."

If I ever do.

"Please, Reverend Mother!"

The prioress looked at him for a long time before shrugging at last. "Oh well, never mind. In the end, it is the Lord in Heaven who decides our fate, not the Lord in Wilburgfos. I will see what I can do for you."

Roger jumped to his feet and had to stop himself from flinging his arms around the prioress's neck. Instead, he breathed a kiss on her hand and smiled at her. "I am eternally grateful to you, Reverend Mother."

The prioress pursed her lips. "Hold your horses, young man. I must first ask Gwennaol if she wants to see you and speak with you at all."

"Why wouldn't she?"

"She's a friendly but withdrawn girl."

"She knows me. We met in the market."

"Yes, I remember. She helped out at our stall for a few weeks. What a coincidence! Then I am sure she will be happy to see you again."

Roger nodded hesitantly. "Certainly, yes." *Eala, what's she going to think when she finds out that I followed her into the priory?*

"She should be in the garden now," said the prioress. "I will see if she has time for you." She stuck her hands into her sleeves and turned round.

"Wait! I may have to come back a few times."

The prioress smiled mischievously. "Do you think so?"

"You said yourself that Gwennaol is very shy. So, it will take a while for her to trust me and tell me everything she knows about my father."

"You cannot possibly come in at the gate every time. Someone might see you and tell your father. Only the Lord can help us then." She eyed Roger up and down. "Besides, you distract the novices every time you visit Adelais."

Roger suppressed a sheepish grin.

"May God turn a blind eye to those occasions," she said with her gaze turned towards heaven. "Wait here."

With his stomach gurgling, Roger wiped his damp hands on his tunic. Now, he had to wait until the prioress would ask him to join Gwennaol – if Gwennaol had time. What if she didn't? Why should she make time for him? They had met by chance at the market, but she would have to agree to seeing him in the priory. He had a pressing reason to speak to her, but why should she hear him out? What was she to make of a man she had only recently met and who was now stalking her all the way to the convent? She would probably be even more dismissive and suspicious, and rightly so.

He swallowed, although his mouth was so dry that his tongue stuck to the roof of it.

"Roger?" The prioress gestured towards the garden. "Gwennaol is waiting for you."

His heart pounding, he took a deep breath and made to set off, but the prioress barred his way with an outstretched arm.

"You have time until you hear the bell chiming for Terce, and you may only enter the garden this one time. If you do not find out what you need to know today, you will have to find another way to speak to Gwennaol."

Roger's pulse was racing. "Thank you, Reverend Mother. I will try my best."

The prioress clasped her hands. "Can you read?"

Roger nodded.

"Good. I will write down for you how you do it. You can pick up the letter tomorrow at the gate."

Had he heard correctly? The prioress wanted to write him a letter about how he could secretly talk to one of the residents of her convent? "God bless you, Reverend Mother. You are too kind."

The prioress smiled. "Now, go." She made a gesture with her head towards the garden. "Or she might think you do not dare."

"I'm very much obliged to you."

Roger stumbled and caught himself just in time to continue on his way with the necessary dignity and reverence.

Ha! I don't dare? What's it with this girl that everyone thinks I should be afraid of her and need to be protected?

He crossed the colonnade that framed the garden and looked around. So this was where the ingredients grew for all those delicacies that Cenhelm had brought to the estate every autumn and that not only refined dishes but were also a treat on their own.

The garden resembled a sea of fresh green and blossoming flowers adorning the trees, bushes and plants.

Four narrow, straight paths of fine sand divided the garden into four equal quarters with a small fountain in the middle.

Between the paths, small berry bushes, various medicinal and aromatic herbs, vegetables and lettuce grew in rectangular beds.

Apple trees spread their branches over the fountain and much of the garden, shading not only the plants but also the convent residents from the sun.

Roger strolled along one of the paths, taking in the scent of lavender, camomile, roses and lilies.

How peaceful it was here! Only the constant hum of bees flying around broke the silence that reigned in this oasis of tranquillity.

Two nuns were silently going about their work among the plants, and yet, Roger had the feeling that someone was watching him as he walked towards Gwennaol at the back of the garden. But when he turned around, both nuns seemed to be solely occupied with the plants around them.

Gwennaol was stooped over a strip of low flowers that randomly stretched their deep blue trumpet blossoms into the air. Her dark hair hung to the ground, shielding the delicate buds from curious glances like a curtain.

Had she not noticed Roger, or did she simply feel no urge to look out for her visitor? In any case, she was fully absorbed in tending to the gentian and allowed nothing to distract her.

Roger stopped beside her and waited.

She paused plucking the weeds, pushed her hair back over her shoulder and slowly straightened up. Her gaze wandered from his dark brown leather shoes over the light-coloured breeches and the dark blue tunic to his face.

He touched his right cheek. Gwennaol had never asked him about the scar before, although it was impossible to overlook the bulging furrow that stretched from his ear to the corner of his mouth. Had she really not noticed it yet? Did she not dare to ask about it? Or had the nuns taught her not to judge people by appearances, so that she didn't care about it?

His heart pounded. How long she looked at him without saying a word! Emma would have walked up to him long ago and flattered him with words and touches.

"Good day, Gwennaol," he said softly, but his cautious smile remained unrequited.

As he looked into Gwennaol's small, round face without his chestnut stallion in the way, he remembered the moment when, after his visit to Adelais, she had looked at him with her sea-blue eyes for what had felt like an eternity. But unlike that day, now, her nose remained unwrinkled. Did that mean she was less suspicious of him than she had been then?

He looked around the garden. Although he assumed that the nuns would keep their mouths shut because of their vow of silence, he wanted to make sure that no one was listening in. One could never know.

When he turned to Gwennaol, her gaze jumped back to his face as if he had caught her looking at something forbidden. Neither her face nor her body showed the slightest sign of embarrassment, though – she was a master at hiding her feelings.

"I'm sorry for following you all the way into the priory, but I really need to talk to you."

"Why?"

He winced. Her tone was sharp as a knife. "What?"

"Why?"

Why? Why? If I tell her that I just want to ask her what she knows about my father, she won't say another word to me. She'll probably leave right away and never want to see me again.

He quickly put on the smile that had brought a bashful blush to many a woman's face and said, "I like you."

Gwennaol looked him in the eye, but neither the colour of her face nor her features changed.

Roger sighed. Why was he still here? This girl was obviously as stubborn as a donkey and too stupid to have a simple conversation.

"Do you always do this?" asked Gwennaol.

"Do what?"

"Chasing women."

Roger gasped. "I'm not chasing women." He threw a glance at their surroundings, praying that nobody overheard them. What if any of this escaped the cloister walls? "What makes you think I need to do that?"

Shrugging, Gwennaol clapped her dirty hands so that the lumps of earth crumbled to the ground.

"Have you lived here long?"

She nodded.

"Do you like it here?" Roger didn't care in the least, but any question was good enough to keep the one-sided conversation going – even if Gwennaol's replies were as meagre as a starved pig.

She shrugged again.

"But you're not a nun." He regarded her from top to bottom. "Why are you here?"

She opened her mouth slightly as if she wanted to say something, but her gaze wandered past Roger's shoulder for a moment, and then she closed her mouth and abruptly lowered her head without having uttered a word.

Roger looked over his shoulder.

One of the two nuns avoided his gaze. Had she given Gwennaol a sign to fall silent?

"Who's that?"

“A relative.”

She glanced at him one more time before bowing down to the blue trumpets again to continue weeding.

Was that it? Was that the end of the conversation, if you could call it that? And he had found out little or nothing. What a disappointment!

He rubbed his palms together and looked over his shoulder once more at the other nuns. “I would like to see you again,” he murmured. *I have to.*

He felt as if Gwennaol had paused for a moment when he said that – or had he just imagined it?

The bell of the church tower struck the third hour. Roger had to leave the priory. His gaze wandered from the steeple to Gwennaol. He rubbed his chin, but the chiming and the girl’s rejection were relentless. “I’ll try to come back soon.”

He slowly took a few steps backwards to see if Gwennaol looked at him again, but she remained hidden behind the curtain of her hair, her eyes firmly fixed on her task.

He turned and left the garden, passing the nun who was a little too eagerly engrossed in her work.

Chapter 19

Roger bent a twig away from his face, ducked and sidled through the lush undergrowth.

Summer was just a month old, but already, the shrubs and plants stretched far into the dusty path that was barely discernible amidst the rampant greenery. Between the closely spaced trees, countless wildflowers crowded the few spots where scattered rays of sunlight fell through the treetops. It was an excellent place for a secret escape route on which one could enter the woods northeast of Wilburgfos almost unobserved. Neither from the peasant houses to the south nor from the northwestern manor house beyond the priory was the path visible, and even less so the place where it came from.

Pushing the last branches apart, Roger squeezed through to the narrow grassy area in the middle of the green thicket.

A low door huddled in the mighty wooden wall in front of him, with a sliding hatch built into it.

Roger wiped the sweat from his face and combed a stubborn leaf out of his hair with his fingers. Then he examined his tunic, plucked off a few burs that were clinging to the rough woollen fabric and smoothed out the folds.

With a pounding heart, he knocked on the door in the way that the prioress had set as his secret identification in her letter.

The little hatch slid to the side, revealing a hole just big enough to frame Gwennaol's face. Dimples flashed on her cheeks, framing her shy smile. "Greetings, Roger," she said softly.

Roger's mouth felt dusty. He had to swallow a few times before his tongue detached from the roof of his mouth and he could speak. "That's the first time you've called me by my name."

"Is it? But we've met so many times by now."

"How beautiful it sounds when you say my name. You should do it much more often."

The dimples deepened. "I'll keep that in mind, Roger."

He smiled.

"What news do you bring from the manor?"

"Nothing good, I'm afraid. Sire Osbern insists on getting the money for the cancelled wedding, and King William has demanded more warriors from England to fight the Frankish king after all."

"Are you leaving?"

"Do you fear for me?"

"Would I have reason to?"

"My father could send me to Normandy, where I might die in battle."

"You mustn't go."

"Would you cry for me?"

"If you leave or if you die in battle?"

"Both."

She looked at him in earnest. "Do you have to go?"

So, she does care for me. She just doesn't say. Roger shook his head. "No. My father already sent Hugues de Borre to Normandy a few weeks ago with two horsemen."

A smile flitted across Gwennaol's face. "So, we'll continue to meet here as usual."

"Yes, we will." He straightened his back with a groan. "Why don't you come out to me so we can talk freely without a door between us?"

"You know I'm not allowed to leave the priory."

"Who could possibly find out? Look around: the trees and shrubs grow so abundantly here that I can barely bend down to the hatch without getting my clothes caught on the branches. Or are you just afraid to leave your sheltered little chamber?"

"I'm not. There's enough room here. Why should I go out?"

"Because it's narrow and dark where you are, whereas where I'm standing, there's light and sun and – mmm!– the delicious smell of the woods."

"It's a prayer room with an altar, candles and a big painting of Saint Mary. It has its own light and smell."

"Why don't you take a closer look at the picture? Do you see the little lever on it? If you pull it, the painting folds to the side and reveals the secret door to the outside."

Gwennaol looked at her side of the door. "There is indeed a small latch. How did you know about it if you've never been in here before?"

Roger smirked. "The secret door and the path have been forgotten by many over the years, but fortunately, not by the prioress. This escape route saved the lives of the convent's residents several times when the Vikings were still regularly attacking the north-east coast of England."

"The door probably won't open if it hasn't been used all these years."

“Wouldn’t you like to try?” Roger’s heartbeat accelerated.

Gwennaol stared at him. “No.”

“Pity. Maybe another day?”

He looked at her expectantly, but she pressed her lips together.

“How long have you actually been in the priory?”

“I grew up here.”

“Then why aren’t you a nun? All girls who enter a convent become nuns.”

“Mammgozh, my grandmother, didn’t want it.”

“Is this the relative you mentioned when we first met in the convent garden?”

“It is. She joined the convent years ago but never insisted that I do the same.”

“Didn’t your father decide what should happen to you?”

Gwennaol snorted. “I have no father.”

“Then what about your mother? What does she say about it?”

She lowered her head so that Roger only saw her dark hair through the hole. He heard a soft sob.

“Gwennaol? Gwennaol!” His gaze flitted across the door. Was there no way to open this cursed thing from the outside? “Talk to me! You’re not crying, are you?”

Two moist eyes flashed at him angrily. “My mother is dead. Am I not allowed to cry for her?” She slammed the sliding hatch shut.

“If your grandmother doesn’t want you to become a nun, why don’t you grow up with relatives outside the convent? What’s the point of keeping you in there if you’re not destined for religious life?” He listened at the latch. “You still there?... Come on, open up again, Gwennaol!”

He tapped the sliding door a few times with his index finger. "I'm sorry. I don't want you to be sad."

The hatch slid open, scratching, and for a while, they just regarded each other without speaking.

"I could look at you for hours." Roger struggled to stifle a grin. "Though I could think of a more pleasant posture for that than standing like an old man in front of that tiny little hole all the time."

A smile crossed Gwennaol's face, flashing her dimples. "I'm not allowed out, and you're not allowed in. You should be grateful we can see each other at all, rather than complaining about it."

"I'm not complaining at all, but I could offer you a very well-kept spot of soil in the woods amidst lush greenery, which is certainly much nicer than your prayer room. Well?" He smiled mischievously at her.

Gwennaol tried to keep her dimples in check. "No, really, Roger, we mustn't."

"Why not? Did the prioress forbid you? She knows that only I am here. No one will know, not even the prioress. And even if she did – trust me – she won't betray us. And in this thicket of trees and shrubbery, no one can see us. Besides, no one knows I'm here... except my friends, of course."

His thoughts went to the clearing in the woods. The number of those who knew about the secret meetings was indeed not as small as he had first assumed. Apart from the prioress and probably Gwennaol's grandmother, there were those who were doing their practice fighting at this moment and were supposed to have his back in case anyone asked about him: Richard, Joscelin and Drogo. Of the three, however, only Richard knew the exact place where Roger and Gwennaol met.

"Your friends?"

"Don't worry. You can rely on them. They would never betray me."

"I have to go."

Roger nodded with a heavy heart. "Yes, I have to go back too before it gets too long. Will I see you again next week?"

Gwennaol nodded. "Gladly."

"There he is!" exclaimed Joscelin louder than necessary, as it seemed to Roger. "It took you a long time to piss."

"Drank too much last night, didn't you?" Drogo asked at least as loudly while fiddling with his weapon belt.

Roger tied his chestnut stallion next to the other horses and approached the mounted messenger, who was watching him with a sneer.

"Do you always take your horse with you when you have a piss?" asked the messenger.

Joscelin rubbed his nose.

"We certainly do." Roger tucked his thumbs into his weapon belt. "It's because of the bears in the woods."

"Bears? What are you talking about? There's no bears in England."

"Not many, that's true. But we saw one recently, not far from here."

The messenger looked around. "What? Near the manor house?"

Roger pursed his lips, nodding. "Those beasts can smell human waste for miles, and they know they'll find plenty to eat where humans live. So, they follow the scent and come to the manor house. That's why we always ride far away from the clearing when we need to relieve ourselves, so we don't attract bears."

With each sentence, the messenger raised his eyebrows further up his forehead.

Joscelin had turned away because of a sudden fit of coughing and patted his chest vigorously.

Roger tried hard to keep a straight face. "But I doubt you have come to learn about our pissing habits. So, what brings you here?"

The messenger closed his mouth and gulped. "Your father sent me. He awaits you in the great hall."

"Why?"

"There's news from Normandy, and your father needs to speak to you."

Roger exchanged a questioning glance with his friends. "I'm coming." He mounted his horse and trotted after the messenger.

Frederic was waiting in the courtyard, and as soon as Roger had dismounted, he waved him over and walked with him into the great hall.

Sitting at a table with folded hands, Sire Geoffrey watched the two until they were standing in front of him. For once, the liege lord had to conduct the conversation without Hugues de Borre, because the latter was still in Normandy with King William and – as Roger had gathered from the messenger – had sent one of his men back to England with news.

The messenger stood apart with a dark-haired man Roger had never seen before. The two were eagerly talking to Sire

Geoffrey's vassals, casting sidelong glances at the liege lord every now and then and quite obviously trying to speak as quietly as possible.

Frederic and Roger took a seat.

Sire Geoffrey looked at the two with a furrowed brow. "Hugues de Borre tells me that King William has invaded the Veuguessin to avenge the insult he received at the hands of King Philippe."

Roger exchanged a glance with Frederic, whose face at that moment had many a worry line added to the wrinkles of age.

His father pursed his lips, and a devilish gleam crossed his eyes as he continued. "King William's troops are destroying the harvest. They're cutting down fruit trees and ravaging the vineyards. All the settlements that get in the king's way, towns and villages, are being set on fire and destroyed by flames."

A disconcerting heat spread in Roger's chest. *Like after his coronation, when he ravaged the entire north for four years because the English wouldn't submit to a king that was forced on them. But the people of the Veuguessin didn't even rise against him. Does King William really believe that God will approve of his actions forever?*

Sire Geoffrey leaned back. "I'll be away for a few days."

"Where are you going?" asked Roger.

"In the meantime, you will support Frederic at the manor and not leave Wilburgfos."

Roger glanced at Frederic, who smiled graciously. "As you wish, Father. Would you tell me where you are going so that I know when to expect you back?"

"I will send a messenger when the time comes. Until then, you stay in Wilburgfos."

"Of course, Father."

How lucky that the priory also belongs to Wilburgfos. Disobeying two orders at once would be asking for trouble.

"I am leaving tomorrow." Sire Geoffrey rose and went to Hugues' messenger and the other men, who looked at him expectantly.

Roger felt a little ashamed because he enjoyed the times when his father was not at the manor and Frederic was in charge, like now. Unlike Sire Geoffrey, the friendly seneschal joked with Dame Edeva and her children and elicited the odd grumpy smile even from thirteen-year-old Tankred. He also remained polite to the vassals and treated the servants strictly but respectfully.

Not surprisingly, Roger was not the only one to bemoan the announcement by a messenger that Sire Geoffrey would return in mid-August. Even worse, Hugues de Borre was also expected back at the manor soon afterwards, and then the pleasant days would certainly be over.

A breath of warm air lay over the fields and grasslands of Wilburgfos at the end of August, into which crickets and birds wove their melodies. Together with Richard, Roger had caught rabbits in the woods and was pleased to ride home with his friend and their shared kill.

In the wheat field next to him, peasants were cutting the grain with sickles and tying it into sheaves. A handful of men and women loaded the upright bundles onto the cart behind a team of oxen to take them to the barns.

Even before the two friends had reached the inner courtyard, they heard the dull rumbling of the threshing flails used to separate the ears of corn from the stalks. Children collected the loose ears and handed them over to the women who sat on the side and separated the wheat from the chaff by shaking and throwing the ears up with large sieves. The sifted grains were then filled into linen sacks, which two servants would later take to the mill at the Fors Bekkr for grinding.

When Roger and Richard entered the great hall, Sire Geoffrey was already sitting at the table with the rest of the family and his vassals, enjoying a piece of roast swan.

A little later, Frederic appeared with a serious expression on his face and hurried to the liege lord.

“Hugues de Borre is back from the Frankish Empire with his men, Sire.”

Sire Geoffrey nodded, chewing, and exchanged a glance with his confidants.

No sooner had the seneschal uttered those words than Hugues came stomping into the room in full armour with his four men. “I bring news from the Veuguessin, Sire.”

The liege lord pushed the food aside and wiped his hands. “You make me curious, Hugues.”

Hugues de Borre puffed himself up and let his gaze wander over those present. “In all of the Veuguessin, there is no stone left standing on another, no field or cattle left to feed the people, nothing in which King Philippe could find pleasure. Everything is destroyed. The enemy troops who dared to invade Norman territory have been driven back by King William, their fortress besieged and the whole town reduced to rubble.”

Sire Geoffrey’s mouth twisted into a sardonic grin. He raised his cup of wine in the air. “Those are good tidings indeed, Hugues. Sit down and let us celebrate this Norman victory over King Philippe and his Frankish curs!”

"That is not all, Sire." Hugues de Borre cleared his throat. "The king had an accident in Mantes. His men brought him to Roem with serious injuries."

Chapter 20

"If you keep improving like this, you might be dubbed in fewer than three years." Oswulf gave his pupil an appreciative nod.

Lying on the grass with all his limbs stretched out and panting, Roger wiped off the sweat that trickled down his skin.

The master of arms had told him a few months ago that he would make him work more, not only on his fighting skills but also on his strength and endurance to make sure that he met the demands of a battle. Very quickly, Roger had found out what this meant for him, such as physical exercises instead of cleaning weapons as a punishment for not following orders.

The female inhabitants of Wilburgfos certainly took more pleasure from these additional exercises than Roger as they gleefully watched the young man take off his tunic and linen shirt and then run round the palisade fence of the manor house five times as fast as he could, as ordered by the master of arms.

"Nobody at the manor can keep up with you," Oswulf stroked his moustache, "whether on foot or horseback, with sword, lance or battle axe."

He put his hands on his back and paced around Roger. "Your opponents here are striplings, of course. They follow the steps and movements that they learned, but they have never had to prove their skill in war. So far, your lack of self-control hasn't done you any harm, for your natural talent saves you – though, even I sometimes wonder how you manage to wriggle out of a tricky situation."

He planted himself at Roger's feet. "However, if you want to hold out in battle against experienced warriors, then you must learn to control yourself and be skilful in your approach."

Roger rolled his eyes. "Yeah, yeah, I know. That's why you still win against me."

"Experience has taught me that imprudence leads nowhere. It's like playing chess: Only those who think their approach through thoroughly, act with deliberation and don't let themselves be distracted by setbacks will emerge as the eventual winner."

Roger lifted himself off the ground and picked up his clothes. "What if you feel you're getting nowhere?" He slipped into his linen shirt.

"It depends with what."

"Or with whom." Roger sighed.

"Are you worried because of your father?"

Roger reached for his tunic. "Not more than usual. He continues to remain silent about his succession, and I have not the slightest idea what goes on inside his head. Frederic does pay more attention that I take on further tasks and give my opinion on certain decisions, but his support alone won't get me anywhere. He is, after all, only the seneschal."

"Then your father would probably like to see you as ruler of Wilburgfos, for otherwise, he would prevent you from fulfilling additional duties. The seneschal would never go against his liege lord's orders or dare to oppose him."

"Frederic is a good man. My whole family likes him." Roger squirmed into the tunic.

"I know... So, if it's not about your father, then who else?"

Roger wiped the sweaty hair from his face, all hot and damp from the exertion.

"You remember Gwennaol, the girl I met at the market just after Easter."

"The girl whom your father wants to keep you away from for some reason and whom you secretly wanted to see again."

Roger smiled. "That's exactly what I did. We've been meeting secretly at the priory since my father forbade me from consorting with her."

"You have actually seen each other several times?"

"I've been visiting her for months."

Oswulf's moss-green eyes flashed. "She must like you."

Roger pulled up one corner of his mouth. "Yes, maybe she does, but it's hard to know for sure, even though she talks a lot more than when we first met."

"I'm glad to hear that."

"If I only knew what she was thinking or feeling, Oswulf! She has recently turned sixteen years old. Other girls chatter away happily at that age, but Gwennaol is as stingy with her words as the king is with his salt cellar."

"She's not making it easy for you."

"Not really, no. Horses and weapons are easier to handle than women. With Gwennaol, neither knowledge nor courage, strength nor skill helps me. Whenever I think she's going to tell me something more about herself and the secret about my father, she falls silent or suddenly has to leave."

"You're not going to give up, are you?" The master of arms beckoned Roger to follow.

Roger adjusted his weapon belt and accompanied Oswulf back into the courtyard. "She'll tell me the secret eventually.

I will not be defeated by a girl after all!" His gaze wandered dreamily towards the convent. "We'll see if I cannot make her talk. So far, I have succeeded with every woman. Maybe God is trying me, and I have to pass this ordeal to be worthy of learning the secret about my father."

"Only those who pass such trials survive. Those who fail must die."

Roger laughed. "You're exaggerating, Oswulf. This is only about a girl, not life and death."

At that moment, Isabel ran crying from the great hall to the chapel.

Roger followed her and found her sobbing loudly and crouching in front of the statue of the Mother of God.

As he knelt beside her, she hastily wiped the tears from her face.

He put his arm around her. "What happened, Isabel? Why are you crying?"

She dried her damp hands on her dress and wiped her face again. "Father wants to marry me off. He thinks that at fifteen years of age, I am old enough and that it is high time he chose a husband for me."

"You're a pretty girl. There are many men at the manor whose faces light up at the sight of you and who would like to marry you."

"Father has very precise ideas about my future husband. He must be a Norman, of course, with sufficient property and influence. I owe him a wealthy and important husband, he says. After all, he has looked after me for fifteen years – ha! Looked after me! He only ever had eyes for William. We were just dirt to him. An English burden he had to carry with him because he took over this manor."

Roger stroked Isabel's back. "Don't worry about it. I'm sure it will take a while for Father to find a suitable man for you."

His sister started to sob again. "How can I not worry when he says he's already found the right man for me? A comte ten years older than you – almost twice my age!"

Roger wondered which would be worse: to become the wife of a rich, old comte or to marry Gilbert FitzOsbern from Scornesbi. Maybe his father just wanted to prevent Sire Osbern from finally getting what he had been demanding for months. Was that why he was in such a hurry for Isabel to get married?

Unable to think of anything comforting to say, Roger rose and pulled his sister to her feet. "Calm down, Isabel. Who knows, this comte might not be as bad as you think."

Sniffling, Isabel left the chapel with him.

From the side, a voice grunted, "Par Deu, you look ugly when you blubber."

Tankred stopped in front of the two with a disdainful look and a basket of mushrooms on his arm.

"And you look ugly all the time," Isabel snapped.

Roger patted his little brother on the head. "What a nasty little creature you are, Tankred."

"Stop that!" Tankred pulled his head away.

"It's just as well that you'll be working as a page for another whole year, so you can improve your manners even further."

"I should be a squire by now. All this woman's work is a mere waste of time for me."

"Oh, is that so? You mean, by virtue of your God-given excellence, your advancement to the rank of squire is long overdue?"

"I am a man, hence it is beneath me to wait on and obey women."

"Aren't you being a little full of yourself, my dear brother? You also forget that one of those women is your own mother."

"She's just an Englesse. In fact, *she* should be serving me, not me serving her. After all, my father is a Norman."

Roger clicked his tongue. "From your manners and bearing, you are a worthy substitute for William. If only you were as good with weapons and horses as you are with insults, one would think our elder brother had miraculously returned to us."

Tankred grumbled a Norman insult and stomped away with his basket so that the mushrooms flew through the air.

When Roger entered the great hall with Richard, the voices of Sire Geoffrey and his vassals filled the air as they were discussing what had for weeks been troubling the Norman lords, great and small, both at their manors and throughout England, and probably in Normandy as well: King William's injuries.

"Is there still no news from Roem?" Roger asked his friend as they meandered past the servants and other new arrivals to their seats.

Richard shook his head. "No. My father said that no one around here knows whether King William is better or not, but they say that he's been unable to leave his bed in Roem."

"Do you think he'll recover?"

"Who can say? King William is strong and powerful, but he's almost sixty years old, and his body is soft and yielding. Even the strength of a king fails at some point."

Roger eyed Richard. Since he had attained the rank of squire, he seemed even more precocious to Roger, though, unlike Tankred, he was very careful not to hurt anyone with his words.

"King William's condition is serious indeed," declared Sire Geoffrey. "Every Norman in England must deliberate how to carry on."

"There is discord between King William and his eldest son, Robert Courteheuse," said one of the vassals. "It seems the king is thinking of giving Normandy to William le Rous. He has always preferred him to his other sons, and I fear that the quarrel with the elder of the two will only strengthen his decision."

"William le Rous is a spoiled and cosseted child!" thundered Hugues de Borre. "He wears his hair long like a woman and dresses like one."

"But he's strong-willed like his father," exclaimed a vassal. "Robert may be brave and skilled in battle, but he's also lazy and has a weak character."

"Precisely. King Philippe had an easy time turning Robert against his father."

"Should Robert survive this campaign, his father will disinherit him. He will not be persuaded to reconcile with him a second time."

Sire Geoffrey wiped away the objections with his hand. "King William will violate neither Norman nor English law. Robert Courteheuse will, as is his due as eldest son, take the ancestral Duchy of Normandy. William le Rous and Henri will have to share England."

Some fell silent, others nodded, still others hummed in agreement or scepticism.

Hugues de Borre looked at Sire Geoffrey. "We must be ready for anything."

Sire Geoffrey nodded sullenly and said, in a low voice but loud enough for Roger to hear it, "I'll be riding north again soon."

The north.

So, that's where his father had recently taken up duties on an unusually regular basis. He never mentioned what he actually did there and where exactly he was going. However, Sire Geoffrey had recently been consulting with Hugues de Borre and his men without Frederic or Roger attending these convocations. The dark-haired man Roger had seen at the manor house last month, before Sire Geoffrey left on a journey, had also returned and was sitting next to the liege lord and Hugues de Borre.

Leaning over to Richard, Roger whispered, "Do you know the man next to my father?"

Richard looked up, chewing, regarded the stranger and shook his head. "No. Who is he?"

"I don't know, but I've seen him here a few times. He's been talking to my father and his vassals, but I don't know about what."

"But I do," cooed a female voice behind them. It belonged to Emma, who was just placing a jug of wine on the table so that her well-filled neckline squeezed past Roger's nose. "He brought news from Robert de Monbrai. I eavesdropped on him talking to your father."

"Robert de Monbrai?" asked Roger. "Who's he?"

Richard waved it off. "An evil man. My father doesn't really like him. Robert is arrogant, loud and hairy. But he's the Comte de Northumberland."

The Comte de Northumberland? "How old is this Robert de Monbrai?"

Richard raised his shoulders. "A few years younger than William le Rous."

"That must be the one Isabel is supposed to marry!"

"She's getting married?"

"Yes, I found her crying in the chapel earlier because Father wants to marry her off to a comte who is much older than her. That must be Robert de Monbrai."

"Poor Isabel. I feel sorry for her."

"Well, I'd be happy if a comte married me." Emma bowed down to Roger as she placed the last loaf of bread on the table. "Or at least a liege lord."

She straightened up with a sigh. "What a pity that the great Norman liege lords are always off somewhere and have no time at all for their wives. But that's where the seneschal comes in at every manor, isn't it? Doesn't only take good care of the manor house while the liege lord's away, does he?" She winked at Roger and walked off.

What else does a seneschal take good care of? Roger wondered, but instead of an answer, he only felt disconcerting looks on his back. When he turned round, some men quickly avoided his gaze, indulging in their food as if nothing had happened.

THE NEXT FEW days reinforced Roger's suspicion that the servants were indeed watching him and whispering about him behind his back.

When he asked some of them about it, they would shrug and protest their innocence – until the day when Sire Geoffrey stood in the courtyard with Hugues de Borre, Frederic and some vassals, while Tankred, the other pages and the younger squires prepared the horses for a hunting trip.

When Tankred tugged frantically at the girth, his horse gave an indignant grunt and began to prance.

"Don't pull on the girth like that, Tankred," said Roger. "You have to be more gentle."

Tankred snorted. "This stupid animal puffs itself up, so that I cannot close the girth." With a mighty jerk, he pulled the strap upwards.

The stallion reared up and galloped away, which two other horses took as an invitation to charge off as well.

Two squires chased after the horses to catch them.

Roger only just managed to hold back his chestnut stallion, who would have loved to follow his companions. "Didn't you hear what I said? I told you to be more gentle!"

"If you know everything better, then *you* can take care of that stupid horse next time."

Frederic put his hand on Tankred's shoulder. "Calm down, Tankred. You're still young and impetuous. One day, you'll be as good with horses as Roger."

Tankred shook off his hand. "Yeah, right. Roger knows it all. Roger can do anything. He's a role model for all of us." He crossed his arms in front of his chest and raised his voice. "But that won't help him, because eventually *I* will be the liege lord of Wilburgfos."

Roger and Frederic exchanged a look.

Frederic smiled empathically at Tankred. "You're only saying that because you're angry with Roger. He's your elder brother and therefore he's—"

"He's not my elder brother."

Tankred threw a defiant glare at the growing number of onlookers.

"What do you mean?" asked Roger.

"You're not my father's son, and therefore *I* am the rightful heir."

"And who do you think my father is, if not Sire Geoffrey?"

Tankred pointed his chin at Frederic. "It's him!"

The bystanders flinched. Roger and Frederic looked surprised.

Frowning, Frederic turned to Tankred. "But, my dear boy, what makes you think that?"

"That's what everyone says at the manor."

Roger planted himself in front of Tankred. "Who's 'everyone'? Tell me their names so I can ask them myself!"

Tankred shrugged. "Some at the manor house. The servants from the kitchen. Emma, for example."

"Since when do you listen to what the servants say? Where did they get that idea from in the first place? One of them must have misunderstood something, and Emma then spread the word without giving it any thought. Just like you, Tankred, who believes such idle talk and even passes it on."

The boy looked at his father, who had paused his conversation with Hugues de Borre and the vassals to listen to the interaction between his sons. "It's not only I who has noticed that you and Frederic are suspiciously close when Father is away. As soon as he comes back, you act as if nothing has happened. Just like last month."

Sire Geoffrey strode into the middle of the circle that had formed around Frederic and the two young men. He looked first at Tankred and then at Frederic, who shook his head incredulously.

"I don't know where Tankred heard these accusations, Sire, but they're not true. I've known Dame Edeva for a long time, and I wouldn't dare to betray you. I swear to you, I have always served you faithfully and honestly, so help me God."

Sire Geoffrey regarded Frederic coolly. "I suppose He will have to when you have to answer for these charges at court."

Frederic gasped. "But, Sire! You don't actually think that I…? Surely, you won't believe these rumours!"

"You will have ample opportunity to show us whether these allegations are rumours or the truth, seneschal." The liege lord turned away and marched back to his vassals.

Stunned, Frederic watched him go.

"This is all a lie." Roger gave Tankred a disparaging look and hurried after his father. "Father, wait! Frederic is innocent. He would never betray you."

Sire Geoffrey briefly glanced at Roger without slowing or stopping. "Then he has nothing to fear."

Roger barred his father's way. "You know that I am your son."

Sire Geoffrey lifted his chin. "You've always been different from William and Tankred. Now I know why."

He wanted to proceed, but Roger stood firm. "None of this is true. Someone is spreading an evil rumour about me so that I won't succeed you."

"We will discuss the matter at the next court session after my return."

"You've been travelling a lot lately, Father, but you never say where you go."

"I have to go to Londres. King William died in Roem on the ninth of September. He was talked into leaving the Duchy of Normandy to his eldest son, Robert, by those present at his death. His second son, William le Rous, will be crowned King of England by Archbishop Lanfranc at Westminster Abbey on the twenty-sixth of September."

That was the longest answer Roger had ever received from his father, but there was little reason to be pleased about it. Who, in addition to Tankred and his father, thought that Roger was not the son and rightful successor of the liege lord? Where had this ludicrous rumour of his illegitimate descent come from, and how far had it already spread? Who would have wanted Tankred, not Roger, to rule over Wilburgfos? And who was so unscrupulous as to use poor Frederic for these purposes, who had dutifully served Sire Geoffrey all his life?

Chapter 21

The Early Mass in the church of St Ansgar of Wilburgfos seemed to go on forever. Was it because Father Leofric was unusually wordy in asking the congregation to pray for the soul of the deceased king? Or because in the same breath, he urged them to confess their own sins and ask the Lord for forgiveness?

For a moment, Roger pondered whom the priest had looked at particularly intensely during his exhortations, but then his thoughts circled again around what was to come. For him, for his mother, for Frederic.

No sooner had the service ended than the churchgoers pushed their way through the heavy entrance gate and out into the open.

Roger made his way to his mother and murmured to her as unobtrusively as possible, "I need to talk to you, Mother. Alone."

Dame Edeva nodded briefly, sent the other women ahead and stayed behind with her son in front of the church. They waited until they were sure that no one could overhear their conversation. Then they strolled back to the manor house at a safe distance.

"What is on your mind, min sunu?" asked Dame Edeva softly.

As usual, she had carefully hidden her long, light blonde braids under her white veil. Compared to the dark green dress with its beautifully decorated neckline and sleeves, her light green eyes looked dull. She had not even reached forty years of age, and yet she looked infinitely tired. She had survived the war for England, endured the loss of her first husband and all her property to the Norman who killed him and then forced himself on her as a second husband, survived the almost annual births and the children lost to the adversities of child-birth or disease, put up with the daily toils in the manor house and with the sons and daughters – not all of them her own – without complaining. And after all this, she was now being suspected of adultery. What sin had she brought upon herself that the Almighty should punish her in this way?

"Did you hear what Tankred said yesterday in front of everyone in the courtyard?" Roger asked.

"I did. Frederic told me about it."

"I doubt Emma started the rumour. Where else could Tankred or she have heard it?"

"Emma loves to talk. Someone could have whispered it to her on purpose because they wanted the rumour to spread quickly."

"But you are innocent. And so is Frederic. What's the point of a trial to clarify that?"

"Your father's honour has been attacked in public. He has no choice. He must also restore his reputation in public."

"How calmly you say that! Are you not afraid of how the trial will turn out? Whoever started this rumour wants to harm you and me. I'm sure they'll do everything to bring about a conviction. Do you know what you would have to expect in that case?"

Dame Edeva laughed pitifully. "Hroðgar! You worry too much." She stroked his cheek as if to reassure a small child not to be afraid of the dark. "The Almighty knows that I have always been faithful to my husband, no matter how he has treated me all this time. God will see to it that no harm comes to me for something I have not done. What would I have to fear from your father? He took my husband many years ago and killed most of my relatives. He already owns my manor and all my land. What else could he take from me? My life?" She shook her head. "He knows that would be of no benefit to him. On the contrary. He may be the liege lord of Wilburgfos, but I am its heart."

Roger let the words sink in for a while. "That means," he finally said, "his anger and revenge will be directed first and foremost against Frederic. But why should he believe the accusations against his long-serving and loyal seneschal? He did not even question Tankred's claims, just as he always blindly believed everything William said. It's as if the rumour suited him to get rid of Frederic and make someone else seneschal – and to exclude me from the succession at the same time."

"That would only benefit whoever took Frederic's place."

"Or someone who wants to prevent Frederic from helping me fight for my inheritance. Because they don't want *me* to be the successor. By way of this rumour, they are trying to get us both out of the way."

Dame Edeva stared at him. "You don't believe Tankred..."

"I doubt it. He probably did hear the rumour among the servants. But I know someone who would have every reason to circulate it."

WHERE HAD THE eagerness gone, with which Roger usually anticipated the weekly trip to the clearing? All he had felt over the last few days was an increasing tightness in his belly, as if he had eaten something bad. But the reason was, of course, not what was put on the table, but rather what was going on around it. The whispering and the looks people kept giving him.

He wiped away the thoughts and accompanied Drogo to the armoury, where they picked up the equipment they needed for their practice session outside.

As Roger was carrying the fighting gear towards the waiting horses, Richard joined him with the snare traps. "Have you spoken to Tankred?" he asked in a low voice.

"What about?"

"About what he said in the yard yesterday."

"What is there to talk about? He heard a stupid rumour from someone and has blindly believed it."

"What did your father say?"

"You heard it yesterday, didn't you?... I'm sorry, Richard. I shouldn't take out my anger on you. It's not your fault."

Richard smiled wryly. "That's all right. Tankred really got you into trouble yesterday."

Roger unloaded a pile of practice weapons next to the horses and looked around. "Tankred is a headstrong and fickle boy. He readily believes things that fit into the picture he has created of people. But he rejects his beliefs just as quickly if it promises to be more favourable for him. What he said yesterday didn't come from him, and it didn't come from Emma either. She would never come up with such thoughts herself. Someone must have insinuated it to her. The question is, who?"

"Why would anyone do that?"

"Because he wants to take revenge on me or my mother? Because he expects a personal advantage from having the seneschal out of the way? Because he takes pleasure in slandering people? What do I know?"

"What would anyone gain by accusing you of not being Sire Geoffrey's son? Our king is... I mean, our former king was not a legitimate son of the duke either."

Roger grinned. "Then I still have a great future ahead of me, you think?"

"No, I mean, yes. Oh, you know what I mean!"

"It's all right, Richard. Nothing has been proven yet. My mother is beyond any doubt and is not afraid of being questioned."

"What about Frederic?"

Roger gave Richard a nudge. "One could think you're already practising for the trial when you should be distributing the weapons on the horses."

He turned to Modig Wiht and checked all his equipment again.

The stallion gave Roger an impatient shove with his nose against the shoulder so that Roger stumbled to the side.

"Easy, Modig," Roger said, patting his four-legged friend on his strong neck. "You need to be patient. I know it's hard. I feel the same way."

From the side, a bright voice lamented, "So do I! I've been patient for so long, and I am so lonely." There stood Emma with wide brown eyes, casually twirling a long strand of hair and licking her lips with a slightly open mouth.

Gulping, Roger looked around.

Joscelin rolled his eyes and disappeared behind his horse.

Emma stepped forward. “I rarely see my big Norman lately,” she breathed, “but maybe, he’ll have some more time for me soon.”

Roger cleared his throat. “Emma, look, we’re about to set off. I’m sorry, I don’t really have time for you right now.”

Emma kept walking until she stood close enough for him to have a good view of her neckline. “I know that, but I’m hoping that very soon, you’ll be able to look after me more, when you don’t have to attend those gatherings anymore.”

“What gatherings?”

“Oh, all that stuff you’d have to do as a liege lord. I’m lucky you won’t need that anymore.”

Roger backed away a little. “What are you talking about? I’m still the eldest son of Lord Geoffrey and therefore the future liege lord.”

Emma frowned. “But I thought Frederic has... you’re...”

“I don’t know where you got this from, but it’s not true, Emma. Lord Geoffrey is my father.”

“Then you will continue to have so little time for me?” The corners of Emma’s mouth dropped.

“I’m really sorry, Emma. You’re a nice girl, and I really like you, but if I’m going to be the future liege lord, I need to be familiar with all that is necessary to run a manor.”

Richard peered around the horse’s backside. “Are you ready, Roger? Oh, greetings, Emma.” He shyly eyed her up.

The kitchen maid followed his gaze, snorting. “What’re you looking at me like that for? Are you wondering how you can get your filthy Norman hands on me? You Normans make it easy for yourselves. You kill off our protectors, and then you divide the manors and the women among yourselves. Ha! Because you can’t have us any other way. It was probably you who told everyone that the seneschal was Roger's father! Because you wanted to take revenge on Roger. Because I wasn't impressed with your advances and your fine Norman ancestry, and because I prefer to get laid by your friend. You'd rather take over Wilburgfos yourself than leave the manor and its women to Roger."

Roger and Richard blushed scarlet. Emma had been loud enough for most of the people in the courtyard to hear her opinions and accusations.

She gathered up her tunic dress, turned and ran into the great hall. Numerous glances followed her before some of them swung over to Richard and Roger.

The two looked at each other. While Roger stood between the horses, somewhat shielded from the greedy eyes and ears of the uninvited witnesses, his friend was on display like goods on a market stand in the open space of the yard, away from the squires and the other residents at the manor.

Awkwardly aware of this sudden bout of attention, Richard shifted from one foot to the other before he resolutely shook his head. "It wasn't me, Roger. You have to believe me."

Roger eyed him. As the youngest of four sons, Richard would have been destined to become a priest. However, the third son of William de Perci was already being educated as a cleric, so he had decided to have Richard brought up as a warrior instead. Was Wilburgfos perhaps one of the lands that the youngest would later take over as liege lord?

Richard took a few steps towards Roger. "You're my best friend, Roger. I would never do anything like that to you."

While Roger was pondering Emma's words, the little redhead came up to him, his hands raised apologetically. "I swear I didn't touch Emma. I don't want anything from her."

Roger suppressed a laugh. "Don't worry. She would have done that for you."

Richard's face turned as fiery red as his hair.

Smiling, Roger patted him on the back. "Enough for now. We should get going if we don't want Oswulf to punish us for being late for the practice lesson."

Joscelin cleared his throat and threw an unobtrusive look behind Roger, who turned round.

Behind him stood Oswulf with his arms folded and his head held high. "He must be a bad man, this Oswulf."

"We were just about to mount," said Roger, "when a little incident occurred that had to be sorted out first."

"So I heard... as did everyone else in the yard."

Richard stood tall so that Oswulf could see him behind Roger. "I didn't start the rumour. Emma must have got it from someone else."

"There's a lot of gossip in the kitchen and the fields, particularly among the women. A careless remark can turn into a rumour fast."

"Someone wants to prevent my taking over Wilburgfos," said Roger.

"Many wars have been fought over succession, Roger. It's nothing unusual."

"Do you know who could be behind it?"

"My guess is as good as yours. What do you think?"

"There are some who have never forgiven me for William's death, even though I am not to blame. They would rather have had William as their liege lord than me."

"Are you thinking of anyone in particular?"

Roger shrugged. "Walter, perhaps, although he tends to ignore rather than discredit me. Hugues de Borre, however, has already made several disparaging remarks about me. Not to mention Father Leofric, who thinks I am the devil himself. But he is a man of the Church. He would never utter such slander as the rumour implies."

"So, that leaves only one of the three."

"The bailiff."

"You have to be careful, Roger. As long as you have no evidence against him, you must restrain yourself in what you say and do. You have a dangerous opponent with a lot of experience."

WITH A SWING of Roger's arm, the scramasax cut through the twigs that stretched across the narrow path. Most of the time, Roger had already been crouching, weaving through openings in the foliage that, without bending the twigs away, were only suitable for someone at least a head shorter and a good twenty pounds lighter than himself.

When he came to another spot that was difficult to get through, he stopped, brushed a few strands out of his face and took a breath.

Was it all worth it anymore? If it turned out that he was indeed an illegitimate son – and a bastard of his mother, not the liege lord at that – Wilburgfos was not his to take over anyway. What use would the secret about his father, his foster father, be to him then? What could a bastard do with it? And yet, his mother had assured him that she had always been faithful to her husband. Why would she lie to her own son?

The hairs on Roger's arms stood on end. He remembered Brandolf and Bjarni and what had been done to them. Yet it was only bad luck that had got them into it all. *Like Frederic.*

He shuddered. With another swipe of his short sword, he parted the branches in front of him and tried to think of something else. Perhaps Gwennaol would brighten up his thoughts. Or should he turn back and put a hold on the secret meetings until a verdict had been reached? Only then would he know if he was not wasting his time on something that could not save Wilburgfos for him.

He pushed aside the last twigs in front of the small clearing. The sliding hatch was open.

Roger crouched behind the bushes as best he could and looked to the left and right. Why wasn't the hatch closed as usual? Gwennaol always waited for Roger to knock before opening it. Was someone else sitting in the little prayer room under the stairs? Had someone discovered Gwennaol there during her regular visits and was now trying to find out why she disappeared for a while in the mornings instead of doing her work? Through the undergrowth, Roger tried to make out who or what was moving behind the opening. He narrowed his eyes. His heart was pounding. He couldn't stay here forever. He had to get closer to the door to find out what was going on.

With his gaze firmly fixed on the aperture, Roger squeezed his way through the thicket and onto the little clearing in front of the secret door. With twigs pricking him in the sides and back from all directions, there was now barely any space left for a man his size.

He bent down and peered through the opening. A single candle was burning in the room, illuminating the walls with a faint glow. Roger saw a piece of the altar that the prioress had mentioned. In front of it was the head of a dark figure, but he could not tell if it was Gwennaol. He heard a low murmur and tried to make out the words. Should he make himself known through the agreed knocks? Or whisper? If the figure was Gwennaol, he would have nothing to fear. But what if it wasn't?

He inched to the side and let his gaze wander along the mighty wooden beams of the cloister. By knocking the sign, he would betray everything and everyone involved in his clandestine meetings. Not only himself, but also his friends who covered his absence, the prioress who had made these meetings possible in the first place, and of course, Gwennaol. For there was no doubt that they would soon find out at the priory that he came to see her. And then? What if his father learned that his son was not only violating his order but had been doing so secretly and regularly for several months? How would he punish him, or, much worse, what would happen to his friends, the prioress and Gwennaol, none of whom were to blame for what he was doing?

Roger turned the signet ring on his left little finger and looked at the symbols on it: tree, sword and axe – the eternal connection and unity of all things; protection, justice and wealth; strength, courage and power. Why was he wearing this ring when he was about to betray his liege lord and put all those who meant well with him in danger? It wouldn't be the first time that his father cruelly punished someone innocent for something that was not their fault. Roger had already been unable to save Brandolf and Bjarni from his father's wrath, even with the support of his friends. What could he do alone? He was not worthy of this ring.

A hiss jolted him out of his thoughts. The sound came from the opening. Roger ducked, ready to make a dash for the bushes. Cautiously, he rose.

"I was expecting you earlier, Roger."

He knew that voice. He jumped up and glanced through the hole. "Gwennaol! It's you."

"What took you so long?"

"There are bad tidings from Normandy and my father's manor."

"I heard that King William died."

Surprised once again at how knowledgeable they all were about worldly events in this small priory, Roger nodded. "Yes. His son, William le Rous, will be our new king before Michaelmas."

"What happened at the manor?"

"There's a rumour spreading about me."

"What rumour?"

Roger bit his lip. He looked deep into Gwennaol's eyes. "They claim that Frederic, our seneschal, is my father. If so, I'm not eligible to succeed my father and have no claim to the inheritance that should be mine after William's death."

"Is the rumour true?"

"Of course not! At least, that's what my mother and Frederic say. My father wants to find out in a court hearing next week whether the accusation against the seneschal is justified. I'll have to try to convince him and the jury that it isn't."

"What will you do if they decide otherwise?"

"I must find a way to prevent them from doing so."

"What if you fail?"

"I'd rather not think about that." He brought his face closer to the opening until he was no more than a few inches away from Gwennaol's face and continued in a low voice, "Whatever happens, Gwennaol, I must see you again. Promise me that you will come to our meetings even after the verdict, whatever it may be. If it weren't for this cursed door between us, I'd take you in my arms now and hold you until you swear it to me by all your Breton gods."

The dimples flashed in Gwennaol's cheeks. "If it matters so much to you, I promise."

"Thank you, Gwennaol. You're a—"

The chiming of the church bell drowned out his words. Gwennaol gestured to him that she had to go.

He nodded and smiled at her with a heavy heart.

Whatever the outcome of the trial, o Lord, let me see her again at least once after the verdict.

Chapter 22

"Well, I think it was a good coronation in spite of it all!" Surrounded by his advisers, Robert de Monbrai rubbed his chubby hands as he strode into the great hall, where a blazing fire and hot, spiced wine awaited him. "It was perhaps a little unexpected, but it was a good opportunity to strengthen old... and new relationships." He raised his cup of mulled wine to the others.

"So, your negotiations were successful?" asked his messenger.

"I would hope so, my good man!" The liege lord slapped the messenger on the back, making him leap forward. "A coronation is always a good occasion to meet the important men of the country and talk to... like-minded people."

"I suppose the newly inherited kingdom and its inhabitants were an important matter to discuss, not only for the king."

"Indeed, they were, even though William le Rous seems to have little concern that his father has divided the kingdom between two sons instead of naming a single heir. He clings to the words of his father, who so decreed."

"One ruler unites. Two rulers divide." The fool grinned at the two men from below.

"Alain le Rous and the Comte de Cestre pledged fealty, as usual, to the new king, but many other barons are displeased with William's decision. They feel left out, cheated out of their property and betrayed," said Sire Robert.

"I would assume most barons will try to secure their lands here in England," said the messenger.

Sire Robert put his hand on the messenger's back and pulled him aside. "They certainly will. The question is, what are they willing to do for it?"

The messenger shrugged. "William le Rous will make them swear an oath of allegiance to him, if he hasn't already done so at his coronation."

"You forget that most of the senior vassals with land in Normandy have already sworn allegiance to his brother, Robert Courteheuse." Sire Robert paused weightily. "And then there is also Odo de Bayeus, whom William le Rous has decided to set free after four years of imprisonment. There'll be many discontented men at court in Wincestre at the end of the year."

The messenger smirked. "Looks like the next Feast of the Lord is going to be very special."

"Which brings me to another task I have for you. After all, we must make sure that we are well prepared, no matter what may come."

Part 5

WILBURGFOS, FROM OCTOBER TO MID-DECEMBER IN THE YEAR OF OUR LORD 1087

Chapter 23

"He is completely besotted with her and is determined to see her again."

"Even against the order of the liege lord?"

"I told you before that he would do anything to achieve his goal. Like a drowning man, he clutches at any straw he can grasp."

"I like that idea. Has he told you what he has done in the meantime?"

"He was rather proud when he told me he was secretly seeing her – and quite upset that he wasn't getting what he wanted from her."

"Indeed, she acquits herself well. And he is persistent, he asks questions, tells her everything that has happened in and around the manor recently. Under other circumstances, I'd say they'd make a beautiful couple. What a pity it will never come to that."

"Even more so with time running out for him."

"So, he knows?"

"The whole court knows. I made sure of that."

"Has he become suspicious?"

"Yes, but he's so obsessed with proving himself as the successor and having the liege lord in his power that he can no longer think clearly about anything else. He insists he knows who's behind the rumour, yet he hasn't the faintest idea to whom he really owes it all."

"You have done well. His wheel of fortune is slowly but steadily turning downwards."

Chapter 24

A few days before the harvest festival on the first Sunday in October, Sire Geoffrey returned home from the coronation of the new King William le Rous. Fewer than two weeks had passed since his departure, and yet it seemed to Roger that his father had aged disproportionately in that time. The reddish-blonde hair, the already fair skin, even the ice-blue eyes – everything looked greyer, paler than before.

Roger knew from his mother and the seneschal that, as a young warrior, Sire Geoffrey had travelled often and for many weeks with the army in England. But that was a long time ago, and the journeys he had made repeatedly in recent months seemed to wear him out. Sire Geoffrey was not much older than the master of arms, but he lacked his daily physical exercise. Was he simply getting old? Was he possibly ill? Or did it have something to do with the fact that two unequal brothers now had to share a single empire, and no one really knew if and how long that would go well?

Whatever the reason, Roger couldn't help feeling that something unpleasant was in the air, even if, to a casual observer, life in and around Wilburgfos seemed to be going on as usual. The days were getting cooler, but fortunately, this year, there was no such rain and cold as last year, when it destroyed most of the harvest. The leaves in the woods, which consisted mainly of mighty oaks, were changing colour and adorned the landscape with a yellow-red band that swept around the green pastureland and the harvested, brown fields. In front of a hut, an old woman sat weaving a basket while two men dismantled the bent coulter from a plough so that the blacksmith could repair it. In the fields, the peasants were sowing wheat and rye. Children were roaming along the unploughed strips, chasing the ravenous crows away with drums, rattles and shouts.

On the outside, everything seemed peaceful, but deep within the people, grew an ominous mixture of curiosity, envy, malice and fear. More and more peasants whispered behind his back or suddenly fell silent when Roger came near them. At first, he tried to ignore some of the wary looks, but the more gossip and gawking there was, the more difficult it became to pretend that everything was all right.

Feeling a little queasy, Roger entered the great hall and beheld the stooped figure of the seneschal, who sat on a chair against the wall with slumped shoulders and a blank stare. He would have loved to help him, but how? He could only wait and pray.

There was still hope for a good outcome of the trial that would decide both their fates today. Apart from the gossip of a kitchen maid, there was no evidence that the rumour contained even a shred of truth. Surely, the misunderstanding would be resolved quickly.

Sire Geoffrey let his bored gaze wander around the room. Beside him, where the seneschal usually had his place as chairman at such hearings, sat Hugues de Borre – just as Roger had thought! The bailiff was already treating himself to a little taste of the position he might occupy and the power that went with it. The rumour was bound to have come from him to speed up the process.

Roger's belly was tingling. The waiting was driving him crazy.

At last, Hugues de Borre opened the court session. He gave the floor to the reeve, who hummed the charge.

"Sire Geoffrey de Bernaium, messires, men of Wilburgfos. We must decide today whether the accused seneschal, Frederic de Lisieues, abused not only the position assigned to him but also the trust of his liege lord and fathered a son with his liege's wife during her husband's and his master's absence."

Those present eyed Roger and then Sire Geoffrey and Frederic as if comparing whom the boy resembled more.

"After losing his beloved wife, Astrid, in the spring of the Year of Our Lord 1068, Sire Geoffrey very successfully fought against the rebels here in the north of England. That same year, he was given the manor of Wilburgfos by Sire William de Perci and married the widow of the former owner, Dame Edeva. We all know what a rebellious and stubborn people the Engleis are, and so it happened that Sire Geoffrey stayed away from the manor for whole months to fulfil his obligations to King William. He assumed that his seneschal, who was in charge of his manor during that time, would do the same and carry out his duties as expected. But when, in the autumn of the Year of Our Lord 1069, Sire Geoffrey was to see his second son after a long absence, and he looked at the child, he began to have doubts about his seneschal's fealty."

The rest of the hearing was tedious and revealed little new information.

None of the witnesses who testified against Frederic could confirm the charge beyond doubt. No one had ever observed the seneschal's making advances to the feudal lord's wife, let alone overheard any suspicious meetings or conversations. Those who were well disposed towards Frederic contradicted the words of his adversaries, and so the entire accusation continued to be based solely on the rumour that had spread among the servants, and which Emma also reaffirmed with a naive smile.

Let's hope that my mother's testimony can convince them! Roger put his face into his hands and closed his eyes. *Gemiltsa me God.*

Unlike the kitchen maid, Dame Edeva appeared before the judges with her chin held high. She placed her hand on the Bible that Father Leofric held out to her and raised the three fingers of the other hand. Then she said in a loud voice, "I, Eadgifu, daughter of Eadgar of Wilburgfos, as Dame Edeva, lady of this manor, swear on the Holy Bible that I have been faithful to my husband, Sire Geoffrey de Bernaium, all the years of our marriage and that I have tarnished neither my own honour nor that of my husband by such outrageous deeds as you dare to accuse me of. God is my witness that Sire Geoffrey de Bernaium, Lord of Wilburgfos, is the father of my son, Roger of Wilburgfos."

She looked at Hugues de Borre with raised eyebrows. He nodded sullenly and indicated that she could leave. Since, as a woman, she was not allowed to attend the rest of the hearing, she left the room altogether but without losing any of her dignity.

After a brief deliberation, the jury returned to the courtroom to announce the following verdict: "We have not been able to agree, Sire. Half of the jury finds the seneschal guilty, the other half considers him innocent."

His hands folded, Roger looked around the large hall as the noise swelled. There was hope after all!

Hugues de Borre ruffled his hair.

Sire Geoffrey had put his fingertips together and was eyeing the jurors disapprovingly.

Then Oswulf stepped forward and raised his hand. As if by magic, all chatter immediately stopped. Everyone stared at the master of arms. Even Sire Geoffrey sat up and looked at him expectantly.

After glancing at Frederic and the audience, Oswulf turned to the judges and the jury. "Men of Wilburgfos. Today, you need to deliberate on the seneschal's misconduct." He pointed to Roger. "And on whether this young man might not be the son of the liege lord, as we, and even Sire Geoffrey, have assumed all these years." The master of arms took a few steps towards the jury. "The accusation against the seneschal weighs heavily, and as you have seen and heard, the witnesses are divided as to whether they should believe the accusation or regard it as foolish gossip from the servants. Even you, most venerated jurors, could not come to a clear decision as to where the truth lies. But if you value that law and order prevail at this manor and that evil deeds are punished, then you must now trust in God. For where man is not able to find the right way, the Lord will help him to do what is right. God sees what is hidden from man. It is not for nothing that we pray, trusting in God, 'Gewurþe ðin willa on eorðan swa on heofonum' – Thy will be done, on earth as it is in heaven. So, should we not, at this very moment, also trust in the Lord and bow to his will?"

"Oswulf sounds like Leofric," Richard whispered.

Roger nodded. "I didn't know he was so devout."

Sire Geoffrey had kept a straight face all the while, listening attentively like everyone else. Now, he took a breath and leaned back. "So, you are proposing a trial by ordeal?"

Oswulf clasped his hands behind his back, as he did on the battleground when he was waiting for his pupils. "The jury can no longer take the decision on your behalf. They have given their verdict, showing that they do not know whether the seneschal is guilty or not. God alone can help us in this situation to find out who is lying and who is telling the truth."

Frederic stood up hesitantly. "But the laws of King William demand an ordeal only for theft, murder, breach of oath and looting."

Oswulf looked at him. "Have you not sworn allegiance to your liege lord and submitted to his will?"

Frederic's gaze wandered back and forth between the master of arms and his liege lord. He was as pale as a dead man. Although it was cool in the hall, small beads of sweat shone on his forehead. "Of course I have. God is my witness that I have always kept my oath to him all these years, even in hard times."

"Yet we have heard witnesses who claim the opposite," grumbled Hugues de Borre. "Since you may have broken your oath of fealty after all, this is a case to which the laws of King William pertain and must be applied."

Frederic wiped his forehead dry with a shaking hand. His breathing was shallow and irregular. "No, not a trial by ordeal! I told you that I swear by God never to have betrayed my liege lord. Is not the oath of a Norman enough for you?"

Hugues de Borre exchanged a glance with Sire Geoffrey.

The latter eyed the seneschal and raised his chin. "Would you confirm this oath in a duel?"

Frederic supported himself on the chair and just about managed to sit down again. "You mean an ordeal by battle? But an oath is enough according to the law."

Roger stepped forward. "Cease this, Father! Don't you see what you are doing to Frederic? He has sworn several times that he has not betrayed you, just like your wife."

Sire Geoffrey squinted at his son. "One crow doesn't pick out the other's eyes."

"Do you not see that someone is clearly abusing your trust to gain an advantage for himself?"

"And, please you, who might this be?"

Roger bit his lip and cast a sideways glance at Hugues de Borre.

The bailiff narrowed his piggy eyes. "I'm warning you. You're in court. Think carefully about what you say."

"What else do you want?" Roger asked his father, "in addition to his oath? Why don't you believe him? What would he gain by lying to you?"

"His son would take what is mine and deprive Tankred of his rightful inheritance." Sire Geoffrey turned back to Frederic. "I accept your oath, seneschal... unless someone challenges you for a trial by water or battle." His gaze came to rest upon Oswulf.

Dear Lord! He's cold-bloodedly sending him to his certain death.

Frederic had followed the look of the liege lord and shook his head in horror. "No, no. Not Oswulf. You cannot do this to me, Sire. Have mercy on me! I am an old man who could never win against the master of arms. Take my money, banish me from your manor and send me away, but do not let me fight Oswulf!"

Roger walked up to the table where his father was watching everything, seemingly unimpressed. “I will fight on behalf of the seneschal. You can see for yourselves that he cannot possibly do battle honourably and according to the rules.”

He cast a side-glance at Oswulf, who stood silently beside him, watching. His moss-green eyes sparkled. Was he proud of Roger’s courage and determination? Or was he looking forward to a single combat against his best pupil in front of so many spectators?

The seneschal groaned in his chair and reached out a hand, trembling. “No, Roger. You don’t have to.” He paused to take a breath. “If it is God’s will, I will fight myself.” He tried to sit up, supporting himself with one hand, while holding the other to the left side of his chest.

“There you see it!” said Roger. “He struggles even to get up from the chair.”

He rushed to help Frederic and was just grabbing him under the arm when the seneschal let out a horrible gasp. His eyes twisted upwards, and with a jerk, his whole body slumped. Roger quickly slid his other arm under Frederic’s back to catch him. But when he knelt down to lay him on the ground, he had only the lifeless shell of the seneschal in his arms. Frederic was dead.

An eerie silence spread through the great hall.

Roger stared into the seneschal’s face. “Frederic?” he breathed, though he realised at that moment that the seneschal would never answer him again, never smile kindly at him again.

Roger’s whole body shook in a wave of anger and pain. He squinted at his father. “You killed him! You watched him die before your eyes. And why? Because of a foolish rumour spreading among blathering servants. This, you are more eager to believe than to trust in your wife and your seneschal. What kind of man are you? You have no feelings. Family, loyalty and trust mean nothing to you. You are no man, you're an animal, and a very bad one at that. I am ashamed to be your son."

Sire Geoffrey folded his hands slowly. "You are not my son. The divine judgement has proven the seneschal guilty."

"What?"

"I will confiscate the seneschal's wealth as compensation for his breach of oath. With regard to you, as of today, you will no longer attend the congregations with me and my closest confidants. You will continue to fulfil your other duties at the manor as expected until Tankred reaches the age to become a squire. As the future Lord of Wilburgfos, he can then take them over from you. You may go now."

Roger stared at his father. He had never loved him, had been angry with him many a time and had cursed him in a fit of rage, but now, a feeling of hatred so profound flooded his body as he had never known before. The blood rushed in his ears, his whole body tensed, the scar throbbed as if it was about to burst open. Was this monster really his father? Or had God verily punished an adulterer with Frederic's death? Roger could not and would not believe that. It simply did not sound plausible for the seneschal he had known and appreciated since childhood.

He lifted Frederic's body and rose. Under no circumstances would he leave the seneschal in this company. He gave his father one last look across the table.

I have suffered your humiliations long enough. You condemned two of my friends out of personal revenge. Frederic had to die because of you. As soon as I find out why you want to keep me away from Gwennaol, we will face each other again. Today, you chase me from the manor like a mangy dog – but soon, very soon, I will be the hunter.

"You will regret this."

He gave the table a good kick, which made his father startle. Without saying another word, Roger turned and left the great hall.

Chapter 25

"He did nothing to save him." Roger paced back and forth in the herb hut where Hild and Lady Edeva usually treated the sick. "How could he ever believe that Frederic betrayed him? The man who has been serving him dutifully for decades."

His mother struggled to rise. Tears were still running down her cheeks, much more than after William's death last year. "Maybe he didn't, but he cannot let his underlings consider him a liar and a cuckold. He has already lost his first wife and his eldest son. He will not let Wilburgfos or even the wife allotted to him be wrestled from his hands by anything or anyone, even though neither ever really satisfied him."

"But why did the rumour come up only now, when I am the one to inherit Wilburgfos? Why not earlier? Father has been away often enough, hasn't he? Why only me? Tankred could just as well be a son of the seneschal, couldn't he?"

"Hroðgar!"

"Forgive me, Mother, but do you not agree that something is wrong here? The rumour is directed specifically against me. Whatever the reason, I must find out why."

Dame Edeva looked at Roger with that look he knew from his childhood, when anger boiled inside the small, sulking boy, and it was only a matter of time before it would be unleashed on the surrounding furniture or wooden structures. And this time, as every time, she said to him, "Promise me you won't do anything ill-considered, Hroðgar!"

And so he did. For he had thought everything through carefully.

Adelais wiped a tear from her cheek. "This is terrible. Frederic didn't deserve such an end. He would never have betrayed him."

"Father doesn't think so. If I only knew who started this rumour, I'd personally wring his neck."

"That won't bring Frederic back to life, but it will certainly bring you to hell, Roger. Talk to the servants. Someone must be able to tell you where the rumour came from or who first spread it. I am sure there are still plenty of people at the manor who liked the seneschal and who want to help you."

"I'm having doubts about that. I'm no longer the son and successor of the liege lord but a bastard of the now-dead seneschal. If they don't talk to me of their own free will, I can't even force them anymore."

"Don't despair, little brother! Your Breton friend will still like you."

"How do you know...?"

Adelais smiled mischievously and looked up to the sky. "The ways of the Lord are unsearchable."

Roger looked around, leaned forward and whispered, "Adelais, you must help me." He told her what he thought about the incident in the court hearing and its background and why he met with Gwennaol. "Couldn't you try to talk to Gwennaol to find out what she knows about Father?"

"You want me to sound her out for you?"

"Yes, maybe. Just a little." He took her hands. "For my sake."

Adelais regarded him for a while. "If I can help you achieve what you want and what makes you happy, then I will see what I can do for you." A mischievous smile flitted across her face. "And if I can pay Father back at the same time, even the better. Ja m'en vengerai par mult fiere vertu."

To quickly end the dispute over the seneschal's final resting place, the disgruntled liege lord finally agreed to a burial at the far edge of the cemetery near the church of St Ansgar. Frederic was buried two days later after a brief funeral service in a small circle. As if in mockery, Sire Geoffrey and Hugues de Borre also attended the service and the subsequent funeral procession, but they were the first to leave as the grave was being covered with earth.

Roger very much appreciated this. He could no longer bear the sight of his father without the hairs on the back of his neck standing up. More than ever, he dreamed of finally having his father in his power and making him pay for what he had done to him all these years as father and liege lord. But for that, he needed Gwennaol, and all the more urgently, because now, time was breathing down his neck. By Tankred's fourteenth birthday at the latest, Roger had to prove that he was not a maternal bastard after all, but the rightful successor to Sire Geoffrey. Otherwise, he would have to leave the manor forever and spend his life at another one.

Would Gwennaol understand the urgency of the matter? Could he freely question her about her knowledge of Sire Geoffrey? Would she then perhaps realise that the answer to that question was the only reason he was meeting her? Would he have to fear that she would become as stubborn and taciturn as she had been in the beginning? If so, it would all have been for nothing. He would lose his reputation, the manor, his friends.

And Gwennaol.

IT WAS DEFINITELY not the undergrowth that made the secret path to the priory so difficult today for Roger. Most of the trees and bushes had long since lost their leaves, so that only the bare branches and twigs were visible.

Like skeletons pointing their bony fingers at me.

Roger shook off the thought and continued on the weathered path, which was barely visible under the decaying leaves. Nature was exhausted, and so was he. Since the seneschal's death, he slept far too little, and badly if he did. He avoided his father and Hugues de Borre as much as possible and only spoke to Tankred if he couldn't help it. It brought tears to Isabel's eyes that she would soon lose her second brother and that she might have to move to Northumberland before the end of the year and leave her beloved family forever. Roger did worry about his sister, but at the moment, first and foremost, he had to make sure he sorted out his own destiny.

Arriving at the wooden door, Roger knocked the secret signal.

The sliding hatch opened, but the smile on Gwennaol's face quickly turned into a frown. "You look tired, Roger."

He approached the opening until his forehead almost touched its edge.

Seen from this short distance, Gwennaol's eyes were even more beautiful – like deep blue water, so clear and pure that you could see your reflection in it.

"I sometimes envy people like you who live in such a small, enclosed and sheltered world. All the falseness, the depravity and death stay outside."

"Don't speak like that! You're scaring me. Has something bad happened?"

"Something is always happening – bad for some, good for others. The old king dies. A new king comes. The old seneschal dies. The new liege lord comes. The bastard leaves."

"The seneschal is dead?"

"He died during the trial, which leaves me standing as a bastard, contending for Tankred's rightful place."

"I always thought you were Sire Geoffrey's son."

"I am, but many put Frederic's death down to divine judgement meant to punish the adulterer. Now, I must try to prove them wrong to convince my father otherwise... You can imagine how difficult that will be."

Gwennaol lowered her eyes. "I don't know your father, but I haven't heard much good about him."

"Who told you about him?"

"Oh, they didn't really tell me anything. Every now and then, they mention his name when it comes to levies or things like that. Nothing I particularly care about."

"Then what do you care about if not stories about my father?" asked Roger with a smile.

Gwennaol shrugged. "Mammgozh tells me much about the time before she entered the cloister."

"She remembers that?"

"Not all nuns enter a convent as girls."

"What does your grandmother tell you about the world out here?"

"Oh, the things women say. Petty gossip for a man. I don't want to bore you with it."

"But I would really like to know more about you and your grandmother. It's always me who does the talking when we meet."

"What should I tell you? You must know from Adelais what we do all day. It's a monotonous life, dominated by prayer times and the same tasks over and over again."

"Why don't you tell the prioress that you want to leave? Why are they keeping you in the cloister if you never want to take your vows?... You don't want that, do you?"

"I cannot leave the priory, Roger. Your father..."

"Forget my father and his orders for a moment and just imagine you could choose if you want to stay or not."

"This is crazy."

"Not at all. Come on, Gwennaol, tell me, stay or go?"

"That's not for me to decide."

"But you can at least think about it. So?"

Gwennaol chewed on her lower lip and regarded Roger. Eventually, she sighed.

"I think I would like to leave the priory," she said softly.

Roger's heart leapt.

"I thank you for your honesty, Gwennaol. Now, let me be honest with you too. Nothing would please me more than to see you outside the priory again someday. Forever."

Blushing deeply, she looked down. "Roger! What are you saying!"

"It's the truth, Gwennaol. You were not meant for life in a convent, were you? So, what are you still doing there? Speak to the prioress! She will help you, and I also promise to try everything to free you."

"You would help me?" Gwennaol murmured and raised her head.

He looked deep into her eyes. "Indeed, I would – even if it cost my life." How he was craving to hug and kiss her now. *If only it weren't for this cursed door!*

"Do you know who might be able to support your claim?" asked Gwennaol.

"No, who?"

"Father Leofric."

The scrawny priest, of all people? "What makes you think he could help me? And that he would actually do it?"

"Father Leofric has been a cleric in Wilburgfos for decades and knows everyone and anyone in the area."

"You mean the man who thinks I'm the Fiend himself because I'm left-handed will come to my aid?"

"He's a priest. It is his duty to help people in need."

"You have a lot of faith in him."

"If we cannot trust a man of God, whom can we trust?"

If she only had this trust in me too! "Why don't you come outside?"

"Outside, where you are?"

"Eala! Did I really say that out loud?... You don't have to come, of course. You can if you want to... Please. Just for a moment."

"I'm not sure. Someone could enter the chamber."

"You can lock the door from the inside."

"How do you know?"

Roger pulled up one corner of his mouth. "An angel told me."

After a short reflection, Gwennaol said, "All right. Wait a little."

She's coming! She's really coming to me!

Roger felt his pulse picking up speed. He gulped. Would she really dare to come outside? All alone with him?

Inside, there were several creaks and squeaks, presumably from the bolts that locked the secret door. Shortly afterwards, the door opened, and Gwennaol cautiously stuck her head out.

Roger rubbed his sweaty palms on his tunic. There she was indeed!

"Come. There's no one here." He folded his hands and smiled as innocently as he could. "Except me, of course."

Gwennaol opened the door just enough to slip through the crack. Curious, she looked at the surroundings around the small mossy patch on which Roger had been standing during their clandestine meetings these last months. A few yellow leaves still clung to the trees here and there. Squirrels hopped across the ground with chubby cheeks, busily gathering food for the winter. From afar, the tapping of a woodpecker could be heard, noisily working on a tree bark.

She closed the door behind her just enough to have a clear view of Roger, but kept one hand on the door, just in case. As her gaze glided over everything she could not otherwise see of Roger through the opening in the door, a coy smile flitted across her face. She quickly glanced at the trees and bushes that framed the space they both now shared. "You really don't have much space out here," she said, looking up at Roger. "You're big."

Roger tried to stifle a grin as he remembered those words coming from Emma's mouth. How different those two young women were! What would Emma have given to find herself with Roger on a grassy patch about as big as the wheel of an ox-cart and hidden among bushes and trees behind a religious building? And what was the first thing Gwennaol thought of when she stood within reach of Roger, with no obstacle in her way? How cramped it was for him here.

"Are you afraid of me?" he asked, trying to calm his pounding heart.

"Why?"

Roger shrugged, puzzled. "Just asking."

"Why did you want me to come outside?"

Because I wanted to see more than just your pretty face. And because I would love to...

He forbade himself from continuing the thought. His hope of ever obtaining his father's recognition that he had fought for so long had already dwindled to a minimum. Gwennaol was the last chance to secure his reputation and inheritance after all. Under no circumstance could he afford to frighten her off with an ill-considered deed. "Why did my father try to keep us apart?"

"I don't know. You tell me." Her gaze suddenly started to wander off. The fingers of her free hand played with the fabric of her tunic.

Just to make sure that something in the surroundings did not worry Gwennaol, Roger looked around. But apart from busy little animals, there was nothing moving in the forest to be wary of. Turning to Gwennaol, he shook his head. "I have no answer either. But my father must have an important reason, otherwise, he wouldn't have forbidden it."

With a glance towards the door, Gwennaol took a deep breath. "Perhaps Father Leofric can tell you something about that too." She opened the door. "I'd better go back inside before someone finds me out here." She lingered on.

Roger's gaze travelled down her body and up again. He didn't want her to leave, but he knew it was time to part. They couldn't risk putting themselves in danger unnecessarily. Not now. "I thank you, Gwennaol."

"What for?"

"For pointing me to Father Leofric. For your honesty. And also for coming outside to join me."

A rosy glow spread on Gwennaol's cheeks. She struggled to suppress a smile but could not hide her dimples. With a fleeting last glance, she disappeared into the chamber and locked the door. Shortly afterwards, her little face appeared in the opening of the sliding hatch. "I wish you good luck, Roger."

I can do with some of that. "Until next time, Gwennaol."

The sliding hatch closed.

I'm hoping to have better news then.

Roger and the other pupils were just cleaning the weapons and putting them back when Oswulf appeared in the armoury.

As usual, he strode along the rows to scrutinise everything. "Looks like making you clean weapons as a punishment has done all of you good. You take excellent care of your equipment. I hope the same excellence applies in battle when you're out there in the clearing."

He sent everyone except Roger away, made sure no one was listening outside and then closed the door.

"The court hearing didn't really go well for you."

"Better than for Frederic."

"Do you think he was your father?"

"No, there's absolutely no reason for that, even though Father readily believed the rumour. If it hadn't been for him, there would have been no trial, and Frederic would still be alive now."

"How do you want to prove to your father that you're the rightful heir to Wilburgfos after all?"

"I will speak to Father Leofric."

"He's wary of you."

"I know. I still have to try."

"Father Leofric is a priest, but his self-denial only goes so far. I could ask Emma to pack you some tasty morsels for him."

"What a splendid idea, Oswulf! He'll gladly open his mouth for that."

"Without a doubt."

Oswulf put his hand on Roger's shoulder and continued in a hushed voice. "You must be vigilant, Roger. The verdict has brought you enemies at the manor, who regard you with scorn and derision. They will try anything to get your father to exclude you from having your say in Wilburgfos, probably before Tankred rises to the rank of squire. You must persevere if you want to prove yourself as your father's son."

Roger nodded. "Thank you, Oswulf. I appreciate your help and good advice. I'll be careful."

Chapter 26

"Don't you think you owe me something for this?" Emma brushed a deep red strand of hair from her cheek. The rain had soaked her hair, and it looked as if she was wiping a thin streak of blood from her face.

Roger took the bag of food and drink and smiled. "I am very grateful to you, Emma." He would have liked to show her his gratitude more openly, but he couldn't. Something was holding him back.

As he was attaching the bag to the saddle, he heard something slump. The chestnut stallion pricked up his ears and neighed expectantly. Roger turned around.

Emma's coat lay in the straw, and the kitchen maid wantonly slid her hands up his chest. "Don't I deserve a little more than that?" She ran her hands along his waist and onto his back as she pressed against him.

Roger looked around, clearing his throat. "I don't think now is a good time." He gently grasped her arms to stop her hands from wandering any further. "People will get suspicious if you are not back in the great hall at the evening meal."

"I said I wasn't feeling well and needed some fresh air... and that it might take a while."

She grasped Roger's buttocks and pulled herself even tighter against him with a hearty grip.

Roger groaned as he felt the tug at his abdomen.

Gwennaol.

He grabbed Emma's hands and pulled them to the front. "No, Emma. I can't."

Emma pouted. "My big Norman can't?" She knelt down while looking at him inquisitively. "Perhaps he would like me to help him a little?"

When she lifted the hem of his tunic, Roger jumped back and held her fast. "No, really, Emma. That's very kind of you, and I do appreciate your offer, but I have to go. And you have to get back too." He tenderly stroked her freckles. "I don't want anything to happen to you because of me." He kissed her forehead and helped her stand up.

With her shoulders slumped, Emma watched Roger pick up her coat. "We'll never be together again, am I right?"

Roger folded her into her coat. He regretted that he could not answer Emma's question in the negative, but he knew as well as she did that it was over. Never again would they meet secretly behind the little chapel for a quick adventure. The pleasant times in Wilburgfos were over. There were his father's order, a dead man and a bastard who would have to fight for his reputation, honour and inheritance if he chose not to simply submit to the accusations.

Roger nodded, resigned. "I thank you for your help, Emma," he said softly, took the reins and led his horse out of the stables to ride to the church of St Ansgar.

"Father Leofric?"

The priest flinched. "What do you want?"

"I need to talk to you."

Leofric drew in his already hollowed cheeks even more, clasped his pectoral cross with his hand and rose hesitantly, his gaze fixed firmly on Roger. "Do you wish to confess your sins?"

Roger glanced around, but there was no one in the church except for the priest and himself. "It's about Frederic."

"The seneschal?"

"Yes. I have some questions."

Leofric curled his upper lip so that small wrinkles formed on his nose. "What makes you think that I, of all people, can help you?" His gaze kept wandering to Roger's left arm, half-hidden behind his back.

"You're a priest. People come to you when they want to praise the Lord and hear from the Bible... but also when they want to clear their conscience and confess their sins." Roger stretched out his left hand and dangled the bag in the air. "I have here an excellent Norman Cidre and some rather tasty mushroom pies from the storerooms at the manor."

Leofric ran his thumb and forefinger along the corners of his mouth.

Roger hid the bag behind his back again and bent down to the much smaller Leofric. "If you help me, the content is yours. If not, I will take it back and distribute it to the poor outside your church."

The priest chewed then gulped as his longing gaze swept from the vanished bag to Roger. "What do you want to know?"

Well, that was easy.

Straightening up to his full height, Roger let the bag hang casually at his side so that Leofric would constantly have the reward for his cooperation in front of him, like the donkey looking at the carrot until it reaches its destination. "You know why Frederic died?"

"It is not for me to question for what reasons the Lord calls His sheep to Himself."

"Answer my question. You heard yourself what he was accused of and why he was taken to court."

"Indeed. He sinned grievously, for he coveted his neighbour's wife and broke his oath towards his liege lord."

"Do you agree?"

"What I think is of no concern. God has already passed his judgement."

"Did Frederic ever mention anything to you that could confirm this accusation?"

Leofric cast a stern look at Roger. "Even if he had, it is not for me to say. I am bound by the seal of confession, and you should not tempt a servant of the Lord if you do not wish to sin."

As if to make sure the bag was still there, he glanced sideways at Roger's left hand.

"How long had you known Frederic?"

"For about twenty years. He came to Wilburgfos with Lord Geoffrey and his kinsmen back then."

"Did Frederic always fulfil his duties, or did you ever hear any complaints about him?"

"I am a man of the church. It is not for me to judge secular matters."

"Answer my question! You are the priest of Wilburgfos and were at the manor house often enough to know how the seneschal behaved."

Leofric ducked his head and looked anxiously at the bag swinging back and forth.

"As far as I know, he never did anything wrong as a seneschal, but I am only a man of God. How could I judge?"

"Did you know that he was in charge of the manor while Lord Geoffrey was away on campaign?"

"I certainly did. I was there regularly in those days to say mass."

"Did you notice anything back then? About Frederic or those who surrounded him? How did he get on with the other residents of the manor? Was there anything suspicious about him?"

Another glance at the bag was followed by the churchman lowering his head. "He... was always very friendly."

"What do you mean by 'very friendly'? To whom? To my mother?"

"He was friendly to everyone, including Lady Edeva. After all, she was the wife of his liege lord."

"Father Leofric, please tell me the truth. Am I Frederic's son?"

The priest looked him straight in his eyes. "Frederic had no children and would never have had any."

"So, I am Lord Geoffrey's son?"

"There was never any doubt about that."

"Which means Frederic died because of a rumour, even though he was innocent."

Leofric pointed to the crucifix and the vault of the church above them. "It is not men but God who punishes us for our sins. To us mortals, it may have looked as if Frederic had died at the judgment of men. But in truth, the Lord punished him."

"Punished him for what? You just said that he didn't touch my mother and kept his oath to my father. Why would God punish him?"

With a suspicious look, the priest watched the bag swinging wildly back and forth with each of Roger's gestures.

"Frederic had other sins upon him that had nothing to do with Lord Geoffrey and his wife."

"Frederic is dead! Now, tell me what sins you're talking about, or I'll throw the bag into the nearest river and you right after it!"

"No, wait!" He crossed himself, clasped his pectoral cross and muttered a few words. Then he folded his hands in front of his chest and looked at Roger. "Frederic was kind, much more so than other men."

"I know that! Frederic always took good care of the younger and lower-ranking folk at the manor house, unlike Father or Hugues de Borre."

Leofric shook what little hair he had left. "You don't understand. Frederic had certain preferences that were not pleasing to God."

"What's that supposed to mean? Kindness that doesn't please God? What are you talking about?"

"He preferred the presence of men to that of women. His marriage to a Norman woman was annulled by the local bishop before he left Normandy. Frederic always tried as much as possible to hide his lewd thoughts. He often came to me for confession and repentance until God decided to finally redeem him from his sins."

Stunned, Roger forgot to breathe as his whole life ran through his head. The moments with Frederic that he and his friends had experienced and enjoyed. How Frederic had entertained them like a father with his stories. How he had praised them when they had done something well and given encouragement when things were not going so well. There was no one else at the manor who had shown such care for the children, who shielded them, at least for a few years, from the scars of war and constant fighting. Whatever Frederic was to people such as Leofric, he was a good man and had not deserved his fate.

Gasping, Roger awkwardly groped his way backwards to the bench behind him and slowly sat down.

He placed the bag at his side while his gaze went into the void. Then he dug his elbows into his thighs and put his face in his hands. His warm breath flowed into his palms and back into his face.

"Are you not well?" Leofric asked cautiously.

"No, I'm not well at all."

Roger should have rejoiced, since he had proof, at last, that Frederic was not his father. But what price did Frederic have to pay for a wrong he had not committed!

Tears welled up in Roger's eyes. His lips trembled. He took his hands from his face and looked at Leofric. "Why didn't you say anything?" He smashed his hands on the wood to his left and right and sprang to his feet. "Why didn't you say anything!"

The priest flinched backwards.

"You were there at the court hearing. You're always there to write down everything that is said during those sessions. Why didn't you tell my father and the jury what you've just told me? You could have saved Frederic's life. You could have preserved justice here on earth. Instead, you kept silent."

For a moment, Leofric's eyes flickered, but a glance at the bag on the bench seemed to instil courage in him.

He straightened himself up, pursing his lips. "Everything confided to me in confession must not be revealed to others.

If I had said something, I would have violated the seal of confession."

"But you just told me!"

Roger flung his arms in the air, trying hard not to go for the priest's throat.

Wincing, Leofric took another few steps back while rubbing his pectoral cross with both hands.

"Frederic was still alive at court, so I couldn't say anything. Now he is dead. But you are alive and wanted me to confirm that you are not Frederic's son. I have given you the proof. If you wish, I will testify to it before Lord Geoffrey. That is all I can do for you."

Roger dropped his arms.

A witness who can prove my legitimacy. That should be enough. For Frederic, regrettably, it comes too late.

He picked up the bag and held it out to the priest. "Here, take this."

Leofric's face and posture relaxed. He let go of his pectoral cross and snatched the bag like a hungry fox being given a chicken.

"I will let my father know that you will come to the manor house tomorrow morning to testify that I am the rightful heir. If you do not honour our agreement, I will tell the Bishop of Eoforwic that you have breached the seal of confession."

Clutching the bag, Leofric shook his head. "Fear not. I will be there."

Sire Geoffrey drummed his fingers on the table. Hugues de Borre let his gaze wander around between the liege lord, Roger and the other vassals, who were idly sitting around, casting yet another bored look at the wooden roof and the walls of the great hall and exchanging the odd whisper.

Fiddling with his signet ring, Roger stared at the entrance, as if the haggard figure of Father Leofric would appear there if he only thought of him hard enough. Where was the priest? He had firmly promised to come to the manor house this morning.

Sire Geoffrey finally sent a messenger to fetch the priest so that the rest of the day's tasks would not be further delayed because of this, as he had called it, futile hearing. Time was oozing.

"Where is he now, your reliable witness?" asked the liege lord, sneering.

"I don't know," answered Roger without taking his eyes off the entrance. "Maybe he's been delayed. He did promise to come."

"You try my patience."

"He'll be here soon, I'm sure."

From the door, someone shouted, "The messenger is back."

A sigh of relief rippled through those waiting. Roger rose and took a breath. Now, everything would be cleared up.

The envoy entered, his gaze wandering over the faces of those eagerly awaiting him.

Sire Geoffrey waved his hand impatiently. "So? Speak!"

"Father Leofric will not come."

Roger frowned. "That's impossible. He promised me when I went to see him at church last night."

The messenger shook his head. "He *cannot* come."

Roger stormed past him. "Then I will personally drag him here by his pectoral cross."

"It's useless, Roger," the envoy called after him. "Father Leofric is dead."

Roger stopped. "Dead? First the seneschal and now the priest?"

Hugues de Borre raised his voice to drown out the chatter that had begun. "Didn't you just say you spoke to him yesterday?"

Shivering, Roger muttered, "He had to die because he wanted to help me."

"Are you sure he was still alive when you left him?" Hugues de Borre questioned further.

"What are you trying to say? Go on then! Don't you want to say what you think, Hugues de Borre?"

"There's no need for that. Everyone in this room knows what I'm thinking. And so do you."

"Father Leofric was alive and well when I left him. Why don't you ask the two peasants who entered the church after me last night if you need proof?" Roger walked up to the bailiff and leaned down to him. "But perhaps someone else overheard our conversation. Someone who wanted to prevent the priest from testifying in my favour. Someone who would benefit from getting me out of the way, just like the seneschal before."

"I think Roger is telling the truth," said the messenger. "I found Father Leofric in his house next to the church. He had no traces of blood or wounds."

He pulled out the bag that Roger had given to the priest yesterday. "But this was lying next to him. Father Leofric seems to have been poisoned."

Everyone stared at the messenger.

Even Sire Geoffrey grimaced. "Poisoned, you say?"

"That's impossible," said Roger. "Emma gave me the bag, and I never let it out of my sight. Maybe the mushrooms in the pies..."

"So, she poisoned the priest," someone said.

"Why should she?" asked Roger. "She would have as little to gain from Leofric's death as I would, for even if some people in this room find it hard to believe, it should be clear that I would hardly poison a witness who wants to testify in my favour." *Or did she want revenge because I have been rejecting all her advances lately?*

"The kitchen maid recently accused Richard de Perci in front of everyone that he was responsible for the rumour about the seneschal," said Hugues de Borre. "He may have tried some more ways to procure a fief for himself."

Roger froze, and before he could utter a word of disbelief, the men euphorically joined Hugues' suspicions.

"He wants to make sure that there is such disorder at the manor that William de Perci takes away the fief from our liege lord."

"Exactly. He's spying on us for his father and is just waiting for an opportunity to usurp Wilburgfos."

"He's going to chase us all away."

Hugues de Borre slammed his fist on the table. "Pernuns dunc ceo tretur! He will not get away with his treasonous acts. We will watch him. At the slightest sign that he is guilty, we will arrest him. Then he will pay for betraying Sire Geoffrey and all of us. Until then, we must be careful. He must not realise that we know what he is up to, or he may escape us."

Roger felt his throat tighten, as if it wanted to stop his heart from leaping out of his agitated body at this point. He closed his eyes. *Richard... No! No! Not another rumour.*

ROGER DID NOT remember how, but somehow, he had ended up at the armoury after this meeting that should have changed his life for the better. Instead of creating hope and trust, his conversation with Leofric had plunged another person into death and fuelled the unrest and suspicion of the residents at the manor house and in Wilburgfos. Nothing had changed about Roger's already bad situation, but he was much more distressed by the outcome that the priest's death had led to a hunt for Richard de Perci. He was his best friend after all, wasn't he? Or was he feigning it all to give himself an advantage at Roger's expense to take over Wilburgfos?

When everyone but Richard had left the armoury, Roger beckoned his friend to join him on the bench. "Sit with me, Richard. I must speak to you urgently."

Richard hesitantly put his weapons aside and took a seat next to Roger. "What's so important?"

Roger looked deep into his friend's blue child's eyes – the eyes that had been looking up at him admiringly for years and whose owner never tired of assuring Roger of his friendship and loyal devotion. "I need to know where you stand."

"What do you mean?"

"Father Leofric is dead. You are suspected of having killed him."

The horror on the little redhead's face tore Roger's heart apart. Would this boy really be able to poison a priest?

"Me?" Richard became pale as a corpse. "Why me? Why should I kill him? I haven't seen him since the last mass."

"When Emma called you a slanderer in front of all the people at the manor house, you protested your innocence.

Perhaps you lied and now wanted to take revenge on her because she recognised your true intentions. And you wanted to prevent Father Leofric from confirming me as the rightful heir so that you, as the youngest son, could secure a good inheritance."

"None of that is true, Roger. I'm your friend, you know that. I would never do you any harm."

"Perhaps you are only pretending to be friends with me in order to find out everything that will bring you closer to your goal. At the same time, you gradually eliminate all those who could dispute your inheritance of Wilburgfos – Frederic, Father Leofric... and even me."

Tears welled up in Richard's eyes, and Roger struggled to keep a straight face, which otherwise he only knew from his own father.

Richard's voice was only a choked, barely intelligible squeak. "I am... I am supposed to... have killed Frederic and Leofric? And you..." His face contorted in pain as the first tears ran down his cheeks, and he slowly slid to his knees before Roger. He folded his hands over Roger's thighs and shook his head while sobbing loudly. "Please, Roger, please! You mustn't believe this. I don't know who put this into your head, but I didn't kill anyone. Neither Frederic nor Leofric. And least of all..."

He lowered his gaze. His slender body shook with each sob. Then he lifted his face, red and wet, and looked at Roger with blurry eyes.

"I'm not here to take over Wilburgfos," he breathed. "My father sent me here to become a chevaler and will then give me a fief near Witebi. I don't need Wilburgfos. But you need Wilburgfos. And I will do everything I can to help you get it. For you are the rightful heir, not only because you are a great fighter, but because you stand up against injustice, against people like your father, who are unjust towards others, including you. And because you are my best friend."

Richard's voice was no more than a hiss, and Roger feared that his friend would collapse from sheer exhaustion and die on his thighs.

He dropped to one knee and hugged him tightly.

Chapter 27

Hastily, Roger swept up the fallen ashes with his hands, stuffed them into the bag and jumped under a table. With a bit of luck, they wouldn't notice the black-grey trail leading from the fire in the middle of the great hall right to where he was.

The footsteps came closer.

"...always known he'd ruin us all," said a voice. "Used the wrong hand even as a child, after all. A servant of the Anti-christ, if you ask me."

"If only the lord had drowned him in the Fors Bekkr as soon as he was born!" said another voice. "Would have been the best for everyone."

"And he's not even his father," the first voice said. "Nor is the seneschal. No, I'll tell you who the father is: a demon visited the lady at night and fathered the child with her."

The second voice groaned. "Who knows who else he'll kill? Even the priest couldn't stop him. The evil is lurking in that boy."

"A danger to us all! Why hasn't Lord Geoffrey chased him away yet?"

"Yeah, should've done so a long time ago. Or better yet, burned him. He must be burned at the stake, this son of the Fiend! The fire will surely cleanse his soul."

"If he has one at all. Already killed two men in cold blood, and one of them a priest!"

"Gemiltsa us God..."

The voices slowly died down.

Roger wiped his damp forehead and stuck his head out of his hiding place.

The two servants were walking around at the rear end of the hall with their backs turned towards him.

With a firm grip on the bag so as not to leave any more traces, Roger crept along the wall on his soft leather shoes, scurried outside and stowed the bag in the armoury before joining his friends.

In the middle of the yard stood the horses, all shaggy with their thick winter coats, despite being well cared for. Pawing impatiently, Modig Wiht greeted his rider with a reproachful neigh.

While Joscelin and the others mounted, Richard hesitated.

"What's wrong, Richard?" asked Roger as he took the reins of his horse.

"Have you noticed how they look at me?" murmured Richard.

Roger let his gaze wander over the courtyard. Some faces turned away hastily, others continued to stare at the two friends.

"They would probably prefer us to ride away and never come back," Roger muttered. "But we won't do them that favour yet." He patted his friend on the shoulder. "Let them gape if they enjoy it. You mustn't pay attention. Many here are simple-minded and easily persuaded by cleverly worded falsehoods. They believe everything a nobleman or a priest tells them."

"Whatever they believe," Joscelin interjected, looking at Richard, "Sire Geoffrey cannot chase you, the son of his liege lord, from the manor without good cause. Your father would certainly hold him accountable for it – and not just for that, when I think of all that has happened here recently."

"Nevertheless, we must be careful," said Roger, "Someone is playing an evil game at the manor. We have to find out who it is and why they are doing it." He side-glanced at the little redhead. "Who knows what they will get up to next?"

"Have you spoken to Father Leofric?" Gwennaol asked the question casually as she pulled her unruly hair back.

Roger looked at her closely. How much longer did he have to keep up this game of hide and seek? Did he even have time for it, the way things were going at the manor? "I need to talk to you out here, Gwennaol."

She paused. "Why?"

"It might be the last time we see each other."

She hesitated for a moment, then her face disappeared from the opening.

Roger heard the bolts creak.

Well, that was easier than I thought. Why didn't I say that before? Maybe we would have got much further by now.

He was just imagining with increasing delight how far that might be, when Gwennaol appeared in the small clearing in her thick woollen cloak.

"What do you mean, the last time? Are you leaving Wilburgfos?"

Roger took a step towards her and was now so close that he could have put his arms around her. Would she let him?

"I bring even worse news than before, Gwennaol. Father Leofric is dead."

"Ma Doue!" Gwennaol clasped her hands over her mouth.

"He had to die because he wanted to confirm that the rumour was false. That's why someone poisoned him."

"Poisoned? That's terrible."

Roger shrugged. "At least I was able to convince my father and his men that it wasn't me who killed him."

"They actually thought that you...?"

"The servants still think it's all my fault. You know..." He waved his left hand. "For some, it was only a matter of time before disaster would strike Wilburgfos."

"Who could do such a shameful deed?"

"Nobody knows at this moment, but many now suspect Richard de Perci."

"Richard? That's your best friend, isn't it?"

Roger nodded.

"But he has nothing to do with it!"

Roger frowned. "How do you know?"

"What?"

"That Richard is innocent."

"How? Oh, I assumed it. Because he's your friend and still so young."

She turned away, wringing her hands.

"I don't think he poisoned Father Leofric either. He has as little reason for it as I do. But someone else must have a reason, and I am sure that this person also wanted Frederic's death. There must be a connection between the seneschal and the priest, and I must find out what that is – before a third person gets killed."

"You mean someone else is going to die?"

"I think so, and I fear that Richard might be next."

Gwennaol turned pale and buried her face in her hands. Her shoulders twitched.

Roger hesitantly put his arms around her and pulled her close. A tingling warmth spread through him as he felt her body against his – a feeling even more beautiful than the tingling before a hunting trip. He could have stayed like this for hours. "Don't be sad, Gwennaol. Everything will be all right."

"I'm so sorry about what happened," she sobbed.

"Don't be sorry. It's not your fault."

"It shouldn't have come to this."

"Nobody could have known it would come this far. We cannot predict life."

"There must be no further deaths, Roger. You must prevent it."

"Don't worry, Gwennaol. I will take good care of Richard. Nothing will harm him."

How cosy it felt to hold her in this embrace! He closed his arms a little more. If only this moment could last forever!

Gwennaol dabbed her face dry with the sleeves of her tunic and smiled faintly. "You are a good man, Roger. You're very unlike what I've been told about the Normans."

"What did they tell you about them?"

"They are ruthless, selfish warriors who think they can take possession of everything – land, soil, animals and people. They bring everything under their yoke and dispose of men, women and children as they please. They know no respect. They have no feelings and only care about their own well-being and wealth. They will do anything for money, and what they don't have, they take with no regard for others."

"And I'm not like that?"

Gwennaol looked up at him. Her face had regained its colour, and a hint of her dimples appeared on her cheeks. "You are different. You're attentive, polite, considerate. You suffer and laugh with your friends and the people of Wilburgfos. And most of all, you care about your best friend's life even though you are in danger yourself."

"Are you afraid something will happen to me?"

"Yes," she breathed, leaning her head on his chest.

She's worried about me. She, of all the girls, who was so dismissive at the beginning.

Gwennaol's features blurred, as if one were staring into a pond into which a stone had been thrown and whose smooth surface was broken by small ripples.

Roger looked at the wrinkled nose of a child whose eyes were piercing him.

"What are you looking at?" he asked, but the little girl didn't answer. "Do you actually know who I am?" He stood tall and spoke with all the pride of a nobleman's ten-year-old son. "I am Roger, son of Sire Geoffrey, lord of Wilburgfos."

The girl hissed something in a language he had never heard before then threw herself forward and spat.

Đis is laðlic!

Roger blinked. Clear as ever, the girl he had taken in his arms earlier was still standing there in front of him. If only he could feel her body really close once more. And perhaps...

He closed the embrace, and as he was slowly bowing down towards Gwennaol, he heard a soft voice whispering in the distance.

"Ur pennadig yec'hed a ra vad d'un den klañv."

He froze. It took him a while to realise that the voice wasn't coming from a distance, but from very close by.

"What did you just say?"

Surprised, Gwennaol repeated her words.

"That's Breton, isn't it?"

She nodded hesitantly.

Roger lowered his arms as something dawned on him. "The Breton girl… We met as children in the priory when my father and I brought Adelais here. You stood in the yard and insulted us. In Breton. That's why I didn't understand you. Then you spat at me. That was you, wasn't it?"

Gwennaol took a few steps back. "I can explain, Roger, but not now."

"Oh yes, you have to. I want to know why you did it. Why do you hate the Normans? What do you know about my father that I don't?"

She shook her head while fumbling for the door. "I must go, Roger."

"Wait!"

He reached for her arm, but Gwennaol dodged to the side. She stretched on her tiptoes to peck him on his cheek, vanished into the little chamber and slammed the door shut.

Confused, Roger stood there, listening to the bolts creaking and wood grinding on wood as the sliding latch closed. When he finally awoke from his stupor, he knocked on the door and called Gwennaol's name several times, but to no avail. The door remained shut.

Chapter 28

In the gloomy December light, dense swathes of fog hung like a heavy curtain over the floodplains of the Fors Bekkr.

No wonder people are seeing ghosts and harbingers of death everywhere.

With a shudder, Roger turned his gaze to the path back to the manor house, which his stallion plodded along in a bored manner.

Behind them rumbled a cart full of logs, pulled by a team of oxen and accompanied on both sides by sweaty peasants. Roger had supervised them in the woods on his father's behalf to procure trees to repair some buildings, as well as gather firewood. The cart and the peasants were followed by the children, with Cenhelm's grandson, little Cedric, in the lead. They had scurried around like little shadows between the trees with their freshly woven wicker baskets to collect the remains of the felling as well as twigs and small branches.

The crash of falling trees still echoed in Roger's ears as he came out of the barn and met his friends in the yard.

"I hate this weather!" Drogo breathed into his hands.

Roger watched the little cloud forming from Drogo's breath. "With everything that has been going on recently, everyone thinks Judgement Day is near. The days are so short and dreary that my father will need a lot more time than usual to travel to Wincestre. But he'll still be faster than Robert de Monbrai, whom he wants to meet there."

"Does he?" asked Richard. "He didn't say anything about it in the meetings."

"He hardly will," Roger replied. "Isabel told me. He wants to seal the comte's marriage to her there."

Drogo snorted. "Isabel deserves a much better husband."

Joscelin raised an eyebrow. "Like yourself, maybe?"

"Why not?" Drogo answered. "My father may not own as much land as this comte from the north, but my ancestors go back to Rollo's kinsmen, who settled in Normandy at that time. My family owns several wealthy manors in England."

Roger eyed the few people who were in the courtyard at the time. "It is indeed strange that a powerful comte should marry a girl from a village like Wilburgfos. I wonder what Father promised him and why they are in such a hurry."

"So, do you know when the wedding will be?" asked Richard.

"Before Candlemas, apparently, so, January, I guess," Roger replied.

"In the dead of winter?" Drogo hopped up and down, shivering. "Does he want to kill Isabel? It's a long and arduous walk up to Bebbanburh, almost to the Scottish border. Why is he doing this?"

"We might learn more about it in one of the next court hearings," Joscelin answered. "Sire Geoffrey will probably also have news from Wincestre then."

"We'll let you know if there is anything important, of course," Richard promised. "Even though I sometimes have the feeling that the men are watching me during those meetings and that not all matters are discussed while I am present.

They've even asked me what my father and the tenants-in-chief think about the new King of England."

"They are trying to sound you out," remarked Joscelin.

"Maybe because my father and his vassals are hiding something," said Roger, "something they don't want you, or your father, to know."

Richard's eyes widened. "Why would they do that?"

"Your father and his liege lord have been serving faithfully both the old and the new King of England," Joscelin replied. "Whatever Sire Geoffrey knows is probably not for the ears of vassals loyal to the Crown."

As Roger and Richard were walking to the stables after dinner, a scream from the great hall froze them.

Roger gulped as the next scream tore the air in the yard.

The two friends rushed back to the hall, cutting through shouts, hasty footsteps and the clatter of wood and metal.

People had thronged to the bottom of the stairs on which Sire Geoffrey stormed up to the private chambers, his cloak billowing.

"What happened?" asked Roger to no one in particular while pushing aside the curious onlookers.

"It's all his fault," someone hissed. "He's in league with the Fiend and brings death to us all."

"Now, go on," Roger demanded, "tell me! Who was that screaming?"

"Don't ask so innocently!" cried a defiant voice. "It was the kitchen maid. She's dead now."

The sentence came down like a hammer on Roger's head. "Emma is dead?"

The silent faces around him were answer enough. He rowed through the crowd like a drowning man and raced up the stairs. After a quick glance at his father, he stuck his head into the room.

"Stop!" cried Hild the healer, who was kneeling beside Emma. "There's a cord in the doorway."

Roger looked down at his feet. In front of the open door was a thick string that anyone entering the chamber would inevitably trip over. Dame Edeva was lying on the doorstep as if someone had thrown her there like an unloved doll.

Cenhelm crouched beside her. "She's alive. She has just fainted, praise God!"

Accompanied by a sigh of relief, Roger's gaze flicked from his mother to Emma.

Her dark red curls spread out in tangled strands on the bloodstained floor, in the centre of which lay the twisted body of the young woman. Beneath her was a net made of ropes with small arrowheads protruding upwards.

"Emma," Roger whispered and stepped over the cord.

At a safe distance from the arrowheads and the net, he dropped to his knees beside the dead girl, whose skin was whiter than ever.

"Emma!"

With trembling fingers, he turned her face towards him. The mingled scratches, blood and vomit blurred the freckles that he loved so much. "How could this happen?"

Hild's eyes were wide, her pupils dilated. She breathed only one word, "Đung."

Đung – wolfsbane. Beautiful to look at, but quick and absolutely deadly even in the smallest quantities, his mother's words raced through his head. When he was little, she had once shown him the most important poisonous plants to beware of when roaming the meadows and woods. Wolfsbane was one of them.

"No doubt the trap was meant for Lady Edeva," Cenhelm said.

Roger startled. "For my mother?"

Cenhelm nodded. "Emma helped her up the stairs and went into the room first. Usually, Lady Edeva retires on her own, but today, she wasn't feeling well. Emma offered to take her to her room. She only wanted to help." Bowing his head, Cenhelm made the sign of the cross.

Hild sobbed. "I hurried upstairs immediately when I heard her scream. Emma was still alive when I found her. She was sweating and throwing up while writhing in pain on that cursed net on the floor. All I could do was sit by her side and pray for her. Death must have come as a relief." Hild crossed herself in tears.

An emptiness spread through Roger that he hadn't even felt when William died. Sure, he hadn't been in love with Emma, but he was fond of her, and seeing her once vibrant body now so lifeless filled him with sorrow and helplessness. "Who did this to her? Why?"

Emma's seductive smile, her soft skin, the secret trysts, the hours they spent together, their passionate touches and kisses – sweet memories that suddenly tasted bitter. How he would have loved to embrace Emma once more! Slowly, he reached out with his left hand to caress the unharmed areas with his fingers. Death had not yet sucked the warmth out of Emma's skin, but her body did not respond to his touch. Not anymore. If only he could bring Emma back to life with his hands!

One last time, he kissed her forehead then rose slowly, closing his eyes and clenching his teeth to hold back the feelings that welled up inside. He felt like he was suffocating and fought for breath. His heart pounded all the way to his temples. A fiery torrent – like the blazing hell fires that Father Leofric had revelled in painting with words in his sermons – consumed the emptiness that filled him. Grief, rage and hatred swirled out of it like an untameable, rearing beast. Out! It had to get out or it would tear his guts and head to pieces.

All tensed up, Roger pulled his scramasax, and for the first time in his life, he recognised something like uncertainty, perhaps even fear, in his father's uneasy gaze.

Then he roared out, like a herd of oxen being mercilessly whipped forward with the bullwhip. Every feeling of pain, fear, anger and hatred he had ever felt, he threw into this scream instead of swallowing it down and silencing it as he had always done before.

Slapping their hands over their ears, Hild and Cenhelm quickly ducked against the wall.

When the pressure inside him had eased, Roger listened, panting. There was no sound around him or outside the chamber. Only his own noisy breathing broke the silence.

Just as Hild lowered her hands and straightened up, Roger let out a deafening scream of attack, whirled around and struck one of the wooden corner posts of the bed with such force that it burst asunder. A well-aimed swing with the short sword slashed the bedding and curtains lengthwise. Everything that stood in his way – a stool, the lid of a chest, a candle in a metal holder – he overturned or smashed with a kick or a blow with the scramasax.

When he paused, sweating and panting, nothing around Emma's body was in the same place as before. Stools and baskets lay scattered among splinters and pieces of wood, while larger pieces of furniture and the walls bore sharp-edged cuts from the sword blows.

Roger's gaze flicked from the chaos in the room past the servants, trembling with fear, towards his father, who stood stiff as a statue at the door, staring at him.

"Are you waiting for your son to come to his senses on his own?" Roger asked, breathing heavily. "Or have you sent for your men to seize the madman raging in your bedchamber?" He put the scramasax into the leather sheath and stepped to the doorway. By now, he already towered over his father, so he looked down at him. "What have you done that so many innocent people have to die so cruelly?"

He slammed his foot on the fateful cord, which snapped with an audible ping. No one would trip over it again and fall to their death. Not today.

"Move out of the way!" Sire Geoffrey shouted down the stairs.

"He brings death and destruction upon us, Sire!" cried someone.

"He's possessed by evil," shouted another. "Lock him up before he kills even more innocent people!"

"He wanted to kill his own mother."

"How many more of us need to die before you condemn him to death?"

"It's all his friend's fault, that redhead!"

"Yeah, he's a traitor. He will kill everyone to get the manor."

Some pushed forward to the bottom of the stairs and waved their fists threateningly, but Hugues de Borre and two other men successfully held their ground amidst the angry crowd.

"Asez!" cried Sire Geoffrey and gestured with his hand. "Make way and let him go. He will leave the manor as soon as possible."

Roger bit his lip. He was supposed to fulfil his duties until Tankred became a squire, but he didn't want to take any risks. It would be better to turn his back on the manor right now, while his father and Hugues de Borre were still able to hold back the disgruntled servants.

Leaning against the doorframe with half-closed eyes, Dame Edeva was in no way able to give her son a proper farewell.

A girl poured her a few sips of wine to help her regain her strength.

Accompanied by the hostile looks of the servants, Roger descended the steps. Some stared at him, others turned away fearfully, still others crossed themselves and folded their hands.

At the bottom, Roger and Hugues de Borre eyed each other.

"I will keep an eye on you," said Hugues.

"And I will find out what's going on at the manor and what your role is – and then I'll return." Roger quickened his steps as the crowd made way for him. He absolutely had to find Richard.

On leaving the great hall, he met Oswulf, who wordlessly accompanied him.

In the yard, Roger stretched his back, taking a deep breath of the fresh, cold air. "Three terrible murders in three months. First Frederic, then Father Leofric, now Emma. What's wrong with this manor, Oswulf?"

"What happened to Emma was an accident."

"She's still dead. And just to think that my mother..." The lump in Roger's throat made it impossible for him to go on. The throbbing of his scar slowly subsided in the cool air.

"I'm sorry, Roger. I know you were very fond of Emma."

"I also liked Frederic, but Father Leofric and I could never stand each other. There must be a reason why all of them had to die."

"And what could that be?"

Roger shrugged. "I have to get away from the manor for a while. I may be next on the list of those to die, but before that, I'm going to find out what Gwennaol knows about my father. She must be the key to everything that has happened."

"You want to go away? Where?"

"I don't know yet. Somewhere where no one suspects me of going and where I'll be safer than here. And Richard too."

"What about Gwennaol? If you go too far, you won't be able to see and talk to her anymore."

"Modig Wiht is a good horse. He'll enjoy longer rides." With a look around, Roger leaned towards Oswulf. "Have you also noticed that some strange visitors have been appearing at the manor lately? Why so many visits all at once? Surely, that's as much of a coincidence as all these deaths. Someone is planning something bigger, and Wilburgfos is part of it. Be on your guard, Oswulf!"

"I'll keep my eyes open. There are still a few things for me to do on this manor, but if I can help you, just tell me."

Roger clasped his shoulder. "I thank you, Oswulf. You are a true friend. I'll let you know as soon as I find out more."

Oswulf's eyes sparkled. "I'm counting on you."

As people's ill will against himself and Richard increased every day, Roger decided to leave the manor even before the feast of the Lord's birth.

On the way to the private chambers, a servant deliberately bumped into him, but Roger gritted his teeth and kept walking. Although it hurt that people gave him an evil look, spat at him and passed him over at mealtimes, punishing them for it made no sense, as was staying at the manor while hoping for things to improve.

He climbed the stairs to the bedchamber and, with a distraught look at the blood patches on the wooden planks, stepped into the room, where his mother and sister were busy embroidering.

Gulping, he closed the door and jutted his chin upwards to avoid staring at the dark spots.

"I know the stains are horrible," said Dame Edeva. "Hild and the women tried everything, but it was impossible to remove them completely. Eala, poor girl. She looked terrible when they carried her away."

Roger sat on a stool and looked at his mother. The failed attack that had cost Emma her life seemed to have affected Lady Edeva more than he had realised. Her skin was no longer pale, but as sallow as the sky before a storm. Her light green eyes resembled the murky, stagnant water of an overgrown pond. Her hands were trembling so much that she kept pricking herself while doing her needlework.

"I need to go away for a while, Mother."

Isabel looked up from her embroidery frame. "You want to leave Wilburgfos? Why?"

"Everyone thinks I'm to blame for the deaths. If I stay, I will probably end up with my throat cut."

Shocked, Isabel almost dropped her embroidery frame. "You mustn't say that, Roger!"

"Eala, Hroðgar!" Dame Edeva put her needlework on her lap. "I know life is hard for you right now. People are frightened. Death has been running rampant in Wilburgfos, and now they see it lurking around every corner. The cold winter and the darkness add to their feelings of doom. Do you really have to leave?"

"I have no choice, Mother, for I may be the next one dead... or Richard."

Dame Edeva nodded. "They are afraid of you and blame you because you are different. But you never were like your siblings. You don't share the lineage with the older ones, and you are more skilled than the younger ones with your left hand than with your right."

She tenderly stroked his left hand until she touched the signet ring. After a moment's hesitation, she squeezed his fingers. "Do you know where you are going?"

"I do, but I cannot tell you. It would be too dangerous. If you have a message for me, tell Joscelin." He took her fragile hands into his. "I still need your help, though. Father shall not cheat me out of the inheritance that belongs rightfully to your firstborn son. I must find someone who knew Frederic as well as Father Leofric did. Then perhaps I can still prove that Sire Geoffrey is my father."

Dame Edeva frowned thoughtfully. "If I am not mistaken, Frederic had two brothers and a sister, though I do not know whether they are still alive."

"Do you know where they lived?"

"One of the brothers belonged to the king's army, like your father and Frederic when they came to England. He went to a manor of William de Perci, but I forget which one. The second brother, Hubert, was a craftsman – what was he again? A stonemason? Saddler? Blacksmith? I cannot remember, but in any case, someone King William needed for his army. He wanted to try and find work in Eoforwic. The sister, Cateline, was still very young when she came to England with her parents. Her father was killed in one of the campaigns in the north, and the mother then wanted to move with her daughter to Eoforwic to join her younger son."

"Eoforwic is big. How can I possibly find Frederic's siblings there? If they are still alive. Otherwise, my journey there and all my efforts will be in vain."

Dame Edeva stroked his cheek and followed her fingers with a sad gaze as they glided gently over the contours of the bulging, scarred flesh. "I have always loved you, Hroðgar. You have your grandfather's English heart, but also Norman pride and the will to win. You are slowly learning to reconcile the two souls in your chest and not let them fight each other. Use your wisdom and your inner voice to guide you. Use the friends you have to get help in your endeavour. And above all, use what Oswulf has taught you in the weapons practice to reach your goal. You wear Kjetil's signet ring. May it guide you to where you will find answers to your questions. May it protect you so you can ensure that justice prevails in the end. May it give you the strength and courage to fight for what you believe is right."

"I thank you, Mother." Roger rose and kissed her hands. "Take good care of yourself! I want to see you whole and hale on my next visit."

"Don't leave me, Roger!" Isabel jumped up, flung her arms around him and buried her face against his chest, sobbing.

"I have to leave Wilburgfos in January to marry Robert de Monbrai. I will never see you again."

Roger stroked her long hair and hugged her tight. "Don't cry, Isabel! I'll return as soon as I can, but right now, my being here is only fuelling unnecessary fears and anger. If I stay, the killing will not stop."

"What if it doesn't stop even when you are gone?"

"It grieves me to leave you behind, but I cannot take you with me. Fear not, Isabel! Your wedding is very important to Father. He will see to it that no harm comes to you so close to your planned union with the comte. As for you, Mother, you should make sure that you are never alone in the next few weeks. Perhaps Father can provide you with one of his men to stand guard."

"As you say, Hroðgar. I will pray that the manor house be spared further misfortune while your father is in Wincestre. Certainly, no one will be so wicked as to spill blood while we celebrate the birth of Jesus Christ."

I doubt that whoever is responsible for the previous deaths will shy away from murder on any day of the year.

"I don't think it will happen either," Roger lied, "but I cannot promise."

Isabel clasped him even tighter. "Then promise me at least that you will be back before I leave."

"I promise. While I'm gone, Joscelin will be able to tell you how I am and what news there is. And if you need a little comfort, Drogo will be happy to help you."

"Drogo? Why Drogo?"

Roger smiled mischievously. "I think he's quite fond of my little sister."

A rosy glow flushed Isabel's cheeks. "Is he?"

She lowered her head bashfully.

"I'd better go now." Roger gritted his teeth.

Isabel wiped her face and struggled to smile. "Good luck, Roger. I will pray for you. Wilburgfos needs a liege lord other than Tankred."

Roger kissed her on the forehead, bade farewell to his mother and left the room, where he bumped into Tankred.

Just as his younger brother was opening his mouth to say something, Roger tapped him on the chest and gave him a stern look from above. "During the celebrations, you will be the only man left of the family. Until I or Father return, you are responsible for the safety of your mother and sister. After all, you have to deserve it to become a squire in three months, don't you? If the slightest thing happens to them, I will hold you responsible."

Without lingering for an answer, Roger hurried down the stairs and out into the yard, where Richard and the armed guard that William de Perci had sent for him were already waiting for him with the horses.

"Are you looking forward to seeing your father again?" asked Roger as they halted in front of the small bridge over the Fors Bekkr.

"I didn't expect to return to Topeclive so soon."

"I would have been just as much surprised if you had told me a few days ago that I would be spending the Feast of the Lord in Sudtone with your uncle. But it is only for a few weeks, and we will meet again here soon. Joscelin will notify us if there is any important news from the manor, good or bad."

"It's still a long time until Epiphany. I will miss you, Roger. So many years we've spent together at the manor, seeing each other every day."

"Don't pull such a face, Richard! We're not parting forever, and it's only a day's ride from Sudtone to Topeclive. It's closer than it seems to you at the moment."

"What about Gwennaol? Will you see her again?"

"I have to, as soon as possible. She is the key to my father's secret."

"Do you think your father has anything to do with the killings?"

"You mean if he's responsible for their deaths?"

"Yes. No. At least not directly, as in being the one who gave the order. Could the secret about your father be the reason why they had to die?"

"Possibly. These strange deaths have indeed only become more frequent since I met Gwennaol. None of them died of natural causes, not even Frederic, who was killed by fear of a divine judgement. If the master of arms had not suggested it, Frederic might still be alive."

"It still frightens me when I think that we could be next," Richard shuddered.

"You'll be safe with your father for now, and so will I at your uncle's manor. Only Gwennaol knows to what extent my father is actually involved in everything."

With a last earnest wish, the friends took leave of each other. Richard rode northwards. Roger took the path to the priory and was soon knocking on the gate.

"I bid you good morning, Roger."

The nun smiled. She had known him since he was a little boy and was used to him appearing more or less regularly at the gate to visit his sister and bring news. For about a year now, he'd had a second reason to pay visits to the convent, and this time, for once, he wanted to ask for admission at the front of the priory.

"And good morning to you, Sister. I have to go away for some time, and I don't know when I will be back. I'd like to speak to Gwennaol before I go. Is it possible to see her?"

"I'm sorry, but Gwennaol is ill and can't have visitors. Her grandmother is looking after her."

"It's nothing serious, I hope?"

"I don't think so, but she is indeed very weak and needs rest to recover."

"Please give her my best wishes and tell her that I will try to come back in January. I would like to see her again then."

"I will do that. She will certainly be pleased."

"Could I still see my sister for a moment?"

The nun nodded. "I'll go and get her."

Roger glanced at the sky. It looked like it would start to snow soon. He would have to hurry.

Fortunately, Sudtone was not far, even if he did not know exactly where to find Richard's uncle. He had never been to that area and didn't know his way around at all. Richard had told him to ride in a slightly south-westerly direction through the woods and then look out for the first large house. That was his uncle's manor.

"How convenient for you! When one of your convent residents is ill, you just talk to the other."

Two mischievously flashing blue eyes peered through the crack in the door.

He couldn't help but grin. "How can you dare think so about me, Adelais?"

His sister opened the door and beckoned him to enter. "So, you are saying you had wanted to take your leave from me anyway before dashing off, even if Gwennaol had not been ill?"

"No, yes, I mean I do not simply 'dash off'."

Slipping her hands into the sleeves of her habit, Adelais raised her eyebrows expectantly. "Then let me hear what you've done wrong this time."

"I am really innocent this time, but it's no longer safe for me at the manor. For anyone."

"What are you talking about?"

"Have you had a chance to talk to Gwennaol?"

"Yes, she told me Father Leofric had been poisoned." Adelais crossed herself. "May God have mercy on his soul."

"There is yet another death."

"What, another one? What on earth is going on?"

Roger swallowed the lump in his throat. "The kitchen maid has also been poisoned, but the trap was actually meant for Mother."

"Someone wanted to kill your mother?" Adelais crossed herself again and clasped her hands. "That's atrocious. Do you know who did this?"

"No, but I'm sure it was the one who poisoned Father Leofric too, and that Frederic's death is also connected to it, even though he wasn't directly attacked."

"How despicable! A murderer in Wilburgfos."

"I will stay in Sudtone for some time with Richard's uncle, Picot de Perci, but I don't know yet when I can come back. In the meantime, you must try to talk to Gwennaol. Ask her what she knows about Father or the people who died. And make sure no one overhears you."

"It will be difficult to get past Morwenna. She guards Gwennaol like a dog guards its bone. Especially since she's been sick."

"You are a clever woman, Adelais. You'll come up with something. Just please don't put yourself in danger. I have already lost two people close to me, don't add a third."

"At least not any time soon." Adelais smiled.

Roger opened the gate. Thick flakes were falling from the sky.

"I'd better go now before I get hopelessly lost finding my way to Sudtone." He took a step forward then stopped. "By the way, do you know Robert de Monbrai?"

"Who was made Comte de Northumberland last year? Certainly."

Certainly! How does she always know everything?

"Isabel is to marry him at the end of January and move north."

"Do you want to leave me any more bad news before you go? Is there anything I should know about Tankred too?"

"Only that in a few months, he will be the liege lord of Wilburgfos unless I can prove in time that Sire Geoffrey is indeed my father."

"I know you can make it, Roger. May God show you the right path."

The gate closed, and somehow, to Roger, it sounded more final than usual.

Chapter 29

"I see the good old bishop is quite incensed by what's happening in England."

Robert de Monbrai sneered at the parchment that his messenger had handed him.

"He's adamant that King William did a great injustice when he imprisoned him. And he is fuming with anger at how much influence the other bishops have gained with the new king in his absence, especially Bishop William of Dunholm. Odo is craving to restore his power and influence as soon as possible. I think, in him, we will have a valuable warrior of the Lord on our side."

He read on. "My uncle says that other important vassals are expected in Wincestre – not all of them ardent supporters of the new king." He wrinkled his nose. "Not least because they will lose some of their lands unless they act soon. Besides, certain peculiarities of our new ruler displease not only the bishops."

"May I assume then that you also intend to spend the Feast of the Lord in Wincestre?"

"My uncle insists. It is a good time to make preparations. You know best how tedious and lengthy it is to send messages back and forth when discussing a major undertaking with other rulers. How much quicker it is to talk face to face! And quick we must be. Something must be done while the king has not yet consolidated his power. For that, we need determined leaders and skilled warriors – and I will have them as soon as I am married."

Part 6

WILBURGFOS AND EVERWIC, FROM MID-DECEMBER IN THE YEAR OF OUR LORD 1087 TO THE BEGINNING OF FEBRUARY IN THE YEAR OF OUR LORD 1088

Chapter 30

"He's getting suspicious. So far, he has no proof, but he is firmly convinced that there is more to it than coincidence."

"We must be careful. He keeps pestering her with questions which unsettle her. She's already made one slip of the tongue, but he didn't notice. It almost seems to me that she feels something like pity for him – and the others."

"Perhaps she likes him more than we thought she would."

"Fiddlesticks. She hates him, like all the others. Anyway, it mustn't be. It would jeopardise everything we want, and nothing is going to stop me this close to my goal. Not even her. I also have to keep an eye on his sister. She has already tried to sound her out. We need more time."

"He told me he was leaving while the rumours against him were circulating at the manor. Maybe that can help us."

"Did he say where he was going?"

"No."

"Then find out."

"It might draw attention to me."

"You are right. Maybe a period of him not visiting her will be enough for her to get her mind back on her task. By no means must he find out her true identity. Not yet."

"He will try to talk to her again soon. Make sure she's ready for more of his questions."

"Don't tell me what to do! I didn't make the mistake. You did."

"A mistake that gets him and his questions out of the way for the time being, which is not too bad, the way things are, is it?"

"We'll see. He has no way of reaching her at the moment anyway. Let me know when you hear from him or find out his whereabouts. Then we'll decide how to proceed."

Chapter 31

As Roger was riding over a thick layer of white, small puffs of smoke rose in the distance between the dense snowflakes. In the middle of the snow, a stately, two-storey building stood amongst numerous peasant huts, like a shepherd keeping a watchful eye over his flock of sheep. Roger pulled the hood of his coat deeper into his face, spurred his stallion and was soon riding past the first snow-covered wooden huts to the rhythmic beats of a blacksmith's hammer on the anvil. Some children, who had been poking around in the snow, stopped to gape at the strange man on the big horse. A dog barked and scratched behind a fence as if it wanted to dig through to sniff the stranger more closely.

"Is this the manor of Picot de Perci?" Roger asked the guard when he reached the mighty gate of the building.

"It is indeed. Ride on!"

A man in a dark woollen coat stood in front of a handful of peasants, checking the baskets of eggs they held out and the pile of wood lying on the ground. As Roger approached the centre of the yard, the man looked over at him.

"A single rider in this weather?" he called out to Roger and walked towards him. "I hope nothing has happened to your companions."

A sword protruded from underneath the man's cloak.

"You need not worry, good man. My name is Roger de Wilburgfos, son of Sire Geoffrey de Bernaium. I have ridden here alone and wish to speak to your lord."

"I am Simon de Kyme, the seneschal. Dismount and go ahead." He made a movement with his head towards the big building beside them and took the reins of Roger's horse. "I'll take care of your mount in the meantime."

Shaking the snow off his woollen coat, Roger entered the great hall, which truly deserved its name.

The heavy wooden beams of the roof rose to a lofty height, encompassing the seemingly endless void between storerooms and the solid stone stairs that led to the chambers on the upper floor. On the opposite long side of the hall, a red-yellow fire blazed. A partition protected it from the cold and the wind that penetrated through the adjacent door. In front of the fireplace, a servant was turning a poker in the flames and smiled as Roger approached, rubbing his hands.

Shortly afterwards, there was a mixture of muffled and rapid footsteps. Like a sinewy hound followed by a watchful herding dog, Simon entered with a companion.

Roger had only seen William de Perci a few times, but the man coming towards him could be none other than his younger brother, Picot: the same light brown, slightly greying hair, the striking facial features, a strong, tall body – only the moustache was missing to make the resemblance between the two brothers perfect. Nor could the kinship with his youngest nephew be overlooked, for Picot had the same big, blue child's eyes with which Richard had so often looked up at Roger.

As Picot approached, he smiled and opened his arms. "Roger de Wilburgfos! Greetings, munsire. It is always nice to have friends visit, especially at this time of year. You are most welcome to put yourself at ease in my home."

"I appreciate your hospitality, Sire, especially with what's going on at my home."

Picot put his arm around Roger's shoulders and pulled him to a table where two cups and a large clay jug stood. The servant, who had just been standing next to Roger by the fire, joined them at the table and dipped the poker into the jug, causing a loud hiss. As the noise subsided, the servant began stirring to warm the liquid contents evenly.

"Richard's messenger brought terrible news." Picot shook his head. "Three awful deaths in such a short time. A poisoner and a murderer amidst the people. And then the incident with the seneschal. These are sad times indeed for the manor of Wilburgfos." Groaning, he slumped onto a chair, which made the same noise as it caught Picot's weight, perhaps because it was about the same age as its owner. "Now, tell me: what can I do for you while you are here?"

"The protection at your manor house is more than enough, Sire. I need somewhere safe where I can try to find out what caused the incidents in Wilburgfos, not only for my own sake, but also so that peace may finally return to the village."

"I understand, and you are welcome to stay as long as you need to. You will take part in the combat exercises while you are here, will you not?"

"Gladly, Sire! A little practice will save me from the wrath of the master of arms when I return to Wilburgfos."

"Your master of arms is an Engleis, is he not? From what I hear, you've been very lucky to have him. What's his name again? Osfrid? Oswald?"

"Oswulf."

"That's right, Oswulf. He seems to have come from a distinguished family. Many of his ancestors are said to have served the kings of this country as valiant warriors, some even as part of the royal household. No wonder he is such an excellent fighter. Did you know that his father fought in the Battle of Pons Belli? The king of the Engleis left him badly wounded at the manor house in Wilburgfos, together with young Oswulf. The boy supposedly took care of exercising the squires under the former master of arms."

The servant put the poker aside and poured them a steaming liquid into their cups. Roger was thirsty from the ride and had to think of Richard, who at that moment was still on his way to Topeclive in this weather, while he himself was sitting here in a dry, heated room with a warm drink. He took a big gulp.

Spiced mead.

A pleasant warmth ran down his throat and sprawled in his belly.

Picot took his cup. "His fighting skills saved his life back then."

"Was he old enough to take part in the battle?"

Picot drank and wiped his mouth. "I'm not talking about Pons Belli. Oswulf's parents and many kinsmen were killed in one of the Norman campaigns in the north of England – those were horrible years, Roger, for the Engleis and us Normans alike. Your father, Sire Geoffrey, led the troops back then. Oswulf's village was attacked, and he fought for a long time with his companion against the Norman warriors. If the Norman master of arms had not persuaded your father to take their young enemy to his manor, I am sure you would not have an Engleis there now to teach the squires. Sire

Geoffrey spared Oswulf on condition that he showed the young men at the manor how to handle weapons, and kept his younger siblings, deployed as workers in various manors and houses, as guarantors. One misstep from Oswulf, and his siblings would suffer the consequences."

"My father coerced him into it by threatening the lives of his siblings?"

"That's how Oswulf came to Wilburgfos a second time, but by then, the manor and its inhabitants were no longer free but under Norman rule, and Oswulf too had to bow to the new lord. After all, not only did his own life depend on his obedience, but also those of his brothers and sister."

"That might explain why he's such a quiet man. He has to work for the one who killed his family and forced him into his service. What about his wife, or was he never married?"

"There seems to have been someone where he came from. I also heard that he became rather fond of a girl who was passing through on her way to Hindrelagh."

"Well?"

"I cannot tell if they ever got married, but as far as I know, the girl drowned in the river barely a year later."

"That's terrible. He always looks as if nothing can shake him, but these experiences must have hurt him deeply."

Roger let Picot's words sink in while taking another sip. "Did you know our seneschal, Frederic de Lisieues, Sire?"

"Well, I knew him as well as any brother-in-arms who fought with me against others. Why?"

"Father Leofric told me shortly before he died why he thought it impossible that Frederic could be my father, but before the priest could make his statement at a court hearing, he was killed."

“I think Frederic was married before he came to England.”

“That’s what Father Leofric told me, but the marriage was annulled by the bishop there.”

“It is difficult to send a messenger at this time of year. The roads are covered with snow, and sailing over to Normandy is dangerous. Even the shortest route takes half a day if the wind is good, up to three on the longer routes; more if there is no wind at all or too much. It can take a very long time for the messenger to return. Do you happen to know if the bishop who dissolved the marriage at that time is still alive?”

“No, but many years have passed since then.” Roger turned the signet ring on his little finger. “Before I left Wilburgfos, my mother told me that Frederic had siblings in Everwic. Do you know anything about them?”

“I don’t, but my seneschal, Simon, rides there regularly to do errands for me. He knows Everwic well and can tell you exactly where to find the best wine and the most delicious food. When the celebrations are over and the roads to Everwic are good enough to use again, you should accompany him into the city.”

Chapter 32

Although Roger enjoyed the freedom at Picot's manor, the separation from his family pained him, especially during these days of contemplation when they all usually spent a lot of time together. He often wondered how his mother, Isabel and Tankred were doing, for he'd had no news from Joscelin so far. Similarly, peasants, merchants and travelling minstrels who came to the manor to offer their services knew nothing extraordinary to report from Wilburgfos. Roger prayed that this was a good sign but doubted that this calm would last and that there would indeed be no more deaths.

He could not wait long anyway, for in a little over two months, it would be the fourteenth anniversary of Tankred's birth, and then, his father would make him a squire. Time was trickling through Roger's fingers like sand. He had to try to speak to Gwennaol as soon as possible, so he decided to go to the priory the next morning.

Gwennaol.

Roger sighed as he thought of the sea-blue eyes. How long had it been since he had sunk into them?

His heart ached.

Even if she's still sick, I might at least be allowed to see her. She is young, and the nuns are excellent healers. She's probably long gone back to her duties. I wonder if she has missed me.

He let his thoughts drift with the snowflakes that accompanied him on the way to Wilburgfos. When he spotted the steeple of the priory, he frowned, overcome with a sudden panic. *What if she hasn't recovered? If she is actually dying? I may never know her secret then, for she will take it with her to her grave.*

Roger slammed his heels into his horse's flanks so that it bounded into a gallop. Arriving at the priory, Roger jumped out of the saddle and hammered on the gate.

A nun opened with a look of surprise. "What can I do for you?"

"I must see Gwennaol. It's a matter of life and death."

"I'm afraid I must not let you speak to her."

"Why not? The prioress herself has given me permission. Let me talk to her! It is urgent!"

"The Reverend Mother is very ill at the moment and cannot receive visitors."

"What, the prioress too? Why is everyone I want to speak to suddenly ill? Is there someone who decides in her place?"

"Sister Agatha is looking after the priory for the time being. Let me ask her if she has time for you."

She closed the door and left Roger standing outside.

He stared uneasily at the grooves in the old wood until the door opened again. But instead of the friendly nun's face from before, a grim woman with narrow-set eyes glared through the slender crack in the door.

"What do you want?"

"Sister Agatha?"

The nun looked Roger up and down. "What do you want?" she repeated.

"I want to talk to Gwennaol."

"Why?"

Why? What does it matter to you?

"Well?" grunted Sister Agatha.

Escaping a wounded wild boar would be easier than getting past this woman. "It's a matter of life and death. I need to talk to Gwennaol before another person dies."

"People die. You cannot prevent that."

"It's about people dying in Wilburgfos, at the manor house. I think Gwennaol knows why."

"How would a mere mortal know?"

Roger rolled his eyes at the sky. *Dear Lord, could you not have chosen a bride for your son who asks fewer questions?* "Please, Sister Agatha! Let me speak to Gwennaol. Consider that you are likely helping to prevent a murder."

"Likelihood is a fallacy, young man. Only God decides what does and does not happen on earth. Hasn't your father forbidden you to see Gwennaol anyway?"

The words hit Roger's belly like a punch. Could a little charm and the prospect of a godly donation maybe persuade Sister Agatha to make an exception?

"So, your hesitation shows me that his order is not just a rumour. In that case, you will understand that I cannot possibly let you go and see Gwennaol. Or let her go and see you."

The blood rushed into Roger's ears. *Let her go and see me? So, does she also know about the prayer room under the stairs and the meetings there?*

He gazed across the floor as if to find the solution to getting past Sister Agatha there. "Fulen þa wyrmes in ðære haligan rode!" he murmured.

"As there is nothing else I can do for you, I will leave you to yourself."

Roger braced his hand against the gate.

"Wait, Sister Agatha! Can you tell me when the Reverend Mother Prioress will be well again?"

"That is in God's hands." She slammed the door.

It took Roger a few moments to regain his speech. "Fulen þa wyrmes in ðære haligan rode!" he roared, kicking the heavy wooden gate. But neither his words or his deeds could reopen the door.

There were only three days left until the sixth of January, the day Roger was going to meet with Richard again. But after the failure at the priory, he desperately needed company and hence rode to the manor house to talk to his friends.

The timing was favourable – Joscelin and Drogo were just carrying the equipment back to the armoury, so weapons practice was over. Roger led Modig Wiht into the stable and sneaked after his friends to the entrance of the armoury, where he said in a deep voice, "Make sure you clean and tidy up the weapons properly!"

"Well, look who's here!" said Joscelin with a whimsical smile, "The prodigal son."

"Oswulf makes us work even harder than usual," Drogo complained. "He thinks that if one of us is missing, everyone else has to make up for it."

"He's probably offended that his paragon of a squire left without his consent." Joscelin winked at Roger. "But at least the practice weapons last longer now, and the surrounding buildings don't need to be repaired after every lesson."

"When are you coming back?" asked Drogo. "You will come back, won't you?"

"Eventually, yes," Roger replied. "It depends on how quickly I find answers to my questions." He sat on the bench and grabbed a rag to help out with cleaning the equipment. "Do you have news from Wincestre? Is Father back yet?"

"He arrived two days ago and called a meeting yesterday," Joscelin answered, gesturing at Drogo to close the door of the armoury. After dipping the rag into the bucket of ashes, he rubbed the edge of a sword. "Some wanted to know from your father what has become of you and Richard after you disappeared without notice. They seemed to be particularly worried about Richard's absence. Hugues de Borre insisted on having his men search for him, but not because he is concerned for Richard's well-being. I think he fears that he will divulge something to his father. What exactly this might be, whether the circumstances at this manor or something else, we can only guess."

"That doesn't get us anywhere," said Roger. "Is there anything else I should know?"

"The reappointed Comte de Kent, Bishop Odo, and the Comte de Northumberland, Robert de Monbrai, were also in Wincestre. The wedding with Isabel has been postponed, by the way."

"Why?" Roger asked.

"Apparently, the king will travel to Everwic at the end of January to attend the refounding of the Benedictine abbey by Alain le Rous. All the distinguished people of the realm will meet there at that time: Archbishop Thomas, Bishop Odo, Robert de Monbrai and his uncle, Bishop Geoffroi de Constantia, as well as Bishop William of Dunholm to name but a few."

"So, there are more important things to prepare for than a wedding." Roger rubbed his chin. "I need to go to Everwic anyway to look for Frederic's siblings. I'll send a message to

Richard to meet me there. Now, I'd better get out of here before Hugues de Borre or Father sees me."

He went to fetch Modig Wiht from the stable and was just about to put his foot in the stirrup when from behind, he heard Oswulf's voice.

"You're too late for fighting practice."

"On the contrary, it's still ahead of me."

Should he ask Oswulf if he had observed anything strange lately? Had Sire Geoffrey or Hugues de Borre started to act differently? Had he also noticed the dark-haired man who had visited the manor house several times now?

The master of arms watched him from under his bushy eyebrows. His huge moustache hid any movement around the corners of his mouth.

Oswulf would immediately suspect that I was withholding something from him. Can I really trust him, or would he tell Sire Geoffrey? Would he side with us, if necessary, against his liege lord, endangering not only his own life but that of his siblings?

Pressing his lips together, Roger mounted. "I must go. Richard is waiting for me."

"That was a short visit."

"Maybe the next one will be longer."

"Good. And then you can tell me what you've found out so far."

Roger eyed the master of arms, an uneasy feeling in his belly. "Certainly."

Chapter 33

A week before Candlemas, the second of February, Roger started preparing for the journey to Everwic. His money pouch was filled with enough silver coins from his last visit to Wilburgfos to pay for an inn and food. Picot's wife provided him with a thick woollen cloak, which would also serve as a blanket in case he could not find a decent place to sleep at night. As for the scramasax, his only weapon apart from the small dagger that everyone carried, he had put it in perfect condition with an experienced eye and well-schooled hands.

As he was crossing the yard in the afternoon to check his horse's equipment in the stable, two poor-looking figures traipsed in through the gate, probably driven out of their beggar's den by hunger. Without paying any further attention to them, Roger went into the stable, checked the leather of the saddle for brittle spots and made sure the bridle was clean and undamaged. His chestnut stallion nickered softly.

"I know, Modig." Roger snuggled against the horse's warm body, patting him on the neck. "You sense that we are going on a big journey tomorrow. What an adventure it'll be! The two of us in such a huge city as Eoforwic for the first time."

Modig Wiht neighed enthusiastically and nudged him with his nose.

Roger stroked his head. "If it were up to you, you'd prefer to set off right away. But we'll have to wait until morning, my good boy."

He ran his hands through the animal's thick winter coat, first over the back, then over the belly and the joints on the legs. It wasn't far to travel, but Roger still wanted to make sure the stallion was healthy with no injuries. Any delays would cost valuable time – and possibly lives. So, they would set off early, as soon as there was enough light so that the horses could tread safely, and they would not have to watch out for nightly robbers and waylayers.

Simon entered the stable. "Do you have a sister who lives in a convent?"

Roger's heartbeat quickened. "Adelais. Has something happened to her?"

"No, but there are two young men in the yard who claim to have been sent by her. They have a message for you and insist on delivering it to you personally."

Oh my God! Something's happened to Gwennaol. She's dying. Or she's already dead. I should never have let that ill-tempered nun turn me away, coward that I am!

"I'm coming."

From a distance, Roger eyed the two sad figures standing like windswept weeping willows in front of the great hall. Had they really walked all the way here from Wilburgfos? The dirty rags they wore had holes and protected them rather poorly from this weather. A few tangled strands of light hair peeked out from under the shabby hoods. The smaller of the two was still very young, perhaps nine or ten years old, and stood close to his older companion, who was probably about Roger's age. Instead of a hand, a stump of an arm protruded from the little one's right sleeve. His large, anxious eyes swept the surroundings restlessly, while his older companion stood motionless beside him with his head hanging.

Roger stood in front of the two.

"Someone from Wilburgfos sent you?"

"Is that you, Roger?" asked the older one. His voice sounded rough, but somehow familiar.

"You know me?" Roger frowned.

"We used to be good friends."

"Look at me!" Roger ordered the older one, who obediently lifted his head and revealed a dirty blindfold. Stunned, Roger stared at him and his little companion.

"What is it?" asked Simon.

"Brandolf," Roger breathed, "you're alive."

He wrapped his arms around his former brother-in-arms and pulled him close. Instead of the once firm, muscular body, Roger felt each and every bone. If Brandolf had not been a naturally strong fellow, the famine that had ravaged England last year would certainly have killed him.

"Your mother and the herb woman tended to our wounds secretly," Brandolf explained as Roger released him from the embrace.

His little brother was a pitiful sight. Small and slight anyway, Bjarni was now merely skin and bones. How Brandolf had managed to keep him alive was a mystery to Roger.

"You know each other?" Simon wanted to know.

"We used to be at my father's manor," answered Roger, "until a court hearing separated us."

"Why don't we go inside?" The young seneschal pointed to the door of the great hall and gently nudged Bjarni forward. "I'm sure you could do with a little warmth and food."

A maid-servant brought warm cabbage strips with crispy bacon and two thick slices of bread for the two guests, who greedily tucked in. Roger watched them eat, struggling to wait until they had satisfied most of their hunger.

"Now, tell me how my sister was able to find you and send you to me with a message."

"Your sister knows us," replied Brandolf. "She asked who we were when we came to beg for some alms that she was giving out."

"She slipped us a gab with bread, cheese and a piece of sausage," Bjarni blurted out with his mouth full.

"And she gave us a letter for you." Brandolf searched through the layers of his clothes with trembling fingers. He pulled a crumpled document out of a pocket and held it over the table.

Roger took the parchment, broke the seal and unfolded the letter. Everyone listened, spellbound, as he read out the following lines:

"*My beloved brother, you should give heartfelt thanks to your two brave friends who, despite snow, cold and hunger, take it upon themselves to bring you my message. These convent walls hide shameful things that you should know about.*

"*On your last visit before the Feast of the Lord, Gwennaol was seriously ill. No one knew what evil had befallen her. Some suspected that the diseases that killed so many of our compatriots last year had now reached the priory in Wilburgfos. Gwennaol's grandmother, Morwenna, watched over her day and night, jealous as a wild sow with shoats – woe be anyone who gets too close to Gwennaol! One day, I heard Gwennaol arguing with her grandmother and repeatedly rejecting the cup the old woman held out to her. The following day, Gwennaol felt even more poorly, and we feared the worst. The prioress was so worried that she told Morwenna she would send for a doctor if her condition did not improve. With a vigorous shake of her head, Morwenna insisted that Gwennaol's health would soon improve.*

"And it did, but at the same time, the prioress fell ill with an equally mysterious malaise. When Gwennaol was well enough to resume most of the normal monastic life, I discreetly asked her about the day I overheard the argument. Believe it or not, her own grandmother had infused her with a herbal mixture that had weakened her to such an extent. When she tried to give her a sip again that day and Gwennaol fiercely resisted, her grandmother accidentally gave her too much. That's why she was in such a miserable state the next day. I think at that point, Morwenna was truly afraid that she was losing her granddaughter.

"I asked her why her grandmother would do such a thing, and Gwennaol told me that she wants to prevent you from seeing her again."

Roger lowered the letter with a snort. "Seo ful lybbestre!"

"Is that what she wrote?" asked Bjarni.

"No. I was just thinking out loud."

"Read on!" urged Brandolf.

"While Gwennaol is recovering, Morwenna seems to have got the prioress out of the way with a similar potion. Now, Sister Agatha rules over us and uses this power wherever she can.

"Gwennaol asked about you. I told her that you were well and that you would come back as soon as you could. She seems to be having a hard time waiting. Va dunc, chevaler preuz et beaus! Hurry up, Roger, or she'll die of a broken heart.

"May the Lord hold his hand protectively over you on your way and push you forward with it, lest you succumb to idleness and let us both stew here in the priory.

"Your loving sister, Adelais."

Roger folded up the letter.

If Morwenna can brew potions that make you sick, she can certainly make even more dangerous concoctions. Poison.

"I must write a letter to be taken to the convent now, to none other than Sister Agatha herself."

He had writing materials and parchment brought to him, sat down and wrote,

> ...I will go to Everwic, yet for how long, I do not know. I will deliver, in due time, the sum of money I promised the prioress for her intercession for my soul and Gwennaol's. See to it that neither the prioress nor Gwennaol suffer another ailment or worse in my absence. If they do, I will use the money to pay a doctor to examine them to determine what disease has afflicted them and how to remove the evil from the convent. I trust you approve of this decision.
>
> Your most humble servant,
> Roger of Wilburgfos

Chapter 34

The next morning, Roger and Simon saddled the horses and led them out into the snow-covered yard.

Picot's cupbearer brought them two coarse woollen sacks of provisions – a loaf of bread, a sausage, a piece of cheese and a full wineskin.

Roger fastened the bag of food onto the pommel of his saddle. "How far is it to Everwic?"

Simon adjusted his weapon belt and sword. His breath left little clouds of mist in the cold, clear air. "About two hours to the outskirts of the city."

"Is it dangerous?"

The young seneschal pursed his lips. "Well, the inhabitants of Everwic need a lot of wood for their castles, bridges and houses. So, the woods are sparse the closer you get to the city, which means you no longer need to be wary of wild animals and robbers hiding behind trees. Besides, there are always many people entering and leaving Everwic at all times of the year, so there is no shortage of fellow travellers. Unfortunately, you can just as quickly find yourself in bad company. Waylayers and thieves lie in wait in the bushes or the narrow streets of the city, even in broad daylight, for unsuspecting travellers."

Roger tapped the scramasax hanging from his weapon belt on his right. "We'll keep them at bay if we have to."

"Be on your guard," warned Picot, who had come with Roger's two friends to take his leave. "Everwic is big, noisy and crowded with people who do not all follow respectable trades." He patted the seneschal on the shoulder. "Simon will reliably guide you through the city. He is a good man who deserves more than the rank and duties of a seneschal."

Picot's words reassured Roger, yet he still felt his belly gurgling as they left the manor.

"I can't believe that a few weeks ago, I was still living in Wilburgfos and now, I'm riding into a huge, unfamiliar city," he said when they had been riding for a while. "Is it true that twenty years ago, nearly nine thousand people lived in Everwic? That is actually several hundred times more than the population in the whole of Cattune."

"Everwic was doing well in those days. Trade flourished, the city grew and attracted many people. Engleis, Northmen and people from many other countries lived there. Some were born and grew up in Everwic, others came there as strangers, wandering craftsmen, traders or travelling minstrels – until the year 1069 of Our Lord, when half of the city, including the minster, was burned down by a large army of Engleis and Daneis to rebel against King William. Everwic has not recovered from it to this day. You'll see for yourself, almost half the houses are empty or derelict."

"But Everwic is still the seat of the king and even has an archbishop. Why doesn't the king choose a less desolate city as a centre of his kingdom?"

"It's still the largest and most important town in the north of England. The old trade and transport routes all lead there, and it is easy to reach the sea and all the important ports using Everwic's two rivers Use and Fosse. Everwic is second only to Londres when it comes to trading. Besides, the king can keep a good eye on the Escoz from Everwic."

By now, only a few trees lined the path and the surrounding white fields, and a cold wind swept across the vast plain, hissing into the ears of the two riders.

To their left, the large, blue flow of the Use glistened in the weak rays of the winter sun. Eventually, between huge ramparts, fortified with palisades, the river forked like the tongue of a snake and flicked out into the town rising before them.

Compared to Wilburgfos, Cattune and Sudtone had already seemed big to Roger, but even those places suddenly seemed tiny.

Again and again, his gaze climbed up the intimidating fortifications, and he had to remind himself more than once to breathe in because he was holding his breath in awe. Never before had he seen such an enormous mound of earth, let alone a building that could have matched it.

As they got closer to the city, the snow-covered ground quickly turned into a slushy, light brown mass in which the tracks of countless hooves, feet and wheels could be seen. Even now, in the deepest winter, quite a few people were heading for the city – how many more might come here when the weather was better and the markets were taking place?

In front of them, two traders with their heavily loaded ox carts pushed the people aside. A small group of minstrels in colourful costumes had lined up at a fork in the road to pocket a few coins from the passers-by with crude songs and breakneck performances. Two peasants complained loudly about the clods of mud hurled at them by the galloping horse of a passing rider.

The path wound to the left over the Fosse, the right-hand part of the flowing snake's tongue, and led them into the city at the southeastern part of the palisade boundary.

So far, Roger's chestnut stallion had willingly submitted to his master's leisurely pace, but the more that people and animals surrounded him and the less room he found for his spacey stride, the more he pranced.

Similarly, Roger's stomach also tingled with excitement, and he had difficulty keeping Modig Wiht in check, however much he stroked his neck or spoke to him softly.

"This is the only way across the river," Simon said, as if to apologise for their riding in this throng towards a narrow wooden bridge with a little toll house and guards.

But Roger totally ignored the bridge, for he was marvelling at the water that stretched for miles on the eastern boundary of the city. "The river is a lake."

"The inhabitants call it either 'li viver le rei' or 'se cyninges fiscpol', depending on which language they speak. When King William wanted to fill the moat of his new castle, he had a dam built in the Fosse just before it flows into the Use. The water, however, rose so much that it flooded the entire area as well as two mills. The good thing is that the flooding also brought plenty of fish into the lake – much appreciated by the local fishermen."

To their right, nestled between the Use on the western side and the dammed waters of the Fosse on the eastern side, sprawled a spacious outer bailey, behind which a giant wooden tower perched on a huge mound of earth.

"It's sixty feet up to the keep," Simon explained. "Whoever wants to climb up there should prepare their attack well. Or raid the other castle instead."

"There are two castles?"

"Indeed, there are. The big castle here on the eastern side of the Use and the smaller one on the western side. It's a little lower, but as you can see, you also have to get over the high palisades first to get into the outer bailey."

How the castle looked down on him! Even the mighty tower of a church was nothing compared to this monstrosity, and suddenly, Roger could relate to how the English must have felt when the huge Norman castles appeared all over the country, wherever King William saw fit. They were indeed awe-inspiring buildings.

The snow-sprinkled houses huddled together like sheep being herded by the shepherd and his dog. So many columns of smoke rose from the roofs that it looked as if an ox plough had made furrows in the sky.

Just in time, Roger noticed that Simon was riding straight ahead, towards the Use instead of following the road that ran alongside the massive castle. "Where are we riding?" he asked, hastily steering his horse to follow him.

"To where the ships land. We're almost there."

As they approached the riverbank, Roger sniffed and looked around. It smelled as if there were a whole army of drenched horsemen standing nearby, but not a single destrier was to be seen anywhere. "Can you smell that too?"

"You mean the smell of leather? That's not unusual when the wind comes from the west. The workshops of the shoemakers and shield-makers lie on the other side of the river."

"Why are we going to the ships?"

Roger struggled to calm Modig Wiht. Directly in front of him was the rear end of Simon's horse, a handful of boisterous young craftsmen rumbled past beside him, and from behind, a merchant pushed his cart forward, clamouring loudly. It was clearly too narrow and too crowded in Everwic.

"My liege lord wants to replenish his stocks of wine and spices. If he sends his seneschal to Everwic, it has to be worth his while."

Along the river, a whole series of smaller and larger ships were anchored on both banks. "What do they sell here?" Roger asked.

"Absolutely everything you would expect to find in such a large city: fish from the nearby waters, wine from the kingdom of the Franks, textiles, wax and oats from the coastal regions of the mainland, and also timber and furs from the lands beyond the sea. Foreign merchants and traders mainly buy grain and wool and often return to their home regions with their ships just as laden as when they came."

"A floating market."

Roger thought of the humble stalls in Wilburgfos. There were no exotic spices or silken robes at the market back home, but it was there that he had seen Gwennaol outside the priory for the first time.

He sighed. He missed her. Hopefully, she was all right.

While Simon kept stopping at one boat after another, exchanging a few words with the owner, Roger tried as best he could to stay out of the way of the people rushing around. Somehow, everyone here seemed to be in a hurry and urgently needed to get somewhere. In Wilburgfos everything was more leisurely. There was always time for a chat. There was no pushing and shoving, no shouting because you couldn't move fast enough on the paths. But here? Roger cringed at the thought of what it had been like in Everwic when many more people lived here.

Simon waved him on. "Come, we must cross to the other side."

Roger was glad to leave this restless place. He spurred Modig Wiht on and took one last look at the hustle and bustle behind him. Everyone hurried along – except for two men in fur-trimmed cloaks and splendid fur caps who were standing next to a fisherman's display with raised eyebrows.

Roger and Simon drifted with the crowd, past closely spaced houses, shops, stores and stalls. The town resembled an anthill, teeming with bustling activity. Simple peasants mingled with noblemen on horseback, merchants with all kinds of goods on their donkeys, craftsmen carrying their tools, and far too many other people. Every spot in the narrow streets was crammed with buildings or people. Roger had simply assumed that the streets in a city like Everwic would be so wide that two oxcarts could have easily passed each other. Now, he found that there was only just enough space for two mules carrying a sack of grain not to bump into each other. Besides, as a rider, you also had to keep your head down to avoid butting it against the low upper floors that jutted out into the streets.

Just as colourful as Everwic's population were also its buildings – newly built and recently repaired houses with neat front sides, half-finished stumps, and dilapidated huts that life had long since passed by. From backyards came the odd grunting of pigs and cackling and clucking of fowl, and here and there stood a few bare, frosted fruit trees. Wistfully, Roger thought of summer in Wilburgfos, of the scent of blossoming flowers, spicy herbs and fresh, sun-ripened fruit. But this pleasant image soon faded as the omnipresent stink of the big city brought him back to reality.

After a small loop along the northern part of the right bank, Roger and Simon rode onto the bridge over the Use, which divided the docks on both sides of the river approximately in half.

"It smells awful here!" Roger waved his hand to dispel the stench that was creeping ever more insistently into his nose. "Are you leading us to the common privies?"

"Not quite, but the tanneries are just a bit further west of here, and this is unfortunately the only bridge to the other side of the river."

"That means we ride back the same way?"

Simon grinned broadly. "You're missing Everwic already, aren't you?"

Roger waved his question off and tried to hold his breath as long as possible until they turned into Skjaldari Gata, which ran south along the river. Instead of dead and decaying animals, urine and rancid fat, the smell of leather dominated the air again.

"I'm going to see what leather goods they offer while you look around the ships," he said.

"All right. We'll meet back here and then ride to the cathedral."

Chapter 35

Roger was standing in front of a workshop, looking at some shields on which the freshly fitted leather skins were drying in the clear winter air, when he heard a voice from behind.

"Can we help you?" The two men who had caught his eye at the fish stall on the other bank of the Use appeared beside him.

"Do you own one of the ships that are anchored here?" Roger gestured towards the docks.

"No, we live here. But you're not from Everwic, are you? Have you travelled far?"

"I'm from Wilburgfos, just a few hours away on horseback."

One of the men nodded. He probably had no idea where Wilburgfos was.

"We know our way around Everwic," the other one said, smiling. "Just tell us what you want!"

"Yeah, come on," said the first. "What brings a young man like you to Everwic?"

"I'm looking for someone."

"Oh, and who's that? I'm sure we can help you find him."

"I would indeed be grateful for your help. Does the name Hubert de Lisieues mean anything to you?"

The first one squinted. "Lisieues, Lisieues – isn't that the shoemaker?"

The other looked at Roger. "You only came to Everwic for a pair of shoes? Surely, that cannot be the only reason for your journey."

"No, actually, I don't want any shoes from him at all. I need to ask him something."

"You ride all the way just for a question?" The man frowned at Roger.

"Ah, I see!" The second nudged the first with his elbow. "He wants to ask him for the hand of the girl he is to marry. Well, if I were her father, I would have you two betrothed immediately. After all, what young man rides such a long way, nowadays, to woo his future bride?"

"No, no. You don't understand. I have a question about his brother. It's important. Do you happen to know where I can find him?"

"You're in luck, my young friend." The first man made a sweeping gesture with his hand towards one of the narrow alleys between the houses. "His house is in that direction, not far from here. Do you want us to lead you there?"

Roger looked around for Simon, who was talking to one of the traders further down.

"Don't worry. We'll send a message to your friend to let him know where you are. It won't take long."

Stepping away, the man beckoned a young boy to come over to him. He gave him some instructions and a coin and sent him off. On returning to his companion and Roger, he pointed at Modig Wiht. "In a town like Everwic, it's quicker to walk than ride, especially in the alleys. Look at us! We walk too, even though we can afford more than one horse."

After a moment's thought, Roger dismounted. "You're probably right. It will do me good to walk for a while. Well?"

"This way." After glancing at the other, the first man set off.

Roger led his horse along, followed by the second man.

"I suppose the celebrations for the Feast of the Lord are much more modest in Wilburgfos than in Everwic, right?" asked the first.

"Probably," answered Roger. "Wilburgfos is only a little village."

"What sort of food did you have?"

"I... I don't know."

"It almost sounds as if you weren't there," said the second man. "Or did you drink so much that you can't remember?"

"I don't drink beyond my thirst. And no, I actually was not in Wilburgfos at the time. Is it much further?"

"Your family must have missed you, no?"

"I suppose so." Roger looked over his shoulder.

Close behind him, the second man was grinning. "And you didn't even go there for a brief visit? How could you do that to your mother?"

"I don't see why this should be of interest to you," said Roger. "Would you stop your questioning now, and lead me to Hubert? I have to get back to the docks soon."

The first man whirled around and grabbed Roger by the throat with one hand. Modig Wiht whinnied and pranced to the side.

"The questioning is just beginning, *Roger de Wilburgfos.*"

Roger reached for the man's hand, but the second man grabbed him from behind and twisted his arms behind his back.

The stallion threw his head up and pulled the reins from Roger's hand.

"How do you know my name?"

"A little birdie chirped it to me. And now, out with it. What was so important to discuss with your mother and your friends that you sneaked onto the manor?"

"How do you know?" Roger tried to get at least one hand free, but the two men held him like the blacksmith holds the iron with his pincers.

"I'm the one asking the questions!"

The man let go of Roger's throat and punched him in the stomach.

Roger folded, gasping for air.

"Answer!"

Slowly, Roger straightened up. "Here's your answer." He kicked the man in the guts as hard as he could.

With a groan, the man staggered backwards a few steps. Modig Wiht reared, whinnying loudly.

"Irn, Modig, ond bring Simon! Retsh!—" Roger's face flew to the side.

The stallion galloped off.

"Leave the nag," the first man said to the other. "We first have to finish off something here. Or someone."

He approached with bared teeth. "Now, tell us what we want to know!"

"What's it to you what I talk about with my mother?"

"You think yourself particularly brave, don't you? Believe me, I made men much tougher than you talk when I was a mercenary." He cracked his knuckles.

"A mercenary. Now, there's a surprise. Who sent you? How did he know I would be in Everwic at this time?" Roger silently wondered who knew about his stay. His mother and friends, of course. Sister Agatha. She was an unpleasant woman, but she was also a nun and would hardly send two mercenaries after him. Oswulf had caught him once on one of his visits to the manor, but Roger had never mentioned to him that he was going to Everwic.

"Never mind to whom you owe our acquaintance," the first man interrupted Roger's thoughts. "Just tell us what you know, and we'll be satisfied – and so will our patron."

"Did he at least pay you well to lie in wait for me here and beat me up? In any case, you can forget about getting an answer from me."

"I wouldn't be so sure of yourself. After all, you don't want anything to happen to your little friend, do you?"

Roger's heart pounded. *Richard.*

He gritted his teeth. "I have no idea who you are talking about."

"Oh yes, you most certainly do. Richard de Perci and you were seen riding off from the manor house together. You cherish your friend, don't you? Wouldn't it be terrible if we had to hurt him to make you answer our questions?"

"You cannot but fail, for he is safe and well guarded. There's nothing you can do to force me, and whatever happens, you will not get away with it. Should anything happen to Richard or myself, William de Perci will track you down, and then, don't count on mercy for whatever you've done."

The man clamped his mouth shut, but before he could strike another blow, Roger smashed his head into the man's face. The attacked grunted, while Roger stamped his heel on the toes of the man behind him and then threw himself forward. His left arm was free at last.

Swivelling to the side, he drew the scramasax and swung the second man, who was still holding on to his right arm, in front of him, the short sword at his throat. "Now, it's my turn to ask questions."

The first man wiped his bleeding nose and glared at him.

"So," Roger said, gasping, "who sent you? Speak!"

"All right." The first man glanced briefly at his blood-smeared hand. Something red was oozing onto his upper lip. "Let's talk like men."

Roger was breathing more calmly, but his heart was racing. *It's about time Simon came! I won't be able to fend these two off much longer.* "Well?" he asked a little too loudly. "Are you finally going to tell me?" His scramasax now touched the throat of his captive.

"Wait!" the man groaned. "Hugues de B—"

"Shut up!" snapped the first man and took a few steps towards the two. "That stripling is too much of a coward to use his knife anyway."

"Hugues de Borre hired you?" asked Roger.

"Yes," replied the second man quickly.

"So what?" said the first. "In any case, you're not really a welcome guest in Wilburgfos, and there must be a reason for that. Apparently, you poisoned the priest and even tried to kill your mother."

"None of this is true! It wasn't me. Who told you these lies? Hugues de Borre, the bailiff, who would love to take over the manor himself? Who wants to get rid of me by sending two scoundrels like you after me?"

The first man pointed to the scramasax with his bloodied hand. "Do you want to kill another one? Haven't you caused enough trouble at home already? That's why you fled the manor, isn't it? Do you think your mother and friends can help you? Or why else did you visit them?"

Roger looked around. There were so many people here – why didn't anyone come to his aid? Instead, people looked away and hurried past. Only a few children were watching from the door of a house.

"Don't come any closer!" said Roger when he realised how near the first man was. He pulled his companion backwards a little, keeping the scramasax at his throat.

The first man sneered at him. "What are you going to do? Cry for help? Even if someone responded to your call, what do you expect? You're not from Everwic, and you have your knife at my friend's throat after punching me until my nose bled. Who do you think they would protect? You or us?" He slowly followed Roger.

"I told you what you wanted to know," groaned his companion, forced to shuffle backwards with Roger. "Take your knife away."

"It's not a knife," said Roger, "but a scramasax that has slit open many a Norman!"

Some people around them gave him a curious look.

"These two men wanted to rob me and beat me up." He stared back at them. "Don't just stand there! Help me!"

A thud knocked Roger backwards. He lost his balance and fell on his back, his captive on top of him. He gasped. A sudden pain drove through his left wrist. His hand opened, and the scramasax fell to the ground. The weight rolled off his chest, then he was yanked up to look directly into the bloodied face of the first man.

"Say your last prayer," the man said through clenched teeth. "You've been playing for time far too long."

A neigh from the side caught their attention.

"Let him go!" someone called.

People stepped aside in awe as Simon rode through the alley on his big bay horse with the prancing chestnut stallion at his side. Modig Wiht was clearly enjoying the attention and threw his head up with another whinny and shook his long mane.

The mercenary hesitantly let go of Roger and eyed the young seneschal. "It's about time you caught your untamed friend. He threatened us with a knife."

"Scramasax, unwita!" Roger pulled his tunic and woollen cloak into place and picked up the short sword.

Simon halted in front of the three. "That's not quite what I saw."

The second mercenary stepped up to him. "He wanted to kill me. If it hadn't been for *him*," he pointed to his companion, "I would be lying in the street now with my throat cut open. Your friend is unpredictable."

"They're both lying," said Roger. "Our bailiff paid them to sound me out and beat me up."

Simon frowned at the mercenaries. "Not unpredictable, but perhaps a little too gullible if he trusts people like you. I already noticed you on the other side. Your behaviour didn't really match your clothes."

One of the men lifted his chin. "You'll be lucky if we don't report you to the reeve and have you thrown out of Everwic."

"And why wouldn't you?" asked Simon, holding out the chestnut stallion's reins to Roger. "Didn't you say someone attacked and threatened you just now? Surely, the reeve has great interest in having peace and order in his city."

The mercenaries hesitated.

"I have done everything I was ordered to do here anyway," said Simon. "So, let us ride to the reeve! You can make your complaint there, and we may get an honest answer to our question."

He picked out four burly men from among the bystanders who had watched everything with their mouths open, slipped them a coin and asked them to help him bring the two mercenaries safely to the reeve.

So, they rode again through the stinking west wind along the great Mikkil Gata road to the bridge over the Use.

"Are you injured?" asked the young seneschal.

Roger shrugged. "My belly and chin will probably ache for a while."

"You got off lightly."

"Yes. I'm glad the boy found you in time. Otherwise, you might have been too late."

"What boy?"

"Well, the one the man gave the coin to. He was supposed to let you know... He didn't actually send the boy, did he?" Roger's heart missed a beat.

"There's one thing you still have to learn, Roger: noble clothes cannot hide an evil mind."

"I should know better by now. Hugues de Borre! I cannot believe it. He pays two mercenaries to lie in wait for me. Did my father not know about it? He discusses everything with Hugues. Can you imagine if he knew about it and did nothing? He approves of an assault against his own son... or at least, that's what I continue to assume, even if many at the manor house are of a different opinion right now."

Chapter 36

With each step on the bridge, the smell from the sea of streets and houses in front of them replaced that from the tanneries behind them. When they reached the other bank of the river, they steered their horses south and followed the four men and the two mercenaries, who were heading for the huge mound of the large castle. There, they were hoping to be able to hand over the two mercenaries to Ralph de Paynel, the newly appointed shire reeve of Everwicscire, and to find out more about Frederic's brother Hubert.

The group crossed the heavy stone bridge that led across the moat past the castle proper into the northern part of the bailey. Roger held his breath in awe. The whole of Wilburgfos, including the manor house, the priory and a few fields, would have fitted into these castle walls! Stables, workshops, barns, storerooms and houses clustered together, and yet nowhere did Roger have the feeling of confinement that befell him in the midst of the streets and houses of Everwic outside the castle walls.

Following the instructions of the guards, they finally found Ralph de Paynel's deputy.

The officer listened to both versions of what had happened with a raised eyebrow then sighed deeply. "If I understand you correctly, nothing was stolen or damaged, no one was seriously injured, killed, treated unseemly or insulted. Am I right?"

"Those two have orders to kill me!" Roger pointed his finger at the two mercenaries. "If you let them off, you'll have two murderers in the city."

"And if you let him off, you'll have a lunatic in town threatening innocent citizens with a knife," retorted the first mercenary.

"Scramasax!" Roger cried. "It's a short sword, not a knife!"

The mercenary pointed at him. "Do you see how short-tempered he is? He's a danger to the city."

"By your leave, munsire," said Simon, "I would like to speak to you in confidence."

The deputy beckoned two guards to take care of the mercenaries then followed Simon, who pulled Roger along, to the side of the room.

"We have been sent by William de Perci, liegeman of the Comte de Cestre," whispered Simon, "to uncover a conspiracy against the king."

Roger gasped. Hopefully, the mercenaries heard none of this, otherwise, he wouldn't leave the castle alive.

"I assume you know that the king is coming to Everwic in the next few days to meet with the mightiest vassals and bishops. He'll be very pleased to learn that you have helped us to fulfil our duty," Simon glanced at the mercenaries, "instead of working against him or obstructing us in our errand. You know what those will face: impeachment, confiscation of property, trial, perhaps even the accusation of being part of the conspiracy themselves – it may be necessary to adorn the gates of Micklelith and Galmanlith again as a warning to others."

The deputy nodded thoughtfully then lifted his chin and marched back to his table.

"I order you to leave the city immediately," he said to the mercenaries. "My guards will escort you to the gate. If they see you again in Everwic within a week, they will arrest you."

Scowling, but without objection, the mercenaries bowed to the deputy's decision and left the room with the guards.

"As for you two," he said, turning to Simon and Roger, "I will give you one week to complete your task here. After that, I can no longer guarantee your safety."

"Jo vus en mercie bonement, munsire," said Roger. "But there is one more thing. I am looking for Hubert de Lisieues. Do you know him?"

"Call it coincidence or fate, but I still have the results of the last tax collection here."

The deputy reached into a stack of parchment, leafed through it briefly then put his finger on a spot in the records. "*Hubert de Lisieues, cordewaner, living in Suteres Gata*," he read out.

"Where is that?" asked Roger.

"Suteres Gata is in the craftsmen's eastern settlement in Everwic," the deputy replied, "just north of the castle and along the viver le rei."

"Then we will pay him a visit tomorrow. I hope my belly and chin will have recovered from the punches by then. Thank you for your help, munsire. Could you also tell us when you expect the king and his followers?"

"Weather permitting, they should reach Everwic in two days."

"Very good." Roger glanced at Simon. "We look forward to being in the same city as our king and his loyal vassals."

As they returned to the huge yard and walked towards the horses, Roger stopped.

"What is it?" asked Simon, turning round to him.

"See those two men in front of the workshop over there?"

With a quick eye movement, Roger pointed inconspicuously in that direction.

"I know one of them. He came to us in Wilburgfos, he's an envoy of Robert de Monbrai."

"The Comte de Northumberland?"

"Precisely. He was supposed to marry my younger sister at the end of January."

"The nephew of one of the king's closest advisers is to marry your sister? You must be joking."

"Not at all. Strange things have been going on at the manor of Wilburgfos for some months. Three people have been killed, and I am blamed for their deaths. They also claim that I am an illegitimate son of the seneschal. Even Richard has been suspected in an attempt to find the one who is to blame for everything. They watch him, they choose their words carefully when he attends the court sessions, and sometimes, he has the feeling that they keep certain things secret from him. And then there is this envoy from Robert de Monbrai, who keeps turning up at the manor house, allegedly because the comte is to marry my sister, as she herself told me through her copious tears. My father and Hugues de Borre use the dead as a pretext to stir up people's hatred against me and Richard. In truth, however, they want to divert attention from their real intention, something they do not want me, much less Richard, to hear."

"So, I didn't actually lie to the reeve's deputy," the young seneschal said, half pleased, half wary.

The envoy took his leave of the other, looked around in all directions and hurried off.

Meanwhile, the one who stayed behind was eagerly discussing over the counter.

"Maybe right now's the time to find out more," Roger said and marched towards the shop.

The man in front of it had a tall and stocky body supported by two strong legs. Dark hair grew on his square head like sheep's wool. Waving his huge, hairy hands about, he complained loudly about the quality of English saddles.

Roger approached him, gazing at the leather goods on offer.

"This is the second time my stirrup leathers have broken. These Engleis are good for nothing. It is no surprise they don't go to war with horses. They can't even make decent saddles."

They are probably not made for your weight.

"I could recommend my saddler to you," said Roger. "I've never had any problems with my saddle."

The giant eyed him disparagingly. "If your beard were as long as your hair, I might take you up on the offer. But by the look of you, your saddle only has to last for the way from your mother's lap to church. My saddle is for a destrier! You probably don't even know what that is."

Roger took a deep breath and swallowed the insults.

"I'm sure my saddler would meet your standards too. He does excellent work, just like our master of arms. But where he lives, the women are also praised for their virtue and skill. With her beauty, singing and handicraft, the liege lord's daughter, Isabel, is said to have beguiled even the Comte de Northumberland, so that the two will soon be married."

"The Comte de Northumberland?"

"Apparently, he is the nephew of one of the king's closest advisers and a very rich man." Roger casually ran his fingers over a pair of leather gloves. "Do you know him?"

"I certainly do."

"Are you aware that some people make fun of the comte? They say it is ridiculous that such an influential and noble man as the Comte de Northumberland should marry a girl from a little village like Wilburgfos. Some claim that he is so ugly that no girl who has ever seen him would want to marry him. Others insinuate that he is only after the girl's dowry. But what could the Lord of Wilburgfos possibly offer the Comte de Northumberland?"

"Do you actually know to whom you are speaking? I am Robert de Monbrai, Comte de Northumberland."

Roger's heart sank into his boots. Why was the comte already in Everwic when the others were not due to arrive for two days?

Robert de Monbrai puffed himself up even more and propped his hands on his hips.

"You will tell me right now who you are and where you got these wild accusations!"

Roger backed away. "I'm afraid I have to leave urgently. Someone is expecting us." He nudged Simon with his elbow. "Let's get out of here!"

The comte grabbed Roger's cloak. "Your name, I said!"

"Gilbert. Gilbert FitzOsbern."

He snatched the cloak from the comte's hand and hurried to the horses with Simon. They mounted and trotted towards the north gate.

"Why did you do that?" asked Simon as they crossed the moat. "Haven't you caused enough trouble today?"

"How should I know that this was Robert de Monbrai of all people? I thought his envoy had simply passed on news from Wilburgfos to another messenger. Let's hope that Richard has been able to find out more in the meantime."

The sun was already beginning to set as Roger and Simon rode into the middle of the city. The Fosse was slowly shrinking back into a river. Where the lake had previously made earth walls and defensive structures superfluous, the city wall now continued northwards, so that the houses were once again fenced in by a defensive ring.

As they rode through the large market area of Everwic, Simon pointed to the left into a frighteningly narrow alley where the roofs almost touched above the path.

Two gutters ran along the ground to the left and right of the sloping surface, and metal bars with hooks protruded from the walls of the houses.

"Do you want to shorten the way?"

Roger peered into the dark tunnel. "Are you serious? What are the hooks for?"

"This is the great meat market, where the butchers hang the pork halves and other pieces of meat to offer to their customers. Looks like they haven't finished cleaning up yet." He pointed to two figures at the back of the alley who were wearily sweeping up the rubbish on the ground.

A breeze swept through the alley and carried to the two riders the smell of rotten meat, decaying waste as well as human and animal excrement.

Disgusted, Roger held his nose. "I think I wouldn't mind taking a different route."

Simon laughed. "The city has quite a few smells to offer, hasn't it? But fear not, by the time the king visits, at the latest, it will all be as clean as if a heavy shower had washed everything away."

Waving his hand in front of his face, Roger spurred his horse. "He'd better not take the same way as us into town. How does it smell here when the sun blazes down onto the streets in summer?"

"Living in a city does have its disadvantages, and yet Everwic is growing. Building and repairing alone offers good work and decent wages to many people, and this attracts even more people and their families."

Roger waved it off. The state of the streets and the number of people and animals that were already crowding them at this time of year was enough for him. "I hope I'll find Frederic's siblings soon so that we can leave this place. Can you imagine what it will be like once William le Rous gets here with his followers?"

"The king won't care. He rides into the city through the great western gate near the second castle and then follows Mikkil Gata to the bridge by the docks."

They turned left, and Roger noted with relief that the streets widened and smelled better. Not long afterwards, they reached the massive shell of Everwic Cathedral, with many industrious hands working to rebuild it.

Simon pointed ahead at a large gate to the left. "That is Galmanlith, Everwic's second great gate after Micklelith. The Benedictines of Saint Olaf hold a weekly market here."

"You mentioned that they adorn the gates of Micklelith and Galmanlith as a warning sometimes – what with?"

"The heads of rebels and traitors. Right, would you like to go and eat something? Or should we keep an eye out for your friend?"

Roger gazed at the sky from which a few snowflakes flurried down on them. "It will take him a good six hours from Topeclive to Everwic, perhaps more, depending on what state the roads are in. I don't think he'll get here before early afternoon."

"Then we still have a little time. Follow me!"

Chapter 37

They headed for the nearest tavern, led their horses into the stable and entered the ale house. A warm mixture of food, beer and smoke wafted towards them. Some of the patrons eyed them with a wary look then quickly lost interest and turned back to their meal.

The two sat down at a free table and ordered two cups of wine and two plates of cabbage soup from one of the maids.

Roger glanced around while fidgeting with his signet ring. "What if Richard doesn't come?"

"Why shouldn't he? You agreed to meet up with him, didn't you?"

"I fear for him. Those mercenaries knew that we left the manor together. They threatened to harm him. Hugues de Borre probably sent a scout after us to find out where we are hiding. Somehow, he found out when I would be in Everwic. Surely, he also knows that I want to meet Richard here. What if he has him waylaid as well? Richard is far too young to defend himself against such ruffians."

"You're worrying too much. Do you really think William de Perci will let his youngest son ride to Everwic alone?"

"The two mercenaries might be lying in wait for him."

"There are many youths moving in and around Everwic. How would those scoundrels know it's him, of all people?"

"They found me."

"Forgive me for saying this, but your hair and scar are quite noticeable."

"Just like a red-haired boy."

"Nothing will happen to him. The mercenaries were only after you. They're not going to take on work that they are not being paid for. Most likely, they don't even know that Richard is coming to Everwic, let alone when and where he will ride into town."

"Hugues de Borre will have sent someone to spy on him too, for sure."

Roger let go of the signet ring and clenched his fists. If only he could see Richard unharmed again soon! He would never forgive himself if he were responsible for something happening to his friend. But one thing was certain: he was not going to let this go unpunished. Back in Wilburgfos, he would confront Hugues de Borre, and his father.

"Now, eat something first, and then we'll ride to the cathedral to look for Richard. He will surely arrive there this afternoon as agreed."

Lost in thought, Roger sank his spoon into the soup. He was indeed hungry, even if he had every reason to be worried after the incident with the mercenaries. But what could possibly happen? The deputy had banned the two scoundrels from the city for a week. So, he would be safe from them here, and by the time they were allowed back in the city, he would hopefully have found out everything he wanted to know and would be well on his way back home. The only thing left then would be to pray that they wouldn't ambush him on the way. After all, they knew in which direction he would be riding.

"Look at me!" commanded a man who appeared with a companion at their table, wearing a finely woven dark blue tunic and carrying a sword. He took Roger's chin in his hand, inspected the right side of his face and nodded to the other man. "Gilbert FitzOsbern? My lord is looking for you. He would like to ask you some questions."

"You must be mistaken, munsire," Simon started, but Roger gestured inconspicuously for him to stop talking.

"I don't think so," said the man in the blue tunic. "A light blonde, long-haired lout with a scar across his entire right cheek. The description fits pretty well, doesn't it?"

"And pray, who are you, munsire?" asked Roger.

"I am Nicholas Beaumont. If you would care to follow me? The comte does not like to be kept waiting."

Roger pointed at his bowl. "Can't you see I'm eating?" *Ðunres hamer on þe heafod! A servant of Robert de Monbrai. Why didn't I make sure no one followed us when we fled from the castle? Under no circumstances must I run into the envoy.*

Nicholas glanced around. "This is hardly the place to discuss certain matters."

"I doubt that I can answer the questions of your master," said Roger.

"Leave that decision to my lord," Nicholas said, audibly annoyed. "Now, take your belongings and come along before I have you dragged out of this tavern."

"You have not the slightest reason for this," said Simon, "so save your threats. If you have questions, ask! Otherwise, let us eat in peace."

"Do you actually know to whom you are speaking? I have been sent by the mighty Sire Robert de Monbrai, Comte de Northumberland."

"And I am travelling on behalf of William de Perci, liegeman of the Comte de Cestre, and have already had someone expelled from this town by the reeve for harassing us this morning. So ask or go away."

Pressing his lips together, Nicholas finally sat down at the table. "Very well then," he muttered and leaned forward. "You have insulted and made a fool of the comte because of his intended marriage to the daughter of the Lord of Wilburgfos. How did you come by this knowledge?"

"Are you saying that no one else knows whom the comte intends to marry?" Roger asked. "Is it not customary for a comte's wedding to be announced everywhere?"

"Answer my question, how did you know about it?"

"I found out by accident."

"From whom?"

"From the future bride." Roger shuddered at the thought.

"Why did she tell you?"

"Oh, it just came about. I happened to be at the manor because... she is my betrothed. That's right, I am supposed to marry her, because the eldest son of the Lord of Wilburgfos died and cannot marry... my own sister anymore."

"She's engaged? Her father never mentioned that when the arrangement was made with my lord. Be that as it may, the engagement must be broken off."

"I hardly think my father will agree to it. It's a beneficial union for both of them." Roger struggled to keep a serious face while making these hair-raising claims. "However, if your lord offers my father part of his intended bride's dowry as compensation, perhaps he will reconsider."

Nicholas laughed out and shook his head. "The master of arms will hardly agree to be shared."

Roger gasped. *The master of arms?*

Nicholas rose. "I will report to my lord what you have told me. I am certain that we will come to a satisfying agreement for all. How long are you staying in Everwic?"

"I don't know." Roger looked to Simon for help.

"We're certainly not going to miss the king's visit," Simon said. "That's why your lord is in town too, is it not?"

"He and many others with whom the king is meeting to lay the foundation stone for the new Benedictine monastery." Instead of a bow, Nicholas nodded to take his leave. "Expect me to call on you any time, messires." With that, he turned and left with his companion.

"The master of arms is Isabel's dowry! If I hadn't heard it with my own ears, I would say that this is a bad joke. So, that's why the Comte de Northumberland wants to marry Isabel of all people, even though he could choose a much richer woman. He uses marriage to buy himself an excellent teacher for good warriors, and my father gets a piece of land in return."

"For what does he now, of all times, need a master of arms who has been at your manor for years?"

Roger frowned. "I doubt it is because his own master of arms has died or because he needs more men to defend his castle against the Escoz."

"Certainly not," Simon said. "There must be a different reason."

"I suspect Oswulf doesn't even know about it, otherwise, he would have surely mentioned it to me. But even if he did know, what would that change for him? His liege lord would have a different name, but that's all. He would still be a prisoner in the manor of his ancient foes. And yet, I would rather have him on my side than on the enemy's."

"You can worry about that some other time. We got rid of the mercenaries, but Robert de Monbrai and his henchmen are in the city. They will soon be looking for you again... Gilbert FitzOsbern." Simon grinned as he pronounced the name. "They haven't seen through your lie yet, but it's only a matter of time before someone finds out who you really are."

"Then come! Richard should reach the city soon. We must get hold of him before someone evil does."

Chapter 38

They rode to the cathedral and steered the horses to a sheltered spot between the mighty church building and the north gate, from where they could easily observe the entrance to the city.

For a while, they watched people come and go, some on horseback, others on the trestle of their heavily laden carts, most on foot.

Finally, two riders appeared at the gate with an inquisitive look on their faces.

Roger was not the only one who immediately recognised his young friend, despite the thick cloak and hood pulled over his head. Modig Wiht also let out a satisfied whinny when he spotted his long-lost dark brown stablemate.

Richard turned the horse to the left and spurred it to trot. “Roger, mon ami!” he called with a bright grin. “At last, we meet again!” Under the hood sparkled the familiar child’s eyes that Roger had not seen for weeks.

“Richard! I am pleased to see you whole and hale. I feared for your life, as Hugues de Borre has followed our every step.”

“I know. He sent a warrior to Topeclive, allegedly because they were worried about us in Wilburgfos. After all, we left the manor without saying when we were coming back. He kept following me around, asking me and my father questions about what we thought of William le Rous and how the new king was ruling the country. They'd sent him to sound me out and find out if I had betrayed them!"

Roger glanced at Richard's companion, who was listening to everything with a serious face.

"This is Nigel," said Richard, smiling. "He's been serving my father for longer than I can remember."

"Are you sure that Hugues' warrior didn't follow you?"

"Not many travel this way at this time of year," answered Nigel. "The few people we saw didn't behave in any peculiar way."

"When Hugues' spy found out that we were to meet here," said Richard, "he insisted on accompanying me to Everwic. But my father eventually sent him back to Wilburgfos after the celebrations for the Feast of the Lord had ended."

"He may have indeed returned to Wilburgfos," said Roger, "but Hugues knows that we are here, and perhaps he senses that we are not here merely to ask about Frederic's siblings. Two of his men attacked me this morning, but what's worse is that Robert de Monbrai is already in town. He thinks I'm Gilbert FitzOsbern and that I'm engaged to Isabel, which is how I found out that the master of arms is Isabel's dowry."

Richard and Nigel stared at him as if deliberating whether to believe him or not. Only when Simon explained in more detail what had happened with Robert de Monbrai and Nicholas did the two nod in amazement.

"We need to be careful in everything we do," said Roger. "William le Rous will arrive in Everwic with his retinue on the last day of January."

"But he will not sign the contracts for the lands and the church until Candlemas," said Richard, "and all the noblemen and bishops will hear mass with him in the church of Saint Olaf."

"So, we have two days to find out from them what, if anything, my father and the Comte de Northumberland are intending to do," said Roger.

"Have you found out anything about Frederic's siblings yet?" asked Richard.

"We know where one of the brothers lives, so, we're going to pay him a visit tomorrow morning. Now, we'd better make sure we find a place to sleep for the night. The encounters during the day have been unpleasant enough. I'm not keen on finding out who roams the dark alleys after the sun sets."

Night was already falling when the four of them saw a building near the docks with a warped sign in the shape of a pig. One of the shutters was hanging on a single hinge, past which light and laughter issued forth from within. The pub had certainly seen better days, but dusk gave the young men no time to be picky.

Roger and Simon entered while the other two guarded the horses.

On the benches at one of the four wooden tables, a few grumpy men in scuffed clothes were loudly enjoying a game of dice, oblivious to the newcomers.

Behind the bar stood a greasy chap with dark hair and coarse, thick hands who eyed them from top to bottom.

"Greetings, munsire," said Simon. "We are looking for somewhere to stay for the night. Do you have room for four travellers and their horses?"

Since the addressed continued to stare at them instead of answering, Roger assumed that, like the peasants back home in Wilburgfos, he did not understand the Norman language.

He was about to ask his question in English when the innkeeper opened his lips and showed a set of teeth with several holes gaping back at them.

"Maybe," he rasped. "That'll be a penny for the night."

"A penny for a single night?" asked Roger. "I can get eight cups of the best wine from the Frankish kingdom for that price!"

"Per head." The host smirked.

"Are you serious? And our horses cost double that, don't they? Feohgifre þeof!"

Roger reached for his scramasax, which he would have been only too happy to poke into the innkeeper's paunch.

"Wait!" Simon grabbed Roger's arm until he let go of the sword hilt. The young seneschal leaned forward and beckoned the host to listen closely. "We urgently need a place to sleep in Everwic for a few nights, but I have a question. I'm sure the reeve has already asked you about it when he collects taxes from you, but do you know what strikes me? How is it that your house is so run down when the prices you charge people for a night's stay are so high? Are you perhaps trying to charge us extortionate prices because we are travellers? Or are the craftsmen of Everwic so expensive that even a well-off innkeeper like you cannot afford them? Or perhaps you don't want to spend the money at all, but prefer to keep it for yourself?" Simon let his gaze wander. "You value your ale house, don't you? Wouldn't it be a shame if you were forced to close it? As far as I know, withholding taxes from the king and his vassals does not go down well. Only this morning, we were talking about this with the reeve of Everwic, when he had the records of the last tax collection in front of him."

The host gulped.

"Anyway, it's late, and I'm sure you have more important things to do than chat with us. As for the price mentioned, I would say a penny for a bed and a cup of wine for all of us together is reasonable, don't you agree?"

"Of course." The innkeeper nodded hastily so that his double chin wobbled. "I'll make you a special price because you're such good customers."

"Excellent! Would you then be so kind as to show us where we can stable our horses and where we will be sleeping? We'll remember you for your exemplary hospitality in our evening prayer and ask the Almighty to protect you from harm."

Wiping his throat with his thick hand, the host pulled his lips into a lardy smile. "That is very kind of you. Follow me."

Chapter 39

"We're in luck," Simon said with a grin as they rode into the town centre the next morning on their way to meet Frederic's brother. "The wind is blowing the stench from the tanneries in a different direction today."

They rode into Koppari Gata, where most of Everwic's craftsmen lived. The tables and displays in front of the shops were laden with works of art and utensils for every taste and requirement – wooden bowls and cups in various sizes, garments made of wool, linen or imported silk, drinking horns, needles, combs and sword hilts made of horn and bone, as well as ornately crafted jewellery, brooches and belt buckles.

"It's over there!"

Simon pointed to a small side alley whose name was carved on a weathered, chunky wooden sign.

"Suteres Gata," Roger read with satisfaction, "the street of the shoemakers."

They asked the first person they met for Hubert de Lisieues and were sent to the last house in the alley.

Roger dismounted, handed Richard his reins and knocked on the door. A little boy opened it and looked up at him.

Roger knelt down at his eye level. "Greetings, my boy. My name is Roger. And who are you?"

"Erik."

"It's a pleasure to meet you, Erik. I'm looking for someone. Is your father at home?"

"No."

"Your mother?"

"No."

"You're not home all alone, are you?"

"No."

Roger glanced at his companions, who were grinning as they watched the conversation.

"Who's there?" a hoarse male voice called from behind.

Erik turned round. "Roger."

"Who is that?"

The little one shrugged. "Dunno."

Roger rose and spoke up, "I am Roger, son of Geoffrey de Bernaium, Lord of Wilburgfos and a vassal of Sire William de Perci. I have come looking for the brother of Frederic de Lisieues."

In the back, there was a muffled thud, chair legs crunched across the floor, someone groaned, and finally, an elderly man with a leather apron shuffled to the door and regarded Roger. "Frederic de Lisieues?"

"The seneschal of Wilburgfos, yes. My mother told me he had siblings in Everwic. Are you Hubert de Lisieues?"

The old man peered suspiciously past Roger and eyed Simon. "You are not from here."

"No, we live about two hours on horseback to the southeast of Everwic."

"Why are you looking for Frederic's brother?"

"There was a court hearing—"

"Has Frederic been charged? By whom, and what are they accusing him of?"

“It’s about a misunderstanding. I have come to Everwic to clear it up.”

The old man nodded, silent and with seemingly no intention to continue the chat inside his house.

“Frederic had three siblings in England,” said Roger. “The eldest brother was a warrior under William de Perci. Then there was Hubert, a craftsman, and a sister called Cateline. The reeve’s deputy sent us here, to Hubert. It seems he is the only survivor of the three.”

“Cateline doesn’t live far from here. She works as a weaver for her husband, a rich textile merchant.”

“So, you see at least your sister regularly?”

“Sometimes.” The old man sighed. “If Frederic had been able to find work in Everwic, I doubt he would have left us. He desperately needed something to do. The separation from his wife caused him a lot of trouble.”

The old man bowed his head, lost in his thoughts.

“I have something important to tell you about Frederic, Hubert,” Roger said softly.

The old man looked up. “You’re bringing bad news, aren’t you?”

“Would you mind if we go inside for a moment? Then I will tell you everything I know.”

After briefly hesitating, Hubert waved him in and closed the door behind him.

Roger entered the workroom.

A fire crackled in the fireplace, its warmth flowing towards him. Only now did he notice how clammy his fingers were as he moved gratefully towards the fire.

On a stool lay a pile of small, oval animal skins, all about a foot long. Six pairs of finished shoes were lined up against the wall. On the worktable was a half-finished single piece that the shoemaker had probably just been working on. The needle was still stuck in the bead of the sole and upper leather.

"So, this is what a cordewaner's workshop looks like," Roger murmured.

The old man shuffled to his worktable. "Before I came to Everwic, I was a saddler for King William's vassals. Over time, I found that the wealthy people of the town preferred to buy high-quality leather goods for themselves rather than for their horses. The barons, rich merchants and traders in particular increasingly asked for better and more durable footwear. Those over there," he pointed at the stool with the little leather pieces, "are cordovan, a select horse leather that lasts long and repels water well."

He sat down with a groan and resumed his work. "This is one of five pairs of cordovan shoes that the king has requested. His father would never have spent so much money on shoes." He sighed. "Times change."

"Frederic would have been proud of you, I'm sure."

"Would? Has something happened to him?"

"He died in my arms during a court hearing. Our priest told me that the Almighty has finally redeemed Frederic from his earthly sins and guilt. Do you know what he means by that?"

Pensively, Hubert stroked the leather of the half-finished shoe.

Roger rubbed his tunic. Surely the old man wouldn't sink into silence now and just get on with his work? "The priest alluded that Frederic preferred the company of m—"

"Frederic always dreamt of the proud heroes from the sagas of our childhood – Alexander, Arthur, Roland," Hubert said, seemingly to himself. "While we adolescent squires relished in discussing the merits of women, he was only ever thinking of his heroes, always evading our questions about women. Once, he got beaten up because he had tried to get close to another youth. Father eventually married him off to a bowmaker's daughter, but the marriage didn't last long. In the end, they both affirmed that the marriage was never consummated. The fact that his wife never had a child was pretty good evidence to support the claim, but there may have been other things. Whatever the case, the then Bishop of Lisieues dissolved the marriage after three years. He ordered Frederic to repent for his behaviour in order to save his soul from the torments of hell. When the Council of Lillebonne, which included the bishop, decided that Duke William should seize the English crown, Frederic received a commission from the bishop. As atonement, he was to accompany the duke to England and there to fulfil his duties for his country, which his nature denied him to do in other ways."

So, it is indeed true. "Frederic was a good man and a loyal and dutiful seneschal."

"Yes, I expect he was. But you certainly did not come here at this time of year to tell me that my brother is dead. What is the real reason for your journey?"

"My father believes that I am Frederic's son and that the latter's death was a divine judgement confirming my lineage. This means I will lose my inheritance and have to leave the manor unless I can prove my father wrong."

"I would gladly help you and swear before your father that you are certainly not Frederic's son. But I cannot possibly leave my shop behind for the time being." He pointed at the shoe in front. "The king will want to collect his goods soon."

"Would you confirm by oath a letter with your words before a scribe by swearing on the Bible?"

"I could do that if you could find a cleric to draw up such a document."

"I will do that and then return to you. I am much obliged to you, Hubert, and I apologize for having come with bad news. I'm so sorry for the loss of your brother. My prayers are with you and Frederic."

Roger left the workshop and returned to his friends.

"Well?" asked Richard.

"I need to find a scribe to corroborate Hubert's testimony."

"That shouldn't be too difficult," said Simon. "Any priest can write, and there's a church on every corner in Everwic."

They asked someone for the three nearest churches and then split up. Roger headed for the church in the immediate vicinity, Richard and Nigel rode southwest and Simon north-east.

The priests in the Church of All Saints gasped when Roger approached them with his request, so he soon found himself back outside the church.

To pass the time, he rode along Koppari Gata and looked at the craftsmen's displays. His friends would have to come by this way on their return, so they couldn't possibly miss each other.

He had almost reached the end of the road when he saw two horsemen turn into Koppari Gata from the big street leading from the castle to the town centre.

Nicholas and his companion!

A quick glance confirmed that there was nowhere to hide, but that would probably have aroused Nicholas' suspicion all the more. So, Roger took a deep breath, straightened up in his saddle and tried to look as confident and self-assured as possible, despite his hammering heart.

"I bid you a very good morning, Gilbert FitzOsbern," said Nicholas, smiling.

"How small the great city of Everwic is that we should meet again so unexpectedly."

"It almost sounds as if you are not pleased to see us."

"Oh no, not at all. With so many strangers around me, I'm grateful for every familiar face. Back in Wil... Scornesbi, everyone knows everyone, of course, so I'm not used to so many strangers around me." *Eala!*

Nicholas' eyebrows twitched, then he nodded. "Indeed, in such a throng of people, you never know whom you can trust and whom you can't."

If only Richard or Simon would come back!

"Anyway, I was just looking for you," Nicholas continued. "My lord wishes to make a proposal to you concerning the dissolution of your engagement and a suitable compensation. I am to lead you to him."

"Oh, I... this is a bad time because I'm still waiting for my friends. We were supposed to meet here."

"That's right, you had a companion when we last met. I'm sure my lord won't mind if you bring your friends along for a chat. He likes to have guests."

"That's very generous of your master, but we still have a few errands to run."

"We might be able to help you."

"No, thank you, that won't be necessary. It's... something completely trivial. Nothing you should waste your valuable time on."

"When are you expecting your friends?"

"Any time, really." *I hope. Where are they, par Deu?*

"Very well, then do what you have to do and come to the castle gate at Sext. I will meet you there and take you to Sire Robert."

"That won't be possible. I mean, I don't know if we will have completed all our tasks by then. Besides, we wanted to look around Everwic before travelling back."

"I thought you were staying until the king came here."

"Indeed, we are, but that day is coming soon."

"I doubt that there is anything among your duties that cannot wait until after noon. So, I'll see you at the castle for Sext."

Đunres hamer on þe heafod! Stubborn as a mule, that man! "Everything concerning the engagement, you must discuss with my father. After all, *he* makes the final decision. Why don't you give me a letter for him? I will give it to him when I return to Scornesbi."

"Sire Robert would like to meet you personally to find out which offer would be best for you."

More likely to see how much he has to spend to buy my sister and the master of arms. "I am deeply honoured by your lord's attention, munsire, but I think you had best speak to my father instead."

Nicholas pinched his lips together and took a deep breath. "Very well then, if you insist. I will tell Sire Robert of your... thoughts and then accompany you on your way back to Scornesbi with a letter from him."

Roger suppressed a scream. This man was worse than a rabid dog that sinks its teeth into your leg and won't let go. It might be better to follow him to the castle after all. The envoy that Roger had seen with the comte in the castle bailey seemed to have been in a hurry. Perhaps he was miles away and there was no more chance of bumping into him, in which case another meeting with Robert de Monbrai could do no harm, could it? "I'd rather not demand this of you. The path leads through woods that are notorious for their waylayers and wild animals."

Nicholas raised an eyebrow. "In case it slipped your mind, let me remind you that I survived travelling from Bebbanburh to Everwic. I should be able to handle a few hours' ride to a nearby village, don't you think?"

"Oh yes, of course. Forgive me if I sounded as if I doubted you. Coming to think of it, I actually like your first suggestion better after all. We should settle the whole matter right here on the spot. Expect me at the castle gate at Sext."

Nicholas smiled. "I knew we would come to an agreement." He rode off with his companion and turned right at the end of Koppari Gata towards the town centre.

Groaning, Roger wiped his sweaty palms on his breeches. What had he got himself into? In a few hours, he would be entering the lion's den under a false name. If only he had known beforehand whom the envoy was talking to in the bailey! Could he persuade Simon to come along to save him from further blunders?

At the end of the street, Richard and Nigel turned the corner.

Richard frowned as they approached. "You look worried, Roger. Have you not been able to find a priest to write down Hubert's words either?"

"I haven't, but that is not the reason for my concern. I am meeting Robert de Monbrai at the castle at noon. His men have just been here and made me agree to it."

"How did they know you were here?"

Roger paused. "That's a very good question. We didn't tell anyone where we were going, did we? Only the reeve's deputy knew we would be here today."

"Maybe he's ordered someone to watch you, after what happened yesterday."

"Either that or Robert de Monbrai also has someone following me." He looked around casually but did not notice anyone acting in any conspicuous or suspicious way. "In any case, our meeting was certainly no coincidence."

"Now, let's hope that Simon was luckier than we were in finding a priest. Then we can leave again soon."

They were riding back to the craftsmen's quarter when the young seneschal met them. He had indeed found a priest who was willing to help.

Roger told Hubert, and a short time later, they were in the church of Saint Salveour.

The priest wrote Hubert's testimony in neat letters on a sheet of parchment, read it out again and then, after Hubert had sworn on the Bible, sealed the entire document with the clerical seal. With great satisfaction, Roger took the document and stored it in his provisions bag.

In front of Suteres Gata, they took their leave from Hubert and eventually left the craftsmen's quarter.

"We've completed at least this task," said Roger, tapping on his provisions bag with the flat of his hand.

"That just leaves Robert de Monbrai," said Simon, "and whatever we find out from him."

Chapter 40

Roger's heart pounded as he and Simon rode over the stone bridge into the castle for the second time.

I am Gilbert FitzOsbern from Scornesbi. I am engaged to Isabel de Wilburgfos. I hope that this will soon be over and that I will leave the castle alive.

They had not quite reached the gate when Nicholas showed up before them.

"Welcome, Gilbert FitzOsbern. I am glad you and your friend have found the time to honour us with your visit." He beckoned two youths to take the horses. "I'm afraid I must ask you to wait briefly. Sire Robert is dealing with another matter, but I will let him know that you have arrived. There is a kitchen over there where you can warm yourselves and have something hot to drink."

He left them standing and walked towards the steep flight of stairs that led to the high castle.

Roger's belly ached. He probably had the mercenary's punches to thank for that – or was it the prospect that he would soon be climbing this narrow path sixty feet up into an impregnable fortress with a possible traitor inside?

Simon patted him on the shoulder. "You look as if you've seen a ghost. Let us go to that kitchen! Something warm will do us good."

They approached the stone building that Nicholas had indicated.

"Unlike his father," a voice came through the tiny window from which wisps of steam twirled into the cold winter air.

"And his brother," said another voice.

"It seems there are other contenders for a hot beverage." Simon peered through the window.

"He may have given the bishop back his goods and his title, but he is taking advice not from him, but from others," said yet another voice. "For someone who used to be the king's first and foremost counsellor, this is a disgrace."

Turning away from the window, Simon shook his head as Roger reached out for the door and put his finger to his lips.

"The bishop is wise and powerful," said someone, "and he still has many influential friends, not only in England but also in Normandy."

"Bishop Odo," Simon whispered.

"Robert will want to get on well with him," said another. "England is a rich country compared to Normandy, and Robert is as lavish with money as William."

Bishop Odo and Robert Courteheuse. One wants power, the other, his father's kingdom. All of it.

"Indeed, and the land he inherited is no longer like the one ruled by his father."

"He will have to fight for his dominion. His vassals are already at war against each other in order to expand their power."

"They swore an oath of allegiance to Robert when Duke William left Normandy for England."

"He's a weak ruler, unlike his father. He takes advice from the wrong people."

"Even his own brother, Henri, called him a traitor because he had allied himself with the King of the Franks!"

"Then what do you make of the rumours that Henri has allegedly given him quite a substantial sum of money from his inheritance?"

"Verily, I've heard that too. Henri is said to have received the western part of Normandy, just where the Comte de Cestre has lands."

"Robert will take land from men who primarily reside in England and give it to his vassals in Normandy to secure their loyalty. As Duke of Normandy, he can dispose of the land as he pleases."

"It would have been better if King William had not divided his kingdom."

"He did what Norman law requires: inherited land for the eldest son, newly conquered land for the others."

The men suddenly fell silent. Had they noticed that they were being overheard?

Roger held his breath.

Simon beckoned him to follow and sauntered away from the building as if nothing had happened. Roger tried hard to look as careless as possible, although he was expecting the kitchen door to fling open and the men to spot them any time. They would quickly be able to figure out why two men were walking away from the window side of a building without having been inside first. Roger quickened his steps and glanced over his shoulder inconspicuously.

"Did you see who the men were?" he asked Simon when they had reached the huts on the opposite side.

Simon shook his head. "It was too dark. Besides, most of them had their backs to the window."

"Sire Robert is ready to receive you," came Nicholas' loud voice from the side.

Roger startled.

"Excellent," Simon said, as calm and collected as usual. "Then let's not keep him waiting."

They followed Nicholas up the hill to the castle, and with every step, Roger felt more dizzy. At the top, the two-storey wooden building lurked like a multi-eyed monster, waiting to open up its massive entrance and swallow them in one bite. If only he could turn around and ride on out of this castle!

In a huge room with a high ceiling, Robert de Monbrai had made himself comfortable at a table and was cheerfully raising a glass to them that looked splendid, even in his paw. "Gilbert FitzOsbern! It's about time we met again to clear up our little misunderstanding."

I had been longing for it too. Roger breathed in deeply. "I am sure we can reach an agreement quickly, Sire."

A servant brought two more glasses and poured them a dark red liquid. Roger thanked him and sipped from the glass. Despite the cold, he was thirsty and – oh yes, he could do with a sip of wine, and such an excellent one at that.

"So, how much do you want?" the comte asked expectantly.

Roger exchanged a glance with Simon. "I don't know. I hadn't act—"

"Well, I think forty pounds should be enough. When I am back at Bebbanburh, I will send someone to pay you in coins, arms and clothing. Where were you from again?"

"Scornesbi, Sire." Roger pressed his lips together. *Forty pounds for the grumpy old man who wanted to chase me from his manor and marry his stupid son to one of my sisters? Never!* "But it is a rough region, full of robbers, waylayers and thieves.

Send your servant instead to the manor house of William de Perci at Cattune. It is further north than Scornesbi, and the road there is much safer. My father will come with well-armed men to collect your gifts at Cattune."

"After he has dissolved your engagement."

"You have my word on that, as true as my name is Gilbert FitzOsbern." Roger hastily raised his glass to his face to hide a grin that was hard to stifle.

"Very good!" Sire Robert also raised his glass, drank and slammed it back on the table. "If only all matters were as easy to finish as this one!"

"I cannot promise, however, that Sire Geoffrey will no longer desire a union between our two houses. We do not wish to quarrel with our neighbours."

"Don't let this trouble you." Sire Robert waved a hairy paw in the air. "Your father will hardly be able to give him a fief like the one he will receive from me."

Roger's laughter froze. "Indeed, he will not."

He rose and bowed to the comte. "I thank you for receiving us and am happy that we have come to an agreement and can part amicably. Now, if you will excuse us, Sire. We still have other matters to attend to."

Nicholas led them back to the front yard and sent for the horses. "I wish you success for your other duties," he said as his two guests mounted. "Let me know if you need any help. I have a feeling we will meet again several times before the king's arrival. You've noticed yourself how small Everwic is and that you always meet familiar faces in the streets." He smiled, or rather snarled – could he sense that something was wrong?

"I appreciate your generous offer," said Roger. "We will gladly accept it if we consider it necessary. A Deu."

He and Simon trotted off, and only after they had crossed the bridge did they slow down.

"*As true as my name is Gilbert FitzOsbern,*" Simon imitated him theatrically then laughed out loud. "You are either very brave or utterly out of your mind."

"Robert de Monbrai seemed to believe it," Roger said, not without pride. "I'm not so sure about Nicholas, though. We will certainly run into him again. He'll see to that."

It was snowing as they rode the rest of the way to the bridge over the Use, where Richard and Nigel were already waiting for them in snow-covered hooded cloaks. When Roger told them what they had found out at the castle, the two looked at him incredulously.

"A battle for power, influence and land," Nigel said, sighing. "That means whoever wants to hold on to their land in Normandy will support Robert Courteheuse, even if he has sworn allegiance to William le Rous."

"That's high treason against the king," whispered Richard.

"Yes," said Roger, "and my father is using the only weapon he has to finally get the reward he's been waiting for for years: the best master of arms in England in exchange for a greater fiefdom."

"Let us eat something," said Simon, "and then we'll split up and ask around in the streets to see if there's any more evidence of a plot against the king."

Richard frowned. "What are we supposed to ask? We don't even know what exactly they are planning, if anything, and who is involved."

"Something casual," Roger answered. "How satisfied they are with their new king, whether they think he will rule England well, and if they know that Normandy is now under the king's brother and no longer part of one and the same realm."

Richard wrinkled his nose. "Do the people of Everwic even care? They are townsfolk, not landowners, and are far too busy going about their business in Everwic. They hardly care what goes on outside the city walls. Those who live here already have several masters who rule over them anyway: the king, his tenants-in-chief and the bishops, who divide the city among themselves."

"Let us hear it from them before we make a judgement," said Simon. "There are places in Everwic where we are bound to get good answers."

Since Roger and Richard spoke both English and Norman, they took over the questioning at the docks.

Simon rode to the monastery of Saint Olaf, whose inhabitants were most affected by the king's visit and the imminent refounding of the monastery.

Nigel wanted to mingle with the people in the castles and ask around there.

As agreed, the four then met in the late afternoon at an ale house near the cathedral to share what they had found out.

"William le Rous does not exactly have the reputation of being a pious and devout man, quite unlike his father," said Simon. "Still, the monks are pleased that the king wants to lay the foundation stone for a new Benedictine monastery. Whether this can win him the favour of the attending bishops and archbishops remains to be seen."

The hostess brought a large tray with cups of beer and bowls of roasted salmon and steamed wild herbs.

Simon waited patiently until she had served everything and left before continuing. "Many churchmen think that

William le Rous looks more to his money than to God unless he happens to have a reason to fear for his own soul."

"Would the bishops rather have his brother, Robert Courteheuse, as king?" Richard asked.

"At least Robert seems to respect the church more than his brother," replied Simon.

"That may be another reason why Bishop Odo is enraged." Roger speared a piece of crispy fish with his dagger.

"Perhaps this is precisely what drives him to Everwic and the refounding of the monastery." Simon shoved the herbs with the dagger onto a piece of bread and put it in his mouth. "What news have you from the ships?"

Richard groaned. "We chiefly found out that the king very much appreciates good food and drink."

Simon laughed. "At least he can't be accused of treating the merchants badly. What do they say about his brother, Robert, and the situation in Normandy?"

"Robert Courteheuse seems to be trying to win over the Norman barons with feasts and lavish generosity, and many are only too happy to oblige. The merchants are slowly selling more again there, especially expensive goods such as furs, silk and spices."

"Robert will not have money and lands forever to buy the barons' loyalty," said Nigel, "but without their support, he cannot rule as Duke of Normandy."

"Robert will do anything to hold on to Normandy," said Simon, "now that he finally has the country in his hands and can rule over it without his father."

"He will need money at some point to secure his rule the way he's doing it now," said Nigel. "Then, at the latest, he will look to England. Eventually, it will depend on to whom the barons break their oath of allegiance, and to which side the powerful bishops fall."

The four exchanged a worried look. Although it was noisy in the room, with all its guests, for a moment, all the sounds of this world seemed to fall silent.

"Do you think England will be redivided if there is indeed an uprising?" asked Richard.

"If the rebellion is successful, maybe," replied Roger, knowing that Richard had to fear this more than himself. William de Perci would never betray his king. Given the number of fiefdoms he held in England, there was much more at stake for him than for someone like Roger's father. The question was whether Sire Geoffrey would not see a rebellion as a favourable opportunity rather than a threat.

"At least as far as the land that will be left then is concerned." Simon ordered another round of ale for everyone. "Some regions in England are still suffering from the effects of King William's campaigns. A second incursion would render the land there entirely useless and harm the population even more. No vassal would be happy with such a fief."

"What about Henri?" Richard wiped his plate with a piece of bread.

The older ones looked at him, puzzled.

"Oh yes, the third brother," said Roger. "What is Henri going to do while his brothers are fighting over their realms? Stand by idly? Support Robert because he has already been given part of Normandy anyway? Or fight for William le Rous because he was born here, unlike his elder brothers? What if the revolt is successful and the King of England is actually overthrown? Won't Henri then want to become ruler of England himself?"

Simon took a deep breath. "Why don't we take a look at the current King of England tomorrow before there is possibly a new one?"

Chapter 41

The next day, they learned from the castle guard that King William would arrive at noon, and it was accordingly busy at the castle gate. Cart after cart passed by, laden with supplies for the king and his mighty guests. Speaking to anyone in the castle now was impossible. Everyone was busy preparing a reception and feast befitting a king. The courtyard was teeming with people, horses and carts.

So, the four rode to the city's magnificent west gate, through which the king would ride into Everwic. In Mikkil Gata, the street that led from the bridge over the Use to the gate, several hooded figures were shovelling away the snow that feet, hooves and wheels had churned up in some places and pressed firmly to the frozen ground in others. The workers removed bumps and sprinkled slippery surfaces with ashes and pebbles so that the king and his followers could enter the city safely on hoof and foot. From the snow, which piled up in substantial mounds at the edge of the street, a few children formed small balls which they threw at each other, squealing and jeering.

A group of men, who had probably been sent by the reeve, made sure that beggars and similar folk went their way and did not pester the noble guests. Women and children with pitchforks, shovels and wooden buckets collected coarse rubbish from the greenish brown snow along the roadsides and gave the filled vessels to a pair of fellow workers, who emptied the contents onto an ox cart.

There was no wind, and yet the breathtaking smell of this cart with its load of rotting waste and excrement hit Roger and his friends from afar and fused with the smell of the tanneries only one street away into an orgy of olfactory cruelty.

Taking a diversion through the side streets, Roger and the others finally returned onto the main road.

Numerous people were already lining the sides, repeatedly stretching their necks towards the gate and talking eagerly among themselves. Between the houses, more people thronged in the street, and there was a fair-like noise and bustle. Were the people of Everwic indeed looking forward to the king's honouring them with a visit and, therefore, greeting him with due pomp and splendour? Or had the ruler's officials simply done a good job of filling the roadsides with so many people in order to create this very impression?

A group of minstrels in front of the gate warmed up their fiddles, flutes, drums, voices and hands one last time to welcome William le Rous with music and song.

Jugglers and acrobats took advantage of the hustle and bustle to earn a few extra coins with their tricks.

A handful of children, who ran noisily along the prepared path, were chased away by an officious-looking man to make way for the distinguished visitors.

Roger and his friends rode to a spot where they had a good view of the gate and waited.

At last, someone signalled to the musicians. They began to play, and the cheering at the gate swelled. All heads turned towards Micklelith.

After numerous warriors in full armour had ridden through the gate, a standard bearer followed. High up on the flagstaff fluttered the red banner on which two golden lions with blue claws and tongues were depicted – the king's coat of arms.

The first shouts of "Vive le rei!" and "Beo ðu hal, leof cyning!" could be heard as an immaculate white stallion with a flowing mane pushed through the gate behind the standard bearer. In the saddle sat a rider with a wide-brimmed felt hat adorned with three long, iridescent pheasant feathers. The ruddy face beneath was framed by reddish-blonde hair that was unusually long for a Norman ruler and king. A wide purple cloak with white fur trim flowed down from the broad neck over the stocky body, covering the horse's flanks and rump but not the considerable royal belly, which, draped in a red silk tunic, wobbled over the weapons belt in time with the horse's movement. On the outside of the leather glove of the left hand, with which the king graciously waved and accepted the homage of his subjects, large rings set with precious stones almost outsparkled the richly decorated gold brooch of the cloak.

"This is our king?" asked Roger.

"I think we all imagined him slightly different," Simon replied. "At least those who knew his father."

With a frown, Roger watched the king smile and wave to his people with his ringed hands.

"Don't you think he looks somehow strange?" asked Richard.

"What do you mean?" asked Roger.

"Well, his clothes are so... so colourful and the jewellery... and the hair... I don't know."

"A king must dress conspicuously to distinguish himself from his vassals and the common people," said Simon. "The more precious and lavish the clothes and jewellery he wears, the more respect he will entice. Having said that, I agree with you that William le Rous does indeed have a rather peculiar taste."

"I hope he has more reasons for being respected than his bird feathers and the colours of his clothes," muttered Roger as the king slowly passed them by.

Right behind him followed three elderly men whose wide-cut purple cloaks with red silk linings covered most of the bodies of their mounts. A purple silk hood enclosed their faces, which, owing to the frosty weather, were gradually changing from red to a colour more in keeping with the rest of the bishop's dress.

"They all look the same," said Roger.

"It may be easier to tell them apart once they've taken off their travelling clothes," said Simon. "But if I am not mistaken, Odo de Baieus has already made a successful step towards regaining his position."

"What do you mean?"

"Look at the animals – a horse followed by two donkeys. What do you think Geoffroi de Constantia and William of Dunholm are riding, and which mount belongs to the royal uncle?"

"So, the struggle for power has long since begun." Roger gazed after the bishops, while the rest of the entourage, mostly armed and in armour, passed by, amidst ebbing cheers. The minstrels joined the procession, with the jugglers and a large number of the spectators following along the roadsides.

Bored, Roger looked back at the gate and startled.

"Well, look who's coming!"

"Isn't that Walter Fossard?" asked Richard.

The rider must have sensed that four pairs of eyes were watching him, for he glanced to the side and, after a moment's hesitation, steered his horse over to them.

With a loud neigh, Roger's chestnut stallion welcomed this change from standing around.

"We haven't seen you for a long time, Walter."

"These are troubled times, Roger. What are you doing in Everwic?"

Roger and his friends looked at each other uneasily. "We are looking for relatives of the seneschal," he replied, trying not to think of the mercenaries, Nicholas and Robert de Monbrai.

"So, how is life as the future heir of Wilburgfos?" asked Walter.

"It almost sounds as if you envy me," answered Roger.

"My father may own larger lands than yours, but my elder brother is still alive. Your realm is smaller, but at least it is yours for the taking."

"If it weren't for the rumour that I am an illegitimate son of the seneschal."

Walter laughed out loud. "Frederic, your father? That's ridiculous. Everyone knows he prefers men to women."

"What do you mean, everyone knows?"

"Did your father never tell you why Frederic actually came to England? He is far too bad a warrior for a Norman commander to have selected him freely."

"You knew it? And my father too?" If only Roger had had something wooden within reach! He would have loved to smash it to pieces now.

Walter raised his eyebrows. "Yes," he said slowly. "Why don't you ask Frederic himself?"

"Because he's dead."

The experiences in Everwic weighed heavily on Roger. First, the assault in the street, then the findings surrounding Isabel's wedding, the conspiracy talks at the castle, the frightening prospect of what lay ahead.

Roger had stopped counting how often he had turned over on his sleeping place. His companions had long since fallen asleep, but he just couldn't get any rest. Too many images were buzzing around in his head.

He sat up and stared into the darkness. From all sides, he heard the rhythmic breathing of the sleeping people. Someone was snoring. A sleeper was noisily moving. Roger would have loved to wander through the night to distract himself. He could do that at the manor house in Wilburgfos, but not in a town like Everwic, where it was too dangerous to wander the streets at night, especially as he would get lost in the maze of alleys and squares. If one was already mugged in the streets during the day, then there was a reason for the curfew after dark, and Roger felt no desire to try and prove the opposite. He had to get back to Wilburgfos in one piece and in his right mind.

He reached for the parchment he had stowed in his provisions bag – the sealed letter from Hubert de Lisieues as proof that Roger was not Frederic's son. He could also repeat Walter's remark. His father would not dare to doubt his words in public, for Walter's father was an important vassal of Robert de Mortain, brother to Bishop Odo and uncle to the king.

But before Roger could settle this matter, he had to ride to the priory and see Gwennaol.

The memory of her made his heart sink. He had often thought of her during his time in Everwic. He missed her like he had never missed anyone before. When he returned, she would have to tell him everything she knew and explain everything. He prayed it was not too late to bring the disaster at the manor to a halt and reveal the secret of Wilburgfos.

But how would he reach Gwennaol? At the secret hiding place, hoping that Gwennaol had recovered and managed to sneak into the chamber at the usual time for their meetings? She would first need to know that he had returned. But what did he have to force his way through the convent gate if the prioress was still ill? Nothing. He could threaten to send for a doctor to examine the prioress, but where would he get one so quickly? In Wilburgfos, there were only wisewomen who used herbs and incantations. He could claim to report to the Archbishop of Everwic about the doings in the priory that had nothing to do with the Christian faith. But what if Sister Agatha didn't bow to his threats and instead continued to deny him access? She had every right to do so. Roger, on the other hand, had to avoid any further delay, because whoever it was that didn't want him to talk to Gwennaol would also make sure that the third murder finally succeeded after the failed first attempt.

But even if Roger could prevent a third death, Wilburgfos would no longer be the same. As it was, England was on the brink of a war to which Robert Courteheuse was urged on by selfish barons and churchmen. Sire Geoffrey seemed to be conspiring with Robert de Monbrai and his followers against the English king. If the supporters of Robert Courteheuse gained the upper hand, Roger's father would get a greater fief. But what if the rebels were defeated, despite their apparent superiority? Then he would be the son of a traitor! He would lose his heritage, his home, his family, his friends, Gwennaol, everything.

And it would be no different if they won.

Roger groaned. Whatever happened, he was bound to lose. There was only one thing left that was worth fighting for.

Chapter 42

"Were your negotiations successful, Sire?"

"Indeed, my good man," answered Sire Robert, beckoning the envoy to him. "It was a truly successful visit to Everwic in many respects." He held out a sealed document to the messenger. "Take this letter and some goods to Cattune. Two of my men and a laden mule are waiting for you in the courtyard. When you have delivered everything, ride on to Wilburgfos and inform Sire Geoffrey that the wedding can go ahead as intended and that I expect him to fulfil his part of our bargain promptly. If all goes as discussed in Everwic, we shall soon need not only sufficient supplies and arms, but also enough men to wield them skilfully."

The envoy bowed. "I am pleased to hear this, Sire."

The comte clasped his hands behind his square head and contentedly leaned against the back of his magnificent chair. "The King of England will soon have to realise that he is too weak to rule this country. We will defeat him and reunite Normandy and England into a single kingdom as it was under his father."

A servant hurried in. "Sire?"

"What is it?"

"I have news from Nicholas Beaumont, Sire. His scout reported to him after your departure from Everwic. He said that the four young men must have left the city the day after the king's arrival. One of them rode north, the other three left the city through the south gate."

Sire Robert shrugged. "What do I care? Gilbert FitzOsbern was foolish enough to agree to my proposal. I never thought it would be so easy."

"He also said that, while overhearing the youths, the name Gilbert was never mentioned and that the one you spoke to in the castle was always addressed as Roger."

The comte let go of his hands and leaned forward. "What are you saying?"

"He finally watched them talk to quite a few merchants at the harbour. He couldn't overhear everything, but they kept mentioning Normandy and King William le Rous. They also went to the castle and the church."

"Never mind."

Sire Robert waved it off and addressed the envoy. "Then you will ride on your own straight to Wilburgfos and tell Sire Geoffrey that the wedding will take place immediately."

"There is a Roger in Wilburgfos, Sire," said the envoy. "He's the eldest son of the lord of the manor, but he has been away for weeks now."

"What does he look like?"

"Tall, with awfully long, fair hair – and a large scar on his cheek."

"What?" The comte jumped to his feet. "How dare he lie to my face? Pretending to be Gilbert FitzOsbern to enrich himself! When you get to Wilburgfos, tell Sire Geoffrey to find his son. And then bring me this Roger!" He raised his hands and clenched them into fists as if he were crushing a lump of earth in each hand. "I will wring his neck with my own hands."

Part 7

WILBURGFOS, FEBRUARY IN THE YEAR OF OUR LORD 1088

Chapter 43

"He knows more than he admits, but I can only guess what he has found out. He has become more cautious and doesn't tell me everything as freely as he used to."

"He's getting more insolent too. Somehow, he must have discovered that someone helped bring about the illnesses. He even threatened to investigate if anything worse happens in his absence. Anyway, there's no need to worry about that now, as he's left for Everwic."

"What's he doing there?"

"How should *I* know? You're the one at the manor house. Why don't *you* know anything about it?"

"He hasn't been there for weeks."

"But you spoke to him in between!"

"Only briefly, and as I've just told you, he's no longer willing to trust me with everything like he used to."

"He's got friends. Why don't you ask *them*?"

"They don't open their mouths either, presumably because he told them not to talk to anyone about what he was doing."

"All right then. So, we'll just have to wait until he's back."

"What if he doesn't return?"

"Stop talking nonsense! Since the seneschal's death, he has been obsessed with securing his inheritance. Sooner or later, he will return to Wilburgfos. We must be prepared for that. As long as people believe he is responsible for the deaths, it will be easy to put him in even more trouble. Who knows? Perhaps, very soon, the liege lord will be forced to condemn, extradite and execute his own son?"

"That would break his mother's heart."

"Only if she's still alive."

Chapter 44

After bidding farewell to Nigel in Everwic, Roger and Richard parted company with Simon after the bridge over the Deorwente. The young seneschal rode on to Sudtone to give his liege lord the news from Everwic. The two friends continued east and soon saw the familiar outline of the priory and manor of Wilburgfos before them.

Roger sighed at the sight. "There we are."

"You sound worried. Is everything all right?"

Roger smiled wearily. "Not yet. But soon. I hope."

"What are you going to do?"

"I must first go to the priory," Roger replied without taking his eyes off the manor house. "Then I will return to the manor house and fulfil my promise. You ride ahead and let the others know we're back, but be careful whom you talk to, and don't mention anything we have found out. Stay with Joscelin and Drogo until I come."

Richard nodded obediently. "I will. You can rely on me."

"I never doubted that."

"I'M COMING. Leave the door alone, for Heaven's sake!" called a muffled voice as it approached the priory gate on the inside. The door flung open, and a panting nun glared at

Roger. "What could be so urgent that you should pound on our gate as if the Fiend were after you?"

Roger lowered his hand holding the scramasax. "Take me to Gwennaol!"

Confused, the little woman with the angry face glanced at the scramasax and the thick branch Roger held in his right hand. "What do you want from her?"

"Just take me to her. Now!"

"No, I won't."

"Oh yes, you will. No nun, however recalcitrant, will turn me away today and slam the door in my face. You have kept me waiting long enough and taken advantage of my reverence for your piety. I have come to see Gwennaol, and will not leave until I have done so."

The nun wanted to close the gate, but Roger rammed the branch into the gap.

"What are you doing?" the nun shrieked angrily and tried to push the door shut.

"Either you open and let me in, or you take a step back before I throw myself against the door."

"Have you no manners at all? This is a place of worship!"

"Ha!" Roger clenched his fingers around the hilt of the scramasax. "The home of a poisoner, more likely. Or did you not know that one of your fellow sisters brews potions that make you ill? That she is not afraid to poison the Reverend Mother Prioress and even her own granddaughter with them as she sees fit? Did you know that? Or did she not tell you about it?"

The little woman yanked the gate open and glowered up at Roger like an ill-tempered goblin. "How dare you insult us and our convent in this way?"

"Because it's true."

Roger pushed the door and nun aside and strode into the priory. "Enough now. Where's Gwennaol?"

"You have no right to do this. Out, I say, or—"

"Or what? Will you call for the witch that this convent protects?"

The nun opened and closed her mouth like a fish out of water.

Roger looked around. "Don't bother. I'll find her, even if I have to search in every corner of the priory."

Apart from the nun and himself, there was no one else around, neither in the corridors, nor in the convent garden, the yard or the adjoining storerooms. But then Roger remembered that, while riding here, he had heard the bell of the church tower. He had not counted the strokes, but about three hours must have passed since they left Everwic. Roger raised his eyes to the sky. The sun was high above him.

Time for the third hourly prayer of the nuns.

He almost ran over the little woman, who then clung to his heels like a shadow in her efforts to keep up with him. Undeterred, he made his way through the portico, past the convent garden and headed for the heavy wooden doors of the nave.

"You are not allowed in there," the nun gasped at a rather unbecoming pace. "You will disturb the prayers."

"I have a valid reason," Roger said and stomped on.

At the entrance, he stopped and put the scramasax back on his weapon belt.

Breathing heavily, the nun threw herself in front of the doors with her arms outstretched. "May God punish you for your recalcitrance. You are not going in there!"

"Yes, I am. Forgive me, sister!"

He lifted the scolding bundle to the side and tore open the doors.

Twenty nuns simultaneously gasped in shock. Roger's pursuer let out an exasperated sigh.

"Roger," said the prioress, smiling.

"Roger?" Sister Agatha rose with a sour face.

"Roger!" Gwennaol shouted from the back row, jumping from her seat.

He crossed himself before the large wooden cross behind the altar, knelt before the prioress and kissed her pale hand. Her pallid face had dark circles under her eyes. Fortunately, the poison had not been able to harm her friendly gaze, which now rested kindly on him.

"Forgive me, Reverend Mother. I will never ever do this again." He stood up and spread his arms. "Gwennaol!"

She threw herself into them with a broad smile and let Roger lift her up and pull her close.

"What is going on?" asked Sister Agatha.

"You're alive," Roger breathed, burying his nose in her hair. "Are you all right?"

"Yes, I am fine. You were gone so long. I thought I would never see you again."

Roger set her down but held onto her. "I promised you that I would come back. I'll never let you go again."

"We'll see about that," said a voice from where Gwennaol had sat. It belonged to a haggard nun with cold eyes.

"Is that your grandmother?" he asked softly.

"Yes, and I think it's time you knew the truth about me."

An evil premonition gripped Roger like the cold waves that had almost cost him his life as a child in the Fors Bekkr.

The wrinkled lips of Gwennaol's grandmother seemed to hide a triumphant grin.

Gwennaol pulled him towards the doors, past a pair of bright blue eyes that winked at him, the angry face of Sister Agatha, the kind smile of the prioress and finally, the distraught face of the little nun who was presumably desperate to find an explanation of this appearance for Sister Agatha.

The two went into the garden where they would be alone while the nuns continued their prayer. Roger had his arm around Gwennaol, afraid that someone might take her away from him again. When she stopped and turned towards him, he slowly let his arms slide around her and pulled her close. A burning heat rose in him, and if it hadn't been winter, his forehead would have been drenched in beads of sweat in no time. Could he at least snatch a kiss from her? The temptation was too great to resist. He slowly approached her face and could already feel the breath coming from her slightly parted lips. Just a little closer. He closed his eyes and felt something on his lips.

"Wait, Roger," Gwennaol whispered as she gently stopped his mouth with her fingers. "I owe you an explanation. Does the name Alain le Rous mean anything to you?"

"Certainly. He is one of King William's most powerful tenants-in-chief."

"He was commissioned by the king after the campaigns here in the north to build a castle in Hindrelagh to watch over the people who were left and to prove the royal power. That was in the Year of Our Lord 1070. My mother was a girl at the time and was on her way to Hindrelagh with my grandmother. My grandfather had been treacherously killed in a battle against Hereward the rebel, and my grandmother thought it best that she and her daughter take shelter with her half-brother."

"Alain le Rous is your great-uncle?"

"Not everyone knew this. Neither did your father, whose manor the two reached in the autumn of that year. There were still many wounded and sick from the campaigns then, so my grandmother was able to put her healing skills to good use. She offered them in return for food and a place to sleep, and in the end, she and my mother stayed in Wilburgfos for the winter. They wanted to continue their journey in spring when the weather would be better."

"What does that have to do with you?"

"Patience, Roger. You will find out." Gwennaol struggled to smile. "Your mother was pregnant then, and she wasn't well for a long time. My grandmother often took care of her, and my mother also tried to help where she could. Your father was disgruntled about his wife's indisposition and was looking for other ways to satiate his unbridled lust. So, it was rather convenient for him that two women were looking after your mother. He forced himself on them several times in his private chambers when they came to look after your mother, and he also harassed them outside the house at unguarded moments." Gwennaol gulped.

"How could my father do this? They were his guests. As their host, it was his duty to protect them from such assaults."

"My grandmother eventually fled to the priory to be safe from your father's abuse."

"And your mother?"

"She refused to come." Gwennaol wiped a tear away.

"You mean she stayed at the manor of her own free will, even though my father was taking advantage of her?"

Gwennaol sniffed. "She loved the young English master of arms. My grandmother betrothed them to each other before she fled."

"Oswulf was to marry your mother? Then it is true what Picot de Perci told me. But if I remember his words correctly, your mother drowned in the river the following year."

Tears were running down Gwennaol's cheeks. "She didn't simply drown, Roger. She threw herself into the river after she had given birth to me and handed me over to my grandmother. She was so ashamed of carrying Sire Geoffrey's child below her heart when it should have been Oswulf's."

She leaned her head against Roger's chest and sobbed loudly.

He embraced the small, trembling body. "So, that's why I wasn't meant to talk to you. He didn't want anyone to uncover his dirty secret."

Gwennaol dabbed her face with her sleeve. "One day, a messenger arrived from Hindrelagh, enquiring about the whereabouts of the two women whose arrival Alain le Rous was expecting. This is how your father learned who his guests were. By that time, your mother had lost her newborn, and my grandmother had fled to the convent. My mother stayed to help Dame Edeva, who was very poorly, and of course, because she loved Oswulf. Your father promised the messenger he would ensure the sought-after women could continue their journey as soon as they were no longer needed at the manor. But he never did because he was afraid of the powerful Breton vassal finding out what he had done. He had my mother taken to the priory quietly to hide his secret from the world. When he learned that my grandmother had taken the veil and that my mother had drowned herself, he thought he was finally safe. He didn't care in the least that she had given birth to his child beforehand."

His child.

Suddenly, Roger realised who he was holding.

"But that can't be possible. It mustn't be. You said yourself that he didn't know anything about you. If he had never seen you before, how did he know that the girl I approached at the market was his daughter?"

"My grandmother always says that I look very much like my mother and that I remind her of her beloved daughter every day."

Except that your father is a Norman whom she hates with a passion for what he did to her and her daughter. And every day, you remind her of that, every day, as long as you live.

Roger thought of what Adelais had written to him, that Morwenna had not flinched from poisoning her own granddaughter for weeks with a potion, just so Roger could not speak to her. How much hatred did that woman harbour and what else would she be capable of? Would she even go as far as to kill people?

"When your father recognised me, he wanted to make sure that I would not betray his secret either. So, he ordered that I was no longer allowed to leave the priory."

"But he failed." Roger almost smiled, but what price did he himself have to pay? "I'm so sorry for everything my father did to you. If I could, I would make amends, but—"

Gwennaol put her finger on his lips.

"No, it's not your fault, Roger. No one can make up for what happened back then, not even your father. But I am sorry for what has happened at the manor and in Wilburgfos because of the past."

He stroked her hair, distraught that he would never again be as close to her as he had been moments before she started to tell her story. He almost wished he had never known the secret of Wilburgfos. But there was no going back. All was lost.

"I am so ashamed of this horrible revenge and everything it has done to you and your family," said Gwennaol. "I don't deserve your understanding and your trust. I am to blame for it all." She burst into tears again.

"You mustn't say that, Gwennaol."

Roger wrapped his arms around her once more, though less passionately than before. After Adelais and Emma, he had now lost the third woman who meant something to him. Seeing Adelais was a joy every time, but Emma was gone from his life forever, and he could not bear to see Gwennaol again, knowing that she would never be his.

When the gate of the priory closes behind me, I will never see you two again.

But there were still the murders at the manor, and his mother was still in danger too.

"I need to talk to your grandmother, but I'll be back," he said and strode back to the church.

Morwenna's words swirled through his mind as he left the priory. With a bitter taste in his mouth, he gazed back once more at the massive wooden building that he might never enter again.

Gwennaol will think that I lied to her and that I never wanted to return after she had told me everything she knew.

He gulped in an attempt to swallow the moisture that welled in his eyes.

But she doesn't know everything. They betrayed and used her just like me.

The brief pang of sadness gave way to a rising anger at the way Gwennaol, who was least to blame, had been treated. If he wanted to somehow make amends for his father's offences against her and her family, he had to fight for Gwennaol now and make sure that the cruel game with her, with him and with the people of Wilburgfos, came to an end.

His chestnut stallion tossed his head towards the manor and neighed loudly.

Roger felt a twinge in his belly. He untied the stallion and patted him on the neck.

"You've always been a loyal friend to me, Modig," he said, lifting himself into the saddle. "So, let's go and get it over with."

Chapter 45

The few servants who went about their daily work outside stared at Roger with surprise and suspicion as he rode into the yard.

"Isn't that the liege lord's son?" he heard one of the men ask as he dismounted.

"You mean the seneschal's son. I thought Lord Geoffrey had chased him away a long time ago."

"What d'you want here?" called the first. "Go back to hell where you came from!"

"Swiga!" ordered Cenhelm. "Get back to work!"

He hurried to Roger, smiling. "It is good to see you well, munsire. Have you good news?"

Roger inhaled deeply. "We'll soon find out, now that I am back home."

He handed Cenhelm the reins and entered the great hall. The warmth of the fire ate into his skin as if his fingers were being struck by a hammer. After hours in the saddle and in the unheated convent, he was frozen to the bone and had to get used to the warmth in the hall again.

He stretched and loosened his stiff limbs.

"Roger, you're back at last!" cried Isabel, jumping up from the table where she was playing Tric Trac with Richard.

Roger willingly succumbed to her embrace.

"Isabel, dear sister. You've become even more beautiful in my absence," he said and kissed her on her forehead. "How is Mother?"

"She's grieving that you left. Are you staying with us now, or do you need to go away again?"

Roger's heart grew heavy when he saw the worried look on his sister's face. "I'm here for now." Soothingly, he stroked Isabel's hair.

She leaned her head against his chest. "I've missed you. Tankred is already acting as if he were Lord of Wilburgfos."

"Where are all the others?" asked Roger. "It's very quiet everywhere."

"They're out hunting with the hawks," Richard replied from the table.

"Did Oswulf ride along?"

"Of course. He's the one exercising the falcons for hunting, so he knows best how to handle them."

Richard and Roger exchanged a glance. Could his friend sense what was going on inside of him?

He didn't want to worry Richard or jeopardise what he intended to do, so he made every effort not to twirl his tunic or fidget with his signet ring.

"So, the prodigal son is back." Tankred sauntered out of the kitchen and stood wide-legged beside Roger. "I thought you had left the manor for good."

"You know, Tankred, it was a relief not to have to put up with your condescending ways for a while. Still, I'm glad to see you alive after everything that has recently happened at the manor." Roger folded his arms. "It's just a pity that the spirit of Christian charity has yet again passed you by during the Feast of the Lord."

Isabel giggled.

"Silly goose," Tankred grumbled, turning back to Roger. "What are you doing here?"

"Well, in case you've forgotten, I live here, but I also came back to make sure that you are all whole and hale."

"Right," Tankred said, nodding. "You've done that now, so you can go away again."

Roger eyed him grimly.

Already next month, Tankred would be appointed squire and groomed to succeed their father in Wilburgfos. Roger would irrevocably have lost the battle for his inheritance if he could not prove his lineage in time.

He reached for the provisions bag. It rustled. The letter from Hubert was still there.

"As I said, I live here, and I have something to do. You will have to put up with my presence a little longer, whether you like it or not, my dear little brother."

With feigned pity, he patted him on the shoulder.

Screwing up his face, Tankred dodged away from Roger's hand. "Stop it!"

"Since you're working in the kitchen, maybe you could bring us something to eat," said Roger. "Richard and I are hungry from our journey and would like to fortify ourselves."

His brother folded his arms. "Get it yourselves! I'm not your servant."

"Tankred!" called Dame Edeva sternly as she descended the stairs from the private chambers. "You are assigned to the kitchen this week. Please be a good boy and do your duty. After all, you want me to report to your father that you are a dutiful page. You know that only such pages are worthy of advancement to the rank of squire, don't you?"

Tankred muttered something into his downy beard and stomped into the kitchen.

"Hroðgar, min sunu. It is good to see you back!"

Dame Edeva bustled over to Roger in her floor-length dark blue dress and embraced him.

"The joy is all mine, Mother. After what happened here in the last few months, I feared for your life every day and have been praying for your safety."

She stroked his cheek. "You are a good boy, Hroðgar. I did not have a moment's peace while you were away. Drogo told me that you went to Eoforwic with Richard. That is a large and dangerous town."

"We had a reliable guide, who accompanied us well and safely. I found Frederic's brother, Hubert. He swore on the Bible and gave me a sealed letter, witnessed and signed by a priest, with his testimony."

Dame Edeva's face lit up. "Đu sægest wilspell, Hroðgar! I hope this will bring your father to his senses."

Roger forced a smile. *This message, maybe, but certainly not what else I have for him.*

The hunting party returned from their excursion shortly before nightfall. The hawks had done well, and Sire Geoffrey's companions contentedly held out to the servants converging in the yard quite a few fowl for tonight's dinner.

Joscelin and Drogo raised their hands in greeting when they spotted Roger and Richard waiting at the edge of the yard.

Richard waved back with a smile, while Roger regarded his friends with mixed feelings. Yes, he was happy to see them safe and sound, but how long would this happiness last? Tomorrow, everything could, no, would change. One way or another.

As his friends approached him and Richard, Roger noticed that Oswulf was watching him. In the pale light, however, it was impossible to see what expression was hidden behind the large moustache and under the hair dishevelled by the hunt.

Tomorrow.

Chapter 46

The next morning, the patchy sky seemed undecided as to whether it would remain sunny or cloudy. The mild weather slowly melted the snow, leaving countless puddles and slippery patches on the uneven, hard ground.

On an ordinary day, Roger would have first gone to the armoury with his friends to get the equipment and then joined them on the battleground. Today, however, was no ordinary day, so Roger dedicated more time than usual to prepare and examine carefully that his weapons were in perfect condition – clean, ready for use, without cracks, breaks or other flaws. He put on the weapon belt and ran his hand over its smooth leather towards the decorated scabbard of the scramasax. His fingers wandered along the carved patterns. If necessary, the short sword would prove to be of better service to him today than to its previous owner. God willing.

In his mind, he turned over the last two years of his life, during which his fate had changed so much.

Fate? Perhaps. Coincidence? No. He knew now that every event after William's death, however small, had been a step that would inevitably lead him into a trap: the befriending by Oswulf, the meeting with Gwennaol, the hints of secrets and confidants, the sudden rumour of his lineage, Gwennaol's growing trust...

Roger gulped. Were her feelings really part of this cruel game too?

Finally, the deaths of Frederic and Leofric. Only Emma's death was the outlier. Here, the trap had failed, but Roger was already in too deep for him to escape.

He looked at the signet ring. Today, the circle would close and prove the eternal connection between people and what happened around them. Justice, the fight against falsehood and injustice, would also be put to the test today, yet whether it would triumph in the end was in the hands of God. And last but not least, strength, courage and power were what mattered today. Did Roger have all the qualities that the tree, axe and sword united on the ring? If not, he would be lost. But at least he would have tried.

He stacked the weapons on the shield and carried them outside.

The others were already on the battleground. Roger laid his equipment on the edge and lined up between Richard and Joscelin.

On the other side, Oswulf was pacing up and down with his hands behind his back. When everyone had taken their place, he strode on a little longer, as he always did when he thought that his pupils had not arrived quickly and orderly enough for the upcoming exercise session.

Roger's heart was hammering.

Oswulf turned to his pupils and eyed them with his head half raised. Sauntering into the middle of the battleground, he straightened up and let his gaze wander over those present until it lingered on Richard and Roger.

"I see the year brings us not only longer days but also more pupils."

"Pupils who have learned a lot while they were away from Wilburgfos," said Roger.

His heart was pounding so hard that he feared the others could hear it.

"Every teacher appreciates when their pupils strive for knowledge outside their lessons."

"It depends on what kind of knowledge."

"Does it? And what kind of knowledge did my pupils thirst for?"

"They had heard about a secret that they felt an urge to uncover."

"Well? Did they succeed?"

"Indeed. But there are still a few gaps that I'm think you can fill."

"Why me?"

"Morwenna told me to speak to you. It seems you know a few things about the recent deaths in Wilburgfos."

"Maybe. Maybe not."

"Then let's find out – now." Roger turned around. There was no going back now.

"What are you doing, Roger?" asked Richard.

Roger picked up his sword and shield – but not those for practice this time – and pushed through between Richard and Joscelin until he stood three steps in front of the other pupils.

Oswulf eyed him curiously. "You want to fight?"

"As you can see, I'm ready."

"Against me?"

"Looks like it."

"Are you sure you know what you are doing?"

"Absolutely." Roger clutched the hilt of the sword.

"What if you lose?"

Roger felt the blood rush through his veins. "I won't."

His voice sounded firm, but he was quivering with anxious impatience inside. He wanted to get on with it, and Oswulf knew it. The master of arms would deliberately delay the fight as long as possible to provoke his agitated pupil into a rash, ill-considered action. Roger knew only too well how this would end. He had to control himself, otherwise, he had already lost the fight before it had even begun.

"You're very sure of yourself."

"I know what I'm fighting for."

"Oh! You know what you are fighting for. Then let's hear your noble goals."

Roger was seething and inhaled so deeply that the fabric of his tunic became too tight for him to continue the breath.

Oswulf's eyes glinted in the early morning sun, as they had done during Frederic's trial, Roger realised.

"I want to know who killed Frederic, Father Leofric and Emma. And who Gwennaol really is."

"What does any of that have to do with me?"

"You know why they had to die, but you're afraid that I might find out and that soon, the whole manor will know."

Silence fell over the yard.

"You seem to have forgotten, in your absence, how to properly assess your abilities, Roger." The master of arms fetched a sword and shield and resumed his place. "Let's see what you remember from practice lessons."

Roger leapt forward and stabbed straight ahead. Oswulf intercepted the thrust with his shield and stepped to the side.

"Gwennaol told me everything." Roger's gaze followed the master of arms, who prowled around him.

"That was her task, and she accomplished it well."

"I also talked to Morwenna."

"Talking will get you nowhere here." Oswulf charged forward with his sword, aiming for Roger's head.

Roger jerked his shield up. Oswulf's sword crashed onto the thick wood. Roger slashed at the unprotected side of his opponent. The master of arms pulled his shield down. A kick against it sent Oswulf staggering a step backwards, but he rebalanced and crept back around Roger at a distance.

Roger blew a strand of hair from his face. "After William's death, I actually thought you were trying to help me, that you were supporting me against my father."

"You've always been gullible." Oswulf's gaze darkened. "And clearly the easier prey compared to your brother. His early death was a godsend."

"I was only a means to an end for you. Just like Gwennaol."

Roger swung his sword at Oswulf's thigh but hit wood instead.

The master of arms thrust the shield, crashing violently against Roger's, then tried to strike Roger's face with the pommel of the sword, but Roger ducked. He gave Oswulf a shove with the shield and aimed for his neck. The sword crashed on the metal shield boss. Oswulf yanked the shield outwards, wrenching Roger's sword arm with it. Roger dodged Oswulf's sword to the side, rolled on the ground and sprang up again.

Oswulf regarded him, snorting. "You look like a pig, and you fight like a pig."

Roger felt the freezing cold slush soak into his breeches and was glad that the coarse woollen fabric of his tunic would keep the thawed snow away from his skin, at least, for a while. "There's no furtiveness in my fighting, unlike in yours. Now, who's the pig?" His heart raced, and his lungs burned from the cold air he sucked in hastily. "You and Morwenna wanted to avenge Solen. You wanted to retaliate against my father for raping and fathering a child with her – Morwenna's daughter and your betrothed – and for making her drown herself in the river because of it. You used me and Gwennaol to secretly carry out your vile revenge."

Oswulf bowed curtly. "It was a pleasure indeed to help Morwenna punish Solen's enemies."

"Everyone at the manor trusted you! You were able to move freely without arousing the suspicion of the inhabitants. Morwenna hated my father, just as you do. That made you just the right person for her to put both of your intentions into action."

"Do I hear envy in your words? Or is it admiration for someone who finally gets what they've been working towards for a long time? Not like you."

Grunting, Roger went after Oswulf again. With loud roars and groans, the two moved across the yard. Out of the corner of his eye, Roger saw that Oswulf was driving him towards the palisade fence, where he would be able to corner him at the end of the great hall.

"Why didn't you just kill my father?" asked Roger breathlessly, as the fight paused again momentarily. "Why did three innocent people have to die?"

"Innocent?" Oswulf snorted and pulled his bushy eyebrows down so low they almost covered his eyes. "They all should have stood by Solen. Instead, they helped your father drive her to her death. Frederic, who happened to observe an assault but preferred to remain silent for fear of his office. Leofric, a man of the church, who did not help Solen after your father's attacks and even accused her of enticing men by her dress and manner, including him, that godless whoreson. Solen was just about able to save herself from his greedy fingers. And finally, Lady Edeva, who witnessed the crime several times but condoned her husband's behaviour. They all deserved to suffer and die as long and painfully as Solen and her mother did. Yes, I killed them. I spread the rumour that you were the son of the seneschal, so that he would be summoned to court and I could settle old scores with him in a divine judgement. I poisoned the wine and food for Father Leofric. Emma helped me well in all this – and more."

Roger closed his eyes for a moment, and Emma's freckled face appeared in his mind. *Poor Emma. You had to die because you wanted to help.* He squeezed his eyelids together to force back the tears.

The master of arms raised the sword and shield. "Frederic and Leofric were only the beginning. Your mother would not have escaped me a second time. I would have got you all eventually. All you cursed Normans."

Roger brought his shield and sword into position. His breeches were drenched with mud, making his thighs clammy. He shook his legs to warm up. "What about me, the son of an Englishwoman? Would you have killed me too?"

Oswulf pursed his lips. "Not immediately. Your father would have regretted the loss of your little brother much more."

"You couldn't care less about the lives of others."

"Neither can your father."

The remark hurt because Roger knew it was true. "You have used both Gwennaol and me as pawns in your diabolical game, but you're going to lose."

"I don't see why. Your brother's death has made it even easier for us. You're young and gullible. A hotspur easily led by words. You made it possible for us to get our revenge after all these years. I knew you wouldn't be able to resist Gwennaol. She's pretty, of course you like her. Your father fell for her mother's charms just as quickly. How unfortunate that she is your half-sister."

Roger had by now regained a good distance from the palisade, but even after several advances, he could not get past Oswulf and into a position of dominance.

"Your father wouldn't have been able to resist Gwennaol either, for she is as beautiful as her mother. But the bait was meant for you. I made sure that you would meet Gwennaol and that her reticence would arouse your ambition. You were to indulge your Norman vanity every time you found out a little more, so that you would fall further into the trap. And how wonderfully you were taken in by her! Now, the poor little fish is wriggling on the hook, and I can slowly pull it out of the water until it runs out of air."

Oswulf lunged forward, pushed the shield between himself and Roger and swung his sword below his waist. Roger stepped to the side to deflect the blow when a sharp pain shot through his lower right leg. Gritting his teeth, he smashed the elbow of his sword arm into Oswulf's face, rammed the sword pommel into his chin and limped backwards a few steps as fast as he could. He didn't want to believe his eyes, but there was blood flowing from his calf over the dirty breeches.

Oswulf moved his lower jaw from side to side and pointed his bloody sword at Roger's knee.

"Looks like your time has come a little earlier than both of us expected. Too bad. I thought you would have liked to see me send your mother and the rest of your loathsome family to their graves."

"You will never be able to have your full revenge," Roger said, panting. "You are part of Isabel's dowry and will go north with her to teach men who will fight for the Duke of Normandy."

"That won't be any time soon." Oswulf calmly regarded the blood on the edge of his sword. "I still have enough time left to finish everything I need to do at this manor."

"I won't give you that time." Roger stood tall. He was dirty and bruised, his limbs stiffening in the damp clothes, and he was painfully aware that his fighting ability had deteriorated markedly after weeks without practice. "Your fate, and mine, will be decided today."

The master of arms sneered. "There's nothing left for you to do, Roger. Why don't you just give up?"

"Yes, there is. There's one last thing."

"And what would that be?"

"I'm going to marry Gwennaol."

"You want to marry her?" Oswulf shook with laughter.

"What are you laughing at?"

Roger took a few steps in his direction. He had to finish the fight quickly before the wound on his leg weakened him too much.

Oswulf's expression darkened abruptly. "She's a liege lord's bastard – the daughter of your father. You can never marry her, for she is your half-sister."

"Now, you are the one who is very sure of himself."

Oswulf's moustache twitched sideways. "If it hadn't been for her, her mother would still be alive. Solen didn't want to kill the bastard, but she also didn't want to be reminded of her tormentor all her life." He lunged forward, whirling the sword around with a swiftness that made it hard for Roger to withstand the onslaught.

Dear God, give me strength! Frederic, Leofric and Emma's deaths shall not go unpunished.

The hammering of the swords on metal and wood echoed in his ears. His left hand had long since ceased to consciously wield the blade, while the incoming blows and thrusts left, right, up, down, were pounding into him.

What will become of Mother and Isabel if Oswulf—

The whirring of a metal blade spinning around another blade cut off Roger's thoughts. Metal grinded over metal. His sword flew into the mud. Oswulf shoved the shield against his stunned opponent. Roger stumbled backwards. Oswulf thrust with his sword. Roger sucked in the air, but all he felt was a dull thud on the shield he had brought before him at the last moment.

Oswulf gasped for air. His hair stuck to his skin in dark strands.

Breathing heavily, Roger struggled to speak. "Morwenna said Gwennaol was marked forever. Just like you." He let the words sink into Oswulf's head while catching his breath and summoning his last strength. "What does she mean by that?"

"What's she supposed to mean? Gwennaol is a bastard of your father."

"But what does that have to do with you?"

"What do I know? You're talking too much." Oswulf approached with his sword low.

The scramasax. "Do you know what I think?" asked Roger as he cautiously drew his short sword from its leather sheath behind the shield.

"Stop thinking and start praying, for your last hour has come." Oswulf took a swing.

Roger braced his arm into the shield. "Gwennaol is not actually my father's daughter."

Oswulf's sword crashed onto the shield. "Whose daughter is she supposed to be then?" He aimed at Roger's left side, which was now without the protection of a sword.

"Yours."

For a tiny moment, Oswulf froze.

Roger threw himself forward with all his weight. The shields smashed into each other. Oswulf was thrown back, the sword falling from his hand. Roger swung the shield over his opposite shoulder and yanked it to the other side, striking Oswulf's head. The master of arms stumbled and fell backwards onto the churned, muddy ground. Roger threw the shield aside. He lunged at Oswulf, knelt on his arms and put the scramasax to his throat.

"My daughter?" Oswulf gasped. "Oh yes, you would like that, wouldn't you? But she'll never be yours. She's your half-sister – a liege lord's bastard."

The hairs of his moustache trembled in the air he exhaled in violent bursts. On the right side of his face, the bony areas on his cheek and above his eye had swollen into bluish purple bulges. Where the thick hairs of his eyebrows or moustache did not cover the skin, Roger's shield had left deep, bleeding furrows.

Roger pressed his lower legs firmly on Oswulf's arms. This was the man he had once trusted. The one who wanted to kill his whole family out of bottomless hatred for a crime long past and without concern for innocents. He had sacrificed everything for this revenge, even his own daughter.

"She's not my sister," said Roger, slashing Oswulf's right sleeve with his scramasax. "Nor is she a liege lord's bastard."

"What are you doing?"

Roger unfolded the strips of fabric. A brown birthmark about the size of a coin appeared. "You're marked forever," he muttered. "So, it is true. She is, in fact, your daughter."

"Đu eart unwita! Morwenna would have known that."

Roger sat up straight, taking a deep breath. "She did."

"What?"

"She knew all along. Many years ago, she treated an injury that you had received in a fight, and in doing so, spotted your birthmark. Hence, you and Gwennaol, your daughter, are both marked forever."

Oswulf shook his head vigorously. "If it were so, Morwenna would have told me the truth long ago."

"Then she wouldn't have got her revenge on everyone she held responsible for her daughter's death. As a healer, she was forbidden to kill, so she needed you. She deceived everyone. Even you, who were so sure of yourself. You are the pinnacle of Morwenna's ambitions. She probably assumed I wouldn't survive the fight against you today. She would have finally killed one of my father's family and at the same time, the unwanted visitor of her granddaughter. You would have been the winner of that fight, but you would have lost your entire battle because you are the one the judges would have punished for killing Frederic and Leofric. Unless I had killed you in battle first. Whichever way you look at it, Morwenna won. Without ever having to leave the priory for it, she got her revenge on the Normans for the death of her daughter as well as her revenge on the English for the death of her husband."

Chapter 47

The eyes of the master of arms were directed at Roger, but they seemed to stare right through him. His mouth was open, without any movement. Between his thighs, Roger noticed that Oswulf's chest had stopped moving. For a moment, he feared that the master of arms had died on him as suddenly as Frederic had in the courtroom. But then a whisper made its way through the thick moustache.

"No, it can't be." Oswulf's moss-green eyes moistened. "She is the daughter of your father, a Norman baron. I must avenge Solen for what he did to her. I must take his family from him, as he took mine from me, my beloved wife, my village, my land, my king, my pride and my honour. That cursed Norman and his cursed followers. Hi sculon gan libbende on helle. He has taken everything from me. Everything I ever cared about." He screwed up his face, pulled his head towards his chest and sobbed, twitching. "Even my child."

Roger marvelled at Oswulf. For the first time ever in his life, he saw the master of arms crying – the one who usually strode over the yard in such an authoritarian manner. Who demanded everything from his pupils, and woe betide them if they did not do their best! The man with the inscrutable face now gave in to the tears he must have hidden beneath his rough shell all these years.

"He's crying," someone murmured.

Many curious and stunned onlookers surrounded the two fighters. Not only the squires from weapons practice looked at them with astonished faces, but Sire Geoffrey and Dame Edeva were also standing there with Tankred and Isabel, and even Hugues de Borre was now approaching with four men.

The master of arms seemed oblivious to all this and instead continued to struggle with his anger and grief.

Roger took the short sword away from Oswulf's throat but continued to kneel on his arms. Maybe the master of arms just pretended to be wailing? He had to be on his guard. After all, an injured wild animal was more dangerous and unpredictable than an unwounded one.

Roger's gaze wandered to his parents.

Dame Edeva wrung her hands. "Eala, Hroðgar! What have you done?"

Sire Geoffrey stood there, with his fists clenched and his nostrils flaring. His eyes were glittering venomously, but they were not directed at Roger; they were aimed at Oswulf.

"Did you hear everything, Sire?" asked Joscelin.

The liege lord nodded, lips pressed together.

Drogo and Richard collected the two swords and Roger's shield. Then they pulled the shield off Oswulf's left arm and put it with the other weapons, at a safe distance from the two fighters.

"He killed them all," whispered someone from the crowd.

"Who?" asked another. "The master of arms?"

"What?"

"I thought it was the son of the liege lord."

"You mean the son of the seneschal."

"The seneschal had a son?"

"Have you no work to do?" Sire Geoffrey snapped at the servants. Then he nodded to his son and said, almost graciously, "You can get up now, Roger. My men will take care of the traitor."

Roger reattached the short sword to his weapon belt and supported himself with his hands to stand up.

Joscelin and Drogo reached under his arms as he groaned and helped him to his feet. The wound on his right calf was burning, though his whole body felt clammy. Supported by both friends, Roger hobbled over to Isabel and Lady Edeva, who looked at him with worried eyes.

"Lieve toi!" commanded Hugues de Borre.

Two men lifted the master of arms off the ground and dragged him before Sire Geoffrey. Oswulf's clothes were drenched in mud, his ash-blonde hair stuck to his head and neck, the swellings above his eye and on his cheekbone now completely covered his right eye, the rest of his face was coated with a layer of blood and dirt. He looked every bit like a beaten opponent, and yet he was still the man Roger had admired for years for his poise and courage. From whom he had learned so much more than from his own father in many tough years. Who had supported him in the difficult time after William's death and encouraged him to go his own way. Who had finally led him to Gwennaol. And who had, all this time, shamelessly abused him for his cruel revenge without arousing the slightest suspicion.

Should he pity or loathe Oswulf in this state? To be sure, without him, Roger would never have come this far, and Gwennaol would never have existed.

But then Frederic, Father Leofric and Emma would still be alive, Roger would not have had to fear for the lives of his family, and he would not have had to fight for his own life in a murderous battle.

Maybe not now, but sooner or later. Without him, I might not even have survived this fight.

With a wrinkle of anger in his brow, Sire Geoffrey regarded Oswulf's disfigured face. "I spared you back then because my master of arms considered you an excellent fighter. I rescued you, an Engleis, from your miserable existence and took you into my manor for you to provide me with skilled warriors, but you betrayed my trust and deceived me. Three of my dependants died at your hands, and you would not have ceased if my son had not stopped you."

Did he actually say 'my son'? Am I then no longer the illegitimate son of the seneschal, but the rightful heir of Wilburgfos? With this battle, have I finally won my father's recognition that was denied me for so many years?

Although Roger felt a surge of pride at the thought, he shivered. The victory over the master of arms and his father's remark had a rotten aftertaste.

Sire Geoffrey lifted his chin. "You know what to expect."

Oswulf laughed out loud. "What could I ever expect from you? You have treated me like your property, a product to haggle and make money with. You have no respect for others and what is important to them. I was young then and agreed to your barter out of fear for my siblings' lives, not because I valued you as a leader, a warrior or as a human being. You are a selfish and cruel oppressor whom I would have done better to kill back then."

Sire Geoffrey's eyes flashed. He drew his sword and put it to Oswulf's throat. "Teins ta lange en coi, engleis! Or I'll cut it out of your insolent mouth right here and now."

"Wait, Father!" croaked Roger. "Hear me out!"

Sire Geoffrey didn't budge or move his sword. "Speak! But be brief!"

Roger cleared his throat. The wound on his leg was bleeding profusely, and his limbs were growing heavy. "As your son, pupil of the master of arms and winner of this battle, I beg you for mercy for Oswulf. I have seen to it that the killing at your manor house and in your fief ceases. That I was able to do so at all is something you owe to your master of arms, who has long taught the best squires at your manor and turned them into excellent fighters. Respect for his pupils and trust in their skills and abilities have made me what I am today and enabled me to defeat my master today. I am grateful to him for that."

Oswulf's moustache twitched at these words.

"I will not let you kill him for personal revenge," Roger said as his strength was failing. "What he has done to his own daughter and others at Morwenna's behest will haunt and torment him for the rest of his life. He will do you no more harm. Banish him from the manor for life, but let him live." *You have no choice anyway if you want to marry Isabel to Robert de Monbrai. Without the master of arms, no wedding and no greater fief.*

Sire Geoffrey's chin tensed. At last, he lowered his sword. "I will consider it. Take him away!"

No sooner had Hugues' men seized the master of arms than Roger groaned.

"Everything's spinning."

With a last glance at the large reddish-brown patch on his calf, he slumped between Joscelin and Drogo.

"Take him to the great hall! Quick!" cried Dame Edeva.

With every step, Roger became less aware of how his friends dragged him across the yard. His leg felt numb, his back ached, and he was freezing. They had not even reached the door of the manor before everything went black.

When Roger came to, he was tucked up in bed in the private chambers upstairs.

In the fireplace, logs crackled in the flames, and on a stool next to the bed stood a cup from which rose mouthwatering clouds of steam.

He was sweating, but when he tried to throw back the woollen blanket, he felt a sharp pain in his torso and lower leg. So, the fight against the master of arms had not been a dream after all. The wounds he had received burned under the thick bandages. Moving his foot hurt, but it was possible.

Relieved that Oswulf's sword blow had done no major damage, Roger sighed. He had faith in his mother's healing skills. She had already helped Brandolf and Bjarni, who had suffered much worse than this. Surely, she would manage to heal his injuries as well, and he would be recovered in a few weeks.

A cool, damp cloth touched his forehead.

He noticed Isabel sitting next to him, dabbing his face. She smiled when he looked at her.

"Roger! You're awake." She bent down to him and kissed him on the cheek. Her long hair tickled his face like delicate threads of silk. "You'll have to stay in bed for a few days." She pointed at the stool. "You've been stirring for a while now – I brought you some soup. It will do you good."

"I thank you, Isabel. Tell me, what happened?"

"You fainted when they carried you into the hall. Mother looked after you as best she could. For two days, she kept vigil at your bedside because you had a high fever. She must have used up all her English incantations during that time. But it seems the Almighty has answered her prayers. Your fever has gone down. Now, let's hope it continues to fall and that your wounds heal well."

"How is Oswulf? Where is he?"

Isabel dipped the rag into a bowl and wrung it out. "Father keeps him prisoner, but he treats him properly. Mother took care of his injuries too." She put the cloth back on his forehead. "Considering it was a practice fight, you were both dealing out frightening blows."

"It was no practice fight, Isabel."

Isabel paused. "You mean… Oswulf wanted to kill you?"

Maybe not yet, but he would have. After killing you all first.

She adjusted the cloth on his forehead. "Why would he do that?"

"It's a long story. I'll tell you when I'm well again."

"I don't have much time left. I'm leaving soon to marry Robert de Monbrai."

Roger gently stroked Isabel's hand. "Don't worry, little sister. If I can, I will prevent this wedding. Trust me."

Isabel's face lit up, and Roger vowed to try everything to ensure that the Comte de Northumberland got his hairy hands on neither the master of arms nor his sister. That irresistible smile would be wasted on the comte, and Roger already knew whose heart it would delight much more.

Chapter 48

After the previous night's snowfall, only the tips of the leaves stuck out from the first tender green of the snowdrops. The snow crunched under Roger's feet as he strolled back to the manor house. An icy wind blew in his face, pushing thick, grey-blue clouds onward. Although the odd sun ray broke through the overcast sky, the yard remained steeped in a dull light. The children didn't seem to mind. They laughed and grimaced in turn as they sniffed at their buckets and baskets, in which, at this time of year, they picked up horse droppings, cow dung and pig droppings. Once the snow had vanished from the land, they would spread their collected treasures as manure on the fields.

In the great hall, the storm whistled through the hole above the fireplace where the flames were flickering. Roger joined his friends who were passing the time with board games. It was long past time for their fighting exercises, but Hugues de Borre, who had temporarily taken over instructing the squires in Oswulf's stead, was still talking to Sire Geoffrey and the master of arms. Moreover, Dame Edeva had strictly forbidden Roger to start fighting again so soon after his injury. It had taken a lot of begging and persuading before, at last, she had given in and allowed him to get up and move around. Now, almost two weeks later, his mother and Isabel were still changing his bandages every day, but Roger felt strong enough to resume his normal life at the manor and perhaps also participate in weapons practice. And above all, to finally ride to the priory and find out if his hope had been justly reawakened at the end of the fight with Oswulf.

Out of nowhere, Hugues de Borre appeared next to the squires. "Your father wishes to speak to you."

Roger limped after him, sat down on a chair opposite his father and beside the master of arms.

Except for a few yellowish purple patches, his face looked the same as before. Only his large moustache seemed even bushier. He had probably been denied even the smallest knife to trim his beard in captivity, to prevent any nasty surprises.

The moss-green eyes scrutinised Roger. "So, you survived."

"Are you pleased, or were you hoping for something else?" asked Roger.

"I have pondered your proposal," his father forestalled a reply, "and consulted with my bailiff. We have decided to grant your wish not to condemn the master of arms. A good friend of mine will take him in at his manor and give him work there."

"Who is this friend?" Roger knew the answer, but he wanted to hear it from his father. "Do I know him?"

"No. He lives on the border with Scotland."

"A vassal of the Comte de Northumberland?" Roger's heart pounded.

"No, it is the comte himself." Sire Geoffrey beckoned to the bailiff. "Now, take the prisoner back and tell him to stand by. I want him to leave for the north as soon as possible."

Oswulf rose. "I will strive under a new lord to give you what you deserve for your decision, Sire."

"Get out of my sight, Engleis!" The liege lord waved his hand angrily.

Oswulf threw a dark glance at Roger.

"Only respect for others leads to good fortune," he said, turning away and leaving the hall with Hugues de Borre.

"I have made another decision," Sire Geoffrey announced, "about the succession in Wilburgfos."

"That is just what I wanted to discuss with you. I brought a letter from Frederic's brother, Hubert de Lisieues from Everwic, and Walter Fossard has also confirmed that Frederic is most certainly not my father."

"I know, I know." His father waved it off. "That rumour was an unfortunate mistake."

In Roger's mind appeared the seneschal's distorted face as he died in his arms. "Frederic died because of it! Yet you knew all along that he was innocent."

"Enough of that. I have decided that you will succeed me at the manor of Wilburgfos."

"Me?"

"You have defended the law and order of Wilburgfos in the battle against Oswulf and have proved yourself a worthy successor."

Roger's head was spinning.

Have I really done that? What law have I restored, then? One that spurns respect for others. An order that, decades later, triggers a cruel private feud that kills innocent people.

He took a deep breath. "I see you have made provision for each of your children. You put Adelais in a convent because your wife died giving birth to her. You marry Isabel off to the Comte de Northumberland because he promised you a rich fief as a reward. You have designated me heir to Wilburgfos, so that Tankred can later take over the larger fief for which you traded off your daughter. But tell me, have you not forgotten a child?"

His father squinted. "William is dead."

"Yes, fortunately. Otherwise, I would never have found out that your illegitimate daughter is still alive."

"What are you talking about?"

"You know who I mean. The girl from the market, who was locked up in a convent all her life to hide her mother's shame, and who you forbade me to see again after you realised who she was."

"You disobeyed my order?" cried Sire Geoffrey.

Roger felt a defiant satisfaction rise within him that his father had actually been oblivious to what had been going on all these months. "How else would I have found out who her father is?"

"She's not my daughter." Sire Geoffrey leaned back with a condescending wave of his hand. "You said yourself that Oswulf is her father. Everyone heard it."

"But Gwennaol doesn't know. She is convinced to this day that she is your daughter, because that is what she has been told all her life. I also know now what the reason was and why you wanted to prevent me from seeing her again."

Sire Geoffrey folded his arms, but his angry stare only spurred Roger on to speak out, eventually, all that he had learned in the last weeks.

"About seventeen years ago, Gwennaol's mother and grandmother had to interrupt their journey to Hindrelagh and stayed longer than intended at the manor of Wilburgfos. However, instead of protecting them and respecting their right to hospitality, you assaulted them several times. Only later did you find out that you had abused the half-sister and niece of Alain le Rous. Fearing that he would hear about your crime, you made sure that both women remained hidden in the priory so that no one would find out about the incidents at your manor. You succeeded in doing so until a year ago."

Sire Geoffrey looked at his son like a cornered animal, warily eyeing its opponent, checking whether escape was still possible or whether it should use claws and teeth to defend itself.

"Once you had made sure that Gwennaol would not leave the convent anymore, you thought your secret was safe at last. Now, you could pursue other ambitions, like the one concerning Robert de Monbrai. His uncle, Bishop Geoffroi de Constantia, suggested to him two years ago, not without reason, that he should become Comte de Northumberland, a powerful position in the north of England, which had been vacant for six years. You knew Robert de Monbrai of old and supported him well because you were hoping for the rich spoils which were denied to you after the campaigns in the north. You do not even flinch from a conspiracy against the king, just to get your way."

Sire Geoffrey slammed his fist on the table. "Teis toi! You don't know what you're saying."

"Oh, yes, I do. I learned a lot in Everwic about Robert de Monbrai and the men he works with – against the king."

"You don't know anything about these things! You've probably heard some gossip and think it's the truth."

"I'll leave that for William de Perci to decide."

"What has he got to do with it?"

"Richard sent a messenger to his father after my fight and asked him to come to Wilburgfos to look into this matter.

You can then report on what has happened at your manor to your liege lord and chief magistrate yourself. He will arrive in the next few days."

Sire Geoffrey's jaws were grinding as if he were crushing up the series of thoughts running through his head.

"After all this time, you may escape punishment for your shameful deeds of yesteryear, but you cannot expect leniency for your treason. There are sufficient witnesses and evidence, and if that's still not enough, we can also question the reeve's deputy in Everwic as to why I was ambushed there by two mercenaries set upon me by my father's bailiff. With or without his knowledge."

A heavy weight fell off Roger's shoulders. He had done what he had to do. He would leave the rest to Richard's father.

He rose and pushed his shoulders back. For the first time, he truly looked down on his father. The arrogance and pride that had hurt and humiliated Roger all these years had now disappeared. All that was left was a defeated warrior who had followed aspirations that had led not to his goals but to his downfall.

"I will not succeed you in Wilburgfos." Roger turned away to join his friends. The conversation was over.

Chapter 49

William de Perci listened attentively to what the residents of Wilburgfos told him about the events of the last weeks and then announced that Roger and Joscelin were to be dubbed the following morning.

Many people flocked to the small chapel that day to witness the solemn ceremony. William de Perci girded each squire with a sword, exhorted them to respect chivalric values and presented them with spurs, shield and armour. The two were now knights of the English king and bound to their lord by their oath of fealty.

Richard and Drogo were also given special honour on this day, for from now on, they had the task of assisting the newly appointed knights in the fulfilment of their duties as their faithful squires. Soon, they would all leave Wilburgfos to serve their new lord.

"SIMON DE KYME, Sire de Wilburgfos – that sounds good to me!" Roger patted Simon on the shoulder. "I'm sure you will be a good liege lord to the people here."

Meanwhile, Tankred and Isabel were watching two men lead away their father. William de Perci forbade a hasty condemnation and insisted on holding the trial in Cattune.

"Keep an eye on Tankred," said Roger to Simon. "A little encouragement will do him good. A few days ago, he was heir to the lordship of Wilburgfos, and now, his father is to be sentenced, his inheritance is taken by someone else, and his own family is leaving him."

"If it comes to what we found out in Everwic," said Simon, "Tankred will have no time to muse. The sooner he grows into his new role as squire, the better for him."

Joscelin joined Roger and Simon with the others and rubbed his Roman commander's nose. "Signs of a rebellion against the king seem to be increasing. The men of William de Perci report that the barons are retreating to their castles and hoarding supplies and weapons there."

Drogo glanced at Isabel, around whom Dame Edeva had put her comforting arm. "What will happen to Isabel?"

"Why don't you ask her yourself?" asked Roger. "She won't have to marry the Comte de Northumberland in any case."

Drogo's gaze flicked between Isabel and Roger, who gestured for him to go over. He wiped his much-too-short hair from his forehead, breathed in and walked over to the two women.

"What about you and Gwennaol then?" asked Simon.

"I will visit her one more time before I leave Wilburgfos for good."

"Is she really Oswulf's daughter?" asked Joscelin.

Roger shrugged. "That's what I hope to find out."

"Do you know what will they do with Oswulf?" Richard wanted to know.

"No, but I would like him to accompany me."

Joscelin raised an eyebrow. "Are you serious?"

"He wanted to kill you and your family!" It was difficult not to notice Richard's concern for his friend on his face.

"I know," said Roger. "His crimes are serious, and he should be punished for them. So, shall we condemn him? Or ban him? If he's outlawed, anyone can kill him without fear of punishment. But then we lose a valuable fighter and teacher. For what lies ahead of us, we need every man we can get. He can serve us well. Perhaps after losing battles against King William, my father and myself, he will finally win the victory he deserves."

"You'd better hurry up and get to your own battle." Simon put his hand on Roger's shoulder. "May you too win the victory that you deserve."

"Could you do me a favour in the meantime, Simon?" asked Roger and told him of his intention.

THE WAY TO the priory seemed infinitely long and, at the same time, far too short to Roger today. A voice in his chest urged him to get to the convent as quickly as possible. Another voice warned him. How could he be sure that Morwenna had not lied to him? Would that be her final victory?

Roger halted in front of the gate and stared at the priory. His chestnut stallion neighed encouragingly and shook his head and mane towards the gate.

"All right, my friend. I'm going." Roger dismounted, patted the horse on the neck and looked doubtfully into his big dark eyes. "I pray to God that the signs are favourable to us."

Modig Wiht nickered approvingly and gave Roger a nudge forward. Roger straightened up, adjusted his weapon belt with sword and scramasax and tapped on the wood.

The gate was not quite open when someone growled, "Not you again!"

Roger looked down into the face of the little nun who had tried in vain to block his way last time.

"Have you learned good behaviour in the meantime, or are you going to shove me aside like a sack of flour again?"

He smiled sheepishly, unfastened his belt and held it out to the nun. "Would you be so kind as to keep my belt for me and tell the Reverend Mother Prioress that I wish to speak to her?"

The nun pursed her lips and eyed Roger suspiciously. She accepted the belt and took a step to the side. "Enter and wait here."

Roger bowed and quickly scurried past the nun in case she changed her mind.

When the prioress appeared, Roger went to meet her.

"I am delighted to see you in good health again, Reverend Mother. My sister told me about bad things happening here."

A worry line flashed up on the prioress's face. "There have indeed been some unpleasant events and discoveries. But I'm sure that's not why you came here."

Roger reached for the small bag he had slipped off when he took off his weapon belt and handed it to the prioress, who received it with wide eyes. "That's right. First of all, I must thank you. I may not be Lord of Wilburgfos, but I still want to keep my promise from last year. Take this gold as a reward for your help. I know you will put it to good use."

"God bless you," she said, marvelling at the bulging leather bag in her hands. "We still have some urgent repairs to do from last winter. But tell me, you haven't come just to give me this?"

Roger bit his lower lip. "I am now a royal knight and will leave Wilburgfos for good. So, I would like to see Gwennaol and Adelais one last time."

"Of course. Gwennaol is taking stock in the storerooms over there, and you will find Adelais in the bakehouse. Now, go before the bell rings for prayer."

Roger kissed the prioress's hand. "Thank you, Reverend Mother. God bless you."

Watching her leave, he took a deep breath, straightened his cloak and made his way to the other end of the yard.

In the second hut, a figure with long dark hair was busy examining the ducks hanging from a metal ring. When Roger softly opened the door and stepped into the room, she turned around. Her sea-blue eyes shone, even in the little light that filtered through the tight wire mesh of the small windows.

"Roger!" She hesitated to come closer but smiled as he closed the door behind him.

"I promised you I would be back."

His heart leapt for joy. He had opened his arms to greet Gwennaol but quickly dropped them as the doubts about her parentage and Morwenna's words darkened his thoughts again. He needed to be sure first. One way or another.

Gwennaol fiddled with the brooch with the three weirdly curled arms on her cloak. "You just disappeared last time after talking to my grandmother. I thought I would never see you again. You've come to take your leave of me."

How she stood there – so close and yet so out of reach!

"I challenged the master of arms to a fight."

"You did what? Why?"

"Morwenna and Oswulf wanted revenge and intended to punish all those who drove Solen to her death: the priest, the seneschal, my mother and father. Even my siblings and myself were to pay for the wrong done to her."

"They would have killed even more people?"

"Nothing would have stopped them. And you were the bait."

"What do you mean?"

"Morwenna raised you for this role from the beginning."

Gwennaol folded her arms. "Right, I know this is about your family, and the murders are terrible, but what you are saying is ridiculous. I was meant to help Mammgozh avenge my mother's death on Sire Geoffrey. Nothing more."

"Morwenna and Oswulf used you, with no regard for your feelings or your life."

"So, you claim that my own grandmother only raised me to use me for her revenge?"

"That's right."

"You're lying!"

"May I remind you that before the Feast of the Lord, your grandmother made you so sick with a potion that you almost died?"

Gwennaol pressed her lips together.

"You were just a decoy, there to make the liege lord's son fall in love with you, only to find out you were his half-sister."

She frowned. "What did you just say?"

He looked at her longingly. How he would have loved to rush and embrace her, kiss her, and whatever else she might have allowed or wished. "That the liege lord's son falls in love, although he can never have her."

"You love me?"

"You have to show me something." His heart was hammering in his temples. In a few moments, his dreams would come true or shatter into a thousand shards. "I want to take a look at your upper right arm. Please!"

"My arm?"

Roger nodded. An army of ants was crawling around in his belly, and a sinking feeling spread over his whole body.

"Why? What's so special about my arm?"

"Just let me see it."

"And once you've seen it, then what?"

Roger was barely breathing. He felt sick. "I don't know, Gwennaol. Please. Just do me this one favour."

He rubbed his damp palms on his tunic.

Gwennaol lifted her chin, silent.

Roger gulped. If she did not comply with his request now, he would never know whose daughter she was.

Slowly, Gwennaol's hands went to the brooch on her cloak, which she hesitantly opened without taking her eyes off Roger. Was she afraid that he would seize the opportunity and assault her, as his father had done with her mother and grandmother?

An unbearable heat shot through Roger's body. He could hardly wait for the answer to his question, and watching Gwennaol undress in front of him was trying his patience. Beads of sweat formed on his skin. He would have loved to tear the cloak off his body to cool himself down, but that would probably have achieved the opposite of what he wanted at that moment.

Gwennaol put her cloak on a shelf, gathered the fabric of her floor-length tunic and pulled it up.

Roger wiped his mouth and looked around hastily. *If a nun comes in now...* Just in case, he took a step back and leaned against the door before he continued to watch breathlessly as

Gwennaol slipped the tunic over her head, giving him a clear view of her exposed legs.

White as milk and not a single freckle anywhere.

Grinning bashfully, Gwennaol hastily pulled her under-dress back down.

Only one more piece of clothing separated Roger from his goal. He would have liked to know what was going on in Gwennaol's head. Did she notice how he devoured her with his eyes while she took off her clothes? Did she see how difficult it was for him to bridle his desire and lust? Could she imagine the agony he was going through?

Gwennaol shivered. "Brr, it's cold."

"Wait."

Roger grabbed the tips of his cloak and stood as close to Gwennaol as modesty and his excitement would allow. With his arms, he folded the sides of his cloak around her. Only her shoulders were left uncovered.

He looked at her expectantly.

Gwennaol threaded her left hand between the two bodies and slid the right side of the neckline over her shoulder and down her arm. His gaze followed her fingers as if they were a hunting prey wandering unsuspectingly while he took aim.

Her hand paused. "Is that enough? I cannot pull it down any further."

He stared at her upper arm. Burning fire and icy storms alternately ate through his whole body. He felt dizzy and sick at the same time. His heart was beating at a speed that even his chestnut stallion would not have been able to keep up with at a stretched gallop.

"Why are you sweating all of a sudden? Are you not feeling well? Answer me, Roger!"

He stroked Gwennaol's arm to make sure that what he saw there was not an illusion; that he could touch it, and it would not disappear. Before Gwennaol could ask another question, he pulled her close and kissed her in a way that would have made even Emma envious. Gone were the doubts, the uncertainty. Morwenna had not lied. Gwennaol was indeed Oswulf's daughter, forever marked with the same birthmark as her father. She was his at last. How long he had waited for this moment! How often he had stood there in the clearing when they met, wishing she would come out so he could look at her, touch her, unhindered! How he had longed to run his fingers through her long hair and over her body, to feel her skin against his.

His excitement rose even more when he realised that Gwennaol returned his caresses.

If only we weren't in the priory...

He paused and opened his eyes. Was that a noise?

Too late! The door opened, and a black habit glided in.

"Oops!" The nun startled, but then a smile crossed her face, and two bright blue eyes twinkled mischievously. "I see the stock inspection is in full swing."

Roger cleared his throat and took a step back from Gwennaol.

"It's not what it looks like, Adelais. Let me explain."

He told her about the talk with Morwenna, the fight with Oswulf and why he needed to see Gwennaol's upper arm. "She is Oswulf's daughter, not our half-sister."

Adelais sighed with relief. "At last, you bring good news! But perhaps Gwennaol should put her clothes back on before Sister Mary comes over. Unless you want to lay your hands on a nun again."

After peering outside, she left the door ajar behind her while Gwennaol threw on her tunic and cloak.

"Unfortunately, there is also bad news," said Roger.

"I knew there had to be more."

"Father will be summoned to court for high treason."

Adelais listened with ever-widening eyes to his account of what had happened at the manor. When Roger had finished, she bowed her head and crossed herself. "What are you going to do now?"

Roger looked at the tips of his feet. He knew he had to take his leave for good and that he would never see Adelais again, whether or not the king's loyal followers could prevent a possible rebellion.

"William de Perci dubbed me this morning. I will go away with the others to Hindrelagh, to Alain le Rous. We must warn the king that his barons are plotting an uprising."

"What about Mother, Isabel and Tankred?"

"Tankred will stay at the manor as a squire, but Isabel is coming with us – Drogo was rather pleased that the wedding to Robert de Monbrai will not take place after all. Mother has decided to renounce her worldly life. She will be glad to see you again after so many years."

"She's coming to join us in the priory?"

Roger nodded. "She loves Wilburgfos and its people, despite everything that has happened to her here in the last twenty years. But she could not bear to continue living in the manor house. The convent offers her a place where she can be close to both the villagers and her family."

"What's going to happen to my grandmother?" asked Gwennaol, frightened. "The prioress spoke to her recently, but Mammgozh has not told me what she has decided."

With a stern look, Adelais slid her hands into the long sleeves of her habit. "The Reverend Mother preferred to wait until she knew whether my brother would make it to the priory again. Now that he is here, she will make a decision as to whether your grandmother may remain here or whether she must leave."

"But where will she go if she must not stay? She has no one left but me and the nuns."

"She abused the sisters' trust," answered Adelais, "and yours too. The only reason she raised you was to use you as an instrument for her revenge. She didn't care about your life. If it had been necessary, she would have..."

She pressed her lips together, but Gwennaol seemed to have understood and slumped her shoulders.

Adelais smiled reassuringly at Gwennaol. "The Reverend Mother will find a just solution, and Roger will take good care of you from now on. It is time you left the priory, for you have been here far too long. You don't belong here."

"You should pack what you want to take with you," Roger said softly.

Gwennaol nodded thoughtfully. "I don't have much. Give me a moment to get it."

She paused at the door and looked pleadingly at Adelais. "Are you coming? I want to tell my grandmother that I am leaving the priory."

Adelais turned to follow her. "I'll accompany you to the gate then. Wait for us there, Roger."

The two women left and headed for the inner yard. Roger watched them with mixed feelings. He was glad not to have to sneak here anymore, even if his visits had mostly been pleasant. He had to leave Adelais behind, but he would take

Gwennaol with him. His old family stayed here; a new life awaited him.

As he put on the weapon belt before leaving the priory, Adelais and Gwennaol approached. Gwennaol was carrying a small bag and fidgeting with its strap.

"May God protect you both," said Adelais, "and grant you a happier life than you have had until now."

Since it was their last meeting, Roger allowed himself to disregard the convent rules and hugged his sister tightly. She would vanish from his life forever. Her loss weighed heavily, and even though another important woman would continue to accompany him, the pain of separation would never quite subside. "I will miss you, Adelais. God bless you."

She opened the door and let Roger and Gwennaol out. "Take care of yourself and Gwennaol, Roger. And remember, the Lord sees everything, and I like to chat with Him."

"I know that, my big sister. Farewell, Adelais."

She smiled, her eyes flashing one last time.

Then the gate fell shut, and Roger locked the moment in his heart to treasure forever.

February was still trying to hold on to winter in its last days, but in spite of the cold, the first bright green messengers of spring were pushing their way through the ground and out of the bare branches of trees and bushes everywhere.

Beside Roger on Modig Wiht rode Gwennaol on a brown palfrey, smiling and with her gaze wandering over the land.

Each time he looked at her, the pain of losing his family receded a little more. He knew he had done what was right. The humiliated, quick-tempered boy had learned much in the last two years. He had Gwennaol to thank for that. *And Oswulf.*

Ahead of them, in the distance, rose the infamous bridge of Pons Belli over the Deorwente, where King Harold had won that memorable last victory for the English. Back then, the Vikings were the enemy to be defeated in order to curb their power in England. This time, however, the enemy came from within.

Roger thought of the signet ring under his leather glove and the symbols on it – the tree, the sword and the axe – and what they meant: the eternal connection of all things; protection, justice and wealth; strength, courage and power. When his mother had given him the ring, he had promised her that he would wear it with pride and prove himself worthy of it. Perhaps, he had now finally fulfilled that promise.

With the roar of the current in their ears, the motley troop of Norman warriors, youths in full armour, and the two young women approached the heavy wooden structure that led across the mighty river with a slight arch. Once they had crossed the Deorwente, they would ride north past Everwic towards Topeclive and eventually to the castle of Alain le Rous in Hindrelagh.

Roger's gaze travelled up the wide wooden planks to the apex of the bridge, where the figure of a horseman loomed. Equipped with a helmet and chain mail, he sat on a medium-sized white horse. A long sword and a short sword hung from his weapon belt, an axe next to the saddle pommel. On his back, the rider carried a shield. With his right hand, he grasped a spear which he had placed on the ground. He had probably been waiting at this spot for some time, but for whom? His armour and weapons indicated that he was not a simple waylayer. Besides, he wanted to be seen, or he would not have blocked the only bridge that led across the river in this area.

"Who's that?" asked Richard, who rode alongside Roger.

"Maybe someone who wants to join us," Roger replied.

About fifteen paces from the bridge, William de Perci halted his troop and called out to the stranger, "Good day, munsire. And who, pray, are you?"

"I was expecting you," the man replied. "A benevolent liege lord told me that I would meet you here."

"Let me talk to him, Sire," said Roger, riding forward at the bidding of William de Perci.

Although he did not take his eyes off the man in front of them, he surveyed the surroundings with a few sideways glances. Perhaps this was an ambush, and the figure visible from afar on the bridge was meant to distract from a much larger force hidden behind the bushes.

Roger stopped. His heart was pounding. He watched his chestnut stallion's ears, trying to sense any small movements and twitches in his horse's body. But there was nothing. Modig Wiht stood there without the slightest sign of alarm, calmly waiting to see what came next.

"You wear a lot of armour for an outlaw."

The man squinted at Roger against the sun. "The outlaw respects no one, and no one respects the outlaw. Anyone can kill him with impunity. His life is worthless."

"So, you prefer your life to be worth something."

"Wilburgfos has shaken off a bad lord in favour of a good one. It has lost its æþeling, but he has won his battle for respect and freedom." He spurred his horse and rode slowly down the bridge.

Roger heard an anxious murmur behind him. He glanced around as the man approached. Had he been too credulous?

The rider stopped his horse beside him, his moss-green eyes sparkling and his huge moustache waggling appreciatively. “It’s a pity you don’t have a beard. You’d be a worthy wearer now.”

Afterword

The barons' rebellion began around Easter 1088. While in England, Bishop Odo de Bayeux and his allies set out from their castles, well stocked with weapons and supplies, to attack and ravage neighbouring lands, in Normandy, Robert Courteheuse prepared to send an invading army to the English south coast.

King William II may have had visual and character flaws, but he was a shrewd and effective strategist and soldier. Instead of letting himself be heckled by the rebels, he mobilised not only his loyal vassals and his English subjects but also those who were still undecided by promising to reward their loyalty to the king with land, money and new, fairer laws. He also personally led the attacks on the rebels, in particular, his uncle, Odo de Bayeux, whom he besieged in Pevensey Castle for six weeks before capturing him.

As luck would have it, bad weather prevented his elder brother's Norman troops from landing, so the English king and his allies managed to crush the rebellion four months after it began.

Bishop Odo de Bayeux was banished for life from England with two of his followers, Eustace de Boulogne and Robert de Bellesme, but most of the barons who had rebelled against the king were allowed to keep their manors and offices. Bishop William of Durham was also banished from the country in a public trial in Salisbury in November 1088 but was restored to his post and lands as early as 1091.

Ultimately, King William II had thus, on the one hand, eliminated his most difficult opponents by banishing them for life, and, on the other, confiscated their lands for the crown without having to redistribute them in order to buy the loyalty of others.

So much for the further course of history. Now, let's take a look at the historical details that I had to remodel a little for dramaturgical reasons. We'll start with Simon de Kyme.

Wilberfoss is closely associated with the de Kyme family, with Philip de Kyme being the first ancestor known by name of the family that resided in the small village until the 18th century. Philip's granddaughter, Margaret de Kyme, was the first to bear the name of the village as a mark of her ancestry in the second half of the 12th century, when she came to be known as Margaret de Wilberfoss, and her husband, Ilgerus of Eggleston, also called himself Ilgerus of Wilberfoss after they married in 1175.

What the owner of Wilberfoss was called in the period in which the novel is set remains a mystery due to a lack of records. However, there was indeed a man named Simon (Symon) de Kyme in the 11th and 12th centuries, whose life and family data unfortunately vary greatly. However, since there are also several Simons in the Wilberfoss line, I have borrowed the name for the (invented) grandfather of Philip de Kyme and included him in the story as seneschal of Picot de Perci.

The historical Walter Fossard, the best friend of Roger's fictional brother, owes his appearance to the fact that his older brother, Robert, born two years before him in 1068 as the eldest son of Nigel Fossard, has a name already used by two other characters in my book. Robert Fossard was the right age to match Roger's big brother, William, but his name would have caused confusion in my story. I therefore took the liberty to make Walter two years older, basically assigning his name to the birth date of his older brother, so that Walter is at the same level of training as William and doesn't have to hang around with the younger squires.

Last but not least, a word about the Benedictine nunnery. Although it was founded before 1153, it did not yet exist in the 11th century – and therefore neither in the time of this novel nor in Book 1 of the Northumbria Trilogy. I count on Saint Benedict to forgive me for having set up his religious community in Wilberfoss at an earlier date due to narrative constraints.

Places

Unless indicated otherwise, placenames are in Old English.

OE = Old English
N = (Anglo-)Norman
ON = Old Norse

Bebbanburh – Bamborough, Northumberland
Cattune – High and Low Catton, North Yorkshire
Deorwente – Derwent, Derbyshire and Yorkshire, river west of Leavening and Wilberfoss
Dunholm – Durham, Durham County
Everwic (Eoforwic OE), Everwicscire (N) – York, North Yorkshire
Fosse – Foss, North Yorkshire, the eastern river running through York
Fors bekkr (ON) – Foss Beck, North Yorkshire, river through Wilberfoss
Galmanlith – Bootham Bar, York's northern gate
Haslinton – Heslington near York
Hindrelagh – Richmond, North Yorkshire
Koppari Gata (ON) – Coppergate, the former craftsmen's area in York during Viking occupation from the 9th to the mid-11th century
Londres (N) – London

Micklelith – Micklegate Bar, York's western gate

Mikkil Gata (AN) – Micklegate, York's main street leading from Micklegate Bar to the Ouse Bridge

Northumberland (N) – Northumbria, Northumberland, County Durham, Tyne and Wear, old Anglo-Saxon kingdom between the river Humber and the river Forth, largely independent from southern England

Pevenesel – Pevensey Bay, East Sussex

Pons Belli (N<Latin) – Stamford Bridge, where the battle between English and Viking forces took place in 1066

Roem (N) – Rouen, Normandy

Sarisberie – Salisbury, Wiltshire

Scornesbi (ON) – Scoreby, North Yorkshire

Sceamoles (OE) – The Shambles, York, the street in which the medieval meat market was

Skjaldari Gata (ON) – Skeldergate, York, the street where the medieval shield-makers were located

Sudtone – Sutton-upon-Derwent, Yorkshire

Topeclive – Topcliffe, North Yorkshire

Use – Ouse, North Yorkshire, the western river running through York

Veuguessin (N) – Vexin, historical county of northern France, halfway between Rouen and Paris, on the then border between Normandy and France

Wilburgfos – Wilberfoss, East Riding of Yorkshire

Wincestre – Winchester, Hampshire

Witebi – Whitby, North Yorkshire

Glossary

Unless indicated otherwise, words and phrases are in Old English.

OE = Old English
N = (Anglo-)Norman
ON = Old Norse
B = Breton

A Deu, qe te gard cors e alme (N) – Farewell, (may God protect your body and soul) God bless you
A tun acort (N) – Agreed
Æþeling – Anglo-Saxon prince, often the heir to the throne.
Als Gernuns (N) – with moustache
Reference to the Anglo-Saxon/English custom of wearing beards. The Normans tended to be clean-shaven.
Aluns (N) – Let's go
Asez! (N) – Stop! / Enough!
Beo ðu hal, leof cyning! – (Be healthy, dear king) Long live the king!
Beo gesund – (Be healthy) Take care
Botelerie – storage room for drinks
Chevaler (N) – rider, in particular a knight
Ço vus di! (N) – I'm telling you! / There you go!
Cum, min sunu – Come, my son

Dameisele (N) – (unmarried) girl
Daneis (N) – Dane(s) / Danish
Destrier (N) – Norman warhorse
Đis is laðlic! – (That's disgusting!) Yuck!
Đu eart unwita! – (You are unwise) You're an idiot! / Fool!
Đu sægest wilspell – You bring good news
Đunres hamer on þe heafod! – (Thor's hammer on your head!) The wrath of God shall strike you!
Eala – Oh! Oh dear!
Exclamation of surprise or pity
Engleis (m), Englesse (f) (N) – Englishman (-men) / the English language, Englishwoman
Escoz (N) – Scotsmen
Feohgifre þeof – (Cattle-greedy thief) Greedy cutthroat
Fiz a putein! (N) – Son of a bitch!
Fulen þa wyrmes in ðære haligan rode! – (May the worms rot in the holy cross) Damn it!
Galwræne yfelsacend! – Lascivious blasphemer!
Gemiltsa me/us God – Lord, have mercy on me/us
Gewurþe ðin willa on eorðan swa on heofonum – Thy will be done, on earth as it is in heaven
God sceal forlætan þe to ðam ecan forwyrde – (May God surrender you to eternal damnation) May you burn in hell
Hi sculon gan libbende on helle – (They shall go living [alive] into hell!) Let them go to hell
Ic eom unwita! – (I am unwise) Silly me!
Ic hine wergðo on mine sette – (I put my curse on him) Curse him
Irn, Modig, ond bring Simon! Retsh– (Recene)! – Run, Modig, and bring Simon! (Quickly) Hurry!

Ja m'en vengerai par mult fiere vertu (N) – (I will take revenge with very great force) I will take revenge all the more resolutely

Jo vus en mercie bonement, munsire (N) – Thank you very much, sir

Le Rous (N) – The red (epithet)

Li viver le rei (N) / se cyninges fiscpol (OE) – the king's fish-pool

Lieve toi! (N) – Stand up!

Lygewyrhta – Liar

Ma Doue! (B) – By God!

Mammgozh (B) – Grandmother

Min sunu – My son

Modig Wiht – Noble-minded/High-spirited creature

Mon ami (N) – My friend

Mon cher... (N) – My dear...

Munsire, plural: messires (N) – sir

Form of address for a man of high status or nobility. See also "Sire".

Par Deu! (N) – By God!

Pernuns dunc ceo tretur! (N) – So, let's (grab) arrest this traitor!

Quei? (N) – What?

Scinlæce – witch, mistress of black magic, in particular summoning evil spirits

Seisisets tut deus! (N) – Arrest those two!

Seo ful lybbestre! – That vicious poisoner!

Si vus plest (N) – please

Sire (N) – Sir

Form of address for the liege lord as opposed to "munsire".

Swiga – Shut up!

Teins ta lange en coi, engleis! (N) – (Hold your tongue still) Watch your tongue, Englishman!

Teis toi! (N) – Shut up!

Tric Trac, Jonchet, Merelle (N) – Norman medieval versions of Backgammon, Spillikins and Nine Men's Morris

Tuché! (N) – Touché! / Gotcha!

Unwita! – (unwise) Idiot! / Fool!

Ur pennadig yec'hed a ra vad d'un den klañv. (B) – A moment of health does the sick person good

Va dunc, chevaler preuz et beaus! (N) – Off you go, brave and beautiful rider/knight!

Valhǫll (ON) – Valhalla

Old Norse mythic home of the warriors who had died in battle.

Vilein Engleis (N) – English peasant

This form of address is ambiguous, as vilein can either simply refer to the rank of an unfree peasant, the most common rank in the peasant class in the feudal system of that time, or be used pejoratively to designate a lout.

Vive le rei! (N) – Long live the king!

(Li) Viver le rei (N) – the king's fishpool

Wæs hal! – (Be healthy!) Cheers / To your health!

An old English toast, usually answered with, "Drinc hal!" – Drink healthily!

Witan – (the wise men) council of the Anglo-Saxon kings.

The Witan advised on political, legal and social matters and comprised a varying number each of bishops and men from the upper nobility. The Witan also decided who would be the next king.

Wordwringa! – (word wringer) sophist!

Acknowledgements

Thank you for reading Roger's story. If you enjoyed the book, please tell others about it by leaving a review on your favourite book portal. It can be as brief as you like, but your feedback is important and valuable for authors and, of course, other readers. Much appreciated!

Be the first to know when my next book is available, and get additional, exclusive reading material by subscribing to my newsletter, *Medieval Motes*, at **www.birgitconstant.com**.

A very special thankyou goes to my editor Miranda Summers-Pritchard for her subtle corrections and for polishing my prose, to my coverdesigner at Damonza, and, last but not least, to John Wyatt Greenlee for redesigning my maps.

FIND OUT HOW THE STORY CONTINUES

The Minstrel's Quest.
Book 3 of the Northumbria Trilogy

Printed in Dunstable, United Kingdom

75315994R00231